ARCADIAN DIVINITY

ELIZABETH WITTEKIND

ISBN: 979-8-9852145-6-7 (paperback)
ISBN: 979-8-9852145-7-4 (hardcover)
ISBN: 979-8-9852145-8-1 (ebook)

Book cover design and interior formatting by Miblart.com

1

The ambulance siren rang in my ears and made them feel like they were bleeding as I took in the scene. The shrill noise from the emergency vehicle stabbed my eardrums as I watched the woman struggle to breathe. She was crushed in her mangled car, unable to get out. She panted heavily and was quickly slipping into a panic.

My eyes tightened as I watched her. I was unable to help the woman or do anything as I stood on the road where the wreck had occurred. It had been a hit and run.

I knew she wouldn't be able to see me. It was impossible for anyone to be able to.

It was hard to witness her struggle though. I watched her blood slowly leave her body as the paramedics finally arrived, along with the fire department.

The young man who had witnessed the accident and had called the emergency services earlier was watching the woman's car. He saw her trapped in her vehicle and couldn't control the tears streaming down his face.

I looked at the woman as she turned her head, looking at the EMTs and the firefighters. They were using the jaws of life to get her out of the wreckage, but I knew that they were going to run out of time. The wreck had caused irreparable damage to her vital organs. The woman had been crushed by the roof of her car, injuring her lungs, and even puncturing one of them. There was blood everywhere from her injuries, and I could hear her raspy breathing as she struggled to stay conscious. I could tell she realized that she was dying.

I took a few steps closer toward the vehicle that was destroyed, walking toward the firefighters. They were using the equipment to retrieve the dying woman.

The EMTs passed me, completely oblivious to my presence. They brought a gurney out from the ambulance, ready to bring the woman to the hospital. They were working hard to save her, even though it clearly wasn't going to happen.

The sound of the emergency equipment rang in my ears as they worked diligently to pull the woman out. I headed toward the vehicle, waiting for the woman to leave the mangled car.

It took a few minutes for them to get her as she was pinned.

I saw it in her face that she was getting pale from the blood loss.

On the side of the road, the bystander was crying.

"Hang in there!" one of the firefighters yelled at her as they continued to slice through the vehicle. "Just hang in there!"

I felt bad for the man instantly. Everyone at the scene was trying their hardest to keep her away from death, but I knew that she was going to lose that battle. There was finally a crunching noise as the car cracked open, allowing one of the firefighters to go in and retrieve the woman. Her brown hair and peach colored skin were covered with blood.

The firefighter gently cut her out of her seatbelt, and I watched him silently as he gingerly laid her flat on the gurney.

"Come on, come on, come on, stay with me," I heard the firefighter quietly say as I edged closer to the wreck. He was watching the woman steadily as he rushed the gurney toward the EMTs. "Stay with me," he said as he continued to talk to her.

The EMTs rushed over to the firefighter, grasping the gurney. They quickly put an oxygen mask over the woman's mouth and nose. Her breathing was slowing though, her face becoming paler. She didn't open her eyes as I walked over to her.

No one could sense me as everyone focused on getting her to the hospital. But she was going to lose her fight.

"Alright," I said quietly to the young woman as her breathing became shallow. I touched her shoulder lightly. "Time to go."

Her chest rose and fell, one last time, before all the life left her. She slipped into a permanent slumber. She passed away silently.

Backing away, I kept my eyes on everyone at the scene of the horrific wreck. I watched them as they moved the gurney inside the shrieking ambulance. Then the EMTs quickly got inside the vehicle with the woman's body. I watched the team frantically take off, the ambulance screaming into the daylight. I stared at the place the emergency vehicle had just been. Then I noticed that the bystander was in the back of a different ambulance. Soon it was just me on the side of the road watching where the accident had taken place.

My thoughts were interrupted when I heard ragged, scared breathing behind me.

I twisted my body around and saw the young woman. Her brown hair was now free of blood, her body no longer broken.

She was perfectly fine. No marks or bodily fluid were on her. She looked panicked when she saw me, and her eyes were filled with tears.

"No. No. No," she said, shaking her head.

I walked toward her calmly. "It's alright," I said softly as I stepped over to her. "You have nothing to be afraid of."

The woman gulped. She was terrified that she had crossed over, that she was no longer alive. Her blue eyes were wide as she stared at me, understanding finally taking hold.

"You're safe now," I said, extending my hand out so she could take it.

The young woman blinked rapidly, before grasping my extremity.

"It'll be okay, I promise," I whispered in her ear, before my gigantic black wings flapped. They pushed us both off the road and into the atmosphere. I held the young woman tight against my chest.

She cried as I held her close. I just embraced her, knowing how scared she was. She was now a Spirit.

A Spirit that would now live in Heaven.

I took a deep breath as I looked at my surroundings. I was on the top of a skyscraper, looking down at the city, at the hustle and bustle below me. I wasn't really paying attention to anything. I was just feeling the breeze blow across my skin, my face.

The sound of car horns filled the air as I stared absentmindedly in the sky, my thoughts going to the young woman that I'd just brought to Heaven.

She'd been scared because she'd left her family behind. She feared how they would cope without her. But above all, she was scared that she'd completely transitioned into a Spirit.

She was safe now.

"Caelum?"

I turned around at the sound of my name, seeing Adiel watching me. "Yes?" I responded, looking at his face.

His dark brown eyes appeared quizzical. "Are you thinking about her?" he asked, advancing toward me.

I nodded, twisting away from him in order to look at the sky again. I could see Adiel come up beside me out of the corner of my eye.

"She was so scared," I said. "She was terrified of dying."

"Mortals are always scared of the inevitable," Adiel said. "Especially death. They're always wondering how it'll be, or if they are going to go to the right place. But you did the right thing, Caelum, you did your duty."

"She's safe now," I said, in almost a whisper.

"That she is," he said, twisting around to look at me. His brown eyes locked on mine. "She's no longer in pain, and you helped her," Adiel said. "Just remember that." He placed his hand on my shoulder. "You're guiding Spirits to the Afterlife. You're doing your responsibility, no matter what. You are doing the right thing. Remember that."

I nodded, understanding his words.

I felt him gently thump his hand against my back before walking off. I could hear wings rustling before I turned around. I saw Adiel take off into the sky, his black appendages flapping behind him.

Adiel oversaw taking care of the Spirits that I brought into the Heavens, while I predominantly stayed on Earth. I moved the Souls of the deceased whenever they crossed over. There were many responsibilities among the angels, and I was tasked with easing the Spirits into the Afterlife.

I watched Adiel as he flew off, wondering in the back of my mind if I indeed was doing the right thing.

But then I just sighed, knowing that I was, and that sometimes the reactions of others were unavoidable. I was helping individuals. I was saving them.

2

I was used to the reactions of individuals that were dying, as well as loved ones who were watching it happen.

Crying, screaming, cursing.... I had seen and heard it all. There were so many ways that people dealt with death. Sometimes people dealt with it lightly, accepting that the individual was in a better place. But then there were others that refused to accept it. They would curse in order to get the feelings of hurt out.

I had also experienced my fair share of the ways that individuals had died, as well as their animals. Shootings, car wrecks, euthanasia, stabbings, cancer, natural causes... I was no stranger to anything, after millennia of moving Souls.

Nothing seemed to faze me anymore. It seemed like I was immune to everything regarding my duty.

I found myself emotionally distant and wary. Emotionally wary because of the way the mortals reacted to the death of another mortal. Because of how they would grieve.

I exhaled as I looked at the scenery, coming back to myself. I extended my wings out from behind me. Then I took off, flying away from the skyscraper on which I had perched.

I sensed I was going to be needed again soon.

As I flew from the skyscraper and toward the ground, I sensed that death was nearby.

I tucked in my wings right as I came across a middle-aged man, who was on the busy sidewalk. He clutched his chest and cried out in agony. A passerby quickly saw this and shouted out in a panic.

"Help! Someone, please, help!"

She put a hand on his back, trying hard to comfort him as another younger man came over. The young man inspected what was going on quickly before taking his phone out and calling 9-1-1.

The older man, though, collapsed, suffering a massive heart attack.

I saw him take his final breath as the young man started doing CPR. I knew though, that his Soul had left his body, and that he had already passed on.

I watched the people as they tried to revive the middle-aged man, doing their best, when there was a voice behind me.

"Hello?"

I twisted around, only to see the man's Soul. He appeared bewildered.

"What is going on? It seems like I just lost consciousness, but now I..."

He stopped. He had trailed off as I looked at him knowingly, before his eyes hit the ground. His body was there and people were trying to resuscitate him. He blinked rapidly before looking back up at me, his brown eyes watching mine.

"Am I.... Am I... dead?" he asked, stuttering a little as his voice caught.

I nodded. "Yes," I said as he looked at the sidewalk, tears beginning to fill his eyes.

As they found mine, he took a deep breath. "Who are you?"

"My name is Caelum. I'm here to bring you to the Afterlife."

The man just stood there, dazed. He couldn't believe that he was not among the mortals anymore. I had seen this look a lot before. "You're... you're...you're an angel?" he asked, his voice trembling.

"Yes. Yes, I am." I extended my hand out before I turned my head curiously. "What's your name?" I asked, trying to calm him down.

"Eric," he responded. "My name is Eric."

"It's nice to meet you, Eric," I said. He smiled a little at my tone, before glancing at my hand. "Everything's alright, Eric, I promise. I'll bring you to Heaven."

Eric looked pale as he watched my eyes. Then he glanced behind me, where a crowd of people had gathered.

The younger man was continuing chest compressions on Eric's body, not knowing that he was gone. It was heartbreaking to watch, but again, I was used to it.

Eric looked back over at me, tears gathering as his eyes connected with mine. He grasped my hand, fully and truly trusting me.

"Come on," I said. "Let's bring you to the Afterlife."

At that moment, my wings came out of my back. Eric stared at the feathers, transfixed at the deep, black color before I wrapped my arms around his body. I got a good grip on him. And then we were propelled up into the sky.

3

"Adiel?"

He turned to look at me, his tanned skin and bald head appearing almost tawny.

"Yes, Caelum?"

I took a deep breath before exhaling in a gust. I stood in the Heavens. I had just brought Eric up here, so I had stayed to ask Adiel a question. I was not in the Heavens a lot, since my home was on Earth. So, I couldn't stay too long. I didn't want to distract Adiel from his duty.

He was the Guardian of the Spirit Realm.

"Do you ever get attached to the Souls? I mean, have a friendship with them? Is that normal for you?" I asked tentatively.

He smiled, the expression taking up his entire face before he answered. "Yes. It is perfectly normal to be attached to a Soul. Why? Would you like to see someone? I can grant them permission if you'd like."

I shook my head. "No. No, thank you. I was just wondering."

I was so used to dealing with what my duty entailed. I never really got close to anyone. It would just make everything gut-wrenching if I did. I was guarded when it came to doing my obligation to the mortals.

Adiel just continued to smile as he looked at me. "Caelum," he started. "Why did you ask that?"

"I was just wondering," I repeated. "This responsibility can be a little bit… difficult to handle at times," I said, stumbling on my words.

"Well, you can always just talk to me if you want to communicate with any Soul. All you must do is ask."

I nodded. "Okay. Well, thank you."

"You're welcome, Caelum."

And with that, I twisted around and extended my wings out, flying out of the Afterlife.

Over the next month or so, I stayed on Earth, doing what I was fated to do. I tried hard to focus as the question that I had asked Adiel kept creeping up in my mind. I gritted my teeth. Embarrassment flooded through me.

One day, as I was bringing the Spirit of an elderly woman up to the Afterlife, I saw Adiel again. A grin spread across his face when our eyes met, before he turned his attention to the older woman. She squinted when she saw Adiel, and I could see a twinkle in her eyes as she smiled at him. She appeared calm as he gently put his hand on her back, guiding her to where the rest of the Spirits were.

"You're safe now," I heard Adiel say as he walked along with her. "Don't worry, you're alright now."

He turned his head toward me as his hand stayed on her back. He wanted to talk afterwards.

I nodded understandingly before Adiel's head twisted back around. I waited patiently, just looking at my surroundings.

Everything was a mixture of extraordinary color. There were white and amber hues surrounding me, while I was standing on top of a cloud. Flecks of gold hit my skin as they dropped from the Heavens like snowflakes.

There was a huge expanse of the Afterlife that was empty. Very faintly, beyond that, I saw the trace of the gargantuan, bright, and speckled Golden Gates. The Gates that were perched on the clouds and were named after the bits of gold that were scattered across the giant fence. They appeared beautiful, welcoming, and non-threatening as I saw them open at Adiel's command. He was still walking with the woman. He grasped her hand gingerly before they both went into the Soul Realm.

Adiel was the Guardian of the Soul Realm. He was the Guardian of the Golden Gates.

When an individual, or animal, died, there was a Gate to pass through. The Soul would reside inside, forever.

I blinked as I looked away from the Golden Gates, peering around at the rest of the scenery.

That was when I saw the Heavenly River nearby. The Heavenly River that was used by Adiel to view Earth when he could not fly down there.

Adiel was mainly tasked to be in the Soul Realm but could occasionally visit Earth if he wanted to.

The River showed anything that he wanted to see.

I walked over to the River, absentmindedly looking in the Water, studying my reflection that appeared in the liquid. I sighed as I saw it.

My blue eyes appeared almost too big for my face, while my dark brown hair was short. My skin was a light color that resembled the inside of a peach. I moved my back muscles as I looked at myself in the reflection, and, within moments, I saw my enormous black wings appear behind me. I smiled as I saw them.

I was happy with my wings. They were everything to me and helped me complete my destiny.

No matter how cautious I was when it came to my duty, I still loved my wings. They were my favorite possession.

"Still loving your angel wings, are you?"

Adiel's voice startled me. I jumped slightly as I saw him heading over my way. He smiled as our eyes met.

I nodded. "Yes."

"Well, that's good. You're recognizing that your responsibility is also your destiny. You love your angel wings, so you realize what would happen if you were to lose them."

I gulped at the thought. If I were to lose my wings, I would be tossed into Hell, and Fall. I would be a Fallen Angel. The thought of Falling terrified me.

I shook my head, coming out of my reverie.

Adiel was watching me closely. "You're not the only angel who is constantly wondering if you're doing the right thing. You're not the only one who thinks about the Souls who've passed on, or who were struggling to survive, only to die. Other angels have these thoughts in their head too," Adiel said, looking at me. "You're not the only one either to doubt your abilities."

"I don't doubt my abilities," I countered. "It's just that sometimes, I wonder about the Souls that have passed on." Like the woman in her mid-twenties that I had brought up from the car wreck…. "I feel like I should have some emotion about them, but I do not want to at the same time. It's a strange feeling."

Adiel just stared at me. "Even a great, powerful angel isn't immune to the mortal emotion. You must, at least occasionally, experience what the mortals are going through. It will help you understand the Soul more. That way, you know how to comfort them, or their family. Caelum," he said, sighing a little before continuing. "You must experience the emotions of the mortals. You must see, hear, and feel what they go through. It will change your entire outlook on your existence, I promise," he said.

He looked at my face as I glanced down at the cloud that I was standing on. I brought my attention back to him.

"Alright," I said. "I understand."

Adiel nodded. "Good. It's important to know that."

He looked down at the Heavenly River, where both of our reflections were. It was the only place we angels could see ourselves, since we were supernatural beings.

We could not be seen by any mortal, or in their mirrors. We were completely invisible, except in the Heavenly River.

Adiel looked at me through the Waters. "See, you can be a part of a mortal's life, just by watching them," he said. His brown eyes were on my blue ones. "You can see how they interact with others. That way you can recognize their personalities, the way they perceive the world. It will help get you through the obligations that you have toward them."

"Okay," I said.

"You can also view any mortal that needs comfort. That, or ones that need to be brought up to the Heavens," Adiel said. "Whatever you need, it'll be here, in the Heavenly River." He twisted his body around to face me. "Caelum, it will help if you get involved in the mortal's lives, even for a little bit." He grasped my shoulder gently, before sighing once more. "Well, I better get back to the Souls. You take care of yourself, alright? Stay safe."

"Alright," I said, before Adiel twisted his body around. He walked off into the Golden Gates of the Soul Realm.

I watched him leave silently before my wings flapped, getting me airborne before I left the Heavens.

I could usually feel the sensation of a mortal leaving the Earth and crossing over. It was a change in the energy that I felt. It was a frequency that only the angels could feel.

It was released right before, during, or after their passing.

There was no sense of time in the Afterlife, or for the angels. Everything was based on the mortal's timeline. A timeline that, to an angel that lived for millennia, was incredibly short.

4

I could sense the change in energy as I landed on the road. I pulled my wings in before walking down the street of the neighborhood.

It was almost like a magnetic pull, and I made my way toward the sensation.

As always, no one saw me as I walked along. I grinned at the children playing in the street. They were young, and were enjoying what they were doing. Being youthful and naïve.

I smiled as I walked along the street silently, before I felt the energy again. It was a nearby house. I walked over to the front yard of the home, stepping on the driveway, before pausing.

Wait a moment. I had been here before. A year earlier, to help a family pet transition to the Afterlife. A dog, a Golden Retriever.

I remembered this because the young girl, the daughter, was extremely upset about the dog crossing over. She had named the animal Lola.

But this family…I knew them. I knew this family.

The woman in her late twenties to early thirties who was a single mother, named Phoebe. She had a now seven-year-old daughter, named Camilla.

I shook my head as all the memories flooded back to me. I had been summoned to a home I'd been to before, which meant that this was going to be interesting.

5

The repetitive sound of footsteps made me turn around. I did so, only to see the little girl, Camilla, racing up the street to her place of residence.

Her brown hair bounced along her shoulders. She ran past the tree I was under, gulping in oxygen and making her way up the front steps.

Camilla quickly opened the door to the house.

I immediately ducked inside as the little girl bolted to the kitchen, yanked open the refrigerator, and found a juice box. She hoisted herself up on the high counter and poked a hole in the top of the drink, and then guzzled it down noisily. She gasped every so often as she was so thirsty.

Camilla must have been playing outside for a while, since she was so dehydrated.

I stayed in the living room, right next to the kitchen, monitoring her as she drank her juice box.

"Camilla?"

My eyes darted toward the sound of the woman's voice. I saw the girl's blue eyes widen at how close her mother sounded, and she instantly pushed herself off the counter as she kept the juice box close. Phoebe appeared in the kitchen, her brown hair in a loose ponytail.

"Camilla, you haven't been on the counter, have you? You know that is where I prepare food. Do not put your butt where we eat."

Her daughter hung her head low, but continued to sip her juice through the straw. "I'm sorry," she said once she was able to speak.

"Don't do it again."

The sound of the wind blowing the door open made Phoebe blink her blue eyes, before she ran past me. She shut and locked it quickly.

"Camilla, you don't just leave the front door open!"

Phoebe then walked back into the living room. She plopped down on the couch that was right next to me, oblivious to the fact that I was beside her.

I watched her quietly as she sighed heavily, before glancing over at her daughter. Camilla was just standing in the middle of the kitchen.

Phoebe turned her attention to Camilla, who now was crinkling the empty juice box in her small hand.

"Honey, you cannot leave the front door open," she said, regaining her composure. "Anyone would be able to walk through, and I don't want that. My duty is to keep you safe, Camilla."

Her daughter nodded. "Okay," Camilla said. "It was just that I was very thirsty. I was running around with Sasha and Ava today."

Phoebe smiled at Camilla's words. "Did you have fun?" she asked Camilla as she slowly walked over to her mother.

Camilla nodded. "Yes, I did," she said. "Ava's little brother even came out to play, too. So, yeah, it was fun. I was thirsty when I ran in here. I forgot to shut the front door. I'm sorry."

Phoebe looked at her daughter for a moment before she spoke. "It's alright. Just don't do it again. I'm glad you had fun with Sasha and Ava."

Camilla nodded, smiling, and then bounded into the kitchen to throw out the juice box. She made her way over to her mother afterward, wrapping her arms around her body.

Phoebe closed her eyes as she felt Camilla hug her and returned the gesture. Phoebe seemed to relax immediately. She pulled away from Camilla to kiss her cheek. "I love you, sweetie. More than life itself."

I smiled at what she'd said, and the young girl just grinned. "I love you too, Mom."

I found myself watching both mother and daughter as they pulled away from each other. Phoebe leaned over, grasping Camilla's shoulders.

"Camilla, I need you to go start your homework. You can do it in the kitchen. I'm going to take a short nap, but I will help you in a little bit."

The young girl nodded. "Okay," she said, understanding.

Camilla went into the front hallway before she ran once more into the kitchen with her backpack.

I glanced behind me, seeing Phoebe smile at her little one, before she made herself comfortable on the couch. She was asleep within seconds. A slight smile made its way on my face as I saw Camilla focus on her work. The little girl stopped every so often to look at her mother, who was now fast asleep. But then the expression melted off my face as confusion took over me.

I could still feel the frequency that meant that someone was going to cross over, that someone was going to pass away. I could still sense it. It was very strong as it radiated from the home. I just didn't know who exactly it was coming from.

I squinted, my eyebrows crinkling in confusion.

What the....?

Both mother and daughter seemed healthy as I stood in the living room, watching the little girl doing her schoolwork. Then I peered over at Phoebe, who was breathing in a natural, normal rhythm as she dozed.

What the...?

I didn't understand.

When Phoebe finally opened her eyes, confusion was drenching me.

I didn't understand it at all.

Someone here was dying, but both Camilla and Phoebe seemed very healthy and strong.

Then why was I here?

Phoebe went to unlock the back door and let the breeze blow through before she went over to help Camilla.

I walked through the backyard of the premises, perplexed as I felt my wings come out.

Why had I been summoned to that home? Both mortals appeared so healthy...

I shook my head to clear it before I pushed myself upward, and I flew off into the sky.

The sounds of the rural countryside hit my ears as I landed in the greenery. Horses munched on grass, while flies buzzed around my head. I waved them away from my scalp as I made my way out of the woods and onto the farm.

It was where I'd decided to go after seeing Phoebe and Camilla. I let a breath out of my lungs.

I couldn't feel the magnetic-pull that meant a mortal was shifting. I'd just come here to look at the scenery, to get away from everything that I was dealing with. At least for a minute.

A horse whinnied in the distance as I walked over to the pasture of the animal. I looked at the creature as my thoughts rattled around inside my head.

I didn't understand what had happened before, with the mother and daughter. Phoebe and Camilla. I didn't get it.

The sunlight beamed down on the landscape as I stood on the turf, pondering over the reasoning behind me being summoned to their home. There was a voice in the distance.

"Caelum," it started. I turned around at the familiar tone to see Adiel looking at me. He took a few steps in my direction before he spoke again. "Caelum, everything happens for a reason."

He knew instantly what I was thinking about.

I opened my mouth to respond, but the words never came out. I took a breath before I tried again. "She's healthy, though," I said. "Both her and her daughter are typical mortals. There's nothing wrong with either one of them. I felt the pull, though. I sensed that one of them was going to turn completely into a Soul. I just don't understand." Adiel walked in front of me.

I watched him, glancing behind his body to see his black angel wings protruding from his back. "There are things that we can't comprehend sometimes," he said. "But it will all make sense eventually, Caelum. I promise."

"Could it be that there is something wrong with the frequency? I mean, I did feel a change. I did feel the sensation near the house, when I arrived in the neighborhood. I didn't see anything wrong though," I said to Adiel, who was just silent as I talked to him.

He waited a few seconds before he spoke.

"There are just some things that make sense in the end, not in the beginning, Caelum. There's definitely a reason why you were summoned to that residence. It might not make sense now, but it will. You just must wait and see."

The horse in the nearby pasture snorted loudly, thrashing its tail around to get rid of the flies that were on it, and Adiel paused.

"Caelum," he said after a moment. "Over the course of time, everything will make sense. I promise. Just continue doing your duty, and you will be fine." My eyes met his as Adiel looked at my face. "Just continue doing your responsibility," he said. "Things don't always turn out the way we want. But everything will be understandable, Caelum, in due time."

I guess that was true. I just had to wait and see how this would all turn out. I turned my head toward Adiel, who was still beside me.

"Thank you," I told him, genuinely meaning it.

He just smiled. "Anything to help you, Caelum. I'll see you later, alright?"

He walked away from me, extending his wings out.

I blinked as I saw Adiel fly up into the sky, leaving me on the ground alone. I sighed as I watched where he left, before I eventually followed him. I soared upward into the skies and left the rural countryside behind.

6

Phoebe and Camilla were on my mind as I flew into the Heavens. I left the Earth behind while I continued to propel myself upward.

I just couldn't stop thinking about the both of them. When I finally got to the Afterlife, I saw Adiel pause, his eyebrows raising as he saw me behind him.

"Have you come to see a Soul?" he asked.

I shook my head, a little out of breath as my heart pounded my ribcage. "No. No, I…" But then I stopped, wondering if I was sure of what I was about to say. I took a breath before starting again. "I want to go to the Heavenly River, Adiel."

He smiled.

"I want to see her. I want to see her, as well as her daughter."

Adiel nodded. "Okay, Caelum," he said.

I quickly walked over to the Water, which was calm, and looked into it.

"Go on, Caelum," Adiel said. "Go check on them. I have to get back to the Soul Realm, but you can stay here if you want. Be safe."

He walked away through the reflection of the River. I glanced up to see him going through the Golden Gates, before he disappeared into the Spirit Realm.

I took a deep breath before looking down at the Heavenly River again. This was all while my heart was pummeling my chest. I could see my reflection in it. My blue eyes, my anxious face... But then I spoke up, in a slightly trembling voice. "Show me Phoebe and Camilla. Show me the home that I was at with the mother and daughter."

The Water churned instantly, and within a few moments, it became smooth. And then the image showed up in the River. The image of Phoebe and Camilla together.

I smiled as I saw them both in the Water.

The River had shown them at that very moment, at their present time.

I focused on the image, studying it. I was trying to understand more about this single mother and her daughter that I'd just visited. I paid close attention as the image quickly became clearer, before I watched the rest of what was going on unfold silently.

7

*C*amilla was excited.

She was sprinting around the kitchen, skipping on her heels. Phoebe shook her head and smiled as she sat on the couch in the living room. She was getting her shoes on as her daughter ran around.

"I guess you're already set to leave, aren't you?" she asked Camilla. The young girl nodded rapidly. "Yep. Yep, I am."

"You're ready to see your Grandma and Grandpa, Camilla?" Again, she nodded quickly.

"Okay," Phoebe said, putting her foot down on the floor again. "Alright, let's go…. Whoa," she paused as she got off the couch, her eyebrows crinkling into her forehead when she stood upright. "Ugh," she said, biting her lip in discomfort before she glanced at Camilla. She quickly changed her expression, instead grinning at her daughter. "Sorry, honey, it's just that my foot fell asleep. Hold on a second," she said, before wincing as she walked around, trying to get the blood flow back in her legs. She paced around before sighing, looking again at her daughter. "Okay," she told her. "It's all better."

Camilla smiled in response.

Phoebe grinned, before grabbing the keys that were on the counter. "Alright, Camilla, let's go see Grandma and Grandpa."

And they both walked out of the house. The garage door opened, before closing as mother and daughter exited their residence.

The image in the Heavenly River went away as the water rippled. Soon, I just saw my own reflection in the liquid. I stared at it, at my blue eyes that appeared perplexed as I realized what I'd just seen.

This woman, Phoebe, she *seemed* alright. Nothing was visibly wrong with her, or her daughter, for that matter.

The only thing that was different was the fact that Phoebe's foot fell asleep, but that alone wouldn't be a cause for concern. That wouldn't cause the energy feeling that coursed through my bones when I saw her. Although, I kept getting that sensation, even just watching the Heavenly River. And I thought I would still have that awareness if I were to go near her, or her daughter, again.

I blinked, coming back to myself.

I just was going to have to watch over Phoebe and Camilla. I had to see what was going to happen to them, while also fulfilling my obligation to the rest of the mortals. I was going to have to multitask.

I twisted my body around from the Heavenly River, instead bringing my wings out and getting ready to leave the Afterlife. Before I did though, I stared at the Golden Gates, whispering, "Thank you, Adiel."

8

"Come on, come on, come on," the surgeon urged as he placed the device on either side of the man's heart. He turned to one of the other doctors, who was operating it. "Send the shock," he said.

The other man did so as I stood behind the surgeon, looking down at the young man on the operating table. I stared at his face, his eyes that were all taped up for the surgery. He was undergoing an open-heart procedure, and his entire chest was open. The electrical pulse soared through the organ to restart it. But I could sense that there was trouble immediately.

"Come on. Don't do this now."

I saw the other personnel glance at each other as I watched. I could see the uncertainty on their faces through the face masks that they were wearing. All the while, the heart monitor was flat-lining. The continuous, loud noise flooded the space.

"No, no, no," the surgeon said again, looking for a second time at the doctor overseeing the heart instrument. "Send another shock," he said.

The doctor obeyed, delivering a light pulse to the patient's heart again, but it was still unsuccessful.

"No, no, no."

But the reason I was here was to bring the man's Soul up to the Golden Gates. The patient was losing his life.

"Again," the surgeon said for a third time.

The other doctor looked somber, but he did what he was told.

The surgeon glanced at the heart monitor, but it was no use as the insistent beeping sliced through the operating room. I could hear his breath catch, and that was when one of the female doctors put her hand on his shoulder.

"Dr. Smith?" she asked hesitantly. "Dr. Smith?"

He just looked away from the monitor, instead gazing into the distance. I could see, through his mask, that his jaw was clenched. He was holding back tears. He exhaled in a gust as everyone else in the room stared at him, bleak looks on their faces. The surgeon spoke in a hollow voice. "He's gone. Turn off the equipment." The man then twisted away from his colleagues, heading toward the door of the operating room. He ripped off the gloves, tearing off his mask in defeat.

I bit my lip as I watched him leave, before I turned to see everyone else exchange sad looks.

One of the women looked down at the young man's body, at his face, before her jaw clenched. "I'm sorry," she said, before she turned off the monitors and followed the rest of the doctors, who had all left the operating room.

They left me alone in the surgical room with the young man's body.

I stared after them, taking a few steps toward the door. I watched as they all took off their face masks, before I heard a gasp behind me. I twisted around to see the Soul of the young man watching me, looking completely baffled. His hair was as black as my wings, while his eyes were a light green. His peach-colored skin was now free of the blood that had been all over the empty shell of his body. He appeared to look very young- maybe in his late teens. "No, no, no," he said, shaking his head as he looked at me. He appeared horrified. "No," he said a second time as he began to blink back tears. He glanced at his body that was still wide open, his heart visible. That was when the water came down his cheeks. "Am I dreaming?" he asked thickly as he looked back up at me. "Please tell me I'm dreaming."

I just watched his green eyes for a few moments before I spoke. "No. No, you're not."

"What...? What...?" the young man started but couldn't continue as a sob choked him. He took a gulp of oxygen before starting again. "What happened?"

I looked at him silently, before peering over at his still body on the table. I took a deep breath before I spoke. "You didn't make it through the procedure," I told him softly as I watched his body. "You didn't make it, and I'm here to bring you to the Afterlife." My eyes flickered back up to his. They were filled with tears. "I'm here to bring you to Heaven," I said, watching his face.

"Who... who are you?" he asked, before pausing. I stayed quiet as he began again. "Are you... you an angel?"

I nodded. "Yes. Yes, I am. My name is Caelum."

He gulped. "Can I just... just... see my parents before you take me?"

His voice was shaky when he spoke, and I nodded again.

"Yes. Yes, you may," I said. "Yes, you may see your parents."

The young man sniffled. "I just... want to say goodbye to them."

"I understand," I said, and I completely did. Some Souls just needed closure.

"Okay, thank you."

"You're welcome," I responded. "Anything to help a Soul."

The young man's green eyes darted to mine. His had drifted to the floor, but he looked up quickly when I said that. He inhaled sharply, exhaling before he began staring at me. I could see a tear run down his cheek. His green eyes appeared completely defeated as he looked at me, utterly raw from the emotion that was engulfing him. "I didn't know that the operation would turn out this way," he said. "I went in for a routine operation, but I didn't make it. I thought that I would. My parents thought so too…" he trailed off. He looked at his still body on the operating table. "My parents though, do they already know?" He glanced at me questioningly.

I was unsure of the answer. I shook my head. "I don't know if the doctors already told your family. But you can definitely go see them. You will be able to see them, but they won't obviously be able to see your Soul or hear you. They will be able to sense you, though, if you touch your parents."

I could tell by the way the young man said the statement that he wanted to see his mother and father. He wanted to touch them. He nodded understandingly before he took a step toward me.

"Okay," he said.

At that moment, there was a doctor with a face mask that came into the surgery room. The man gulped as he saw the young man's body on the table. He sniffled as he gathered up the bloody equipment that was nearby. Then he ducked out of the room, a sob in his throat.

"Come on," I said, motioning for the young man to follow me.

He gulped. He was behind me as we walked out of the rooms that only medical personnel could be in, before we made it into the waiting room. He inhaled sharply as he saw who I realized was his mother and father. They were sitting in the chairs of the waiting room, appearing anxious. His mother bit her lip, breathing heavily as her foot tapped the floor insistently. His father was leaning forward, his head hanging as he gripped his skull with his hands. They hadn't been told yet.

I watched them quietly, and I could see, out of the corner of my eye, the young man come up beside me. His glistening green eyes were glued on his parents.

Footsteps in the nearby hallway made me turn. I saw the surgeon for the open-heart procedure walking over to the young man's parents. He cleared his throat as he approached them. The mom elbowed her husband to get his attention, since he still was leaning forward. He glanced over at his wife, before they both noticed the surgeon. Expectant looks were on their faces as they stood up from their chairs.

The surgeon took a deep breath, blinking for several moments before he spoke.

"We did everything we could, but unfortunately, his heart was not strong enough. We used all our capability to save him, but he didn't make it," he said, to which I could see both of the parent's eyes widen. Tears began to gather as the surgeon continued. "We tried to restart his heart, but it wouldn't move again," he said.

The young man's father threw his head forward. His forehead scrunched up in an expression of utter agony as the doctor's words hit him. He gripped his skull again, this time appearing to look like he was going to rip out his own hair. The mother breathed deeply, before she began crying, tears streaming down her face. The father turned toward his wife, enveloping her in a hug.

"Please accept my condolences," the surgeon said, taking one last glance at the mother and father before walking out of the waiting room. I could hear him sobbing once he got close to the area that was only for the employees, and then he disappeared.

The young man beside me turned to watch the surgeon, before twisting back around to see his parents. They were now crying on each other's shoulders.

"Lucas…" the mother said thickly. "Poor…Lucas," she bawled, gripping her husband hard, while he remained silent, completely overcome with emotion. A garbled sound erupted from her throat as she sobbed, her stomach spasming against her husband as he embraced her. They just stood there, in the middle of the waiting room, holding each other for several minutes.

The young man beside me, Lucas, was crying along with his parents.

I turned to him as fresh tears stained his face. "You can go to them," I said, motioning toward his parents. "Go on."

Lucas gulped, his chest hiccupping slightly as he looked at me. Then he sighed, taking a few steps toward his family, who had broken apart from their hug. They began to wipe their eyes.

Lucas made it right in front of his mother, before he glanced behind him, looking at me. I nodded, encouraging him to continue what he wanted to do. "Go on," I said.

Lucas twisted back around, gazing at his mother's sad face, before leaning forward. He enveloped her in a hug. I could see her expression change almost immediately at her son's Soul's touch. She blinked rapidly, confusion showing on her face as she felt the energy change. Her raw eyes crinkled as the feeling took over her, and then she inhaled quickly. She gasped as Lucas spoke in her ear. "Bye, Mom. I love you," he said, and then pulled away from her gently. She had an expression of complete bewilderment on her face as Lucas went over to his father, repeating what he'd done with his mother. "Bye, Dad. I love you, and I'll miss you."

He stepped away from both of his parents then, twisting around to look at my face.

I just stared at him, before he turned his body to look again at his parents, who appeared shocked. They stared at each other, before the father spoke in a raspy voice.

"Mary, did you feel that?"

Lucas' breath caught as he realized that his presence had been felt, and I smiled, looking over at him. He smiled back at me.

"I did," his mother responded, nodding rapidly. "I did." She sniffled, before clearing her throat and wiping her eyes.

I peered back over at Lucas, whose eyes were glistening again. He seemed to be more relaxed as he smiled through his tears. He was smiling at his mom and dad as they hugged one last time. Then the parents broke apart, sniffling.

I watched them for several more seconds, my thoughts instantly going to how they had reacted to their son's Soul.

Mortals could sense both the Souls and the angels, if we chose to have our presence known.

I blinked as the realization hit me. I was going to have to talk with Adiel again, talk to him about this.

I found myself looking at the parents of Lucas while I was lost in thought. The sound of one of the doctor's shoes squeaking against the floor made me come back to myself. I took a deep breath before I turned to Lucas, who was still right beside me. I put a hand on his shoulder.

He glanced up at me.

"Lucas, it's time to go."

He nodded understandingly. "Okay. Thank you for letting me say goodbye," he said.

"Anything to help a Soul," I responded, echoing what I had said earlier.

Lucas grinned at me, and I smiled back at him. I was happy to help him. He found closure, seeing and hugging his parents.

It helped him so that he could now move on to the Afterlife.

I tapped Lucas' shoulder. "Lucas," I said, "we have to go."

Lucas twisted around to look at me, right as I felt my thick wings come out of my back. "Wow," he said, admiring the black color as his eyes widened.

I smiled as I saw his facial expression, before extending my hand out. I held his green eyes with mine. "Are you ready?"

Lucas sighed again. He nodded, grasping my hand.

"Okay," I said, wrapping my arms around him. "Let's go." And we flew up into the Heavens.

9

A diel was waiting as we entered the Afterlife. He must've seen us coming from the Heavenly River. He grinned kindly as he saw Lucas, who looked meek when he saw Adiel.

Then Lucas smiled nervously. "Hello," he said as I took my arms away from him. "Are you…. another angel?" Lucas asked.

Adiel continued to have the warm expression on his face. "Yes. Yes, I am. My name is Adiel. I'm here to bring you to the Spirit Realm. Caelum here, he brought you to the Afterlife, while I will watch over you." Lucas turned his head to look at my face, before the Soul brought his attention back to Adiel. Adiel had a calming expression in his eyes, a warm smile. "You're safe now," he told him.

Lucas breathed deeply, exhaling in a gust. "Will I… will I be able to see my parents?" he asked, before clearing his throat, and starting again. "I mean, will I be able to view them, keep up with their lives, even though I'm not there anymore?"

My eyes snapped up to Adiel's as I heard that question. I was wondering the same thing. Sometimes things were different for Souls, so I didn't know what Adiel was going to say.

He nodded, listening to Lucas' words, and I blinked. "Yes. You will be able to view your family. That Water over there," he pointed to the Heavenly River nearby, "will help you see your relatives whenever you want, if that brings you peace."

Lucas' face lit up at Adiel's words. That was certainly going to bring him peace. Lucas' green eyes drifted over to where the Heavenly River was, staring at it for several seconds. "I just...miss them already," he said.

Adiel watched him. He nodded. "Well, you'll always be able to see them, if you ever want to."

Lucas brought his eyes back to Adiel's. "Thank you," he said.

"You're welcome," Adiel replied in a kind tone. "My duty is to make sure Souls are comfortable in their new environment. Now," he said, twisting around toward the Golden Gates that were behind him. "Are you ready?"

Lucas glanced at the Gates, his eyes bulging before he regained his composure. His gaze shifted to Adiel before he nodded. "Yes. Yes, I'm ready."

"Good," Adiel said. Lucas walked in front of him, with Adiel following close behind.

And they both walked off, toward the Golden Gates.

10

"What are you thinking about?" Adiel asked as he came up beside me. I glanced up at him, bringing my attention away from the Heavenly River.

I'd been staring in the Waters, lost in thought while watching my reflection. I was thinking about how Lucas had touched his parents, how they could feel his presence.

"About... the young man before," I said, reiterating my thoughts that were in my head. "He hugged his mother and father. He made his presence known. Could... could angels do that too?" I asked.

Adiel's brown eyes seemed to sparkle. "Yes, we can. Not only can Souls do that, but angels can as well." He was about to turn away, but then his forehead wrinkled as a thought came to him. "Is it the mother and daughter that you're thinking about?"

My eyes darted up to his, before I swallowed hard. "Yes."

I should've known that he already knew where my thoughts were. I just couldn't seem to stop thinking about Phoebe and Camilla. Bringing Lucas to the Afterlife seemed to continue the thoughts of them. I couldn't get them out of my head.

"Caelum." I looked up as Adiel said my name. "Both Souls and angels can be sensed by the mortals whenever we want them to. We both can't be seen. You must be careful if you want to do that, for an angel, at least."

I nodded understandingly. "I know," I said. "I get it."

"Just be careful," Adiel repeated.

"I want to see them again," I said, the words seeming to spill out of my mouth as I watched his brown eyes. "I want to visit them."

"Then go see them," Adiel said. "Go visit them, Caelum. Just don't forget your obligation to the rest of the mortals."

I swallowed hard against my throat at what he said. "Okay, I'll do that," I responded as Adiel stared.

Even though they wouldn't be able to see me, I would be able to see Phoebe and Camilla. I would be able to check on them. I felt a little nervous, which, for an angel like me, almost never happened. I had never really felt this emotion before. But I pulled through it as my wings erupted from my back. I flew out of the Heavens, leaving Adiel behind.

11

I landed right in the front lawn of the familiar house as I saw the children playing in the street.

"Mom?"

I turned around to see Camilla peering through the window, at the commotion in the road. I could hear the little girl through the home, though the front door was shut.

"Mom, is it alright if I go play?"

I couldn't hear Phoebe's response as I walked up the front steps. The entrance to the house opened quickly as she ran outside. I swiftly went inside the home, looking behind me as the girl turned back around. She had forgotten to shut the door again, but luckily, she ran back to the front steps. She closed the front entranceway before it clicked, signifying that it was indeed sealed. I heard her footsteps as she ran across the driveway. They disappeared as she moved farther away, running to the street. A grin was on my face as I turned toward the hallway of the house, but it faded as I noticed that all the lights were off in the home. The scene appeared gloomy.

Then I noticed Phoebe in the kitchen. She was sitting at the table, her elbow on it as she put her hand over her forehead. A frustrated expression was on her face before she shut her eyes.

My forehead scrunched as I looked at Phoebe. What was going on with her?

I gulped worriedly, my emotional state switching as I saw Phoebe's expression. The grin on my face had changed to a look of dread. My heart was thudding my ribs as I immediately walked over to her.

I felt my intestines loop in knots as I saw her head in her hand. She was breathing in a slow, rhythmic pattern.

It was almost like she was meditating.

Her name was on the tip of my tongue even though she wouldn't be able to hear me. The way she was acting was so alarming. But then she moved her palm away from her face, and I noticed the hand tremors that went through her extremity. They made it impossible for her to keep it steady. She tried to fight the tremors, and I could see her bite her lip in concentration, but she couldn't stop the shaking.

That was when I noticed the greeting card that was on the table. Phoebe had been trying to write a card to her mother.

I could see the other one that Phoebe's mom had written as I peered over at it. I attempted to understand exactly what was going on, and stared at Phoebe, alarmed. She gasped in a lungful of air, when suddenly, she began crying.

Tears started running down her cheeks, cutting trails into her flesh. I instantly felt my heart sink at the sight.

Of course, I wasn't expecting anything happy by coming here, since I came to mortals to ease them into the Afterlife. Even though that was my duty, just watching Phoebe struggle with an issue that I didn't exactly understand… It was heartbreaking.

I didn't know what was going on with her. I still felt the magnetic-like frequency that was emitted when a mortal crossed over. When they transitioned completely into a Soul. It was almost like it was tugging me closer and closer in the house.

I blinked repeatedly, taken aback. This was just so strange....

Phoebe continued to sob for several seconds. Tears were hitting the greeting card that was on the table, before she quickly stopped. She gazed through the kitchen to look at the front door. I followed where she was looking and realized there were footsteps near the house. Camilla was running back to the front door. Phoebe inhaled sharply at the noise. She instantly wiped her eyes as I turned my attention back to her, and Phoebe immediately got up from the table.

Carefully, she pushed away from it before attempting to stand. She was able to slowly with a grimace of pain. She bit her lip a second time.

I recognized that expression. Her foot had fallen asleep again. Oh, no.

Something was wrong with Phoebe.

The fact that this was no coincidence and that Phoebe was in pain quickly dawned on me.

I inhaled deeply as I backed away from her. I let Phoebe pass as she exited the kitchen, before the front door opened. Camilla bounded inside. I could see Phoebe grit her teeth as she tried to get the blood flow back in her legs, and then she spoke, calling out to her daughter.

"Camilla, you're back already?"

"Yes. Everyone went inside to eat. I didn't realize that it was time for dinner, Mom."

Phoebe blinked, her forehead scrunching together in bewilderment. Her eyes darted around, not exactly looking at anything as she realized what Camilla had said.

It was clear that Phoebe had forgotten. "It's dinnertime?" she asked quietly to herself as she went into the kitchen again. She glanced at the clock that was on the stove nearby.

It was six-thirty. It was the mortal's daylight savings time, which meant that it was still light out, even though it was late.

This must have confused Phoebe. She inhaled. Phoebe had forgotten. Which, from what I could tell, was unusual for her.

Phoebe's distraction was so palpable that I could almost feel it. She twisted back around to look at Camilla, who was staring at her mother expectantly.

"Umm, honey, I'm sorry about that. I forgot to make something tonight. But… but," she trailed off for a moment. My heart was pounding my ribs. "We can have something special," she finished.

Phoebe made her way over to the freezer.

It didn't escape my notice that Phoebe was walking with a limp on the way over to get the food.

She opened it. "Who do I know who loves pizza?" Phoebe said happily. Camilla squealed, skipping into the kitchen, and smiled.

I would have been smiling along with Camilla, but she was oblivious to the danger that her mother was in. That made everything that Phoebe was going through incredibly scary. Camilla was clueless.

Wait…

I paused as I thought for a moment.

Wait…

The sensation, the energy-feeling that was now coursing throughout the home was there because…because… of Phoebe. Her actions were now making sense as I blinked, beginning to understand what was happening. That was why the energy, the pull was so strong. It was Phoebe.

Phoebe was… She was…slowly dying.

My eyes widened as the realization slammed into me. The force of it hit me like I had been struck by a large vehicle.

The energy was present because of Phoebe.

But…. Camilla… Her little girl… What was going to happen to Camilla?

My breath caught as I turned my attention to the daughter, suddenly worried for her future. What was going to happen to Camilla when her mother passed?

My eyes darted from Camilla to Phoebe, and, to my shock, they began watering. The thought of the little girl enveloped my mind. Little Camilla…

Just the mere thought of her being without her mother made me cry. This, like being nervous, almost never happened.

I had never really gotten attached or drawn to a Soul, or a mortal, the way I had been with Phoebe and Camilla. And yet I blinked away tears, sniffling as I watched Phoebe turn around to look at her daughter. Camilla was sitting by the kitchen table.

"Camilla, we're going to be eating a little bit late," she said. "Why don't you go watch some TV? You can watch that cartoon you like so much."

"Okay, Mom," she responded happily, hopping off the chair before disappearing into the living room. She found the remote control and sank into the couch. Camilla navigated and settled on an animation.

The little girl put the remote control back, and then laid against the couch, enjoying the show.

I stood on the carpet of the living room, watching Camilla for several moments before looking back over at Phoebe. She looked at her daughter as she stood in the kitchen, her attention on Camilla. But then I saw tears begin to well in her eyes.

"No. No. No," I found myself saying out loud, even though Phoebe and Camilla would not be able to hear me. "No, don't cry."

But then my eyes started tearing up as I saw the look of utter terror on Phoebe's face.

Phoebe knew that something was wrong with her. She just didn't know what it was, nor did she know that whatever she was struggling with was going to take her life. Phoebe just knew that she was sick.

It was almost like I could read her mind, the way she stared at her daughter. She was terrified of what would happen to her.

What would happen to Camilla?

I sniffled, gulping back tears as I stared at Phoebe, who was now crying silently. Tears were streaming down her face.

She continued crying, and then just took a deep breath as she attempted to calm down. She breathed in and out, slowly, rhythmically. In and out. In and out.

Afterward, she disappeared, running upstairs into her bedroom. A mixture between a cough and a sob was in her throat.

I watched her quietly as she left, before regaining my composure and glancing over at Camilla, who was still watching her cartoon. The daughter was content.

I wanted so badly to follow Phoebe, but I resisted the urge as I stayed behind. I walked instead to the kitchen, going and viewing what was on the table. I gritted my teeth together as I looked at the greeting card on the table - the one Phoebe had attempted to write in.

The writing on the other greeting card was in print, not cursive, so it should've been easy to read the card that replied to it, but Phoebe's was illegible. I couldn't read the card, at all.

I squinted, thinking back to her hand tremors, and realized that that was probably the reason she'd been so upset.

But what was going on with her?

She was obviously sick, now I could see that. She was sick with something.

I stood in the kitchen, lost in thought as I looked down at both greeting cards. I was thinking about Phoebe's ailment.

The sound of the oven beeping startled me. I jumped.

Camilla turned her attention toward the noise, before she hopped down from the couch. She turned off the TV and ran over to the staircase.

"Mom!" she yelled. "The oven is ready!"

"Okay, honey. Thank you!" I heard Phoebe call back. "I'm coming."

I heard footsteps as she came down the stairs, and I backed out of the kitchen as she entered. She swiftly put the food in the oven.

It was when she turned back around that I noticed her raw skin. She had been sobbing.

Oh, Phoebe, I thought as I saw her face, *you poor thing.*

And then I paused.

I'd never really thought like that before. For a mortal, or a Soul. But here I was, crying and worrying about this single mother and her little daughter. Everything regarding Phoebe and Camilla was the start of a new feeling.

I guessed that my heart was no longer closed off when it came to these mortals. My heart was beginning to melt.

"It'll take several minutes to cook, sweetie," I heard Phoebe say to Camilla. I shook my head, coming back to myself. "Go and finish your show. I'll let you know when it's done. Or…" she stopped for a moment before continuing, "the oven will beep when the pizza is cooked."

My head went to the side slightly, questioningly, at the way she trailed off. I had a feeling that it was because of her ailment.

But what was it? What was she struggling with?

"Okay, Mom," Camilla said cheerfully. Phoebe smiled at her, even though I could see that it was a forced expression. She was in pain. Emotional pain.

I stood in the living room, silently watching as Camilla passed me. She went and sat down on the couch again before turning on her animation. I brought my attention back to Phoebe, who breathed in deeply to collect herself. She twisted around toward the refrigerator. She got a juice box for Camilla, and a water pitcher for herself. She went over to get a drinking glass from the cabinet, walking over to the table to get set up for their dinner.

I watched her movements carefully as she put the napkins out, studying her. I was extremely nervous for her, suddenly.

"Mom?"

I looked up to see Camilla staring at her mother from the couch that she was still on.

"Yes, honey?" Phoebe turned around from the drawers to look at her daughter.

"Can I turn on the lights? It's a little too dark in here," she said.

Camilla was right. It was incredibly dark in their home. Too dark.

"Sure," Phoebe replied. "You can turn the light back on."

"Is your head still hurting?" Camilla asked tentatively, to which my head snapped over to look at Phoebe.

My head moved so fast I thought I was going to get a crick in my neck. Now she had a headache?

She shook her head, looking at her daughter. "No, Camilla. My head isn't hurting anymore. But thank you for asking."

"You're welcome. I just wanted to know if you were feeling better."

"Well, I am," Phoebe said.

The young girl grinned at her mother, and then got up from the couch, heading over to the light switch. Camilla turned on the illumination. The brightness instantly soaked the living room, before Camilla walked up to Phoebe, wrapping her arms around her.

"Aww, thank you, honey," Phoebe said, returning the hug.

I stared at both Phoebe and Camilla, who then went over to the kitchen table, waiting for their dinner. I looked at Phoebe, studying her behavior, trying to see if anything else was out of the ordinary. There was nothing though as the oven finally beeped.

I watched as the mortals that I'd been looking after ate their meal. That was when my mind went from Phoebe and Camilla to Adiel as I studied them.

Instantly, I had a desire to speak with Adiel about this, about these mortals that I was now preoccupied with. I just had never had this happen before, me being so drawn to them. It was a strange sensation, but at the same time, it felt like I was protecting them. It felt that way, even though that wasn't my duty.

I ducked out of the home as Phoebe opened the back door after dinner. She had gone outside to see the rest of the sunset. I had to get back to the Heavens, to talk with Adiel. I took a deep breath through my lungs as I felt my wings extend, and then I was propelled into the sky.

12

Adiel was waiting for me when I flew into the Heavens. He opened his mouth as I landed in front of him. "I saw you coming," he said.

So, he most definitely saw me at Phoebe's house. He must've seen everything.

"Did you... did you see what happened?" I asked him, reiterating the thoughts that were inside my head.

Adiel nodded. "Yes, I did, Caelum. I saw your reaction as well. You spoke out loud to the mortals, even though they weren't able to hear you."

"Did I do anything bad?" I wondered.

Adiel shook his head. "No, Caelum. You didn't do anything wrong. You are beginning to get involved in their lives, in the lives of the mother and daughter. That is a good thing. It is better to be involved with a mortal, or a Soul, then to never have an attachment at all."

"She's...Sick," I said, my voice catching slightly as I looked at Adiel. "Adiel, she's sick. I just don't know what it is. But...." I stopped, taking a breath to steady myself, "she has a little girl that she's going to leave behind. What...? What....? What is going to happen to little Camilla?"

I stared at Adiel, since my eyes had hit the ground.

Adiel sighed, before he spoke. "Caelum, there are many mortals that can help that little girl in case of an emergency. In this case, it would be the mother's death."

Just the word *death* made my eyes tear up. Adiel noticed this and placed a palm on my shoulder.

"Caelum, there's always the girl's father, or the grandparents, who can take care of her."

I blinked at what he said, trying to compose myself again. I sniffled.

"But…. but how will she remember her mother? Camilla must have the memory of Phoebe. The child is only seven years of age."

"Well, then, both of us can help with that," Adiel stated. "I can grant Phoebe permission to leave the Soul Realm in order to be with her daughter. This is for a limited amount of the mortal's time. You can help her go to Earth and see Camilla. That way, it can give both you and Phoebe peace of mind. The Heavenly River will always help as well. It's exactly like what I told Lucas. He wanted to see his parents. The Heavenly River will show you whatever you wish to see from Earth." Adiel stared at me. "Look at me, Caelum," he said, and I did. "That child will never forget her mother. I promise you that. I can grant Phoebe's Soul permission to see you anytime you want," he said. "There's just a limited amount of the mortal's time that she'll be able to be on Earth to see her little girl, her little Camilla."

I nodded, and when I turned to look at Adiel, he was watching me. A thoughtful expression abruptly took over his face.

"What?" I asked as he turned his head to the side slightly. He was thinking.

"Caelum, have you ever been inside the Soul Realm, been inside the Golden Gates?"

I blinked, suddenly taken aback.

"Umm, no. I cannot remember the last time I was there."

Maybe I was there millennia ago, when I had first gotten assigned to take Souls to the Afterlife, but that was a thousand years ago, so I couldn't remember.

I shook my head, coming back to myself.

"No," I repeated. "I can't remember, Adiel. I'm sorry."

"You don't have to be sorry," he said. "Just..." he started, before twisting around, gazing at the Golden Gates that were behind him. "Come with me. It'll help you feel better. I have a surprise. Someone wants to see you."

My forehead crinkled in confusion.

What? What did he mean? Someone wanted to see me?

"Adiel, what are you talking about?" I asked as he began walking. But I followed closely as he advanced toward the Gates.

"Just follow me," he said. "You'll understand once we get inside."

I shook my head in bewilderment, before I just decided to go along with him. Based on what he had said, though, I guessed I was going to go along with what he was saying.

13

I took a breath through my lungs as I looked at the Golden Gates. They were *a lot* bigger than they seemed. They went high above me, disappearing into the whiteness of the Heavens. I reached out to touch the Gates. Adiel smiled.

As soon as my fingers touched them, I could feel the magnetic-like pull that meant a Soul had crossed over. It was radiating from the Golden Gates, the sensation. It drenched them, and I twisted around to look at Adiel.

"It's because of the Spirits. Every single one of the Souls is inside here, which is why the feeling is so strong," he explained.

I nodded as I heard his words.

"Now," Adiel said, looking in my eyes. "Are you ready to go through the Gates?"

"Yes," I responded as I brought my attention back to them. I looked through the structure to see what appeared to be white fog settled behind them. "Yes," I repeated. "Yes, I'm ready."

Adiel placed his hand on my shoulder in a comforting gesture. Then he stared at the gigantic barrier which kept the Souls safe, at the Gates that were in front of us. He murmured the words, ones that only the angels knew, and I watched in amazement as the Golden Gates opened. They slowly unlatched as Adiel turned to face me, motioning toward the inside of the now open barrier for the Souls.

"Come on, Caelum," he said. "Let's go."

My heart was pummeling my ribs as he turned around. I followed close behind him as we entered the Soul Realm.

I had no idea what to expect next as I walked into the protected area. My eyes were on Adiel's back the entire time, studying his body language carefully. I had no idea what he had been talking about before either, when he said that there was someone who wanted to see me. I trusted his judgement though, so I kept up with him as he advanced deeper into the Realm of the Spirits.

My thoughts rattled around inside my brain as I made my way over to him. I walked with him as we moved through the Realm.

I stopped where I was as Adiel paused, motioning toward the vastness of the Soul Realm. I squinted, confused, as I looked ahead of me. I shook my head at Adiel, who turned to watch my face.

I couldn't see anything, or anyone, in front of me.

All I could see was the white fog that seemed to drench the Spirit Realm, the portion of it that we weren't in yet.

"What is it?" I asked Adiel, who just began to grin. "What's going on?"

But again, Adiel smiled, his brown eyes sparkling. He twisted around to the white fog. My forehead wrinkled in confusion.

That was when the sound of heavy panting hit my ears, followed by the sight of the fog dispersing slightly. A medium-sized figure bounded toward Adiel.

He laughed as the figure headed over toward the both of us, and that was when a gasp soared through my lungs. The figure came out of the low-hanging clouds.

The figure… It was a dog. But not just any dog. It was Lola. Phoebe and Camilla's Golden Retriever who had passed away a year before. It was the Soul of Lola that was bounding toward Adiel happily.

"Come here, Lola," he said, his grin now radiating throughout his entire face. The energy soaked his body. "Good girl. You're such a good girl." He thumped his hand against Lola's side, rubbing her ears as she went up on her hind legs, licking Adiel's cheek.

He laughed, and I felt a smile come across my face as the dog saw me. She wagged her tail rapidly.

She made her way toward me before she licked my hand, walking in circles around my body.

Adiel turned his attention to me as he laughed again. Lola was now on the ground of the Soul Realm, on her back as she showed me her belly. A laugh got stuck in my throat as I looked back up at Adiel, who was grinning.

"Well, go on," he encouraged.

I leaned down and scratched her underbelly, laughing once more as Lola moaned in contentment.

"Aww," I said as she shut her eyes, momentarily relaxed. "You are a cutie."

"I thought that she might help you," Adiel said, causing me to look up.

I nodded at him, smiling. "Thank you," I told him.

"You're welcome, Caelum. Anything to help you feel better."

And I knew he genuinely meant it.

I'd really been upset thinking about the fact that Phoebe was dying. But the Soul of Lola was helping me get through the emotions that I'd been dealing with.

She was making me feel serene. All the stress had seemed to leave my body when I played with her.

The Golden Retriever got up from the ground, causing me to get up from my crouch. Lola abruptly got on her hind legs, licking my cheek.

"Oh, Lola," I said, a grin on my face as I felt the dog's tongue on my skin. "Thank you, sweetie."

Adiel's eyes were soft as I looked back up at him after rubbing Lola's ears. "She can help you," he said. referring to Lola as the dog walked up to him. He petted her head gently. "Whenever you're feeling upset, you can come in the Golden Gates, and see Lola's Soul. Just be sure to let me know," Adiel said.

"Would… would I…. be able to bring her to Earth with me?" I asked. Maybe if Camilla and Phoebe felt the presence of their former pet, they might have peace of mind about her.

I remembered how Camilla had reacted when the Golden Retriever had to be euthanized. This was after Lola was hit by a car. The dog's legs had been shattered by the vehicle, causing irreparable damage. Any movement would cause Lola to whimper in agony. It had been difficult for Phoebe to even get the dog into the car to bring her to the vet. She'd been found in the road, bleeding profusely.

I'd seen a lot of reactions of people to the death of a loved one, but I never could quite shake the memory of six-year-old Camilla at that particular moment. She'd been crying so hard that she'd literally vomited. She'd been shaking so horribly at the stress of the fact that her doggy, a Christmas present two years before, was going to cross over. I was there, in the room at the back of the vet hospital, as Camilla said goodbye to Lola. I remembered that she'd kissed the top of the Golden Retriever's head, saying goodbye before she'd been ushered out of the room by her father.

That was the only moment that I'd ever really seen him. Right before Lola had passed away.

It was once Camilla was out of the room that Phoebe said bye to Lola. She had been upset as well about the fact that the dog was going to cross over. Phoebe had begun petting the Golden Retriever, comforting Lola as she whimpered, and that was when I saw the vet come to the front of the dog, near Lola's legs.

I didn't watch as the vet inserted the needle into Lola's front extremity. The vet put her out of her misery.

All I had been focusing on was Lola, as she'd slowly taken her last few breaths.

I'd touched Lola's shoulder as she'd passed away, and, within a few moments, I'd seen the Soul of the Golden Retriever right behind me.

Lola had been in the Soul Realm, inside the Golden Gates, ever since.

I blinked, coming back to myself, away from the memory that was taking over me. I cleared my throat, my eyes on Adiel.

"Can I bring her to Earth with me?" I repeated. "It would help Phoebe and Camilla greatly."

Adiel grinned. "Yes, Caelum. Yes, you can. It's exactly like what I said about Phoebe. I can grant Lola permission to leave the Spirit Realm. It works for animals as well, not just humans."

I smiled.

I was going to do that. At some point, I was going to bring Lola to Earth. This was in order to see Phoebe and Camilla. It would help Phoebe certainly. It would help reduce her stress levels. She'd been worried about Camilla, so Lola's Soul would be a way for Phoebe to decompress.

I knew the way that most mortals reacted to their pets, after millennia of helping them cross over to the Afterlife. Mortals, they could get very attached to their animals.

"Caelum?" I looked up as Adiel said my name. "Caelum, everything's going to be alright."

I brought my eyes up to his, before a snore resounded from the ground. I grinned, glancing at Lola's sleeping Soul. I watched her chest rise and fall as she breathed.

"Caelum," Adiel said a third time. I turned my attention back to him. "Everything will be okay, no matter what happens."

I guessed that that was true. Even with Phoebe and Camilla, everything would work out. No matter what, little Camilla would never forget her mother. Both Adiel and I would make sure of that.

That fact made me feel a lot better, especially now since I'd seen Lola. She'd calmed me down, making me understand that everything would fall into place eventually. It would all make sense at some point.

I sighed as Adiel blinked, an understanding expression on his face. He squinted, staring at me for a few moments before he brought his brown eyes to Lola. The dog was still snoring on the ground of the Afterlife.

He grinned at the sound Lola was making, and then crouched down on his knees. He leaned forward and petted her sleeping Soul. "Caelum," he said, his eyes still on Lola. "You're going to be okay."

I knew Adiel was right as I heard his words. I realized that what he was saying was true. That everything would work out in the end. There was truly nothing to be afraid of.

14

I stood on the carpet of the home, watching as the middle-aged, brown-haired woman suddenly bent over in pain. She grasped her head in her hands, and her forehead was scrunched as agony overcame her. She crouched down on her knees, screaming in the living room of her house.

I blinked at the loud noise as she crumpled to the floor. Her peach-colored skin appeared incredibly pale as she lay there.

There was absolutely nothing I could do as she began to lose consciousness.

I stood on the floor, watching her for a few seconds. I waited to bring her Soul to Heaven, when I suddenly heard a door open, followed by footsteps across the nearby hardwood.

"Mom?"

My head snapped up as I heard the voice of the woman's grown child.

"Mom, where are you?" She paused for a few moments, before trying again. "Mom?"

The daughter's voice got confused when she didn't hear an answer. She came into the living room, a gasp escaping her lungs as she saw her mother's crumpled body on the carpet.

The young woman was maybe mid-teens to early twenties, with peach-colored skin, and dark brown hair. Her eyes were blue.

"Oh my God, Mom," the daughter said, her eyes wide as she began to panic. "Mom," she repeated, shaking her mother's shoulder gently. "Mom, can you hear me?" she asked as she continued. "Mom…" she trailed off, her voice breaking.

But then, I could see the middle-aged woman's eyes open. She appeared disoriented. She stared, wide-eyed, at her daughter, almost as if she couldn't see her.

"Mom. Mom, thank God," the daughter said, putting her head down in relief. She saw her mother lock eyes with her.

But the relief was short- lived as her mother blinked rapidly, appearing confused. She couldn't see her daughter, even though she was right in front of her.

"Mom?" the daughter asked. "Mom?"

The middle-aged woman continued to look, before she muttered something unintelligible.

The daughter squinted, trying to understand what was going on, when the middle-aged woman's stomach suddenly spasmed.

My eyes narrowed as I tried to understand the woman's ailment. Her stomach spasmed a second time.

Her daughter looked at her, alarmed, before she recognized what was going to happen. The mother was going to get sick to her stomach.

"Bathroom," she said quietly, so softly I could barely hear her. She had to say it again for the daughter to understand her. "Bathroom," she repeated. The daughter nodded, and then quickly got her mother up from the carpet. The woman stumbled slightly as she clambered up from the floor. She was completely disoriented as the grown daughter put a hand on her back, guiding her toward the nearby restroom. I followed them silently.

The woman, the middle-aged mother, had just gotten to the toilet when she'd moved the seat of the commode. She then proceeded to abruptly, and violently, vomit everything in her system.

"Mom," the daughter said as she saw her mother throw up. She shook her head in a panic. "Mom," she repeated, dazed, before she blinked. She grabbed the cell phone that was in her pocket, immediately calling 9-1-1 as her mother continued to wretch into the toilet.

I watched both the grown daughter and mother silently as the daughter said the details of the mother's symptoms to the dispatcher. Then the young woman hung up, pulling the phone away from her ear once more to dial another number.

Meanwhile, the middle-aged mom was getting paler and paler by the moment. Her head was resting on her arm, which was on the side of the commode.

I sighed as I saw the sight. The mother appeared miserable.

"Caleb, I need you to get here now. Something is wrong with Mom," I heard the daughter say into her phone. "I found her unconscious, but now she just vomited." She paused as Caleb responded. "Yes, I'm with her right now. I just called the paramedics, but you must get here fast. She's getting pale, and there's something really wrong. Just… You must come right away, okay?" And she quickly hung up, putting the cell phone into her pocket before she walked over to her mother. The daughter rubbed her mom's back, trying to make her as comfortable as possible.

My heart was pounding as I watched the grown daughter. I caught her gazing up at the ceiling of the bathroom, tears in her eyes as the mother vomited once more into the toilet.

The older woman groaned, glancing up at her daughter for a moment before saying something to her. Again, whatever she'd said was unintelligible.

Her daughter just stared at her, shaking her head in bewilderment. I saw tears cut trails into her cheeks. "Mom, I don't... don't...know what you're saying," she said, beginning to cry. "I don't understand you." Then she peered behind her, toward the bathroom door. I knew that she was waiting for her brother to come by. "Come on, come on. Caleb, where are you?"

She was waiting on her brother, and, of course, the paramedics.

There were several gut-wrenching moments that passed as the mother gasped for breath. Then she turned to look at her child, who was crouched beside her, choking on sobs. The mom couldn't recognize her own flesh and blood. The woman couldn't even see her own daughter.

"I'm... I'm sorry," was all the grown daughter could get out, before there was a loud slamming in the other portion of the home. Someone came inside.

My head snapped up at the noise, my attention diverted.

"Naomi? Mom?"

A male voice rang out through the once silent house.

"In the bathroom!" the daughter, Naomi, yelled thickly. "We're in here!"

Footsteps quickly resounded in the hallway, before I looked up to see Caleb come into the bathroom. His face immediately went white as he saw the sight of his mother and sister. His blue eyes were wide as he took in the scene.

His short red hair seemed to make his pale skin even lighter. He stood there for a few moments, dazed.

Naomi's voice rang throughout the room, snapping Caleb out of his thoughts. "Caleb, go outside and flag down the ambulance! They need to know we're in here! Tell them that she's having trouble breathing!"

I blinked as I heard her words, turning my attention to the mother, who was gasping for oxygen. She still appeared delirious.

Caleb gulped, nodding almost robotically. He disappeared, sprinting for the front door as Naomi tried supporting her mother, but it was difficult for her.

Naomi finally just put her mother's arms around her own shoulders, lifting her up from the bathroom floor. "Come on, Mom. Come on," I heard her say quietly as she propped her mother upright. The mom was clutching the sink. "Come on." By now, Naomi was crying so hard that I thought that she was going to vomit as well. She steadied her mom. Naomi's hand was on her mother's back.

I could almost hear the statements that she was saying in her head.

Stay calm. Just stay calm.

It was a few moments later that I heard the front door slam, the rushed footsteps, and the sound of voices. It was the paramedics. They had arrived.

"When did this start?" I heard one of the EMTs say as they darted into the bathroom. Naomi's scared face looked up at them when they entered.

Caleb just looked at his sister, not knowing the answer. "Naomi, when did you find Mom like this?"

"Umm, maybe two or three minutes before I called you," Naomi replied, sniffling as she looked in the man's eyes. "She was just on the carpet when I found her, and then she vomited. She's not making sense either," she said. "She's not speaking right."

Two other EMTs came into the bathroom with a stretcher, gently easing the middle-aged woman onto it. They put an oxygen mask over her mouth and nose. The paramedics brought the mother out on the stretcher, working hard to keep her stable and alert.

Once they brought her out, one of the EMTs walked with them. Naomi and Caleb followed close behind.

I walked behind them quietly.

"How old is she?"

"She's fifty-six."

"Any history of high blood pressure, or heart problems?" he asked.

"High… high blood pressure," Naomi said thickly. "There's a history of it in our family. Mom told us once."

"Is she allergic to anything?"

"No. No medications or anything else," Naomi replied.

"Is she disoriented?"

Naomi nodded. "Very. It's almost like she didn't recognize me. She'd started gasping, too." The EMT looked at both Caleb and Naomi as they all made their way outside. They were near the ambulance that was open and had blinking, flashing lights. "We must get her to the hospital right away. You can follow along behind us."

Naomi's eyes drifted to the inside of the emergency vehicle that her mother was in, staring at her body for a few moments before she looked away, stricken.

"We have to go," the EMT said, walking away from both Caleb and Naomi. The other emergency personnel had secured the middle-aged woman inside the back of the ambulance.

I managed to get inside the open emergency vehicle. I heard the front passenger side door slam when the EMT climbed in the ambulance.

Then they were off.

I didn't have to be outside the emergency vehicle to know that Caleb and Naomi were right behind it as they drove. I could sense that the grown children were following the ambulance.

Millennia of moving Souls helped me understand mortals a bit.

I knew that both of them would be headed to the hospital as well. But Naomi and Caleb were going to be heartbroken.

I stood by the middle-aged woman's head as I looked down at her, and I waited for her to turn into a Soul as she lay there in the ambulance. That was when I saw her blue eyes open. She appeared confused. She blinked, before her eyes seemed to settle on the EMTs, who were right beside her.

One of them swiftly leaned forward, checking the pulse in her neck. "Ma'am," he said, looking at her face. "I'm right here, Ma'am. We're on the way to the hospital right now."

The ambulance was screaming as it moved through the road; the siren blaring noisily.

I could tell by the way the woman looked that she wanted some comfort. Some comfort in the process of transitioning fully into a Soul. And I would help her. I would make sure that she would be the only one who could see me also.

I just had to remember what Adiel told me. I had to be careful if I wanted to be sensed, or visible to a mortal.

I had to make sure that I was only visible to the woman that was dying. No one else would be able to see me.

I promise I'll be careful, Adiel. I closed my eyes, reciting the words. I knew it would make me visible to the woman as I stood in the back of the ambulance.

It was an old one, one that I had remembered when I'd first been given my obligation. That was when the ambulance finally stopped.

I heard the mortal woman gasp right before I opened my eyes. I instantly felt a smile come across my face at the noise. The dying woman, she had seen me.

"We're here!" I heard one of the EMTs yell as he got out of the front of the ambulance.

I glanced up at the sound of the emergency vehicle's doors opening, before I slowly walked out with the paramedics. My eyes were on the middle-aged woman's the entire time.

Her eyes were still glued on mine as I felt my wings become visible.

I wanted to make sure she knew that she was safe, that I was going to take care of her. That I was an angel.

The woman gasped again as she saw the feathery appendages, and I smiled as I walked along the road. I followed the paramedics as they made their way toward the nearby hospital.

"Mom?"

I twisted my head around to see both Naomi and Caleb immediately getting out of their car. They had driven together to the emergency room. Exactly like I knew they would do.

"Mom...."

Naomi sniffled as she saw her mother on the stretcher. Her eyes were as raw as uncooked meat. She watched her parent being brought into the ER, and she ran up to where her mom was. Caleb followed close behind her. His hand went on his sister's shoulder then, stopping her before she could catch up to the paramedics.

She twisted her head around, staring at him for a split moment like he'd lost his mind.

"Naomi," he said, "I think we should go into the waiting room."

She paused, thinking, before nodding. "Okay, Caleb."

Naomi sighed, before I saw them walk off, to a separate portion of the hospital that was only for visitors. I noticed then that we were at the entrance of the emergency room.

I heard the middle-aged woman's heavy breathing as I brought my attention back to her. She'd been watching me the entire time with her blue eyes.

I followed close behind the stretcher she was on as we entered the hallway. She stared at me through the oxygen mask that she was wearing.

It was around this time that the doctors that were already in the hospital stepped in, coming to the woman's aid as the paramedics stepped back.

"What happened?" one of the male doctors asked the nearest EMT.

"The patient was passed out, then vomiting, and she wasn't speaking correctly. This is all according to her grown daughter. She has high blood pressure, but she isn't allergic to any medications. Now her eyes are open, but she seems delirious."

The doctor nodded, glancing once at the middle-aged woman for about a heartbeat. This was before he and some other assistants brought her into the emergency room.

That was when I knew it was time.

I smiled at the woman's blue eyes that were still glued to mine. I calmly extended my hand out toward her, as the doctors wheeled her into the room.

"It's alright," I said, looking at the middle-aged woman warmly. "It's okay."

She extended her arm out toward me, which confused the personnel that were beside her. They couldn't see me of course, so they looked bewildered.

But I knew the woman was ready. She was ready to fully become a Soul.

Her hand touched mine, and that was when I saw her take her last breath. Her chest rose and fell one final time, before her hand fell on the edge of the apparatus that she was on.

The doctor closest to the middle-aged woman noticed her hand fall to her side, and immediately spoke.

"Ma'am?"

There was no response as the woman's body lay there. She had passed away.

The doctor approached her, feeling for a pulse against her neck before he blinked. "No. No. No. No," he said, shaking his head rapidly. The other assistants in the emergency room exchanged uncertain looks as the doctor began chest compressions. "Come on. Come on."

But after several moments of trying, the doctor began to falter, since the woman wasn't regaining a heartbeat. He backed away, bringing his hands away from her chest. He sighed, glancing at his assistants.

They exchanged looks again, before peering over at the woman's body that was still on the stretcher.

The doctor inhaled quickly, his breath catching before he spoke. "We have to go tell the daughter and son," he said.

The assistants nodded, their heads bobbing up and down almost robotically before they all left the room. I was soon the only one left in the ER room with the woman's body. She still had the oxygen mask over her mouth and nose.

"I can be the one to tell them," I heard the doctor say as he passed the room, along with the assistants.

"Yes, doctor," one of them replied, before their footsteps disappeared around a corner. It was a few moments later that I couldn't hear them anymore.

I was alone with the woman's body. That was until I heard a gasp behind me.

I twisted around to see her Soul staring at my face, a look of bewilderment mixed with awe in her blue eyes. She opened her mouth to speak, but nothing came out as she shook her head, slightly dazed.

I just stood there patiently, waiting for her to talk.

"You..." she began, "you really are an angel," she said.

She was still looking at my wings. They were still out of my back.

I nodded as the woman latched eyes with me. "Yes. Yes, I am. I helped you transition completely into a Soul," I said. "You were so sick before, and unconscious, when your daughter found you."

The woman blinked, taken aback for a few moments before coming to the present. "You saw that happen?" she asked.

"Yes," I replied. "I saw you collapse to the carpet, and when your daughter and son came to your aid. I saw everything happen."

"Will I be able to see them? Will I be able to see Naomi and Caleb, to say goodbye?"

"Yes," I said automatically. "Yes, you will."

The woman took a deep breath before attempting to ask a question. She stopped, and then started again. "What's... what's your name?"

I smiled warmly. "My name is Caelum," I said.

"Well, Caelum, thank you for giving me the opportunity to see my daughter and son before I go with you. I appreciate it."

I just continued to smile. My expression was soft. "You're welcome. Anything to help a Soul."

The woman looked at me, and then sighed.

I walked forward, and I could see that her eyes were wet with tears.

We both made it out of the emergency room and through the hallway, until finally we reached the waiting room, where Caleb and Naomi were. They looked extremely anxious.

I glanced over at the woman who was by my side. She was crying, tears streaming down her face as she wept.

I squinted a little at the sight of her sobbing, before I twisted around just in time to see the doctor come into the waiting room. He was walking toward Naomi and Caleb. I saw the gut-wrenching expressions on both the grown children's faces as the doctor told them that their mother didn't make it. It was once he had walked off that I gestured to the Soul beside me, motioning toward her children.

"Go on," I said. "Go see them."

At that, the woman sniffled before looking into my eyes.

"I promise, everything will be alright," I said.

She nodded, understanding my words, and then went over to see Naomi and Caleb. They were hugging each other tightly. Naomi was crying into Caleb's shoulder, while he was just hugging her. He was sobbing silently.

I watched quietly as their mother's Soul approached them. I watched Naomi's eyes crinkle in confusion as she felt her mother near her. Naomi pulled away from Caleb as she felt her mom's presence, and that was when the mother seized her chance. She hugged both of her children, holding them close to her.

The woman embraced Naomi and Caleb as they looked taken aback. She then pulled away from them, twisting around to walk back toward me. She had almost made her way to me when I heard Naomi sniffle, and then gasp.

"Caleb?" she asked. "Caleb, did you feel that too?"

Their mother stopped in her tracks, looking right at me as she heard her children talk behind her.

"Yes, Naomi," Caleb responded. "Yes, I did feel that."

Immediately, I saw their mother's face light up, all traces of sadness gone from her. She smiled, beaming, before she suddenly ran to me. She took me completely by surprise as she wrapped her arms around my body, hugging me tightly. "Thank you," she said thickly into my shoulder. "Thank you so much."

I blinked. I had never really had this happen to me before. I'd never had a Soul hug me like this.

But I rubbed her back affectionately, comfortingly. "You're welcome."

15

"Caelum, are you okay?" Adiel's voice floated into my consciousness. I blinked, coming back to the present. "Caelum?" he asked again.

"Yes. Yes, I am," I responded, looking into his brown eyes.

I'd just brought the Soul of the woman up to Adiel, for him to bring to the Golden Gates.

It was after she was gone that I'd been lost in thought.

"I was just…. just… thinking," I said.

My mind was on Phoebe and Camilla again, specifically Phoebe.

I'd really been thinking about the similarities between her and the Soul.

About the Soul of the woman who'd been suffering from a horrific headache before collapsing. About how she'd been sick to her stomach violently, and then wasn't able to speak coherently.

I was thinking about it all, about the similarities between Phoebe and this other Soul. I blinked again, as I stared into Adiel's eyes.

"What, Caelum?"

He saw the realization hit me, saw my expression change, and followed me as I quickly made my way over to the Heavenly River.

I paused when Adiel stopped me, putting his hand on my shoulder. "Caelum, what's going on?"

I turned to face him.

"It's Phoebe and Camilla. Really, it's just Phoebe," I said to Adiel. "She's been having symptoms similar to the Soul that I just brought up to Heaven. I think… think… that something similar is going on with Phoebe. Something's wrong with her brain."

Adiel stared at me, soaking in my words. "You want to look in the Heavenly River to check on her?" he asked.

I nodded. "Yes. Yes, I do. I want to see how she's doing now."

Adiel took his hand off my back. "Well, Caelum, you go ahead and check on her. If you need any help, you'll know where to find me. I must get back to the Souls," he said. He turned away, toward the Golden Gates, and I watched as he walked to them. He disappeared.

If I need anything, I know where to find you, I thought as I twisted back around, toward the Heavenly River. *I'm sure I'm going to need you soon, Adiel.*

I took a deep breath through my lungs, attempting to steady myself as I saw my reflection in the Water. Then I said the two names that had been on my mind. "Show me Phoebe and Camilla."

"Where is it? Where is it?" Phoebe asked quietly as she sorted through the drawer of socks. "Come on, Phoebe, where did you put it?" She went over to the light switch, and immediately, illumination flooded the space. Phoebe squinted uncomfortably, even though it wasn't incredibly bright. She gritted her teeth, before going onto her hands and knees to look underneath her bed. "Come on. Come on. Where is it?"

"Mom?"

Phoebe looked up as she heard her daughter's voice. "Yes, Camilla?"

"Am I going to Grandma and Grandpa's for a long time?"

There were footsteps in the hallway, and then Camilla was there, looking at her mother. There was a full backpack on her shoulder. She was also holding a full duffel bag with her other hand.

The child was packing up her schoolwork as well as her clothing. She was going to be with her grandparents for a while.

Phoebe sighed, looking at Camilla. Phoebe got up from the carpet, instead leaning over to talk to her young child. "You're just going there while I get some things sorted out," she said, looking into Camilla's blue eyes. "Grandpa will be picking you up from school until I get back and see you, okay?"

Camilla nodded, acknowledging her mother's words, before she opened her mouth again. "But why do I have to stay with Grandpa for so long? I'm spending a lot of time with him."

Phoebe nodded.

"Yes. Yes, you will be," Phoebe said. "The problem is, Camilla, that I don't know how long it will take. I don't know how long it will take to do the things that I need to do."

Camilla scrunched her eyebrows in confusion before speaking.

"What is it that you need to do, Mom?"

Phoebe sighed, looking away for a few moments. She faced her daughter again.

"I need to go see a doctor, honey, and Grandma is coming with me. I don't know how long everything will take. Grandpa will take care of you until I get back, okay? I need you to behave for him."

Camilla nodded. "Okay, Mom," she said. She leaned forward, enveloping her mother in a hug.

Phoebe closed her eyes as she hugged her daughter. Then she broke away from her. Phoebe rubbed the middle of Camilla's back affectionately as she spoke to her. "Camilla, have you seen my necklace anywhere?" she asked her. "I was looking for it everywhere, but I couldn't find it. It's the special one."

The little girl's face lit up as she realized what her mother had asked her and nodded rapidly. "Yes, Mom. I've seen it." Camilla squinted, thinking, and then walked over toward Phoebe's dresser that was by her bed. She picked up a necklace that was on the top of it. "It's right here."

Phoebe smiled as she saw her daughter hold the jewelry in her hand. The little girl gave Phoebe the necklace, and Phoebe shook her head, sighing as she took it. "I've been looking all over the place for that," she said. "Thank you, Camilla."

Camilla grinned as Phoebe leaned down and kissed her daughter's head, and then made her way over to a nearby mirror. Phoebe clasped the necklace around the back of her neck before it fell in front of her chest. The pendant was a dog pawprint. It fell right above Phoebe's heart.

The mother stared at the pawprint for a few moments. She grasped it, holding her hand close to her as she became lost in thought. She twisted around afterward, blinking as she came out of her reverie, and looked at Camilla. "Are you ready to go, Camilla?"

"Yes, Mom. I'm ready."

"Okay, honey," Phoebe said. "Let's bring you to Grandpa's for the week."

Camilla picked up the duffel bag that was on the floor as Phoebe put on her shoes.

"Alright, Camilla," Phoebe said after she stood up. "Let's go."

The Heavenly River rippled as the image of Phoebe, and Camilla disappeared. Soon, I was just staring at my own reflection. I looked in the Waters, my mind wandering as I watched my own blue eyes.

So, Phoebe was going to go to the doctor, and was leaving Camilla with her parent for the week, while Phoebe's mother went with her.

It must've been a specialist that she'd been referred to. Especially if the trip there, as well as the appointment, would require Camilla to be with Phoebe's parent for the week. And if it was a specialist that Phoebe was going to see, that meant that I'd missed seeing her when she went to the doctor the first time. The first time when the initial appointment was, when the specialist was recommended.

I'd missed that first appointment…

I shook my head, shaking away the bad sensation that had been stored in my gut at the thought.

Now, Phoebe was going to see another doctor…

I had to see what was going to happen next, with both Phoebe and Camilla. I had to watch over them both.

I looked at myself in the River for a few moments before I spoke. "Show me Phoebe and Camilla again."

Phoebe quickly locked the front door to the house as Camilla walked over to the car in the driveway. The little girl opened the unlocked vehicle, tossing both her duffel bag and her backpack inside.

Camilla clambered inside the car just as Phoebe joined her daughter. "Got everything?" the mother asked her.

The small child nodded. "Yes, Mom. I have everything I need."

"Alright," Phoebe said. "Buckle up."

Camilla pulled the seatbelt over her body, securing it on the other side of herself.

Phoebe smiled at her child, and then kissed the top of her head. She shut the car door before getting in the driver's seat. Phoebe sighed, putting the keys in the ignition. "Alright, Camilla. Time to see Grandma and Grandpa."

16

The Heavenly River returned to normal. The image faded from the enchanted Water.

I watched the now reflective pool of liquid for several moments before I found myself blinking again. I'd become lost in thought, staring at where Phoebe's face had been.

She'd appeared uncertain, nervous, about going to visit her parents with her daughter in tow. But she had no choice. She had to see the doctor, the specialist, and had to take Camilla to her mother and father's home. Phoebe had to figure out what was going on with her body.

I breathed deeply as I stood there, next to the Heavenly River. I thought about Phoebe and Camilla, and then turned toward the Golden Gates, where I knew Adiel was. I knew that I was going to repeat myself as I stared at the Gates, but I didn't care.

"Thank you, Adiel," I said, before I extended my wings, and flew out of the Heavens.

Over the next few days, I couldn't seem to stop my mind from wandering. I couldn't keep Phoebe and Camilla off my brain. It was like the image of the single mother and her child were seared into my consciousness. Every time I blinked, I saw the anxious blue eyes of Phoebe; her face contorted in an expression of worry.

Phoebe... Poor Phoebe...

Adiel seemed to notice that I couldn't really focus as well, when I'd brought a Soul up to Heaven that was an elderly man. An elderly man who'd passed away from kidney failure. He had refused treatment, refused to go to the hospital, saying he was ready to leave the World and that he'd lived a full and wonderful life. But I couldn't really focus on what the older man had gone through, even though his organs had failed.

My mind was consumed by Phoebe and Camilla, and the specialist doctor that she was soon going to see.

"Caelum?"

I glanced up to see Adiel staring at me. He had just brought the Soul of the older gentlemen through the Golden Gates, while I'd been standing near the Heavenly River. My brain was overwhelmed by Phoebe and her small child.

"Caelum, you're thinking about them again, aren't you?"

I sighed. "Yes, I am. I just can't seem to stop. About Phoebe especially."

I didn't care how that sounded, the way I'd just said that. It was Adiel I was talking to. I didn't have to worry about the way I sounded when I spoke with him.

"She's headed to the doctor, a new specialist, this week, and left her daughter with her parent. She's scared, Adiel," I said, looking into his eyes.

He stared at me, listening to what I'd just said.

"I know," he responded. "I saw her too. I have been watching her as well, in the Heavenly River. I saw her go to the initial appointment, saw her explain her symptoms. The doctor referred her to a neurologist. That is the specialist that she is going to see."

My eyes were glued to Adiel's. I hung onto every word that he said.

It took several moments before I could speak. "You…. you saw Phoebe?" I asked.

Adiel looked at me. "Yes, Caelum. I saw her and her mother."

"Where… where are they now?"

"They're at the neurologist's office," he said.

17

It didn't take long to get to the neurologist's building. All I had to do was follow the sensation that had been radiating from Phoebe, through the liquid of the Heavenly River.

I threw my wings out behind me as I landed on the asphalt.

My heart pummeled my ribcage as I entered the facility, but then I felt the tension leave my gut as I peered around the waiting room.

Phoebe was there, sitting in one of the chairs. She clutched her purse nervously, with her mother beside her. Her mother must have driven her daughter here, since Phoebe was having symptoms.

Oh, Phoebe, I thought. *You poor thing.*

"Phoebe?" We both looked up at the sound of her name being called. One of the women behind the desk moved the sliding glass, glancing at her. "Phoebe, you are going to have to fill out a little bit of paperwork before the neurologist sees you. Since you are a new patient here, we must add you to our system," she said.

Phoebe nodded understandingly. "Oh, of course. Sure, I'll fill it out."

She grabbed the clipboard that the woman gave her, before the woman spoke again.

"Just be sure to fill out the paperwork to the best of your ability. We need to know all your symptoms, your family history… Everything you can think of."

"Yes, of course," Phoebe said again. "I'll give it back soon."

The woman smiled at her, and then was just about to move the sliding glass back. She paused, focusing on the necklace that Phoebe was wearing. "That's very cute," she commented.

Phoebe looked up, smiling as the woman nodded toward her pawprint necklace. "Oh, thank you. Our dog Lola passed away a year ago. Before she was put down, we had her paw imprinted. This was given to both my daughter and I after Lola passed. It's very special," she said. "Now, she'll always be with us."

The woman smiled. "Well, that's quite a story," she said, glancing at Lola's pawprint one last time. She looked at Phoebe, who brought her attention to her once more.

"Thank you for the paperwork," Phoebe said. She went and sat down, looking at the clipboard as she began to fill out the forms.

I moved over to where Phoebe was sitting, along with her mother. I stood near her as she marked up the papers. Leaning over slightly to look at them, I watched Phoebe as she filled out the forms.

She had written her name, Phoebe Bright, and was checking the boxes under the word *Symptoms* on the paper, when I felt the familiar gut-wrenching sensation that I thought had left me. The symptoms Phoebe was checking on the form was almost all that were listed. Numbness or tingling, headaches, mental confusion, vision changes… The list went on and on.

A knot coiled its way into my stomach, grabbing my intestines. I found myself getting incredibly anxious as Phoebe filled out the rest of the paperwork. I looked straight at Phoebe as her eyes were down, but she was preoccupied.

I tried gazing into her blue eyes, but that was when she exhaled, standing up and bringing the clipboard with her.

The woman behind the counter brought her attention to Phoebe as she walked up to the desk. "Thank you," she said after she slid the glass away, which allowed her to get the papers. "The neurologist will be with you shortly."

"Okay," Phoebe said, nodding.

And then she sat down in the chair, waiting patiently for her name to be called.

18

"Phoebe Bright!"

Both of our eyes snapped up at the sound of the woman's voice in the waiting room.

"I'll be right out here when you're done, okay, sweetheart?" Phoebe's mother said.

"Okay, Mom."

Phoebe smiled as she stood up, going over to the woman. The woman stood in front of the door that led to the hallway and the patient rooms. A clipboard was over the woman's chest as she held it close to her.

I followed Phoebe as she walked over. The woman spoke as she saw Phoebe inhale nervously. "It's your first time here, isn't it?" she asked, to which Phoebe nodded, looking into her brown eyes. "Well, Dr. Spark will be sure to take good care of you. You filled out the forms? All the way through, correct?"

Phoebe nodded as I watched her, studying her body language.

The tightness in her chest seemed to disappear as she breathed out. She was getting more relaxed.

"Yes," Phoebe said. "Yes, I did. I filled them out the best I could."

The woman nodded understandingly. She paused for a few moments to flip through the paperwork that was attached to the clipboard. "Alright, Ms. Bright," she said, bringing her attention back to Phoebe, "let's bring you on back."

Phoebe sat on top of the examination table, her elbows on her knees. Her legs were crossed, her purse behind her.

I sighed as I watched her. I stood in the corner of the patient room.

Poor Phoebe....

Her eyes darted from side to side as she took in the look of the room, and that was when I saw her catch what was on the wall.

It was the certification that Dr. Spark, the neurologist, had. It proved his credentials, that he was in fact qualified to do what he did.

Phoebe stared at the certification for a few seconds before she brought her eyes away from it, instead looking around the room again.

I stood in the corner of the area, watching Phoebe silently in the closed, empty space, when my heart dropped to my stomach.

Oh, no, I thought as I swallowed hard against my throat.

Phoebe had inhaled sharply, suddenly grasping her head in immediate pain. "Ugh," she said, visibly writhing in agony as her eyes squeezed shut. She rubbed her head with her fingers, trying to soothe the area. I was breathing heavily as I stared, before she finally took her hand off it. Phoebe blinked to come back to herself, and I felt my heartrate go back to normal. She inhaled deeply, exhaling slowly. "Just be calm, Phoebe. The neurologist will know how to treat you. You are going to be fine. Just stay calm."

I stood on the floor, watching Phoebe for several moments, when there was a voice on the other side of the closed door.

"Yes, I have the papers, thank you. I just picked up the clipboard."

The knob to the patient room moved, and then the doctor was there. He smiled warmly at Phoebe, who still appeared anxious. She smiled through her nervousness though as her eyes met the doctor's brown ones.

"Hi," Phoebe said, her voice shaking slightly. She paused, clearing her throat, and brought her hands up on her knees.

He watched her silently, before sitting in the chair opposite her, watching her face. "Nervous?" he asked.

A breathy laugh escaped Phoebe's lungs, and she smiled at the doctor, nodding.

"Well, you're in good hands, no matter what happens," he said. He extended his hand out in a kind manner. Phoebe grasped it. "I am Dr. Isaac Spark. I am the neurologist here and will do everything I can in order to make you feel better, or diagnose you, if the need arises."

"It's nice to meet you, Dr. Spark," Phoebe said.

Phoebe and the doctor talked for a long time.

Dr. Isaac was very attentive to her concerns, listening to what her symptoms were… He even brought out tissues for Phoebe when she spoke about Camilla. About how terrified she was for her daughter. He just calmly told her afterward that she shouldn't get too ahead of herself.

Phoebe nodded understandingly, and I sniffled along with her as a tear fell from her left eye, running down her cheek.

Phoebe was making me cry, over the fact that she was scared about her daughter, and ultimately, about the fact that she was going to pass away from something. Something that was slowly killing her.

A sob went through me as I stared at Phoebe, stared at her scared face, and that was when she spoke. "Okay," she said, understanding the doctor's words. She took a moment to gather herself again.

Dr. Isaac squinted a little when he saw Phoebe's expression but sighed as he saw her calm down. It was after he did that that he took a small flashlight out of his white coat pocket. "Well, Phoebe, let's start your physical examination."

She nodded, sniffling. "Alright," she said, sitting up straight and looking at the doctor as the light shone in her blue eyes. Phoebe attempted to squint at the bright illumination, and that was when I felt my heart drop again.

Dr. Isaac squinted, his forehead scrunched together in confusion and concern. But that expression wasn't on his face for long, since Phoebe was staring at him. He quickly regained his composure.

Dr. Isaac put the small flashlight back and then stood up, asking Phoebe if she could do the same. The neurologist checked her balance, her coordination, everything that would seem off if she was battling something.

I watched silently, in the corner of the patient room, as Phoebe struggled to keep her balance. Suddenly, it seemed like she was getting weaker.

The doctor checked her coordination. Whether she could touch her nose with her hand, and my throat closed with sobs when Phoebe was having trouble with that simple task.

It was after that that she brushed one of her arms with her other hand, wincing slightly.

Dr. Isaac was immediately alert at the change in her expression. "What is it?" he asked.

"It's my arm. The numbness is now there and in my hands. It used to be in my feet, but now it's in my upper extremities." She paused, before she spoke a second time. "And now it's… it's… in my feet again. Ow," she said, clearly in discomfort.

The doctor blinked, taking in the information before he spoke again. "Sit down, Phoebe. I want to do a reflex test now."

She did what he asked her, and then the doctor brought out a little device that he used to tap her kneecaps. They barely moved.

Dr. Isaac's eyebrows scrunched together. "Phoebe, can you not feel this?" he asked as he tapped her knees lightly with the device.

She blinked, before I saw tears well in her eyes. "No. No, I can't. Not really."

He squinted, thinking, before he glanced back up at Phoebe. "Alright, we're going to stop that for now," he said, putting the device down on the nearby table.

He looked at her face. I could tell by his expression that he was worried for her. "One last final test, and then we're going to be done, okay?"

"Okay," Phoebe said.

Dr. Isaac backed away from her so that she could slide off the table. I could see him keeping a close eye on her as she did so. "We are going to check your vision with a simple chart. Can you see the one on the wall?" he asked, pointing to the eye chart that was across the room.

Phoebe nodded, and then she spoke. "Yes. Yes, I do."

The tight sensation in my chest seemed to become even more prominent. I watched the doctor walk up to the chart. He instructed Phoebe to cover one eye with her hand.

She did so, and then he began to point to the letters, nodding as Phoebe got all of them correct with her left eye, before she switched, covering up that eye so that her right one could get tested.

Dr. Isaac was looking confident as Phoebe read the first few ones. He looked happy as I read his body language. The tension in my stomach decreased as I stared at him. But then a sharp inhale from Phoebe made my head snap toward her.

Phoebe....

"Umm.... Umm..."

"What is it, Ms. Bright?"

"It's my vision, it's getting blurry. I can't see the letters right now. And now my..."

But she was interrupted by immediate pain. She winced automatically.

The doctor took all of a heartbeat to understand what was going on. He instantly came to her side, putting his hand on her back as she doubled over in agony. "Ms. Bright? Phoebe?"

My heart pummeled my ribcage as I stared at both the doctor and Phoebe, before she sighed, looking back up at him. "Sorry," she said, her eyes on Dr. Isaac's.

"There's nothing to be sorry about," he responded automatically, placing his hand on her shoulder as he helped her into an upright position.

I watched them both closely, my eyes beginning to water as I saw how nervous Phoebe was.

"Are you alright now?" Dr. Isaac asked her.

"Yes. It's just that… just that… these headaches have been off and on for a while now, along with the other side effects. That's why I got referred to you."

The neurologist stared at her, listening to her words. "Can you still drive alright? Has this been happening while you are driving?"

"Yes, I can still drive okay, and no. No, it hasn't."

I could see the relief in Dr. Isaac's brown eyes as he exhaled. "Well, that's good," he said as he guided Phoebe toward the examination table. "Alright, Ms. Bright," he said, letting go of her when he knew that she could stabilize herself. "We are done with our appointment. But because of what I have seen today, I'm concerned about a few things."

At this, Phoebe held her breath, her eyes becoming glued to the doctor's.

"I want you to immediately get an MRI, since you are already here and have been having symptoms. We must give you a consent form and then we will get you in the room, okay?"

"Will it be a long procedure?" Phoebe asked.

"It will take about forty-five minutes to complete the MRI," he said, to which Phoebe nodded. "Okay, Ms. Bright. Just hang on while I get a consent form and then we will get this going."

Phoebe sighed and then spoke again before the doctor exited the room. "Would someone be able to tell my mother where I am? I don't want her to be worried."

Dr. Isaac turned, looking at her. "Yes. We will let her know."

Then he turned away, going to get the form, while Phoebe just clutched her purse nervously.

It took a few minutes for the doctor to come back with it. Phoebe signed the piece of paper, and that was when Dr. Isaac left the room, saying goodbye to her.

19

P hoebe took a deep breath, steadying herself as she sat on the examination table. I stood in the corner of the room, watching her body language carefully. She pulled her phone out of her purse, checking the time.

It was ten-thirty in the morning.

I watched Phoebe as she waited anxiously for the doctor to come in to see her. I knew it wasn't the neurologist that was coming in soon.

Since Phoebe was getting an MRI, it was going to be a different doctor, one who would perform the scan, and then another individual that would look at the images.

I'd been in hospitals and been an angel long enough to understand these kinds of procedures, like the one that Phoebe was going to undergo.

But that didn't stop me from feeling uneasy about her. I could sense her nervousness about the whole thing.

I silently gazed at her as she sat on the table, as she unknowingly faced me. I stared at her peach-colored skin, her crystal blue eyes, her freckles that looked like chocolate sprinkled all over her cheeks…

I stopped myself.

What was that, Caelum?

My breathing hitched for a moment, my heart skipping a beat. Now, I couldn't stop noticing how beautiful Phoebe was…

She blinked several times before twisting her body around. I shook my head, coming back to the present.

The sound of the doorknob turning caught our attention as we both looked at it, and I inhaled. I tried to calm my pounding heart. I saw the doctor come in. He was smiling warmly. He sat down in a chair opposite Phoebe. "Hello, Ms. Bright," he said. "My name is Dr. Mark Ray. I'm the technologist will be performing the MRI this morning. I just wanted to discuss a few things with you before we go ahead with the procedure."

He watched Phoebe's face. She nodded understandingly. "Okay," she said.

"Do you have any metal piercings? We need to make sure, for your safety, that there is nothing that could interfere with the MRI or potentially harm you. There cannot be anything of that nature near the scanner."

Phoebe shook her head.

"What about perfumes, dyes, or hairsprays?"

"No, none of that either," Phoebe said.

She was bare-faced and natural today. Natural and stunning.…

I blinked as that thought went through my mind.

"Alright, then. The only items that are metal would be inside your purse, I assume?" the technologist asked.

"Yes," Phoebe said. "I made sure that I didn't bring any jewelry with me. I don't have any makeup on either."

"Okay," Dr. Ray said. "Did you have any sedatives prescribed for you? I did not see any in the chart that had your information.

I just want to make sure that I have talked about everything before we start."

"Yes, I completely understand," Phoebe said. "No, I wasn't prescribed a sedative. I'm not claustrophobic." The doctor blinked, nodding. "Alright, well, I'm going to bring you back to the locker room where you can store your valuables. You can also change into a gown. Anything with metal or wire must come off, okay? That means undergarments as well. You can only wear the hospital gown, anything underneath it must be cotton. We don't want you to get seriously injured."

I saw Phoebe blink, and then she opened her mouth to speak. "Yes, I understand," she said.

The doctor paused for a moment before talking again. "Were there any questions you had for me before I bring you to the locker room?"

I gazed at Phoebe's face, her bright eyes as she looked at Dr. Ray. She shook her head a third time. "No," she said. "I'm ready."

"Well then, Ms. Bright," Dr. Ray said as he got up from the chair and opened the door. "I'll show you to the room."

And I followed them both outside and toward the lockers.

20

"Here we are," Dr. Ray said as we made it to the room. It was a bigger area than the one that we were in before. This allowed the lockers to be in there, while there was wide open space in the center, allowing for the person inside to change.

Dr. Ray backed out of the locker room. Phoebe took one of her purse straps off her shoulder and took her phone out. She turned it off and put the device back. That was when she looked up, and a nurse came into view, smiling.

"Hello, Ms. Bright," she said, her chocolate brown skin glowing. The woman had incredibly white teeth. "I'm Yvonne. I have your gown for you."

"Oh, thank you," Phoebe said, taking the blue hospital outfit from her.

"Just put your things in the lockers before you put the gown on. Make sure that everything is off, except cotton, before you come back out, okay? We'll be waiting for you outside."

Phoebe nodded. "Alright. I'll be right out."

Yvonne grinned at her before she turned around, exiting the locker room.

I followed close behind Yvonne, before I twisted around for a moment. Phoebe turned on the light switch, shutting the door and locking it with a quick snap.

Yvonne, Dr. Ray, and I all waited for Phoebe to get changed, and after a few seconds, I saw the doctor go off into another separate gigantic room.

Hmmm, I thought as I watched him leave, *that must be where the MRI machine is.*

I squinted, before I walked after the technologist, curious.

Sure enough, that was where it was. A massive machine that took up an enormous amount of space in the room. There was a tiny extra area on the side of the space, with a clear panel and without a door that the doctor could just walk through. That was where the technologist would be able to see the images being taken, as well as where he could speak to Phoebe.

I'd seen these machines before, since I was an angel and I'd seen *a lot* of things over the millennia. In this instance though, it gave me pause.

It really was a tremendous thing, what Phoebe was about to go through. Getting an MRI was a big deal.

"Okay, Ms. Bright," I could hear Yvonne say from a distance. "Just follow me and we'll go into the room where the scanner is."

"Alright," I heard Phoebe say. Footsteps were on the floor as they advanced closer. I stepped backward, away from the machine and over toward the wall. There was a good view of Phoebe and Yvonne as they were coming in.

Yvonne was in front of Phoebe as they headed inside the colossal area. Yvonne was in her nursing outfit while Phoebe wore a blue hospital gown.

The material of it was loose as it covered Phoebe's body, part of it coming down slightly on her chest. It exposed a bit of her flesh. Her long brown hair cascaded past her shoulders, her skin light and clear...

My heart fluttered as I saw Phoebe, and that was when my eyes were suddenly on the piece of skin that was showing. It was right where Lola's pawprint necklace would've been, settled right over her heart.... I couldn't stop staring at the base of her throat and the top of her sternum...

"Here we are, Ms. Bright," Yvonne said, breaking me out of the reverie and bringing me back to the present.

I shook my head, blinking. My cheeks abruptly felt like they were on fire.

Phoebe's timid voice soaked my arteries as she spoke up, and I looked straight at her as she did so.

"So, I just need to get on that table, then?" she asked, her voice soft as she glanced up at Yvonne.

"Yes," the nurse said.

I peered over at the MRI machine, seeing a small portion that was outside of the contraption.

Phoebe would have to go sit down on it, and then the table would be brought inside the scanner.

"I'm sorry," she said as she looked at Yvonne again. Her eyes had been locked on the device, taking in the entire thing. "I've never done this before. This is my first MRI, so I apologize. I'm a little nervous," she admitted.

Yvonne looked at Phoebe, smiling a little. "Well, it's going to be alright. You're in good hands today. The one thing about the scanner is that it is going to be loud while taking the images. So, we will play some music for you when you're in there. It will help with nerves as well and hopefully will calm you down."

Phoebe nodded understandingly at Yvonne, who just looked at her. "Were there any questions you had for me, or for Dr. Ray, before we start the procedure?"

"Well, yes, actually," Phoebe said, to which Yvonne blinked, waiting patiently. "When will I get the results back from the MRI?"

"Usually, it takes about a week for the radiologist here to interpret the images."

Like I knew would happen, there would be a technologist helping with the MRI process, with the photos being taken. That was Dr. Mark Ray, while there was the radiologist that would help view the images and help diagnose Phoebe.

There were many individuals at this facility to help her find out what her ailment was.

"Any more questions?" Yvonne asked.

"No," Phoebe said. "No, I'm ready now."

Yvonne smiled warmly. "Alright, Ms. Bright," she said, glancing over at the table that was outside the scanner. She then turned around to look at Phoebe. "Follow me."

Yvonne walked over to the MRI device, Phoebe right behind her.

I could sense the nervousness that was drenching Phoebe as Yvonne gestured toward the table. Phoebe took a deep breath before she advanced closer to it, and then turned around to sit down. She relaxed on her back, watching Yvonne, who looked down at her calmly.

"Okay, Ms. Bright," she said. "I'm going to put some head-phones on you before we start. Hold on while I get them for you." Yvonne walked off, into the small area where the technologist - Dr. Ray - was waiting patiently. She returned with black headphones in her hands. "Ms. Bright, I'm going to place these on you, and then we can start. If you need to talk to us, or if you are feeling light-headed or dizzy, just speak up while you're in the machine. We'll be able to communicate with you. There is a microphone inside. Be sure to stay as still as possible, okay? The MRI is very sensitive and the images could be blurred with any sort of movement."

Phoebe nodded at everything Yvonne had just said. "Okay," Phoebe responded. "I understand."

"Alright," Yvonne replied, bringing the headphones into Phoebe's line of sight. "I'm going to put these on you - we will play classical music through them- and then we will start the MRI." She leaned forward, extending the headphones out so they fit the entirety of Phoebe's head and ears.

I saw Phoebe sigh as Yvonne pulled away from her.

Phoebe's eyes closed. She inhaled deeply, exhaling slowly.

My heart was thudding my ribs as there was an abrupt noise that erupted throughout the room. The table began to move, bringing Phoebe inside the massive device.

Yvonne stared as Phoebe was brought inside the machine, waiting until the sound stopped. She looked at Dr. Ray through the clear glass panel. She walked over to join him inside the area, away from the MRI scanner.

Which meant that I was the only one near the device.

I gulped as I watched the massive machinery, hoping that Phoebe wasn't going to be scared...

"Okay, Ms. Bright," I heard the technologist say. My eyes snapped over to the area where he was. "We are going to start now. Just try to be as still as possible."

"Alright," I heard Phoebe's voice through the booth that Dr. Ray and Yvonne were in.

My insides felt like liquid, and I closed my eyes, trying to steady myself. I opened them again, staring at the MRI machine.

I was just worried about Phoebe, about the prognosis that this MRI would lead to... I hoped she wasn't too anxious, inside that device....

There was a loud sound taking over the entire room as the MRI started. I brought my hands to my sides, trying to calm the tremors as I continued to look at the device.

My eyes were glued on that machine as the scan began.

I was paying attention so intently that I was startled by Dr. Ray talking through the device, speaking to Phoebe.

"Ms. Bright," he said, "hold on for a second. There's something happening with the machine."

"Is it something that I'm doing?" she asked. She sounded slightly panicked.

My heart skipped a beat at the change in her tone.

"No, it's not you," Dr. Ray said reassuringly. "It's just that the scanner seems to be acting up. It isn't getting the images correct. They are incredibly blurred. Almost as if there's something near the device..."

"I'm not moving," Phoebe said from inside the machine, to the technologist. He squinted, confused.

Then he peered over at Yvonne, who was standing beside him.

"Yvonne, will you go and check to make sure that there's nothing near it? I just want to make sure that everything's alright."

"Yes, Dr. Ray," she said, walking out of the small area and going into the room where the device was. "I'll check it."

I turned my head to the side, squinting as the nurse made her way around the machine. She checked all around it, before she frowned. She hadn't noticed anything.

Wait a moment, I thought as I saw Yvonne sigh, frustrated once she couldn't see anything. *I think I know what's going on...*

I was the only one in the area with the MRI scanner, so it could only be one thing. Or, in this case, one supernatural being.

Me. I caused this.

The fact I was in the room with Phoebe was causing the device to malfunction. It could sense my presence, even though the mortals couldn't.

Yvonne went back into the small area, joining the technologist once more, and I saw her shrug her shoulders at him. "I looked everywhere around the contraption. There's nothing that's disrupting it," she noted, to which Dr. Ray just looked at her, stunned.

"It's still not picking anything up correctly. There must be something wrong."

"There isn't, Dr. Ray."

Yes, there is, I thought. *You just can't see it.*

I slowly turned my head around, glancing at the MRI device. I walked over toward the small area where Yvonne and Dr. Ray were. I made my way out of the room with the colossal machine.

"Wait a minute," Dr. Ray said, blinking as I silently moved behind him. I looked at the computer monitor that had the images of Phoebe's brain.

He was right. The light blue images were incredibly blurry and partially twisted, as if something had physically moved them while she was inside the contraption.

That something was my presence.

But now, since I was inside the area where Yvonne and the technologist were, the sensation was no longer there. The computer attached to the machine seemed to sputter one last time, before it went back to its natural rhythm.

"Everything's okay now," Dr. Ray said, staring at the computer screen that now appeared normal. He was confused, but also relieved. "Alright then."

He twisted around to glance at Yvonne, who looked just as perplexed as he was.

Dr. Ray pushed a button in order to speak with Phoebe, who no doubt was getting incredibly anxious. "Ms. Bright?" he asked. "Phoebe?"

"Yes?" she responded, her voice loud and clear in the small space.

"Everything's okay now, we're not having issues with the machine anymore. We are going to continue with the brain scan, alright? Just stay as still as possible."

"I understand," Phoebe said, before Dr. Ray took his hand off the button that he'd been pressing. Instead, he started the MRI contraption again.

The noises were incredibly loud as Phoebe got her brain scanned. I saw the images pop up on the computer that Dr. Ray was in front of.

The images, even though they were in focus this time, appeared to be a little bit off. Something was wrong with Phoebe's brain as I stood there, watching the images from the MRI machine go into the computer. I felt my heart rate quicken.

Oh, no, I thought as I saw her organ. *No. No. No. No.*

From what I could tell, there was an abnormal mass in her brain.

I knew from millennia of moving Souls and being in hospitals that something was *very* wrong. I instantly felt bile speed up my throat, and I was wary to swallow as I looked more carefully at Phoebe's brain.

And that was when I realized what the mass was. It was a tumor.

21

I didn't know how long I was standing there in the small area behind Dr. Ray and Yvonne. I was staring at the computer screen that was attached to the MRI machine.

My blood seemed to stop flowing inside my veins, and I blinked, my breathing short and sharp. I couldn't inhale properly as I realized what was happening.

Phoebe had a tumor. Phoebe had a…a… brain tumor.

"Okay, Ms. Bright," Dr. Ray finally said, breaking me out of my thoughts. "Phoebe, we are done. I'm just going to bring you out of the machine, alright? Are you feeling okay?"

"Yes," Phoebe replied from inside the scanner. "Yes, I'm feeling fine."

"Good," the technologist said. He glanced over at Yvonne, who walked into the room to help Phoebe. "I'm going to bring you out of there now," Dr. Ray repeated, before he pushed a button.

There was a sudden sound throughout the large room nearby as the table came out of the MRI scanner.

I looked up, my heart in my throat, before I went and watched as Phoebe was brought out. A few moments went by as she was moved, and then… She was there.

She looked relieved that she was out of the small, enclosed space. I could see it in her eyes.

Yvonne stepped forward, leaning down and grasping the black headphones that were over Phoebe's ears. "There we go," Yvonne said absently as she took them in her hands. "You did a great job, Ms. Bright," she continued as she helped Phoebe off the table. Yvonne held Phoebe's hand until she could stand on her own. "Now, it'll take a few days to get the results from this appointment. The radiologist will have to look over them, and then will send them to Dr. Isaac Spark, so that he can talk with you, okay?"

Phoebe just nodded.

I could tell that it was a lot of information for her to soak in, but so far, she was doing great.

Long story short, she was going to have to wait for the results, and then the neurologist would meet with her about the prognosis from the MRI. The prognosis that was... the brain tumor. It was a brain tumor.

Even though it would take the radiologist time to diagnose Phoebe, to look at the scans of her brain matter, I already knew it was something bad. I'd been around long enough to recognize the pictures.

I knew what it was immediately, even if it would take time for the mortals to view the images.

Just the thought of a mass inside Phoebe's head was enough to make me sob, but I held it together as she saw Dr. Ray come out of the small area. He walked over to her and shook her hand kindly. "It was nice to meet you today, Ms. Bright," he said, sounding sincere.

"You too," Phoebe replied, before she brought her extremity to her side.

Yvonne smiled as Phoebe twisted toward her, and then Phoebe walked behind Yvonne. She followed Yvonne out of the MRI room, heading over to the lockers.

I walked behind them as they left the area. Yvonne opened the door to the locker room for Phoebe, before Phoebe turned around, thanking her and then turning on the light. She shut the door with a sharp click.

Yvonne walked away from the room, instead advancing down the hallway while she waited for Phoebe.

I followed Yvonne, waiting patiently as Phoebe got changed back into her clothing.

After a few minutes, the locker room door opened, and she came out dressed in her clothes with her purse on her shoulder.

Yvonne smiled as Phoebe met her eyes. "Well, Ms. Bright, it was nice to see you today," she said calmly. "You can go up front to see the receptionist, alright?"

Phoebe nodded. "Okay, thank you so much." Yvonne just grinned.

"You're welcome. Dr. Spark should be contacting you within the next week to discuss the results."

"Alright," Phoebe replied, smiling.

Yvonne gestured toward where the desk was. "Just go up there, and the receptionist will help you. Bye, Ms. Bright," she said, shaking Phoebe's hand before she walked off into the hallway.

Phoebe adjusted the purse straps on her shoulder, and then went over to the receptionist's desk. She showed her insurance card. She smiled at the woman behind the sliding glass, afterward going into the waiting room.

Her mother was tapping her feet insistently on the carpet, biting her lip before she saw Phoebe.

"Phoebe!" she said, relieved when she saw her daughter. She got up from the chair, hugging her. "Are you all done? Are we all ready to go?"

Phoebe nodded. "Yes," she said.

"Alright then, honey," her mom replied, adjusting the purse on her shoulder.

And they both walked off, into the parking lot.

I inhaled deeply as I watched them. I walked after them, following Phoebe with my eyes as she advanced across the lot and went into her vehicle.

My heart was pounding so hard my pulse was in my head. Tremors were taking over my hands, while sweat was beginning to bead along my hairline as I saw Phoebe's mother start the car.

Phoebe…Phoebe…

The sound of the vehicle caused me to blink, and then she drove off, heading toward the hotel that was nearby.

I watched her car quietly as I saw them both leave.

Phoebe…

22

One afternoon, I'd been summoned to the hospital bed of a young man on life support from a motorcycle accident. His family was by his side, along with a young woman who didn't look like the rest of them. I guessed that she was his girlfriend. She held his hand as he was on the apparatus, unconscious.

The young man on the cot had monitors attached to him through the wires that surrounded his body. A neck brace was there, cushioning the back of the area. There was also a tube that ran down his throat.

The entire appearance of the young man was incredibly unsettling, jarring. But, after millennia, I had gotten used to the look quickly.

The sound of the machines filled the air as I took in the scene. I was so used to the noises though, that they faded into the background.

I stood on the other side of the apparatus that he was on, across from the girlfriend that was holding his hand.

"John," I heard her say, a sob in her throat as her fingers ran across the back of his extremity. "I love you."

I paused at the words she had just said. Even after all this time, I was still mystified by the mortals, at the human emotions that they had. I stopped for a few seconds, before I touched John's arm. I immediately felt the magnetic sensation that meant he'd completely become a Soul.

Right when I touched John, the machines began to beep, taking over the space.

The young woman and the parents blinked, just as the doctors and nurses ran into the room.

"You all have to get out now," the doctor said. He walked in and put his hand briefly on the woman's shoulder. Tears filled her eyes. "You have to go."

A gasp behind me made my body twist around, and I saw the Soul of John. He appeared drastically different from his body on the hospital bed. Free of the wires and tubes, he looked healthy, with blond hair and brown eyes. John just stared at me, wide-eyed. "Am I...? Am I...?" he started, before clearing his throat and beginning again. "Am I dead?" he asked.

I looked straight into his eyes. "Yes. Yes, you are."

I had the feeling of my black wings coming out of my back as I spoke to him, and I saw John's expression change. He gasped. "You're an... an angel," he breathed.

"Yes. Yes, I am. I'm here to bring you to Heaven. If you want to say goodbye before we leave, you are free to do so."

John blinked, twisting toward where his still body was on the hospital bed, swarmed with wires and tubes. He appeared taken aback by seeing the doctors tend to him. But then he looked at me. "I would like to, thank you," he said. "Amber..." I saw John gazing into the hallway, where the young woman was. She was turned away from everyone there, facing the wall. She was crying.

"Amber," John said, watching her. "Oh, Amber…" He trailed off, his voice catching. He was crying silently as he saw his family members and girlfriend lose control.

"John. John. John," was all the parents kept repeating. They were outside as well, clutching each other. Amber blinked back tears.

John turned to look at me, and I nodded. I knew exactly what he was wondering even though he didn't say anything.

"Go ahead," I told him. "Go say goodbye."

John sniffled, a tear running down his face as he walked over to his parents in the hallway. They were still clutching each other tightly, crying. He twisted around toward me, taking a glance at my face.

"Go ahead," I said. "You can touch them."

John brought his attention back to his parents, whose eyes were blood red from sobbing so much. He hugged them both hard. "Bye, Mom," he said. "Bye, Dad. I'll miss you both."

I saw their expressions change as John embraced them, and then he pulled away, taking in their nonplussed faces.

I smiled as John turned to look at me. His face was a jumble of shock and awe, but then the look changed as he saw Amber suck in a breath.

She cried, tears streaming down her cheeks. "Bye, John," she said in a thick voice. "I'll miss you."

Amber turned away from the wall, instead looking unknowingly at his Soul. John was just staring at her wordlessly.

I saw him look at his girlfriend for maybe two moments before John reacted to her anxious state. He leaned forward, taking Amber's head in his hands, and kissed her.

I heard her gasp as she felt the sudden sensation of John, but just stood completely still. Her eyes were closed as she felt the energy of her boyfriend. It was several moments before he broke away.

He ran his thumbs over her cheeks as she looked ahead of her, staring blankly at him as he wiped away her tears. "Bye, Amber. I'll miss you too," he whispered into her lips. "I love you," John said to his girlfriend, before he brought his hands down to his sides. He turned away from her and glanced at me.

I brought my eyes toward Amber, who had a surprised, perplexed look on her face.

I peered over at John, who nodded. He was ready to leave.

"Alright," I said. "Let's get out of here."

"Okay," John responded.

My wings unfurled before we went up into the Heavens.

Adiel was waiting when John and I made it to the Afterlife. He was over by the Heavenly River, no doubt watching what had just happened. He nodded, smiling as he acknowledged John.

"Hi," Adiel said, a warm expression on his face as he saw the Soul.

John blinked, glancing first at me, and then at Adiel.

"Are you... an angel too?" John asked Adiel.

Adiel nodded. "Yes. I'm the Guardian of the Golden Gates. I will watch over you in the Soul Realm, which exists beyond the Gates. Caelum here, he brought you to the Heavens from Earth. That is his duty. My duty is to keep you safe inside the Spirit Realm."

John squinted.

"A Spirit and a Soul are the same thing," I told him, and he glanced over at me.

"Oh, okay," John said, understanding. "What's that do?" he asked, gesturing over to the Heavenly River.

"That is the Heavenly River," Adiel said. "That is a body of Water that is enchanted, and can help you see whatever, or whoever, you wish to see. If you wish to use it, just let me know and I will grant you permission to spend time out here. Caelum, he can show you how to use it. He uses it himself."

I blinked, my eyes immediately connecting with his.

Adiel instantly saw this. The way I'd reacted wasn't missed on John either, who I saw peer over at me out of my peripheral vision.

But I just inhaled, exhaling slowly. "I do, as you said Adiel, bring the Spirits to the Afterlife."

I paused, looking over at John. "I like seeing the mortals and the way they live. It's easier to watch over them before bringing them up here, to the Heavens," I said to him, gulping as his brown eyes watched mine.

"Oh, alright. Yeah, that makes sense."

I brought my eyes back to Adiel, who seemed to grasp how nervous I was. "Come on," Adiel said to John, grabbing the Soul's attention and looking over at the Golden Gates behind him. "Come on. I promise, it'll be alright."

John peered over at me, and then at Adiel. He nodded. "Alright," John said, and then he followed Adiel as he entered the Spirit Realm.

23

"What were you so nervous about before?"

My head jerked upward immediately at the sound of Adiel's voice. He'd just brought John to the Spirit Realm.

Adiel calmly made his way toward me, his brown eyes focusing on mine. "Are you alright?" he asked as I blinked, feeling suddenly flustered. I made eye contact with him. "Caelum?" He squinted, appearing worried.

I just watched his eyes. "I'm just…just…" But I couldn't finish. Instead, I started again. "I thought you were going to bring up Phoebe and Camilla. I thought you were going to tell John about them."

Adiel's eyebrows furrowed. "Caelum, I wouldn't do that. The way you feel about her and her daughter are completely your feelings. I'm not going to tell that to a Soul, no matter what happens between you and Phoebe."

I blinked as Adiel said her name, but it felt as if a gigantic rock was lifted off my chest.

He wouldn't tell a Soul about what was going on between a mortal and me. I would rather that it be kept between myself and Adiel.

Kept quiet.

I sighed, before glancing over at him, since my eyes had hit the ground. "So, you were watching what had happened in the hospital?" I asked Adiel.

"Yes," he said. "I saw you there with the Soul of John, as well as his body. You did the right thing, letting him say goodbye. That is the best thing that an angel can do for a Soul, allowing closure." He twisted around, staring at me. "Closure is very important, for both of us. Angels and Souls."

I blinked, looking at Adiel for a few moments before I breathed deeply, remembering the brain mass. Phoebe…. It was her organ. The thought of the tumor suddenly hit me like a hurricane.

"Caelum?"

I didn't answer Adiel as I walked past him, my insides abruptly feeling like the interior of a fire pit.

"Caelum?" he repeated.

I brought my eyes to his at the tone in his voice, staring into his face as I struggled to breathe. "Ad…. Adiel," I stammered. "Adiel, she's… she's…" But I couldn't finish. The lump got the entirety of my throat, causing it to close. Water quickly began to leak out of my eyes, cutting trails into my cheeks. My head hung low, and a garbled sound got released from my throat. I started shaking uncontrollably, my stomach spasming as my lungs fought to take in oxygen.

No. No. No. No. Phoebe… I thought as I cried.

Through my tears, I saw Adiel walk toward me, his feet edging closer since my eyes were hitting the ground. "Caelum?" he asked, to which I stared at him, my body exuding defeat. "Oh, Caelum," he said, calmly putting his arm around me. "It's Phoebe again, isn't it?"

I just looked at him, my silence speaking volumes as I stood there, my eyes and cheeks raw.

"What is happening with her?" Adiel asked. "I saw that you were at the neurologist's office, in the back with the MRI scanner, but I didn't see everything. I didn't see the images of her brain."

I sniffled, blinking before I spoke. "She has a… mass on her organ. Phoebe has a tumor. I recognized it on the scan before the doctors did, and now she must wait a week to find out the results, the prognosis."

She had to wait, only to be crushed by what the doctors had found…

Adiel brought his arm down to his side, but stayed close to me as he processed my words. "Other than that, did the MRI go okay?"

"Well…. well…" I stuttered, before I regained my composure, looking in Adiel's brown eyes. "Well, the scanner sensed my presence, even though the mortals couldn't see me. The images were incredibly blurred and unreadable. I had to move inside the little booth so Phoebe could get her MRI. She was nervous, but besides that, the scan went well. I saw the images of her brain though. It's what she has that's… that's… getting to me."

"Her mother was driving, right?"

"Yes, and from what I can tell, she's going to be driving back home to see and pick up Camilla soon. But Adiel," I said, anxiety soaking me. "Phoebe has a tumor."

Adiel sighed, listening to my words, and looked at me silently. He blinked, watching me calmly. He squinted, thinking. "Caelum," he started, and I just looked at him. "Caelum, do you love her?"

My eyes widened as they focused on Adiel's.

"There has to be a reason why you're so dedicated to Phoebe, why you're always wanting to see her, to be in her life."

Heat rushed into my face, burning my cheeks. "I.... I...." My words got jumbled as I tried to speak, but I couldn't get anything out correctly. I breathed deeply, and then looked at Adiel, who was just staring at me, his eyebrows raised.

I'd... I'd never... I'd never been in love before. Not really.

Being an angel meant just bringing up Spirits to the Heavens, not... not... falling in love with them, or mortals. But I guessed that that was the rule that I'd instilled in myself, not one that was for the angels.

Adiel continued to observe me silently, his look causing me to become flustered.

"I.... I... Maybe," I finally got out, managing to speak.

"It's okay," Adiel said reassuringly. "It's okay to have feelings for a Soul, or a mortal. You're not the first angel to fall in love."

My heart raced at his words, and I just watched him as he spoke.

"Caelum, I saw your reaction to Phoebe when she came out in her hospital gown. I saw it all in the Heavenly River."

My eyes hit the ground in embarrassment, but Adiel put his hand on my shoulder, and I looked back up at him.

"It's alright, Caelum. Everything is okay. You are not doing - and haven't done - anything wrong."

I stared at Adiel, looking at his face, before I sighed, the embarrassment instantly leaving me.

"Everything's alright," he repeated.

And I knew, from the tone of his voice, that he was right. I hadn't done anything wrong.

"So, are you going to go and see what Phoebe is up to now?" Adiel asked.

I *was* planning on it....

"Yes," I said. "Yes, I was. I want to make sure that she's alright."

Although I knew that she was now dying of a brain tumor, I wanted to see her...

"Caelum?"

I blinked at the sound of Adiel's voice.

"I know that you care about Phoebe, but I need to remind you of something."

My forehead scrunched together in bewilderment. "What is it?" I asked.

"Be careful, and be safe," he said. "Mortals *can't* know of our existence, unless they are truly dying. That is the only time they can view us. Nobody else that is living can know, alright? I just want to make sure that you understand. If you were to make yourself visible to a healthy mortal, you could jeopardize the entire existence of us angels. You must not do this, *you must not.* Do you understand? Only make yourself visible to mortals that are going to fully become Spirits, alright? Promise me, Caelum," Adiel said, a slight urgency to his tone.

I blinked at the sudden switch in his voice, but I still nodded, looking him straight in the eyes. "I promise, Adiel."

He continued to stare at me, as if to make sure that I comprehended what he'd just said. Then he leaned forward, hugging me. "Alright," he said once he pulled away. "I must get back to the Spirits, Caelum," he stated. Then he turned and walked away.

24

P hoebe was going to be headed home soon.

Hopefully, everything would be alright with her trip back…

Hopefully, Camilla was doing alright without her mother or her Grandma…

Camilla must've been missing them both terribly…

I blinked, bringing myself back. I just wanted to make sure that Phoebe was feeling alright. I was worried about her. I guess I was… I was… in love with her. She had melted my once cautious heart, enveloping my mind… Phoebe…

My thoughts began to trail off again, before I cleared my throat, yanking them back to the present.

The one thing that I did want to do was be there for Phoebe. This was when she was going to be with her father, her mother, and her former partner. I wanted to be present when she discussed her wishes with them.

I knew that was what she was going to do. I'd been an angel long enough to know that most mortals liked to tell their families what was going on with them, as well as their final wishes.

But I felt like I needed to watch over Phoebe, protect her…

I just had to- and was going to- be there for her, even though she wouldn't be able to see or hear me. I was going to be with her throughout everything that happened.

25

The steady beeping of the monitor slowly began to change. The young woman's heart switched its rhythm.

I slipped into the hospital room quietly, gazing at her face from across the area. I could tell that she was incredibly sick. She was skin and bones, her peach-colored flesh as pale as a sheet. She was also bald, her head and body barely covered by a knit cap and hospital gown. But she looked peaceful, pain-free, as she passed away. Her eyes closed in eternal sleep.

The machine's noise morphed into an insistent, constant signal that meant that her organ had failed. The loud sound didn't go unnoticed as I twisted around. Within moments, I saw the nurses and doctors flood the space.

They tried to revive her, but it was no use as they crowded around the bed she was in, attempting CPR.

The young woman was no longer among the living.

A gasp made me twist around, and that was when I came face to face with the Soul.

She appeared drastically different from her body. She was healthy- maybe in her late teens - her skin was glowing, while her blond hair was thick, reaching her elbows. Her eyes were blue.

I blinked at the change, between her Soul and her pale, ill body.

She stared at me, and her eyes were wide. I looked back, knowing how stunned she was.

I stood there, quiet, waiting for her to speak.

"What....? What...? You're an... an... angel," she stuttered. She took a step closer to me as she peered over at her body that was now slumped against the hospital bed, lifeless.

I'd brought my midnight black wings out of my back, to show her who I was. I nodded at her words. "What's your name?" I asked her, trying to calm her down.

"Umm... Rachel," she said, stammering. "What's yours?"

"Caelum," I said, studying her face calmly. "May I ask what you were going through? Why were you in the hospital?"

Rachel blinked, as if she still couldn't process what had happened. Then she latched her eyes on mine. "I... I have... had... leukemia. It had spread throughout my body. I'd had it for a while, and had been receiving chemotherapy. Apparently though, it didn't work, and the cancer... the cancer killed me." Rachel sounded sad - and shocked - at the same time.

"I'm here to bring you to the Heavens," I said, to which she blinked. "Is there anyone that you'd like to say goodbye to before we leave? You can if you would like."

Rachel blinked, almost in disbelief, and then shook her head.

"No, I don't have anyone. My parents are... are... at home. I recently had to start the treatment at the hospital once it began to spread. They're not here, so no. I don't have anyone." Her voice caught at her last sentence, and I could see tears beginning to fill her eyes. "I'm... I'm... sorry," she said, a sob in her throat.

"There's nothing to be sorry about, Rachel," I replied as I saw her features become contorted, sadness engulfing her.

She wiped her skin quickly with her hand, embarrassment taking over her. But I sighed, advancing toward Rachel, and looked into her scared eyes.

I leaned forward, bringing my hands around her body as I hugged her.

Rachel's sharp inhale resonated in my ears, her breath hitting my shoulder. I just continued to hold her close as I attempted to comfort her. Finally, Rachel just let go of her emotions, crying into me.

But I didn't pull away as she sobbed. I didn't do anything else as her tears went onto my clothing.

I just hugged her tightly, until she stopped. It took a while.

I held her close, determined to make her feel better.

"Caelum, are you feeling alright?"

I looked at Adiel, who'd just come back from the Golden Gates. He'd brought Rachel into the Spirit Realm. "Yes, I am. I'm just thinking…" I trailed off. "It's not about Phoebe and Camilla though," I said, to which Adiel raised his eyebrows slightly.

"What's wrong then?" he asked, walking toward me.

"I'm thinking about…. about… the Souls. I'd never willingly hugged one before, but I did that with Rachel. I'd willingly comforted her when she cried. That… was the first time I'd ever done that," I told Adiel, who blinked calmly.

"Caelum, that's a good thing. You're finally feeling the mortal emotion, starting to grasp it. With Phoebe especially, but also with other Souls. No angel can be immune to everything mortals experience. It's great that you're beginning to understand and comfort the mortals, and the Souls. You're doing a good thing, Caelum." Adiel looked at me, his brown eyes on mine. "You're finally letting Souls and mortals in," he said, smiling slightly.

I nodded. I guess I was doing that.

I was finally understanding the mortals, and the Souls. I was finally grasping their ways.

26

"Speaking of Souls and mortals, where is Phoebe right now? She should be on the way to see her Camilla, correct?" Adiel asked.

I scrunched my forehead together, attempting to think. "Yes," I said, my thoughts going to Phoebe. "Yes, she should be headed back home now, and be back tonight. If not, she's staying somewhere before she completes the drive back."

Nervousness quickly crept in my body as the thought of Phoebe staying overnight at another place entered my mind. But her mother was driving a long way. It would be almost impossible for them to make it back in one night, no matter how fast her mother was driving.

That was the one thing that Phoebe wasn't thinking about- or had said wrong. Either way, it would take Phoebe a while to get back to her daughter.

I just hoped that Camilla was still alright…

"Caelum?" Adiel asked, and I blinked, coming out of my reverie. "Are you worried for her?"

I stared at him. I was *always* worried about her, and her little Camilla… I nodded. "I'm constantly thinking about her - and Camilla- no matter what I do. Right now, I'm just worried about her diagnosis. How her family will take it, as well as the fact that her symptoms are… are…worsening."

First her feet were falling asleep, and then there was the sensitivity to light, and, finally, the headaches that had crept up on her… It *all* had me worried.

Adiel sighed. "No matter what happens, Caelum, it's going to be alright. I know it's tough sometimes, watching someone slowly die, but some angels have to do their obligation, and bring Souls to the Afterlife. Bringing the Souls to the Heavens is easy. It is mostly watching the mortals pass away that's the hard part."

I took a deep breath.

That was true. He was right. But Adiel was always right.

He came close, thumping me on the back. "Caelum, everything will work out in the end, I promise," he said.

I looked at Adiel and sighed. He was always right.

"Do you need anything else before I go back to the Spirits?" Adiel asked.

I shook my head. "No. No, I don't, but I'll let you know if I do," I said as I watched him. "I'll come by the Golden Gates if there's anything serious."

Adiel nodded. "Alright, then. I must go back inside the Gates." He smiled before bringing his hand up on my shoulder, squeezing it affectionately. Then he walked away without another word, leaving me by myself.

I sighed. I knew that I had to check on Phoebe- that I wanted to, rather- and I also wanted to make sure that she was safe, that she wasn't having any more terrible symptoms of the brain tumor.

I knew from experience and being in hospitals that they could be particularly nasty and harsh to deal with.

I had the urge to check on her through the Heavenly River.

My heart was thudding my ribcage as I made my way over to the charmed Water, before I looked at my reflection. My blue eyes and my peach-colored skin were visible through the liquid. "Show me Phoebe Bright," I said, making sure that I was speaking clearly. "Show me the single mother."

A sigh exited Phoebe's lungs as her mother made it into the parking lot of the motel.

They were both exhausted as she went into a spot that was available. Her mother turned off the vehicle and then got out of the front seat, opening the back door before getting their bags. Then they walked to the motel, the sky as black as ink as they moved. They were going to stay there for the night.

The Heavenly River moved as Phoebe disappeared, leaving me to stare at my own reflection.

I brought my eyes away from the Water, thinking.

So, Phoebe was staying overnight at a motel, since it was taking a while to get back to Camilla. She was going to stay at various places until she was back home.

And I was going to watch over her, and her mother, the entire time.

Using the Heavenly River, I was able to oversee what was going on with Phoebe, to make sure that she hadn't had anything go wrong with her trip. That she was safe.

It turned out that everything went alright. There was nothing to worry about. The only drawback about the trip was that it took a lot of time to get back home. It took quite a bit longer than Phoebe expected, but that fact made her much more excited to see Camilla.

Phoebe was really looking forward to seeing her daughter, and, of course, her father. But she was really missing her little girl.

I could tell as I watched her when she drove home that all she was thinking about was Camilla. Phoebe missed her terribly.

It was days later, in the afternoon, that I finally saw Phoebe and her mother turn into the familiar neighborhood. I saw a smile on Phoebe's face as they came through.

I smiled along with her as her mother parked in the driveway, while the front door of the house opened. Phoebe exited her car, and that was when her parent was there, a grin on his face as he took in the appearance of his daughter.

Phoebe's smile radiated throughout her face, when there was a sudden sound behind her father.

A grin came over me as I watched all of this in the Heavenly River, knowing what was going to happen next.

Phoebe was going to see Camilla.

27

"**M**om?" Camilla's voice was behind Phoebe's father as she came into view, and then a smile came over her small face. "Mommy!" she yelled, excitement soaking her as she ran down the front steps toward Phoebe. "Mommy, I missed you," Camilla said, hugging her mother's body tightly.

Phoebe leaned forward, embracing Camilla, and kissed the top of her head. "I missed you too, sweetheart. So much." She waited until Camilla pulled away from her and looked at her face before she spoke again. "You haven't been misbehaving for Grandpa, right? You've still been good for him?"

Camilla nodded. "Yes, I've been good for him, Mom," she said, to which Phoebe looked over at her parent to see if her daughter was telling the truth.

He nodded, smiling. "She was very nice the entire stay," Phoebe's father said, coming down the front steps into the driveway.

"Fantastic," Phoebe said, glancing back at Camilla. "That is excellent news."

Her small daughter met her eyes, looking happy, and then she looked at her questioningly. "Mom, how was your visit to the doctor? Are you sick?" Camilla asked.

Phoebe's parents were focused on their daughter as she crouched down on her knees, briefly glancing at her father before staring into Camilla's eyes. "Well, it turns out that, I don't know yet. I had a brain scan, and I won't know what I have until the doctor calls me back, honey. I don't know," Phoebe repeated, and Camilla's eyes widened.

"Is your brain okay?" she asked naïvely.

"It is right now, Camilla," Phoebe said. "But I won't know the results from the scan until the next few days."

"How did the MRI go?" her father asked, coming down the steps to join his wife in the driveway. He stood next to her as she put her bag on the pavement.

"It went well," Phoebe said, nodding at him. "It took a long time, but other than that, it went well. There was one portion of it where the doctor thought that there was something near the machine. But then it turned out to be nothing. I just continued getting the MRI. I had to wear headphones though, since it was so loud."

"It's great to hear it went okay." Phoebe's father said, and then squinted as he thought about something. "Would it be alright if we all go inside and talk?" he asked abruptly, switching the conversation. "Or are you in a rush to get home?"

Phoebe blinked, and then shook her head. "No, we can go inside," she said, looking down at Camilla.

"Can we eat ice cream?" her little daughter asked. Phoebe laughed.

"Is there any in the freezer inside? And did Camilla eat lunch?" she asked her parent. He nodded at both questions, grinning at his granddaughter.

"Then yes, Camilla, you can have ice cream," Phoebe said, and her daughter smiled widely.

"Yay!" she yelled, to which Phoebe shook her head. A grin was on her face as she glanced at her parents, who both were wearing the same expression.

Then Phoebe followed them as they walked up the front steps and into the home, shutting the door behind her.

The River Water rippled as the scene disappeared, leaving me to stare at my own reflection.

So, Phoebe was finally back with her parents, and Camilla, but her mother and father both wanted to talk with her.

I suspected that the conversation was going to revolve around the one that Phoebe wanted to have with them, and Camilla's father. Possibly about the MRI, or maybe about what would happen after the MRI results came back....

I inhaled quickly as I brought myself back to the present, as I looked into the Heavenly River. "Show me Phoebe Bright again," I said to the charmed liquid, and it quickly churned, until an image popped up in the Waters.

I focused intently on it as it came into view, determined to find out what would happen next.

Camilla waited patiently for her mother. She was smiling, before she turned to her grandmother, who was standing right beside her. "Grandma, may I go get the ice cream?" she asked.

Phoebe's mother grinned at Camilla.

"Yes, you can. Just be careful. Put it on the counter so it can thaw out a little, okay? Don't try to scoop the ice cream out yet. One of us will help you."

Camilla continued to smile, her excitement drenching her as she ran into the kitchen.

Phoebe's mother looked over at her husband. "Mark, would you just make sure that she gets it out alright?"

"Yes, Susanna. I'll be right back."

And he disappeared after his granddaughter.

Phoebe grinned as she stood on the rug in the front room. She was still gripping the door handle. She took her hand off it as she watched her father walk after Camilla, and then glanced over at her mother. She motioned for her daughter to follow her into the nearby dining room.

The Water rippled as it switched the image. My heart was pummeling my ribs as I saw the change. It took only half a moment, and then the liquid settled down, becoming calm again.

I watched the River closely as Phoebe and Susanna showed up in the clear fluid. I sighed, before I focused my attention on them, my insides feeling like liquid.

Susanna turned on the light in the dining room as she entered, flooding the area with illumination.

Phoebe squinted at the brightness, before she just stood there, in the hallway of the house. "Umm, Mom," she said, clearly in discomfort. "Can you tone down the light? It's bothering me."

Susanna's eyebrows wrinkled together in worry. "It's another headache, isn't it?"

Phoebe shook her head. "No, it's that I'm more sensitive to light at the moment. I don't have a headache right now, but I might if it continues to be bright like this." She groaned. Her eyes were narrowed.

Susanna quickly went over to the light switch, turning it off before going into another room, twisting the lamp light on.

It wasn't as bright as Phoebe and her mother went into the area. "Is this better?" Susanna asked Phoebe, who nodded.

"Yes, it's alright now. That other one was just too much."

Phoebe sighed, glancing around the space.

They were in the living room. Susanna and Phoebe sat down on the couches, on opposite sides. All in all, the space appeared nice, cozy, and welcoming.

Susanna looked over at her daughter, about to say something, when Camilla bounded into the room. Mark walked behind her.

Phoebe glanced at her mother for a moment before she turned her attention to her daughter, who had plopped down on the couch beside Phoebe. "Camilla, honey, Grandma, Grandpa, and I all need to have a conversation. It's going to be important, but boring. Why don't you go in the room you're sleeping in and make sure that everything is packed up in your bag. You can eat ice cream once we're all done talking. I'll come to your room afterward, okay?"

Phoebe brushed a tendril of Camilla's hair back behind her ear. Camilla nodded understandingly. "Okay, Mom," she said, before sliding off the couch. "I'll go get my things."

"Thank you, Camilla," Phoebe said as her daughter walked off.

A few seconds later, there was the sound of a door shutting.

Phoebe brought her attention back to her parents, who were both now sitting on the opposite couch together, waiting to talk with their daughter. Phoebe took a deep breath, and then opened her mouth to speak. "I know that a lot of stuff has been going on for the past few months now," she said. "And that I've been having the headaches and other issues that sent me to the doctor in the first place. Then there was the neurologist. I know that you would like to talk to me about something regarding that, but I would much rather save it for when I talk to both of you and Derek. This is once I set up a day to meet with him. I will certainly let you know the date, that way you can join."

Mark and Susanna shifted a little as they heard Phoebe's words, and then her father spoke. "It's just that..." Mark started, but then stopped, pausing to clear his throat. He began again. "We're worried about you, Phoebe, and we were just wondering about... about... the custody arrangement." Mark seemed to blurt the sentence out, although he was having trouble with it. "If anything were to happen," he said, taking a deep breath. "We just want to know what you put in place."

Phoebe stared at her parents for several moments, and then blinked as she processed the words. "I know that you love Camilla very much, as do I, but I don't like the way you are jumping to what needs to happen if I... I... were to pass away," she finished. There was a catch in her voice. Phoebe cleared her throat, and then went on. "There still are a lot of things that need to happen before we go over the custody arrangement. The main thing being the MRI results. Afterward, if I do, in fact, have something wrong with me, I will be willing to talk about it. Right now, though, it is too early."

Susanna spoke up as Phoebe paused to take a breath. "What was it that you wanted to talk about with Derek, then?" she asked.

Phoebe looked at her mother. "If he would be able to take Camilla some days, if I need more treatment. What to do if I need another brain scan done. It is totally possible. I also just wanted to give Derek more time with Camilla. He is her father. But I wanted to talk with *the both of you, and Derek, about that. I just want what is best for Camilla."*

"We do too," Mark said.

Phoebe nodded, knowing that her parents meant well. "After I get a phone call from the neurologist's office about the results, I will be talking to all of you. I don't want to right now, though. It's too early to tell," she said, with a tone that signaled the conversation was over.

Phoebe's parents sighed as they looked at their daughter. They sat there, watching her, and it was several moments later that Phoebe spoke up. "Now, I want some ice cream. How about both of you?" she asked her mother and father, who blinked.

"Yes, I'll have some," Mark said, looking at Susanna.

"I'll have some ice cream as well," she said, nodding as they both got off the couch.

"So, all of us want the frozen dessert," Phoebe stated. "Well, let me go get Camilla." She walked out of the living room, instead going down the hallway.

Susanna and Mark glanced at each other nervously, before there was a knock on the door down the hall.

"Camilla," Phoebe said. "Camilla, it's time for ice cream! I know you want some!"

The little girl laughed, the sound soaking the house as she opened the door. She bounded down the hall with her mother behind her.

"Let's get some ice cream," Phoebe said, looking at her parents before going into the kitchen, following Camilla. "Let's all have a treat."

The enchanted fluid rippled as the scene evaporated, and I blinked as I took in my reflection.

Phoebe didn't know the results yet, from her MRI, but she would know within the next few days. And then after that, she was going to speak with her family, and former partner, Derek.

I looked up from the Water, thinking about the whole thing...

I knew exactly what was going to happen now. I would be there for Phoebe.

28

A bird chirped from the tree that was right near the driveway. The large plant provided shade for me once I landed in the grass. I pulled my wings into my back as I walked along Phoebe's property. The sun shone down from the sky as I stepped onto the sidewalk.

It was a few days later, and I wanted to check on Phoebe. To make sure that she'd gotten her phone call from Dr. Isaac...

She'd made it to her home by now, her car was in the driveway. I knew that she was inside, along with her daughter.

I breathed deeply, trying to steady myself, as I glanced into the window. Trying to look in...

I could see the interior of the home, but I couldn't... couldn't... see Camilla, or Phoebe, even though her vehicle was present.

My eyes narrowed as my forehead scrunched together. Where was she?

I couldn't see her, at least from where I was, standing in the grass. I blinked, before I walked forward, onto the front steps leading up to the door. I tried to get a better view of what was going on.

I couldn't see Phoebe, or Camilla... Where were they?

I squinted, thinking for a few moments, before I remembered something.

There was a window on the side of the home, right by the living room. I could just look in there to check on them.

If I would be able to find Phoebe and Camilla…

My intestines writhed in knots as anxiety began to swallow me whole, but I gulped, determined to do what I came to do. My breathing picked up as I headed down the steps, instead going over to the side of Phoebe's house. This was where, sure enough, there was a window.

The blinds were up, exposing the interior of Phoebe's living room.

I peered inside, trying to locate her, when I saw Phoebe on the couch. She was fast asleep, her bare feet on the piece of furniture as she breathed rhythmically, slowly.

She appeared so peaceful, beautiful in her sleep…

I swallowed hard against my throat to regain my composure, and it was a few moments later that I saw, out of my peripheral vision, long brown hair bouncing.

Camilla. She was in the home too.

It felt like a gigantic rock had been lifted from my chest as I was finally able to breathe normally.

Camilla leaned forward, crouching down to put her schoolwork in her bookbag. She glanced over at her mother in the living room, who still had her eyes closed. Camilla just looked at Phoebe, watching her as she slept, and then grabbed an extra pillow that was on the other couch nearby. The little girl brought the soft cushion over to where Phoebe was, putting it behind her mother's head the best she could without waking her. Camilla then backed away, not wanting to disturb Phoebe.

Aww, that's so sweet, I thought as I watched her. *Camilla, you are too cute.*

The child sat down on the other couch, kicking off her shoes, and sprawling out across the furniture. She was lounging on her back, when she sighed. Then she closed her eyes, settling down to copy her mother.

I don't know how long I was standing there, looking into the window that allowed me to see Phoebe and her daughter, who both were now lost in unconsciousness. It must've been a while though, because I got startled by a tree branch breaking in the wind.

I turned around, looking at my surroundings, and then shook my head to clear it. Twisting my body toward the window again, I took one last look at Phoebe and Camilla. I walked away, ready to fly up to the Heavens, when there was a sudden, sharp, insistent ring that echoed throughout the house.

I stopped in my tracks. It felt like I'd been struck by lightning as I slowly turned my head, bringing my right ear closer to the nearby open space. Meanwhile, the phone rang throughout the interior of Phoebe's property.

Come on, Phoebe, I thought as my breathing began to quicken. *Come on, Phoebe. Pick up the phone. Pick up the phone. Pick up the phone.*

I couldn't help it. I ran back over to the window, peering in right as Phoebe woke up.

Her eyes widened immediately as she swore under her breath, and she instantly got up from the couch, running to the phone in just the nick of time.

"Hello?" she asked in a raspy voice, and then quickly cleared her throat. "Hello?" she tried again.

Out of my peripheral vision, I could see Camilla wake up. She looked curiously at her mother, who just put her index finger to her lips when her eyes connected with Camilla's.

I knew what that meant. Be quiet.

Shh, Camilla, I thought. *Just be quiet.*

The young daughter just stood there silently, waiting, and watching her mother as she was on the phone.

No doubt with the neurologist, or the neurologist's office....

"Yes, this is Phoebe," Phoebe said, bringing my attention back to her. "Oh, hello, Dr. Isaac," she said, to which my heart painfully skipped a beat.

She was about to get the news....

I gulped nervously. My feet shifted uncomfortably as my eyes were glued on her.

She sat down in a nearby chair as I saw her eyes expand quickly. Her breathing became hitched.

Oh, no, Phoebe, I thought as I saw her twist away from Camilla.

Phoebe inhaled abruptly, but then walked over to a desk in the kitchen to grab a pen and some paper.

She sat back down, scribbling some information before she sucked in a breath sharply again. Then Phoebe spoke into the phone.

"So, I'm going to need to come back?" she asked, trying to keep her voice as steady as possible, for Camilla's sake. "O.... okay. Thank you so much for getting back to me. I will call you back to schedule another appointment once I've discussed everything with my family. Thank you again, Dr. Isaac," Phoebe said. She sounded like she was on the verge of tears. "Okay, bye," she said, nodding. She then hung up.

I couldn't see her face. She wasn't looking in my direction as my stomach tightened uncomfortably.

Instead, Phoebe was looking outside through a kitchen window. Her back was to me. It was several, silent moments before Camilla spoke up.

I blinked, shifting my focus to her. She'd been staring at Phoebe throughout the phone call, waiting patiently. She spoke.

"Mom, what's the matter?"

Camilla could sense that even though Phoebe's back was turned, that she was upset.

"That was the doctor, honey," Phoebe said, and then turned around. Her face was stricken, her eyes filled with tears.

Just the sight of her expression was like a knife in my gut.

"It turns out that…. that… I'm…I'm… sick."

Camilla stood where she was, blinking in disbelief. "So… so… your brain is hurt?" she stammered, struggling to get the words out as she saw her mother's face.

Phoebe nodded. "There's something wrong with it, sweetheart. I'm going to need some more treatment. I must schedule another appointment with the doctor, honey."

She was choking on sobs as she spoke. Her voice was incredibly raspy, and then…. she broke down.

Phoebe crouched down on her knees and began to cry.

Tears began to flood down her face as she sobbed. She shut her eyes, dissolving into the agony, when Camilla abruptly ran up to Phoebe. She wrapped her tiny arms around her mother, comforting her.

"Mommy. Mommy. I'm here, Mom," she said.

Phoebe held her daughter close, kissing Camilla's head, and then squeezed her tightly. Phoebe looked like she was never going to let Camilla go.

They were hugging for a long time.

29

"Adiel? Adiel, are you there?" I stood in front of the Golden Gates, staring through them, at the white mist that surrounded the inside of the Soul Realm. "I want to talk to you."

"Yes, I'm here."

I heard his voice float back toward me. Within moments I saw him appear, with Lola at his side.

I grinned as I saw the dog, getting quickly reminded of Phoebe, and Adiel smiled as he saw that I was looking at her. My eyes drifted over to his as I backed away, allowing him to say the words.

Afterward, he turned to Lola, who instantly sat on the ground of the Spirit Realm. "Good girl, Lola. Good girl," Adiel said, before walking toward me, advancing out of the Golden Gates. He watched me for several moments, and then he spoke. "What is it, Caelum? Is there something troubling you?"

I shifted my feet a little, uncomfortable. I had just come back to the Afterlife, had just seen Phoebe fall apart from her phone call with Dr. Isaac, had just seen Camilla hug her mother…. "Yes, actually," I said, sighing and then bringing my eyes to his. "It's Phoebe, and Camilla. Phoebe just found out about the tumor, and she's devastated. I… I… want to comfort her in a way, so I… I… wanted to ask you if I could bring Lola with me to Earth."

Adiel's face immediately lit up, his brown eyes seeming to sparkle. "Yes, you can do that, Caelum. It can only be for a few hours though. After that, the Soul will start to fade away and then will show up in the Spirit Realm again. I would need to grant her more permission after that, and the whole process would start all over again. So, the rule is, only a few hours. After that, you must come back to the Afterlife, okay?"

I nodded, understanding.

"When would you like her to join you on Earth?" Adiel asked.

"Umm…Well," I paused as I thought. "I would want her when Phoebe starts to talk with her parents, and Derek. I want to bring some comfort to her life and Camilla's, since this is a stressful time for them." I exhaled in a gust. "I'll let you know when I need Lola. I wanted to tell you about everything beforehand."

Adiel nodded. "Well, that sounds good to me, Caelum."

He glanced over at the Golden Gates for a moment or two, and then looked at me, thinking. "How is Phoebe?" he asked.

I stared at his face, then I spoke. "Not very good. She got the phone call from the neurologist, Dr. Isaac. She was crying when she found out about the tumor, and was clutching Camilla as well…" I found myself trailing off, and then Adiel sighed, which brought me back. "But they're not doing good, both Phoebe and Camilla. I just want to comfort them with Lola," I repeated.

Adiel smiled as he heard my words. "Well, that will certainly help them both. Their dog's Soul is an excellent source of company."

That part was true. Just the sight of Lola made me smile, as I looked beyond the Golden Gates, into the Soul Realm.

Lola was panting. Her tongue was lolling out of her mouth as she saw me watching her. The Golden Retriever appeared to be smiling.

She was adorable.

The happy expression was still on my face as I brought my eyes back to Adiel. He was watching Lola too, before he looked at me. He nodded understandingly at the words that I'd said before.

"Okay, Caelum. If you want to bring her to Earth with you, then I will allow it." He put his hand on my shoulder, and then spoke again. "I will do anything I can to help you, you know that, right?"

"I do," I said, looking him in the eyes. "I do, Adiel."

30

The woman and man were huddled together, crying as they sat next to their small child. He was engulfed in wires. A tube was down his throat, the life support machines clicking and beeping as his parents sobbed.

I could hear his mother speak between breaths.

"Garrett…. Garrett…. Garrett…." she said, trailing off when a horrible sound broke through her throat.

Oh, you poor things, I thought as I saw both parents. They were clearly in distress for their child. *I'm so sorry.*

But I was there to bring another Soul to the Afterlife, no matter how large or small they were.

I twisted around as I heard a doctor and a nurse both come into the room. They saw the mother pull away from her spouse, sniffling.

"So, what is it?" she asked, her voice rough. "What's the prognosis for our Garrett?"

The nurse turned her attention toward the doctor, who was right beside her. The doctor inhaled, and then sighed.

"Umm…. I regret to tell you this, but it doesn't look good for Garrett. His prognosis isn't looking well. Based on the symptoms that he experienced a few days ago when he came in, it has been determined that he is... is... not going to survive."

The father stared at the doctor, as if he couldn't understand him.

"It's the swelling of the brain. The encephalitis, it has quickly become deadly. We've tried everything we could, but I'm afraid that...Garrett won't wake up."

Even I found myself tearing up a little as I turned around to look at the small boy who was in a coma, Garrett.

He was so tiny, so petite... His time on Earth had been so short-lived...

But, on the other hand, it was his time. His time to completely become a Soul.

I knew then that I had to do my duty. I had to bring Garrett up to Heaven. I blinked slowly, exhaling, and then focused on the little boy that was surrounded by the machines.

He was so small....

I realized that my hands were shaking when I advanced closer to Garrett. A tightness was in my chest as I gently placed my seemingly gigantic hand up onto his shoulder.

That was when I noticed that Garrett's head was bulged. His brain was swelling. Swelling horrifically.

Immediately as I touched him, the monitor went off, reacting to the fact that the little boy's heart was flatlining.

I felt a twist in my gut, almost as if someone had pushed a blade into my intestines....

His mother and father's anguished cries were behind me as I brought my hand back to my side. I paused for several moments, wondering if I had, in fact, done the right thing, when I heard a tiny voice behind me.

"Hello?"

I heard Garrett, and I twisted around to see a little boy standing behind me. He was maybe around seven years of age, with bright blue eyes and dark brown hair. He looked vastly different from his body that was attached to the life support equipment.

He appeared to be the same age as Camilla. That similarity made my heart jump.

Garrett, though, looked incredibly sad and confused. He turned back toward his parents, who were distressed. His top lip trembled as he saw his mother and father sobbing, but then he stood up on his tiptoes, managing to see his now lifeless body.

Garrett's face contorted into an anxious expression instantly. I saw him inhale, beginning to panic, when he looked at me, squinting.

Right as he opened his mouth, I knew what he was going to say. I felt my thick, black wings protrude out of my flesh. They flapped behind me before I brought them in front, so they were on either side of my body.

I crouched onto my knees, my wings visible as I stared at Garrett, seeing all the expressions flash across his face.

Wonder, curiosity, fear....

"It's alright," I told him as his eyes grew wide, as he saw my wings. "I'm safe, and you are as well."

"You're...an angel?" he asked, blinking as if he couldn't believe what he was seeing.

"I am," I said. "My name is Caelum, and I'm here to bring you to the Heavens."

I reached my hand out calmly, and the boy's eyes watched it. Then, he glanced back up at me.

"Are you a good angel?"

I grinned at the curiosity of the small child. "Yes. Yes, I am. I promise, everything's okay."

Garrett peered into my eyes with his blue ones, thinking, before he heard his mother cry out in agony.

Instantly, I could see Garrett's eyes begin to glisten. But he continued to stare at me, as I held my hand out toward him. "It's alright, I promise," I repeated as I watched Garrett, his small stature, his tiny body.

He blinked, a tear running down his cheek, when he abruptly darted toward me. He wrapped his petite arms around my middle like a vice.

I inhaled sharply, taken off guard, but then I just calmed the boy down, rubbing his back affectionately as he cried into my clothing. "It's alright, little one. It's alright."

I held him close to my body as he sobbed, looking up from the ground to see the doctor and nurse advancing toward Garrett's body.

They were going to turn off the equipment. Which meant that it was time to leave.

"Garrett, Garrett," I said in the small boy's ear, getting his attention.

He paused, pulling away from me slightly so that he could peer into my eyes.

"What is it?" he asked in his tiny voice.

"It's time to go, okay? We need to leave now. You must come with me," I said in a calming manner.

Garrett studied my eyes for maybe two moments before he sniffled, moving his hands from my middle to my neck, allowing me to pick him up.

I grinned as I realized just how comfortable he was with me. I straightened myself up from my crouch, positioning Garrett on my arm and holding him securely with the other hand. "We're going to leave now," I told him as he met my eyes again. "Hang onto me, okay?"

He nodded, and then grasped my neck tightly.

"Okay, Garrett, time to go," I said, and I walked out of the patient room with the child in my arms.

I glanced down at Garrett as I entered the Afterlife. His face had been buried in the crook of my neck, while his arms were still around it.

He'd been tired from crying and the process of coming to the Heavens.

In the distance, I saw Adiel coming toward me, his mouth extended in a wide smile when he saw my little companion.

I grinned back at him right as Garrett moved his head off my shoulder, gripping my neck tightly as he saw Adiel.

Garrett yawned, rubbing one hand over his eyes, and then blinked as he watched Adiel carefully. "Who... who are you?" Garrett asked tentatively. He was still clutching me.

Adiel smiled warmly at the small boy, taking a few steps forward. His thick, black wings came out of his back as he did so.

Garrett gasped. "You're an angel too?"

Adiel nodded wordlessly.

I turned my attention to Garrett, who faced me then. "Garrett," I said. "You're going to go with him to the Soul Realm. You'll be under his protection. He will keep you safe."

Garrett stared at my face, and then blinked, twisting toward Adiel. "What's your name?" Garrett asked him.

Adiel looked at the boy calmly. "My name is Adiel. I will protect you from now on," he replied. "I'll watch over you."

Garrett glanced over at me with an unsure look on his face, almost as if he was checking to make sure if Adiel was telling the truth.

I nodded at the small child. "It's okay," I told him. "Adiel's safe, I promise."

Garrett peered back over at Adiel, who had a relaxed expression on his face, and then turned back toward me. "Can you let me down, please?" he asked, to which I crouched down on my knees, letting the small child go.

He grinned at me, and that was when I saw that he was missing some of his teeth.

Oh, he's so cute, I thought as I saw him walk over to Adiel, who was now crouched onto his knees.

"Hi," Adiel said to Garrett, who replied quietly.

"Hi," he said softly, and then grasped Adiel's hand that was extended out.

Adiel then straightened himself up, and walked off toward the Golden Gates, with Garrett's hand in his.

I watched them both leave, smiling at how cute it all appeared to be. That little boy was so adorable, and Adiel was so sweet with him…

I sighed and then turned around to the Heavenly River, ready to check on Phoebe, when a thought came to me.

There were similarities between Phoebe and Garrett, since Phoebe had a brain tumor, and Garrett had encephalitis, which was inflammation of the brain. Both had an ailment that had affected the same organ.

I wondered if there were similar symptoms between the two…

I stood in front of the Heavenly River, lost in thought, when I finally blinked, coming back to the present.

Phoebe. I had to check on her. I wanted to see what she was going to do now that she'd heard from Dr. Isaac.

Glancing at my reflection in the Water, I quickly spoke up in the firmest tone possible. "Show me Phoebe Bright."

31

*P*hoebe was crying. Crying so hard that she appeared to be a visible wreck.

She paused for a few moments, gasping for breath as her diaphragm spasmed, and sniffled. She grabbed a box of tissues on her dresser, blowing her nose noisily, before she fell backward onto her comforter. She landed flat on her spine.

Phoebe stared up at the ceiling, seemingly lost in thought as she stayed there, alone in her bedroom. Tears streamed down her cheeks as she looked up, not really focusing on anything.

She inhaled slowly, before letting the breath out, seeming to calm down.

Phoebe blinked, and straightened herself up on the bed, grabbing the phone that was on her dresser. She dialed a number, and then waited for a response on the other end. "Hi, Mom," Phoebe said, her voice slightly raspy. "I got the results from Dr. Isaac. It's not good. They found something." Her voice caught on the last part, but she pushed through the pain. "Yes, I'm going to call Derek right after I hang up with you. I'll see when he's available to meet, and then will call you back, okay?" Phoebe nodded at what her mother said on the other end. "I'm just scared, that's all," she replied to her parent. "I don't know what will happen next. I'm going to have to contact the neurologist again once I speak with you, Dad, and Derek, but I don't *know what else will happen. I'll find out when I get there. But one thing at a time." Phoebe paused. "Alright, I'll talk to you later. I have to call Derek. Okay, I love you, Mom. Bye."*

And Phoebe hung up, her hands shaking as she did so. She closed her eyes for several moments, and then dialed Derek's number.

After a little while, she spoke. "Hi, Derek," she said. "I hope you're alright. I just wanted to talk to you about a few things. It turns out that I'm not doing well. The neurologist found something wrong. I'm going to need to schedule another appointment with them once I talk to you and my parents about this, and a few other subjects." Phoebe nodded at what Derek said. "Okay, so you'd be able to meet up with us? I would like to coordinate with everyone." She waited. "Okay. When would be a good time for you? Saturday morning? Alright, that sounds great. Would you be able to come to the house?" Phoebe blinked as she stopped, listening to Derek. "Alright then, thank you for agreeing to this. I'll see you on Saturday, Derek. Bye." Phoebe pressed the button on her cell phone, ending the call, and threw it on her bed beside her.

There was a sudden knock at the door, and Phoebe smiled. "Come in, Camilla," she said, to which it opened.

Camilla ran to her mother, hugging her. "Hi, sweetheart," Phoebe said.

The daughter pulled away slightly from her, but then Phoebe just held her tight, as if she didn't want to let her daughter go. She held onto Camilla, not knowing what was going to happen next. Phoebe was terrified.

The Water rippled back to normalcy, and I looked up from the River, thinking about what I'd just seen.

Phoebe was scared, and she had set up the date to meet with Derek. No doubt now, she was calling her parents back to let them know the plan.

They were going to be meeting up and talking about this very important topic. The topic being…. being…. Phoebe's brain ailment.

I sniffled at the thought, blinking to bring myself back.

This was going to be interesting, having everyone together. And I was going to be there to support Phoebe.

32

"Caelum, are you alright?"

I looked back up at Adiel, since my eyes had hit the ground. I had been thinking about the meeting with everyone. With Phoebe's parents, and Camilla's father. I had been preoccupied with the thoughts. I blinked. "Yes," I said. "I'm okay. My mind is just on Phoebe, that's all. Like always."

It seemed like she was constantly consuming my thoughts.

"Did she have her meeting with her family yet, and her daughter's father?" Adiel asked.

I looked in his eyes as I responded. "No. No, not yet, but she will see everyone on Saturday. I wanted to go to Earth and be there. I wanted to bring Lola with me also."

Adiel smiled. "I can certainly help you in that regard."

I grinned back at him. "I knew you would."

My eyes shifted from Adiel to the Golden Gates that were behind him. My brain quickly became enveloped with the thought of Garrett. My breathing caught a little as I focused on the Gates, and I saw, out of the corner of my eye, Adiel peer over to where I was looking.

He squinted, before facing me. "Caelum, is it the small boy that you're thinking about?"

I nodded, not taking my eyes off the Golden Gates.

Garrett was just a tiny child, like the way Camilla was....

"Well," Adiel said, "he's doing fine. Lola is taking care of him." A laugh shook through his throat, and I smiled as I brought my eyes back over to Adiel. "Everything is, and is going to be, okay, Caelum. I promise."

I felt like he was consistently telling me that. Maybe he was. Or maybe I constantly needed the reminder.

Whatever the case, he was always repeating himself in that regard. But I knew it was true. Everything was going to be okay.

33

The sound of the waves breaking surrounded my eardrums as I stood on the wet sand. I was in front of the water, letting the seafoam gather around my bare feet.

I'd been standing on the beach for a few hours now, just watching the sunset. I was thinking about what would happen the next morning with Phoebe and Camilla. Also, it was about the talk that Phoebe wanted to have with her family and Derek.

It all must've been incredibly nerve wracking for her, knowing that she'd agreed to speak about a lot of things that were actually quite personal. That was why I was going to bring Lola down to Earth the next morning, bring her down to attempt to make everyone as comfortable as possible.

The orange-pink sky drenched my vision as I saw the sun cross in front of me, a gigantic orb of light that settled in front of my line of sight. That was when I sighed, knowing that I was doing the right thing. I was comforting the mortals.

The magnetic sensation emanated from the Golden Gates even though they were closed. I blinked several times as I stood in front of them, looking up, only to see the Gates tower out of my view. I was never going to get used to them.

"Caelum?"

My head snapped to the side, glancing through the barrier that was in front of me.

"Caelum, have you come to see someone?" Adiel asked, coming out of the white mist.

I nodded as he smiled, backing up from the Gates so that he could open them.

He closed his eyes as he said the words, and that was when they unlatched. They went toward Adiel. He sighed as he opened his eyes back up again, watching mine.

I shifted a little, nervous, before I stated why I'd come to the Golden Gates. "I.... I.... came to ask if I could get Lola. I wanted to bring her to Earth with me," I said, my heart thudding my chest as I spoke. "It is the day that Phoebe will be speaking with everyone. I just want her to be calm."

It was the next morning, Saturday.

I just wanted to comfort Phoebe the best way I could...

Adiel smiled, and then nodded understandingly. "Okay, Caelum. Follow me," he said, motioning toward the interior of the Soul Realm. "We have to go find her first."

I gulped, and then walked over to him, before we both advanced through the white mist. We navigated through the Spirit Realm as the Golden Gates shut behind us.

A child's giggle brought a smile to my face as I walked through the mist with Adiel. I could see a grin spread across his face as well when he heard the noise. Then he laughed, peering over at me, his face wide in a smile. Motioning in front of himself, pointing toward the white fog, he brought my attention toward what was in the distance.

I paused. I managed to see a tail wagging, spreading the dense clouds of substance everywhere.

"Lola! Lola!"

I heard another giggle, and then glanced over at Adiel, only to see him looking straight ahead.

I followed where he was focusing, only to see Lola and...and... Garrett. They were playing together.

The child was sitting on the ground of the Spirit Realm, while the Golden Retriever was licking his face, her tail wagging rapidly in her excitement.

I couldn't help it when I saw them. I smiled. "Aww," I said, grinning. "That's so cute."

Adiel walked forward, before crouching down on his knees.

Lola turned toward Adiel as she saw him come out of the white mist. She ran over to him, whining in her ecstatic state. She bolted around Adiel in circles, and then bounded over to Garrett, sitting near him with her tail sliding across the ground, stirring up the fog.

Garrett glanced over at Lola before twisting his body around, turning toward Adiel and I as I walked out of the mist.

I copied Adiel, locking eyes with Garrett as I crouched onto my knees.

Lola continued to stay close to the little boy, but she was still wagging her tail, her gaze on Adiel and I.

"I need to borrow Lola from you," I told Garrett in a calm, relaxed tone. "I'm going to take her to Earth with me. I'm going to bring her back afterward though, I promise."

I could tell that Garrett was already very attached to the dog, that she was helping him.

The child looked into my eyes, hearing my words, and then nodded. He peered over at Adiel.

Adiel smiled as I glanced at him. He was on my left side. "Is that alright?" he asked Garrett.

The boy looked at him, thinking. Then he responded. "Yes," Garrett said. "Yes, that's alright. You can do that."

Adiel grinned. "We'll bring her right back to you, okay?"

Garrett nodded wordlessly, his blue eyes darting between Adiel and I.

"Alright," Adiel said. He glanced over at Lola, who began whining, shaking excitedly. Adiel brought himself up from his knees, straightening up before he smiled at the Golden Retriever. She immediately got up from the spot on which she'd been sitting, instead walking over to Adiel and I.

The dog licked our hands as she walked toward the both of us, and that was when I twisted around, facing Garrett.

"We'll bring her back soon, Garrett," I told the small child, who locked eyes with me. "We'll be back."

The boy blinked, and then I turned, walking away, following Adiel and Lola. I advanced through the white mist of the Soul Realm.

34

The sight of the Golden Gates made me stop.

I turned to Adiel, who was staring ahead. He looked at me, grinning as Lola whined. I smiled as I watched Adiel look down at the Golden Retriever, before he crouched, touching her head with his hands. Then he closed his eyes, reciting the words that meant Lola's Soul would be safe on Earth.

I watched Adiel silently, and then my eyes drifted over to the Retriever, who appeared so calm and well-behaved.

She just sat still as he said the words. Afterward, his brown eyes opened, and he turned toward me. "Now," he said, "you can bring Lola's Soul to Earth. Just remember, a few hours at a time, alright?"

I nodded. "Okay," I said.

I peered over at Lola, who licked my hands once more, and then sat down beside me, waiting. It was as if she knew that she was going to be coming to Earth. "Are you ready?" I asked her as I leaned down to pet her. I rubbed her ears, watching Lola relax, before Adiel walked ahead of me, stopping in front of the Golden Gates.

He shut his eyes, reciting the words to open the barrier. Within moments, I saw the Gates open. He twisted around to face me, his eyes opening again. He motioned to the outside of the Golden

Gates, and that was when I knew that it was time. Time to bring Lola to Earth.

I nodded at Adiel before I brought my attention over to Lola again. I petted her head lightly, speaking softly to her.

"Lola, come on, girl. We're going to see your owner's house."

At this, the Golden Retriever's head tilted, almost as if she was contemplating what I was saying.

"Do you want to go see Phoebe and Camilla? Do you?"

Their names made my insides feel like water, but I ignored the sensation as Lola's ears perked up. She stood, bounding toward me.

I smiled, glancing over at Adiel, who just grinned. "Have fun," he said, a laugh in his throat.

I looked at Lola, who was now right beside me. She was ready, willing, and eager to follow me anywhere I went. This was certainly going to be fun.

I stared right in front of me, looking at the Golden Gates, and then began walking outside of the Soul Realm. Lola was right behind me. Taking a very deep breath, I turned toward Adiel as I exited the Spirit Realm, before the Gates shut in front of him.

He nodded as he looked at me encouragingly. I knew what he meant as he did.

Go on.

I looked down at the Golden Retriever beside me, who just had her eyes glued on mine. She watched me calmly. "Come on, girl," I said, putting my arms underneath the dog so I could get a good grip on her. I would fly with her in my arms.

Lola didn't resist as I picked her up off the ground of the Heavens. She did lick my left cheek though as I brought her up to my chest.

"Aww," I said softly. "You're so sweet, Lola. Hang on, now, okay?"

And I felt my wings come out of my back as I held her tightly, flying out of the Afterlife.

I landed right in front of Phoebe's house, right on her front lawn as I leaned over, gently putting Lola on the grass. I smiled when she licked my cheek again. "Lola, you're so sweet," I said, rubbing her ears gently. I twisted around to Phoebe's home afterward, watching it uncertainly. I didn't know what to expect from the meeting that Phoebe had set up.

I stood on the grass, moving underneath the tree that was by the driveway. I walked in the shade, my eyes focusing on Phoebe's property. I had no idea what to expect next.

A glint of sunlight against one of the house windows made me turn. A car pulled up into Phoebe's driveway, breaking me away from my reverie. The car engine cut off once it was parked, and I blinked before I saw a brown-haired man step out of the vehicle, looking apprehensive.

I squinted, before I finally put it all together.

This man was... was... Camilla's father. This man was Camilla's father.

I felt the blood in my head pulse against my skull as I realized who he was. I wasn't jealous; I was just... just... nervous about how this would all happen, this meeting that Phoebe had set up.

I'd been an angel long enough to know that not all romantic relationships ended well. I just was hoping that everything would work out well for Phoebe, that nothing would be awkward for her…

Derek crossed in front of his car before he stepped onto the walkway toward the front door, appearing slightly nervous. That was when I saw his blue eyes blink. He had just walked up the steps to ring the doorbell when I saw him squint. The window blinds on the inside of the home moved quickly. This was accompanied by an excited squeal.

I smiled, and I looked down to see Lola's ears perk up in interest.

"Daddy!" Camilla yelled. I could hear her even though I was outside.

Derek chuckled, grinning as he heard his daughter.

"Daddy's here, Mom!"

There were a few seconds as Derek waited by the front door, and then it opened, revealing Phoebe.

I stood there for several moments, my heart racing as I took in her appearance, but then Lola whined excitedly. This caused me to shake my head. I glanced down at the Golden Retriever, who was sitting patiently, waiting for a command. She looked up at me as I saw her. "Come on, Lola," I said. "Let's go."

Crossing to the driveway before making it over to the sidewalk, I advanced as Phoebe kept the door open, talking to Derek for a few moments.

I whistled softly to Lola, who instantly came up to me. "Lola, sweetie, sit down."

She immediately did what she was told, and I smiled.

Adiel was right. She was so well-behaved.

I brought my attention back to Phoebe, who was talking with Derek, but then she was interrupted by the sound of bounding footsteps.

Phoebe smiled, moving slightly away from the door to allow her daughter to go through it.

Camilla giggled as she saw her father, and I glanced down at Lola again to see her tail wagging across the sidewalk.

Aww, I thought as I saw her. *She's happy to see Phoebe and Camilla again.*

"Daddy!" I heard Camilla squeal, and I saw Phoebe smile as she watched her daughter in Derek's arms.

"Hey, Camilla," he replied. "Are you being good for your mother?" he asked her. He rubbed Camilla's back affectionately as he looked into her blue eyes.

"Yes," his daughter said. "Yes, I am."

Derek glanced at Phoebe for confirmation, to which she nodded. "Well, that's good," Derek said, before letting Camilla down on the ground.

I stood on the end of the walkway, at the beginning of the front steps. I took everything in, when I saw Phoebe squint.

Oh, no, I thought. *Not again.*

"Derek, why don't you come inside?" Phoebe asked, blinking at the sunlight that was beginning to stream through the door, into the front of the home.

Derek looked at Phoebe, who appeared uncomfortable. She seemed to be getting a headache as her eyes narrowed.

My breathing hitched as I saw the change in her, my pulse pounding in my head.

"Sure," Derek said. "Come on, Camilla," he told his daughter, glancing down at her. Phoebe backed away, allowing Derek and Camilla to enter.

I peered down at Lola. She was still waiting patiently.

"Come on, Lola," I told her. "Let's go."

And I quickly went up the steps, following Derek and his daughter inside Phoebe's house. The Golden Retriever was right behind me.

35

I stepped inside with Lola, just as Phoebe closed the door. It cut off the sunlight.

Instantly, the house looked incredibly dreary, dark.

Phoebe blinked, going over to a light switch so that it illuminated the room that they were in. "Sorry," she said to Derek. "I've been having... having...headaches. Bright lights seem to make me more sensitive."

Derek just stared at Phoebe, but I could tell by the look in his eyes that he was uneasy. "It's alright, Phoebe. Don't worry about it."

She nodded, before she glanced down at Camilla, who was still at her father's side. "Camilla, you can stay out here, but after Grandma and Grandpa come, I'm going to need you to go in your room and clean it up, okay? I need to speak to them, and Daddy, privately, alright? I'll let you know when we're all done. I'll come to your room."

Camilla nodded her small head. "Okay, Mommy."

"You can play with your plushies too," Phoebe continued. "I'll let you know when we're done, though."

Camilla nodded again.

Phoebe sighed, bringing her attention to Derek, who I noticed had been staring at her the entire time that she'd been talking with

Camilla. Phoebe bit her lip, holding her emotions together as she watched Derek's eyes.

That was when I knew that this meeting that she'd set up was going to be an emotional one.

I twisted my body around when I heard a car engine, only to see a light darting across a window outside. I automatically knew then that Susanna and Mark were in the driveway.

Phoebe didn't have to speak for me to know that she was nervous about this whole situation.

But I was going to help her. I was going to help Phoebe any way I could.

"Grandma! Grandpa!" I heard Camilla yell excitedly, running over to the window blinds and moving them to peer outside. "They're here!"

A grin made its way across my face at her happiness.

Her love was for both her parents, and her grandparents.

I smiled as I watched Camilla, but then blinked, realizing that I would have to move away from the door. I quickly did, Lola following me quietly. She sat as I walked over to the nearby staircase.

I glanced down at the Golden Retriever, whispering to her even though everyone around couldn't see or hear me. "Good girl, Lola. Good girl," I told her.

She looked up at me before her tongue lolled out of her mouth. It appeared she was smiling.

I laughed. She was so well-behaved.

The sound of feet on the steps leading up to the closed front door made me look upward, staring as I heard the knock on it. Phoebe's parents were here.

I stole a glance at Phoebe as she calmly brushed Camilla's shoulder before going and opening the door, welcoming her parents inside of her home.

They both smiled at Phoebe, and then at Camilla, who darted over toward them.

"Hi, Camilla," Susanna said.

She hugged her granddaughter before glancing up at Derek, who just stood, watching Camilla.

Susanna gave him a cordial smile and then went over and stood by him.

I grinned. They had a good dynamic going on between them. It was one of the better relationships that I'd seen, that I'd encountered, after a romance had ended.

Which meant that all of this would be easier for Phoebe.

Camilla had wrapped her arms around Mark as he watched his granddaughter.

"Have you been behaving for your mother?" he asked her.

She smiled, nodding. "Yes, I have."

"Good," he said, kissing the top of her head.

Then he turned to his wife and Derek, smiling a little at him before I heard Phoebe sigh. I turned to see her walking in the middle of the room. I heard her breath hitch slightly, but then she cleared her throat, beginning to speak. "Okay, so now that you're all here, we can go into the dining room to talk."

Phoebe blinked for a few moments, as if in a daze, and then looked over at Camilla, who was still beside Mark. She raised her eyebrows slightly at her daughter, before Camilla looked at her grandparents.

"Bye," the little girl said to them. She waved at Derek, who just smiled at her.

"Bye, Camilla," he said as his daughter walked throughout the home, going into her bedroom.

I watched her leave, and could still hear her footsteps before the door closed.

After it did, I brought my attention back to Phoebe, who still looked visibly nervous.

Oh, Phoebe, I thought. *It'll be okay. It'll be okay.*

She inhaled deeply, and then spoke.

"Thank you all for coming. I appreciate it. There was some news that I received, not too long ago, and I needed to discuss a lot of things with all three of you. This would be regarding both Camilla, and myself. This is heavy subject matter though, so I want to sit down for this conversation."

Mark and Susanna nodded wordlessly in agreement, while Derek just looked at Phoebe.

And then all four of them: Mark, Susanna, Derek, and Phoebe, went to sit in the nearby dining room.

I followed close behind, Lola right beside me.

36

I stood next to Phoebe as she brought her eyes down to her hands. She uncomfortably laced her fingers together, then took a deep breath, bringing her extremity up to her hair. She cautiously tucked a strand behind her ear. I was standing behind her as she pushed herself underneath the table.

The light was dimmed for Phoebe's sake, while everyone else: Mark, Susanna, and Derek, was on the opposite side of her, facing Phoebe as she shifted uncomfortably in her seat.

Come on, Phoebe, I thought. *You can do this.*

She paused, taking a deep breath, and then spoke. "I wanted to say thank you to you all for coming here and meeting with me today, if I… if I…" she trailed off a little, and my heart skipped a beat, "haven't said so already," Phoebe finished.

My heart rate resumed its normal rhythm, but then my forehead scrunched together in worry. Was she forgetting things?

"The point is, that I'm glad you're all here," Phoebe said. "I figured I had to talk to you all about what's been going on with me, and how I want things to continue. I also wanted to talk about Camilla, and how I wanted her to be taken care of. I would love to say that everyone here gets along cordially, so I expect you all to act that way with the plan that I would like to talk about. This is both for Camilla's sake, and for mine. I would like everyone to continue being respectful of me, and Camilla, and my decisions that I have made. All of you are needed, no one will be left out, and all three of you are vital to me, as well as Camilla. You're all going to be part of the plan that I have in place."

Phoebe paused before continuing. "I am willing to answer any questions you have, but I want you to respect my decisions for the major things that I will be discussing, okay?"

Mark and Susanna nodded wordlessly, while Derek laced his fingers together, blinking and then staring at Phoebe. She looked at Derek, who nodded along with her parents.

I watched him carefully, studying his body language, waiting for anything that might make Phoebe uncomfortable, but there was nothing from him.

He just watched Phoebe. He was listening carefully to her, being respectful.

This was a good dynamic that they all had. They were all being nice to each other.

"Alright," Phoebe said, causing me to focus on her. "I found out, about a week ago, that I'm going to have to go back to the neurologist as soon as I can. It turns out that… that… the MRI results weren't as well as I'd hoped." She stopped, gathering herself together, and then went on. "I will need to go back, and if I need additional treatment, which is a possibility, I would need you all to take care of Camilla. You all would need to take turns depending on what your schedules are."

Phoebe glanced at her parents. "Mom, Dad, if you both can't take Camilla one weekend, then Derek will." She glanced at her daughter's father. "I will certainly try to pick her up whenever I can, but if I can't, I expect you all to help. Is that fair?" she asked, to which her parents and Derek all said, "Yes."

"Alright," Phoebe said, nodding a little.

There were a few moments of silence, and then Susanna spoke up. "Phoebe, dear, do you know what they found from the MRI results yet?"

She looked worriedly at her daughter before Phoebe cleared her throat, making sure there wasn't a hitch in it. Then, she spoke.

"The doctor said that the radiologist had found something. I need to go back as soon as possible."

Susanna blinked as Mark sighed. Derek fidgeted a little in his seat.

Derek then asked a question. "Does Camilla know? I mean, obviously she knows that we all came here, but does she know why? Does she know about the results?"

Phoebe nodded. "Yes, she knows, to the best of her ability. To her, my brain is... is... sick. That's the way she understands what is going on with me. But yes, Camilla knows. I will talk to her about the decisions that will be made today. I also expect her to behave for all three of you. But she has been behaving lately, so there are no worries from me about that."

Mark spoke. "We've only ever wanted the best for you, honey, no matter what your decision is."

Susanna nodded along with her husband's words. "Yes, definitely," she said.

Derek then spoke up. "I'll help any way I can."

I noticed Phoebe lock eyes with him, looking thankful.

Sure, they weren't in a relationship anymore, but they could still co-parent with Camilla without any issues. That wasn't going to be a problem.

"Now," Phoebe said. "All I know right now is that I need to go back to the neurologist for another appointment. I don't know any other details besides the one that I already told you all. Once I do, though, I will be telling the three of you. Again, everyone here is vital, both to me, and to Camilla. I'm going to need you all to work together for me so that Camilla can get what she needs, as well as myself. Do we all understand?"

Mark, Susanna, and Derek all nodded simultaneously. "Yes," they all said together.

Phoebe watched Derek, who blinked when she focused on him. "Derek," she said. "Your mother and father are welcome to see Camilla as well whenever they want. Tom and Katherine can certainly come by if they wish. They've always been excellent grandparents to her. If you are comfortable with that, I would like them to see Camilla. Would that be alright? That's really your call."

Phoebe looked at Derek, and he nodded. "Of course. Camilla can certainly see my parents. They were asking about you, too, Phoebe. They wanted to know how you were doing."

"Did you tell them about me?" she asked.

Derek gave her a powerful gaze. "I told them that you had an MRI, and that I was seeing you today. They just wanted to make sure how the mother of their granddaughter was doing."

Phoebe smiled. "Well, your parents have always been so kind to me, even after our relationship ended. To be honest, Derek, I don't know what the future holds. I don't know what's going to happen, which makes everything scary. Both what I'm going through, and what has the possibility of happening. I don't...don't... know how this will all turn out, but the point is, that I want everyone to work together, for my sake, and Camilla's. That is all I ask."

Mark, Susanna, and Derek all looked at each other, seeming to agree with Phoebe as they exchanged glances.

Derek nodded as he brought his attention back to her. "Alright, I promise," he said.

Phoebe gave him another thankful glance, and I smiled from where I was. I'd moved to the side to see her expressions.

Everybody was going to work together so that Camilla and Phoebe were taken care of.

"So," Phoebe started again. "If my parents, for whatever reason, can't take care of Camilla, Derek," she said, studying him. "You will. Do we all understand?"

Derek looked at her, before responding. "Yes," he said. "I'll also tell my parents about Camilla. That they'll be able to visit too."

Mark and Susanna nodded, both looking at their daughter.

"We promise to take care of little Camilla," Susanna said. "We'll take care of her and all hope that you'll be alright in the long run."

Phoebe smiled at her mother. "Thank you, Mom. I appreciate it."

Phoebe sighed, glancing at her parents, and then at Derek.

"Well, that's what I wanted to discuss with you all. I'm not going to be able to consistently take care of Camilla, or pick her up from school, so I wanted to just say what I expect from the three of you."

Susanna extended her hand out across the table, grasping her daughter's. "We promise," Susanna said again.

Mark nodded, while Derek watched Phoebe carefully.

Phoebe inhaled, glancing at everyone across from her. "Thank you," she said.

And that was when I knew that everything was going to work out for Phoebe.

Derek, Mark, and Susanna were all going to work together to help her.

37

L ola licking my hand tentatively caused me to look down at her. I smiled as I saw the Golden Retriever's tongue loll out of her mouth. She really was such a good dog.

I leaned down to rub her ears, and continued to smile as she shut her eyes in contentment.

You're so sweet, Lola, I thought. *You are too cute.*

Phoebe pushing the chair out from the table was what brought my attention back toward her. She got up from the chair as everyone else copied her. Phoebe exited the dining room, instead going through the house, and I instantly knew what she was doing. She was getting Camilla.

Derek, along with Susanna and Mark, stood up and went into the front room. They were waiting for Phoebe to come back. Derek sighed, glancing at Phoebe's parents.

"I promise, I'll take care of Camilla when I have her. I'll do everything to the best of my ability."

Susanna smiled, walking over to him and enveloping Derek in a hug. "I know you will," she said, and then backed away from him.

Mark brought his attention to Derek, before leaning forward and thumping his shoulder affectionately, not unlike, I realized, the way Adiel would behave with me.

I instantly felt content as I saw the exchange between all three of them.

This was great for Phoebe. It meant that everyone was going to be getting along.

A smile passed through all of them before I heard a door open. A few moments later, footsteps skipped across the floor, and I grinned.

"Daddy? Grandma? Grandpa?" Camilla asked, before her tiny frame showed up in the front room.

"Yes?" Derek responded. Susanna and Mark both smiled at their granddaughter.

Phoebe walked into the area as Camilla continued to talk.

"Is everything okay?"

Derek squinted, crouching down on his knees to get on her level. "Yes, honey, everything's alright. We just had to speak with your mother, that's all. It was an important thing that we were talking about. It was also about you."

"Is it about Mom's brain? Is it because her brain is sick?"

Derek glanced up at Phoebe, whose eyes instantly tightened. She spoke.

"Yes, Camilla," Phoebe said as her daughter twisted her little body around to look at her mother. "Yes, Camilla. We just want the best for you. That's the most important thing out of all of this."

Camilla turned to look at her father, who nodded at Phoebe's words. Then she ran to him, hugging his body.

"It was nice seeing you today, Daddy," she said, holding him close. "I missed you."

A small smile came across Derek's face, and he rubbed Camilla's back affectionately. "I've missed you too, sweetheart," he said, and then pulled away from her to look into her face. "You behave for your mother, okay?"

Camilla nodded.

"Okay," he said, and then glanced at Phoebe, who just was staring at her daughter.

"We love you very much, Camilla," she said, crouching down on her knees right as Derek straightened up.

Phoebe gazed into her daughter's eyes.

"We all love you very much, Camilla," she repeated. "We want you to know that."

Her small child nodded. "I do, Mom. I know that."

"No matter what happens, I'll love you forever," Phoebe said, and I felt a lump build in my throat as water started to fill her eyes.

Camilla squinted at the sight. "Oh, Mom," she said, wrapping her hands around her. "Don't cry."

Phoebe pulled her daughter close, rubbing her back as she glanced at her parents and Derek, who were all watching her. Phoebe's eyes glistened as she looked at all of them.

I knew what all this meant. Even though Phoebe's parents and Derek had agreed to take care of Camilla, I knew what that look was. I'd seen it before.

Phoebe was beyond scared of the future, of what was to come. She was terrified.

38

"How did it go?" Adiel asked me after I flew back up to the Afterlife with Lola in my arms.

I let the Golden Retriever down on the ground before I answered him. "It went alright," I said, rubbing Lola's ears, and then glanced up at Adiel's face. He was steadily watching me. "Everyone got along. The plan is for Phoebe's parents to take Camilla when Phoebe can't, and whenever they can't do that, Derek will. There were no arguments either. Phoebe made all her important points, and then spoke about her MRI results and the phone call from the neurologist. She just said that she was going to make another appointment after the discussion."

"That's excellent to hear that Phoebe has a great relationship with her parents, as well as with her daughter's father. Everything will go a lot smoother when they all get along. Caelum," Adiel said. I'd brought my eyes to the ground. I looked at him again. "Caelum, this is a good thing. It'll be easier for Phoebe now."

I nodded understandingly as I watched Adiel's face, studied his eyes. "I know," I said. "I'm just…. just… nervous."

At that last word, Adiel spoke at the same time I did.

I blinked, and he smiled slightly.

"I know you are," he said. "But you have to trust that everything will work out in the end."

"I'm still working on that part," I admitted.

Adiel came up to me, putting a hand on my shoulder. "I know you are, and I know that this is difficult for you. If you have to speak about anything, you know where I will be," he said, glancing down at Lola. She was sitting patiently on the ground of the Heavens. "Hi sweet girl," Adiel told her, rubbing Lola's ears and smiling when she shut her eyes in contentment. "How was she on Earth?" he asked me. His gaze was still on the Golden Retriever.

"Well," I started, "she was, like usual, very well-behaved. But I thought I would need her because of the situation that Phoebe was in. I thought that Lola could help, but it turned out that I didn't really need her. Lola was great company, even though her presence wasn't needed."

"Well," Adiel said, turning and looking at me, "it was the thought that counted, Caelum. You did a good thing, and everything went well, which is great. Even if Lola was not needed, she still is an excellent Soul. Now, if you don't mind, I have to bring her back to the little boy, Garrett. He's probably waiting for her to come back."

A grin spread across my face at the thought of Garrett, and I nodded. "Okay," I said understandingly. "Yeah, you don't want to keep him waiting. He seemed very attached to her."

Adiel smiled, petting the Golden Retriever again. "Come on, Lola," he told her, who automatically got up and wagged her tail. "Come on, let's bring you back to Garrett."

The next few weeks passed in a blur.

I continued to do my duty, guiding Souls to Heaven, but, like always, Phoebe and her little girl were consistently in the back of my mind.

Adiel wouldn't say a word as I flew up to the Afterlife with the Souls. He would just give me a knowing look and then glance over at the Soul, before he would calmly go over to them, introducing himself. He would be very gentle with them, making sure they weren't scared. Afterward, he would guide them to the Golden Gates, smiling at me.

I knew he knew that I was distracted by everything going on with Phoebe and Camilla, since I didn't really talk to Adiel that much, only nodding when answering his questions. But he didn't say anything about this. He would only bring the Souls to the Golden Gates wordlessly. I was quiet for a long time.

"Caelum?"

I glanced up at Adiel, tearing my eyes off the Heavenly River, where I'd been staring.

He sighed before he looked into my face. "You love her," he said.

It wasn't a question. It was a statement.

My heart pummeled my chest, hurting my ribs as I watched him.

"Umm…. umm…. yes," I finally responded, feeling heat rise through my cheeks. I kept my eyes fixed on Adiel's, instead of bringing them down to the ground. "Yes. Yes, I do," I said, taking in his expression.

He appeared calm, composed. "When are you going to see her again?" he asked, curious.

I blinked, thinking. "Soon, maybe tomorrow. I wanted... wanted.... to bring Lola with me again."

Adiel smiled, the expression taking over his entire face. "Okay, Caelum. I'll grant her permission again, to be on Earth. Whatever brings you peace, I will do for you."

I looked into his brown eyes, searching them, but only found his kind look. There was nothing in his eyes that made me think he was being mean.

Well, he couldn't be rude. He was an angel. He would lose his wings if he was.

But there was just a genuine, kind sense about him. Even more now than I'd ever known.

I stared back at Adiel, thanking him silently.

"Anything for a friend," he stated, and then grinned, grasping my shoulder. He looked at me for a few moments. Then he walked off in the direction of the Golden Gates.

39

My hands shook slightly as I brought my gaze to the Heavenly River, my thoughts automatically going to the single mother that was sick, and her small daughter. I wanted- *needed*- to see them, to check on them.

I stared into the Water, watching it for a few moments before I spoke up. "Show me Phoebe and Camilla."

Camilla was hugging Phoebe, her little arms wrapped around her mother's body in a vice-like grip. "I love you, Mom," she said, pulling away in order to look at Phoebe's face. Camilla blinked as she watched Phoebe, who had been crying. The mother's eyes were rimmed in red, her cheeks puffy.

"I love you too, sweetheart," she replied to her daughter. "I'm just… scared, that's all. I don't know how this will all turn out, honey."

"Well, I'll be with you, Mommy. No matter what, I'll be here, Mom."

Phoebe smiled through her tears, and she sniffled. "Thank you, Camilla. That is very thoughtful of you."

Phoebe pushed a strand of hair back behind Camilla's ear, and the child smiled. "Mom, you're going to be okay, no matter what."

Phoebe kissed the top of her daughter's head. "You're so good, Camilla. You really are such a sweetheart," she said, pulling Camilla close to her chest, enveloping her. "You really are."

The River rippled automatically as the Water moved away from the image, finally settling into a smooth liquid within a few moments.

Blinking rapidly, trying to make sense of what I'd just seen, I heard heavy panting behind me. I turned around, only to see Lola running toward me happily, with Adiel right behind her. I grinned, glancing at Adiel. "Thank you," I told him as I petted Lola's head absently, feeling the Golden Retriever lick my hand.

"You're welcome, Caelum. Now, where are you going to go?"

I sighed. "Phoebe was looking sad as she held Camilla. They both appeared to be at their house. I was going to go over there, to check on them."

Adiel nodded, taking in my words. "Well," he said. "Just be careful."

"Alright," I said, bringing my attention back to the Heavenly River, which was now smooth and imageless. The thought of Phoebe sobbing was enough to make me emotional…

Adiel must've caught that thought of mine intuitively, because he said, "Caelum, everything will work out."

I glanced up at him.

"You just must remember what your duty is. To bring Spirits to the Afterlife. But, Caelum, it'll be alright."

Adiel sounded calm, collected. The words coming out of his mouth were making sense.

I finally nodded, then looked at Lola, who was waiting patiently for me. "Alright, Lola," I told the Golden Retriever, and I could see Adiel smile out of my peripheral vision. "Let's go see Phoebe and Camilla."

40

The sky was overcast as I landed on the driveway to Phoebe's home. Lola was in my arms.

The Golden Retriever licked my cheek before I let her down, and I grinned at the sensation. "Aww, Lola. Thank you, honey."

She immediately whined once her feet hit the nearby grass. She'd realized where we were.

The grin widened on my face as I saw Lola's reaction, but then it abruptly disappeared. I was instantly nervous for Phoebe as I focused on the closed front door.

My pulse was in my head, the blood pumping through my skull as I looked at Phoebe's house. My chest hurt, and I realized that I'd stopped breathing.

Quickly, I took a deep breath, trying to steady myself before I brought my hands to my sides, straightening my body. I glanced down at Lola, whose tail was wagging. Her tongue was lolling out of her mouth.

Somehow, seeing Phoebe and Camilla's former dog's Soul gave me the strength to keep going. I sighed, taking in a lungful of oxygen, then I brought my eyes back to the residence. "Alright, Lola," I said, my voice and hands shaking slightly. "Let's go inside."

I walked up on the steps leading to the front of the house, my body trembling as I did so.

Lola followed close behind, sitting and waiting once she got beside me. Her tail was wagging across the ground, and I grinned. "Aww, sweetie. You're so excited."

I brought my hand up to her. She licked my extremity, and I looked at the Golden Retriever. I tried hard not to succumb to the nervousness that was building inside me.

It'll be okay, Caelum. You'll be alright. You're just going to check up on them. You're okay.

I gulped, and then heard footsteps running toward the door.

"Okay, Mom," I heard from inside. It was Camilla. "I'll be outside."

"Alright, honey!" I heard Phoebe yell back. Her voice had gotten incredibly close. "Just come back if it rains or if no one else is there, okay?"

"Alright, Mom!"

I stepped away just in time to see the front door open and tiny Camilla bound outside, skipping down the steps in her excitement.

Lola whined when she saw Camilla, her tail moving rapidly along the ground, but stayed put as she saw the little girl run off.

I quickly ducked inside the home with Lola before I heard and saw Phoebe. She was coming up to the front room. I turned around to see Camilla run to the front steps again, grasping the door handle. She then closed it.

Camilla's footsteps receded, and I caught a smile from Phoebe as she turned around, instead going through the house. The house though, it was suddenly cold. I shivered, peering around.

Like before, when I'd been here, the lights were out, making everything appear extremely dark. Dark and ominous.

This all made the nervousness creep back into my veins. The darkness, the way it was so cold....

This wasn't going to be good, whatever was going to happen. I was getting a bad feeling in my stomach.

I swallowed, anxiety engulfing me as I followed Phoebe into the kitchen. Lola was right behind me.

41

Lola's panting and footsteps grounded my thoughts as I walked along. Although, anxiety seemed to still drench me. The cold, the darkness. Everything made me feel on edge.

The Golden Retriever's sounds were keeping me from falling apart.

As if she knew what was going on with me, she pressed her body into mine, leaning against my legs. Her long, fluffy tail hit my side as she licked my hand, and I smiled slightly when Lola's bodyweight shifted.

I petted her head with my other extremity, attempting to calm us both down. "It's alright, honey," I told Lola. "I'm alright. Everything's okay."

A steady rhythm of inhaling and exhaling caught my attention, and I looked up at Phoebe. She was in the kitchen. She was looking extremely anxious, and I felt my heart drop into my stomach as she squealed, running over to the sink.

Instantly, I felt the need to comfort her, to hold her hair if she vomited. I suddenly cared so much for her. But I could do nothing.

I just had to stand there, in the middle of the room, with no way to help.

Phoebe stood over the sink, quickly looking clammy and sweaty as she blinked, trying hard not to vomit.

I finally walked up to her in the dark area, my eyes on her even though she wouldn't be able to see me.

Her eyes were wet, but a piercing, crystal blue. Phoebe truly was beautiful, even though she was struggling.

I wanted to help her so badly...

Phoebe stared out the window leading to the backyard from the kitchen, staring absently for several moments before she blinked rapidly, appearing confused.

I squinted, abruptly feeling uneasy. This wasn't good. This wasn't good at all.

Phoebe's arms started to jerk slightly as I watched her, and that was when I heard Lola whine. It was a grading, uneasy sound, one that made my eyes snap downward.

I stared at the Golden Retriever. "What is it, girl?"

My eyes focused on Lola, before I heard Phoebe gasp. Now, she was truly trembling, almost uncontrollably. Then my eyes were glued on her. She *was* shaking uncontrollably. She wasn't able to stop the movements that were going through her frame.

My breathing changed automatically as I watched Phoebe, worry soaking me. Lola's whine interrupted me again. This time she even got up on her hind legs, licking my face. Then she ran around me, quickly moving in circles.

My eyes narrowed as I saw Lola, and then I glanced at Phoebe, who was clearly in discomfort. I glanced down at Lola, who was now panting heavily.

That was when it suddenly clicked. Lola was trying to tell me something. She had picked up on whatever was bothering Phoebe.

Phoebe was in distress, I realized, as she instantly paled, quickly looking like she was going to vomit again as she leaned over the sink. She was there for a few moments before she inhaled quickly, instantly appearing fearful. She started crying, and that was when, to my shock, I saw Lola run up to her former owner, quickly rushing around her body.

I stood in place as I watched Lola's behavior. The Golden Retriever suddenly barked. It was a sharp, nervous sound. One that told me something bad was going to happen.

Phoebe, of course, couldn't sense or hear Lola, but it made me jump as I realized that the dog was trying to warn me of something.

Lola twisted around, looking at me before barking again. She came over and licked my hand insistently.

I blinked, seeming to come out of my daze, when Phoebe abruptly darted out of the kitchen, into the living room. She ran onto the carpet. Tears were streaming down her face, and she shook. She quickly dropped to the floor, falling against the soft ground.

Lola barked sharply, rushing over to Phoebe, but she had already succumbed to the seizure as I came into the living room, staring in my dazed state.

Phoebe had begun to convulse, her body twitching and trembling. She was being ripped apart by the shocks, but the severity of the seizure had caused her to immediately become unconscious.

It was several moments before I could even move, but then my muscles unlocked. I ran over to Lola, who was now laying down next to Phoebe.

Lola looked back at me, her breath coming out of her furry body quickly as her whine shook through her throat.

Meanwhile, Phoebe was still shaking, tremors tearing her body apart.

I leaned down toward the Golden Retriever, touching her head and feeling the sensation of the dog's tongue on my face. I suddenly realized it was damp with tears. I'd been crying, and didn't know it. I sniffled, wondering if this was it, that this seizure was what was going to kill Phoebe, cause her to cross over. Then I saw her body instantly become still. The shocks evaporated from her frame.

Lola turned her head around, licking her former owner's cheek, trying to wake her up.

My heart was in my throat as I watched Lola closely, and was thankful that Phoebe had collapsed to the carpet on her side. That way she didn't choke on her own saliva. My heart racing inside my chest, my eyes were focused on Lola as the Golden Retriever continued licking Phoebe's face. Lola edged closer to her former owner, keeping her warm. The dog even lifted her paws over Phoebe so she was completely covered by Lola's fluffy body. Lola whined, licking Phoebe's cheeks, glancing at me periodically. I petted Lola's head, my body numb as I stared at Phoebe, who was still unconscious.

I was crouched down on my knees, tears streaming down my face as I saw what was in front of me. I resisted the urge to touch Phoebe's head as she laid on the floor, unresponsive, protected by her former dog's Soul.

Phoebe was breathing. It was just that she was still gone in a deep slumber, which made me uneasy. She was still taking in oxygen though, which was a good thing. I just wanted her to *wake up*.

Come on, Phoebe, I thought. *Wake up. Wake up. Wake up.*

She was unconscious though, her body still except for the fact that she was breathing.

Uncontrollably, I began to sob, leaning on my knees, crouching over Phoebe's chest as I watched Lola lick her cheek. The Golden Retriever tried to wake her up, but Phoebe wasn't budging.

Phoebe's eyes stayed closed as Lola whined insistently. The noise made my insides squirm, when I abruptly heard footsteps near the door that was now closed.

My heart rate spiked as I realized that it was Camilla.

Camilla. Camilla. The little girl…. She was going to see her mother, collapsed on the carpet…

But there was nothing I could do as I heard the daughter open the door and run into the front room.

"Mom?"

I heard her little voice as I stood, unable to do anything as I heard her skip into the kitchen, totally oblivious to what had happened to her mother.

My heart pounded my chest, my breathing rapid as I saw Lola's tail wag at the sound of Camilla's voice. "Mom?" Camilla asked, trying to locate Phoebe. "Mommy, where are you?"

I still couldn't see Camilla since I was in the living room. Lola barked, an anxious sound that rang through the area.

"Mom?" Camilla asked again, and Lola barked a second time. Even though she wouldn't be heard by the daughter, Camilla still walked into the living room eventually. She sounded and appeared perplexed. "Mom?"

I twisted my head around just in time to see Camilla standing in the middle of the carpeted area, her mouth open in surprise.

"Mom, what's…?" she started, but then stopped, realizing her mother couldn't hear her.

I stayed put, crouching down on my knees, seeing Phoebe breathe. Her eyes though, remained closed.

Camilla walked up to Phoebe cautiously, leaning down and shaking her shoulder in the process.

Lola's whine erupted through her throat as she saw the tiny child. The Golden Retriever licked Camilla's cheek, unable to contain her excitement.

The whole scene that played out in front of me was enough to make me cry.

Phoebe was completely unconscious, drool slightly on her face. She was on the carpet in the living room, where Lola was positioned right on top of her. The Golden Retriever attempted to keep her safe and warm. The dog's body heat was helping Phoebe.

This was all happening while the dog was licking Camilla's cheek, as Camilla was shaking Phoebe's shoulder.

"Mom," Camilla said, her voice first begging, and then abruptly hitting a pleading tone. "Mommy, wake up."

The crack in her voice was enough to make my eyes water, and then the little girl repeated herself before going over to the other side of Phoebe, where I was.

I backed up as Camilla tried to wake her, but it was no use.

"Mom," the daughter said, her voice thick, and then I saw her pause, blinking quickly. She ran to the kitchen, sprinting back in what seemed to be a split moment, with an object in her hand.

I squinted, looking at it for a bit before realizing what it was. It was Phoebe's cell phone. It must've been on the kitchen counter.

With trembling hands, Camilla called the emergency services.

I blinked, partly stunned by this turn of events, but stayed still as Camilla spoke into the phone.

"Hi. I'm on my mom's cell phone right now," she started in her tiny voice. "My mom, she's not waking up, and she's on the soft floor of the room with the TV. She's drooling, and not answering me. I think this is an emergency, but I'm not sure," she finished, pausing as the operator talked to her. "Yes. Yes, she's breathing. Mommy's just not waking up. Okay, I'll stay with her." She paused to breathe, and then spoke again to the person on the other end of the phone. "Umm, the address is... umm..." Camilla took another deep breath, trying not to lose control, before she told the person where Phoebe's house was. "…. that's where we live," Camilla finished. "Alright. I'm going to stand by Mommy. Yes, the door is unlocked. I was…was… just coming in from playing outside and I saw her like this."

Camilla sounded like she was going to shatter into a million pieces. She reached out, touching her mother's sweaty forehead, brushing her hair back, when I heard a gasp. My eyes widened as I saw Phoebe's eyes open. Her breathing accelerated as she took in her surroundings.

Immediately, Lola began licking Phoebe's cheek, but Phoebe didn't register it at all. "Camilla?" she asked hoarsely, but Camilla immediately told the operator about her mother.

"Mom is awake now. Mommy is awake now," she said. "Okay, I'll stay with her. Okay, I'll do that."

The little girl sounded very sure of herself as she hung up the phone, instead gazing into Phoebe's face. The mother just appeared bewildered, and fearful. "Camilla, honey… what…?"

But Camilla got up from her crouch, running out of the room. "Stay there, Mommy! Don't move!" the little girl called. There were a few moments as the rest of us: Phoebe, Lola, and I, were all left alone.

Lola began licking Phoebe's cheek again, trying to keep her awake.

Come on. Come on, Phoebe. Stay awake.

And then things began to change. Camilla came back after a while. Heavier footsteps entered the room, signifying that the EMTs had arrived.

"Camilla, what's going on sweetheart?" Phoebe asked, still incredibly disoriented. She gulped as she saw the paramedics behind her daughter.

"Mommy, they're here to help you."

Almost as if she understood that assistance had arrived for Phoebe, Lola instantly got up from her former owner's body, instead walking over to me.

Me, who was just standing in the corner of the dark room, still and in shock.

Lola sat down next to me, rubbing her head into my leg to grab my attention.

"Good girl. Good girl, Lola," I told her, petting her body, and then kept my eyes on Phoebe. She was now being propped up onto a gurney.

I watched Phoebe being brought out of the living room before I saw one of the EMTs come over to Camilla, leaning forward and getting on her level. Then the woman spoke to the little girl. "You're a very good daughter, alerting us about your mother. I think she'll be okay, but we still will take her to the hospital for safety, alright?"

Camilla nodded, and then spoke, sniffling slightly. "Mom... Her brain is sick. Mommy's brain is sick. She went to the doctor a while ago, and there...there was something wrong. Does this have anything to do with that?"

The EMT scrunched her eyebrows together, trying to think, but instead appeared nonplussed. "I have no idea, honey. Possibly, but to be honest, I don't know."

Camilla inhaled quickly, on the verge of a sob.

The EMT put a hand on the girl's shoulder, trying to comfort her. "We'll find out sweetheart, okay? We'll see what we can figure out."

She paused, and then looked in Camilla's damp eyes. "We'll see what we can find out, honey," the EMT repeated.

Camilla nodded, seeming to trust the woman.

The feeling of a wet snout pressing against the back of my hand caused me to glance down at Lola, who was nudging me with her muzzle. She whined, and that was when I looked into the distance, seeing the lights from the ambulance dance across the overcast surroundings outside. The front door was still open.

I peered back over at the Golden Retriever, whose eyes were glued to the outside, beyond the door. The dog was clearly on edge.

I sighed, taking one last glance at Camilla and the female EMT before I walked over to the door, my eyes instantly burning from how bright the ambulance lights were, scanning the sky.

Lola walked ahead of me, bounding down the steps, before looking back. It was almost as if she was checking that I was following her.

I did so, advancing forward into the chilled outside, petting Lola's head afterward. Then I noticed Phoebe on the gurney.

She was still disoriented, but awake. She was talking to another EMT. He was asking her about Camilla, about a number he could call so that Camilla could stay with someone while Phoebe was in the hospital.

"Her father, Derek. He can take her," she said, her voice still slightly hoarse. "He should be able to."

The EMT nodded, while another woman came up to him.

"We have to get going," she said.

"Okay," the male EMT said, and then twisted to Phoebe. "What is his number?" he asked her, pulling out a clipboard that was nearby.

Phoebe told him the number for her daughter's father; the man wrote it down quickly, and then turned around, toward the front door that was still open.

Right as he did so, the EMT that had been talking with Camilla came out of the house.

The female EMT looked behind her. Camilla stopped when she caught the paramedic glancing at her. "Sweetie," she started, watching the little girl's eyes. "You're going to have to stay here, alright? Just until…" she trailed off as she was interrupted by another paramedic who spoke in her ear. "You're going to have to wait until your father gets here, okay?"

Camilla nodded her small head, before going over and sitting on one of the front steps. She settled down, her elbows on her knees, the ambulance lights spinning around the overcast sky.

I peered around at the outside surroundings, and that was when I noticed that all the commotion had drawn a crowd. People were in the street and coming out of their houses to see what the issue was.

Turning back toward Camilla, I saw that the EMT was speaking to her some more. "Honey, you're going to have to stay here, okay? There's a police officer that will keep you company, just until your dad comes to get you, alright?"

Camilla nodded understandingly.

As the EMT spoke, an officer came out of his parked vehicle, the lights flashing and spinning around.

That was all the atmosphere was suddenly, a bunch of whirring, dizzying brightness.

He walked right past me, over toward the small child, while the paramedics nodded at him silently. He glanced at them quickly before giving them all a nod back. Then he focused again on Camilla, who didn't appear frightened of the officer.

The doors shut on the ambulance as the paramedics all got inside the vehicle, and then they were off, driving into the gloomy surroundings.

My heart was abruptly in my throat again as I saw the EMTs leave. I wanted to be with Phoebe, but I also wanted to wait for Derek, to make sure that he was going to be able to pick up Camilla.

Every fiber of my being was making me go see Phoebe, but I ignored the sensation as I saw Camilla on the front steps, waiting patiently.

I had to stay before I could go see her mother. I had to make sure that Derek was going to come and get Camilla. I waited, with Lola beside me, while the police officer and the little girl were by the front steps of Phoebe's home.

It seemed like I waited for an eternity.

42

The sight and sound of the familiar car parking shook me out of my reverie. I twisted around.

My breath caught in nervousness as I saw Derek exiting his vehicle, darting up to the front walkway. Camilla got up from where she was, running over to her father and wrapping her arms around him quickly. My eyes tightened as I heard her sob into Derek. He bit his lip, glancing over at the policeman. "Thank you so much, officer!" he said. Then he looked down at Camilla, who was still crying into him. "Camilla, honey, what happened?"

"Daddy, I'm not sure. I saw Mom asleep on the carpet, and she was drooling." She looked up at her father, the whites of her eyes raw.

Derek squinted as his daughter continued to speak.

"I called 9-1-1 and then while I was on the phone with them, she woke up."

Derek shook his head, not entirely understanding, before he peered into Camilla's face. "Well, we're going to the hospital, and seeing her, okay? We're going to meet your Grandma and Grandpa too. They said that they were on their way there when I was coming to get you. We're going to go see your mother."

Derek brought his attention to the police officer, who had come up to them. "Could you help? I need to go see her mother, and I need to go there as soon as possible. Would you be able to show me the way?"

The man nodded, and I felt the nervous knot in my stomach dissipate.

Okay, I thought. *Everything's going to be okay.*

Now Camilla was taken care of.

I sighed as I saw her get into the backseat of Derek's car, watching as he got in the driver's seat.

The police officer got into his vehicle, and then led Derek out of the neighborhood, while people watched, dumbstruck at how the events unfolded.

My heart pummeled my ribs as I saw them leave. Lola's whine caused me to peer down at her, before I put my hands underneath her body, pulling the Golden Retriever close to my chest. "Come on, girl. Let's go," I told her as I held her tight.

My wings unfolded, and then, moments later, I was airborne, climbing into the atmosphere.

Adiel's worried face greeted me as I flew up to the Afterlife.

I leaned over, setting Lola on the ground before immediately going to the Heavenly River.

She bounded beside me, panting heavily. Adiel stroked her head absently, and I could see him looking at me out of the corner of my eye, right as I commanded the Water. "Show me Phoebe Bright."

The ambulance made it to the entrance of the hospital, to the ER, the lights erupting through the foggy surroundings. The vehicle parked before the paramedics got out, opening the back, and took Phoebe out.

She appeared groggy as I gazed into her face. She looked pale, confused, but other than that, healthy. Well, healthy as much as she could be.

As she glanced at the EMTs that were bringing her inside the hospital, I noticed the name of the building.

I was focusing so much on the fact that I could go and see Phoebe that I didn't even catch the discomfort on her face. That was until I heard her inhale quickly. She abruptly grasped her head as she was wheeled inside, on the gurney.

"Ma'am?" One of the paramedics watched her face until Phoebe opened her eyes back up. "Are you having a headache?" he asked.

She scrunched her eyebrows together, the top of her forehead crinkling. "Yes. Yes, I am. It just... just won't go away..." She trailed off as the doctors at the door of the hospital took over. The EMT looked at the main doctor, nodding at him, before I saw the hospital employee peer down at Phoebe.

"You have a headache?" the doctor asked.

He must've heard Phoebe talk to the paramedic.

"Yes, sir," Phoebe replied. She moved slightly on the gurney, in discomfort. "Wait...." she said abruptly. All the employees wheeling her into the hallway looked at each other, appearing alarmed. "I can't... can't... see...." she said, to which one of the nurses spoke. "Ma'am? Ma'am?"

But there was no response as Phoebe lost consciousness. She was still for maybe two moments, and then she was engulfed in convulsions that shook her body, ripping it apart. Her eyes rolled in the back of her head as she moved uncontrollably, and that was when everyone around the gurney began to hurry as fast as they could into the ER.

The main doctor began to shout demands at the nurses as he immediately put Phoebe on her side while she was on the gurney. This was all while she flopped around wildly. The sight was terrifying.

"We need to get her in the emergency room now!" the doctor yelled.

They turned into the area just in time for one of the nurses to run into the hallway. She grabbed another doctor passing by and asked him if he had a certain anti-seizure medication, and where it was. The doctor's dark, chocolate brown skin seemed to get lighter. His skin paled, and then he rushed out. He ran out of sight as the woman glanced back over at her colleagues, that were now trying to keep Phoebe from hurting herself, trying to keep her steady.

"Come on, come on," the main doctor said, watching Phoebe as she continued to have the seizure. "Come on. Stop. Stop. Stop."

The other nurses ran out of the room, immediately obeying the doctor's orders. He was shouting, scared for Phoebe, as he saw her convulse.

"I need that medication!" he shouted into the hallway, where people were scrambling.

Phoebe needed that medication. And she needed it now.

43

My wings were out of my back even before the Heavenly River rippled, the scene that had just played out disappearing into nothingness.

My heart was racing, my breathing rapid. My insides felt like they were on fire.

I glanced at Adiel, who just gulped. Even he seemed taken aback by what he had just seen. He knew what I was going to do before he spoke. "Be careful, and be safe, Caelum."

He seemed to know how insistent I was in leaving to go see Phoebe. And he seemed to respect it.

Adiel stepped away, and then with an abrupt nod, I was flying out of the Heavens, my thoughts completely focused on the mortal woman that I was looking after.

My feet hit the pavement outside the hospital as I landed, pulling my wings automatically into my back. Immediately, I saw a nurse coming out of the doors to the emergency room. I quickly advanced toward the ER, catching up to the nurse right as she left them.

She exhaled in a gust, and I blinked, realizing that she was the same one who had talked to the other doctor about the anti-seizure medication. The nurse seemed to relax. It seemed like she was calming down as she looked back at the ER ward.

Which meant that Phoebe had gotten the medicine she needed. Which meant that she was stable.

I breathed a sigh of relief as I realized this. I continued through the hospital doors.

Come on, Phoebe. Where are you?

I scanned my surroundings, wondering where she was, before I caught sight of the main doctor that had been by her side. He had a calmer expression on his face than he'd had before. He'd been so stressed by the image the Heavenly River had had. He walked out of the emergency room.

"How is she, sir?"

I peered over at the nurse, who was staring at the head doctor, waiting for a response.

"She's stable, but we're going to need to get a CT scan immediately."

"Is she responsive?"

"Yes. We gave her the medicine she needed to stop seizing, and she's awake, but very tired."

Phoebe was tired…

She was getting sicker. Sicker and sicker….

I turned at the sound of a familiar sigh, and my blood turned to water. My insides seemed to melt. Instantly, I relaxed as I walked into the room.

Phoebe was on a hospital bed, propped up on a pillow. Her finger had a monitor on it, connecting her pulse to a machine, while she had an IV in her arm. Her blue eyes scanned the area as I entered. My heart rate quickened as I saw her face. She was so gorgeous…

But I just exhaled as I walked into the corner of the room, glad that she was awake. Awake, but visibly fatigued.

She was exhausted, her eyelids drooping as she scanned the area. Phoebe blinked sleepily, but then focused on the doctor that came into the room. "Ma'am?" he asked, walking to her bedside. "Phoebe?"

Phoebe's eyes latched onto his as he approached her. Still, she appeared incredibly drowsy. "Yes, doctor?"

"Phoebe, I'm afraid you had a seizure. We had to give you some medication, but we would like to carry out some more tests."

Phoebe's eyes started to glisten, and I sniffled as I saw her begin to tear up. But then she looked at the doctor with wet eyes. "Camilla. Camilla," she said, repeating her daughter's name one last time. "How is she?" Phoebe blinked, abruptly confused. She twisted her head from side to side, almost as if she was trying to find her little girl. "Where is she?"

"She's with her father. I think your parents are with them. They are all in the waiting room, I believe. I'll check."

The doctor disappeared for a few moments, leaving Phoebe and I alone. He walked out of the room, talking with one of the other nurses before coming back quickly. He met Phoebe's eyes as she stared at him, tired but anxious at what he was about to say. He nodded, looking at her. "Your daughter is in the waiting room, along with her father. Your parents are there too. Everybody is safe, including you."

I saw the tension leave Phoebe's body. She breathed a sigh of relief. "When will I be able to see her?" she asked.

"Once you've rested, but we're going to need to get a CT scan of your brain. We need to figure out the cause of the seizure."

"I already had an MRI a few weeks ago," Phoebe said, her words slightly spilling into each other since she was so tired. "The neurologist told me that they found something. They thought that it could've been a tumor."

Her eyes glistened again, and I resisted the urge to go over and comfort her.

The ER doctor nodded, but then focused on Phoebe, who was fighting to stay awake. "Ms. Bright, why don't you rest for right now? We'll see about getting your relatives in here a little bit later. I still want a scan done, but for right now, I'll let you sleep," he said, looking into her tired face.

"O… okay," she said, before she put her head on the hospital pillow, closing her eyes. She was asleep in moments.

My footsteps echoed through the hallway of the emergency room, even though no one would be able to see or hear me. I made it out of the ER quietly. I heard a TV running in the distance, which meant I was almost at the waiting room.

"Daddy?"

A grin spread across my face as I recognized that tiny, little voice.

"When will we be able to see Mommy?"

Camilla's tone exuded worry, and I made it to the waiting area just in time to see Derek hug his daughter. "I don't know yet, honey," he responded as he held her close.

Even though I'd just smiled when I'd heard Camilla, I felt my insides squirm at the desperation in her voice. By the way she was breathing quickly, she was choking on a sob.

Poor Camilla, I thought as I saw Derek pull away from her, watching her now red eyes.

"We'll be able to see her soon, sweetheart, okay?"

Camilla nodded. She blinked several times, and then twisted to look, seemingly, right at me.

My heart skipped a beat painfully as our eyes connected, but then I heard footsteps behind me, and realized that the little girl had been staring at the ER doctor. I inhaled deeply before turning and peering over at him as he advanced toward Mark, Susanna, Derek, and Camilla.

"Are you Phoebe Bright's family?"

Susanna nodded as everyone turned their attention to him. "Yes. Yes, we are," she stated, and they all locked eyes with the doctor.

"Well," he started, "Phoebe seems to have had two seizures today. She had one when she arrived here, but she is stable now. You," he crouched down on his knees to get to Camilla's level. She focused on him. "You possibly saw her after she'd had her first seizure. You did the right thing, calling 9-1-1. You saved her."

"When will we be able to see her?" Mark asked.

"Soon," the ER doctor replied, straightening himself up again. "She's resting right now. We'll have her moved as soon as she wakes up."

Derek nodded, gathering everything that the doctor had just said. "Thank you," he said.

"You're welcome," the doctor replied. He walked away, disappearing into the hallway.

Every one of Phoebe's relatives watched him leave. They all appeared to exhale. I knew then that it was time to go.

Camilla, Derek, Mark, and Susanna all seemed to be calm for the moment. And Phoebe seemed to be okay for right now.

That meant that I could leave. But, like always, I would be back.

My wings appeared quickly, and I swiftly flew up to the Afterlife.

44

"**P**hoebe is doing a lot better now," I told Adiel once I pulled my wings into my back.

He probably already knew that though, since he was right by the Heavenly River. He nodded as he took in what I said. "Well, I'm glad Phoebe is alright, at least for right now," Adiel replied. "Even though some of our duties are to guide Souls to the Heavens, it still brings me joy to hear that one of the mortals is safe. I also know that it makes you feel better that she is safe."

I watched Adiel's face as he said that. He knew he was right.

I was just constantly thinking about Phoebe, about her small daughter, about... about... her brain tumor. I inhaled quickly as I pulled myself away from the thought.

Adiel peered over at me for a few moments, seeming to understand that my mind was wandering. "The mortals, and their emotions, are truly amazing, Caelum," he said. "It's excellent that you are now opening up and experiencing more of their feelings."

I guessed he was right. I knew Adiel was correct about one thing; that Phoebe, for right now, was safe. Safe and in a slumber.

After she slept, she would be moved out of the ER, get a scan of her brain done, and then see her family. Hopefully, she would be released from the hospital soon...

Even as I thought about it, I had a horrible sensation in the pit of my stomach.

What if she continued to struggle with the effects of the brain tumor? What if she had yet another seizure?

My mind began to wander as the terrifying thoughts circled around it.

No. No. No. No. Phoebe…

I blinked as I felt Adiel's hand on my shoulder, and I looked up. "Caelum," he said. "Caelum, everything will work out. No matter what happens with Phoebe, everything will be alright," Adiel finished, repeating the words that he'd said to me once before.

I inhaled, and then nodded at his words. I understood what he meant.

Everything would be alright.

45

As I suspected, Phoebe got her brain scanned, got out of the ER, and got to see her family soon after she was moved. She was able to go home within the next few days with her mother driving her, and saw the neurologist again after she returned home. She had spoken to the doctors once she'd gotten her brain scan. She indeed had a mass on her organ. Both the CT scan and the MRI had confirmed that.

Phoebe was levelheaded once she had gotten on the phone with Dr. Isaac, explaining what she'd been through, and had scheduled a new appointment with him. Phoebe was ready for everything that the neurologist wanted to talk to her about.

Thankfully, none of my horrible thoughts ever came true. She didn't have a third seizure, and for right now, she appeared stable.

Like always, I saw everything happening with Phoebe in the Heavenly River. I did so while I was fulfilling my obligation to the mortals. I continued to bring the Souls up to the Heavens, to Adiel, who, as usual, was silent when I came up to the Afterlife. But then again, he was always silent when it came to me. He knew that I was preoccupied with Phoebe and Camilla. So, Adiel didn't say a word. The one thing that Adiel didn't do though, was judge me, which I was grateful for. He didn't seem upset by the fact that my focus was mostly on the mortal woman and her daughter.

If anything, Adiel seemed understanding, maybe even supportive of the fact that I cared about Phoebe. All he would do was grasp my shoulder, watching my eyes wordlessly before letting it go.

He was not judgmental. Adiel understood.

"Adiel?"

He turned his head around, peering into my face. He appeared calm.

"Yes?" he responded.

"Thank you," I told him, and I meant it.

He wasn't being mean. He was being kind to me no matter what happened to Phoebe, and whatever I did to watch over her. I was incredibly thankful for that.

Adiel just scrunched his eyebrows together, before smiling. "You're welcome."

He seemed to know what I was talking about. He was always good at knowing what I was thinking.

Adiel got serious as he looked at me. "You know that you can talk to me about anything, right?"

I nodded. "Yes. Yes, I know that," I said.

"Alright," Adiel responded. "I just wanted to make sure you knew."

Adiel really did care about me. He really, truly did.

"Caelum?"

I shifted my focus over to Adiel. My focus had been on the Heavenly River.

He squinted a little, thinking. "Caelum," he started. He breathed in deeply, before continuing. Adiel, for what seemed to be the first time in his entire existence, seemed uncomfortable. "I have something to tell you."

I blinked rapidly, taken aback. First, I was caught off guard, then I was alarmed. Anxiety took over me, my voice shaking slightly. "Ad...Adiel, what are you talking about? What's...?"

I trailed off, only for him to stop me.

"No. No. No. No," he said, watching my eyes widen. "It's just that...that... Caelum, I haven't told you everything that you probably should know."

"About what?"

"About how... we shouldn't... shouldn't be visible to the mortals."

My eyes widened again.

What was Adiel saying? Was he saying that there was a way to become visible to them? Visible to...My heart thudded my chest. Visible to Phoebe.

Was there a way?

"Adiel, are you saying there's a way that I can actually see her?"

Meet her...

"Yes, Caelum, there is a way."

I gulped. "Why didn't you tell me this before?"

"I...I... didn't realize how much you cared about Phoebe, or little Camilla. That was until she was admitted to the ER. Rule number one is to not reveal yourself. It would be incredibly dangerous for us if we were to, but if angels keep their wings hidden, they're safe." Adiel looked up into my eyes, since his had been down on the ground of the Afterlife. "You can meet Phoebe," he said.

Meet Phoebe... Meet Camilla... Be among the mortals...

"What's the rule?" I asked Adiel.

"You must keep your wings hidden the entire time you see anyone that isn't dying. There are special words I can teach you. You can see her, though. You can finally be visible to Phoebe." Adiel's eyes shifted to the Heavenly River, peering into the Waters. "You can also see yourself the way the mortals see you. You will be able to view yourself in their mirrors."

I looked at Adiel's eyes through the River.

I was interested in that. I was *very* interested in that.

46

"So other angels have this ability?" I asked Adiel, wanting to know more about the subject. "The ability to walk among the mortals?"

Just the thought of it made my heart skip a beat.

"Yes," Adiel said. "The words are used by the Guardians of the mortals."

I knew what he was talking about.

The Guardian angels. The ones who protected the mortals from death.

"The Guardians can be visible among them, or not at all. It just depends on the way they want to do their duty. The words though, they wasn't really made for an angel whose duty is to bring the Souls to the Afterlife. But it'll still work the same way it would with a Guardian angel," Adiel said.

My heart raced at his words, as I stared into his eyes.

I could finally *meet* Phoebe....

"Caelum," Adiel said, pulling me back to the present. "No matter what you do, whether you are among the mortals or the angels, well, you know."

I knew what he was going to say.

Be careful and be safe.

I leaned forward, hugging Adiel. "I will, Adiel. I promise."

"You're not…. not…. mad at me, are you?"

I scrunched my forehead together, pulling away from him.

"Why would I be mad? You're just doing your duty. It's okay."

For the first time, it seemed, I was comforting Adiel.

He just locked eyes with me, before nodding.

"Okay, Caelum." He sighed, looking relieved. "Okay."

The heavy breathing of the older man filled my ears as I slipped into the room of the hospice house. The noise sounded incredibly raspy and rough.

I automatically knew that there was something wrong with his lungs. The way he was taking in air was way too labored. The elderly man was extremely weak.

He wasn't going to be among the living much longer.

I blinked as I walked over to his bedside, seeing the flowers that were on his dresser. The staff here was making sure that he was cared for.

I found myself staring at the man, peering into his face as he slept, and that was when I noticed the nasal tubes that were under his nose, the cannula that was giving him the oxygen he needed. The machine that he was hooked to steadily released the airflow, but I knew that he wasn't going to need it much longer.

I glanced around the room, peering into the hallway, before I realized that it was all empty.

It was nighttime, and the hospice house that I was in was going to close soon.

I sighed, exhaling slowly before I advanced toward the elderly man, watching him as he struggled to breathe properly.

It was his time to become a Soul.

I made it to the right side of his bed as I focused on his sleeping face, reaching over and touching his right shoulder. Instantly, I saw the man's chest rise and fall one last time. I brought my hand back as I retreated, stepping onto the carpeted floor, and then looked at the man's body that was tucked in the bedsheets. He was lost in a permanent slumber.

I stood there, on the soft ground, watching him. Then I shook my head slightly, looking outside the bedroom and into the hall. That was when there was a voice behind me.

"Hello?"

It was shaky, confused, and scared.

But the breathing was steady and rhythmic as I twisted around, and I let my wings come out of my back in order to calm the man down.

As I turned toward his face, his forehead wrinkled in confusion, before realization slammed into him.

"You're safe," I said, as the older man struggled to comprehend what was going on. "Everything's alright."

He blinked, and then took a deep breath. "What's your name?" he asked, looking stunned.

"My name is Caelum," I said, taking in the man's appearance.

His breathing was no longer raspy, his face no longer covered with the nasal cannula that was giving him oxygen before. He looked healthy, his body no longer under stress.

"I'm here to bring you to Heaven," I told him. He blinked, peering into my face as I brought my hand out in front of me. I waited for him to grab it.

The man gulped, staring at me with his green eyes, and then took it.

I smiled warmly as he brought his extremity to his side, but continued to look into my eyes, seeming amazed.

"What's your name?" I asked him.

"Isaiah," he said. "My name is Isaiah."

"It's nice to meet you, Isaiah," I said, truly meaning it as I glanced behind his Soul, peering over at his body that was now empty.

Isaiah turned to look at himself tucked in the bedsheets. His body appeared peaceful, calm. Isaiah twisted around, back toward me, looking into my face. "I had emphysema. It was at its end stages. I knew it was going to kill me. I just didn't know when it would happen. I...I..." Isaiah trailed off for a moment, thinking, before coming back to himself. He sucked in a breath, struggling as he watched his body. "I shouldn't have put my family through all of this..."

I knew what he meant.

He meant the hospice house, and his death. He appeared stricken as the thought consumed him. "My family...my daughter... my wife..." he said thickly, beginning to cry. "They shouldn't have been put through all of that..."

I just stared at Isaiah, listening to him as he broke down.

"My...my... family..." he sobbed. "My poor family..."

"You will be able to see them up in the Heavens, Isaiah. You'll be able to visit them, if you wish. I can bring you down here again so you can do so, if that's what you want," I said.

He looked at me, a tear running down his face, before he nodded understandingly.

"Is there anyone that you would like to say goodbye to before we leave?" I asked.

Isaiah shook his head. "No. Everyone is at home. I'm alone here." He gulped in oxygen, and then peered into my eyes. "Are you sure I'll be able to see my loved ones?"

I nodded. "You will, I promise."

If I lied, I could lose my wings.

"Promise," I repeated as Isaiah sighed deeply.

He nodded in acknowledgment.

"Now, Isaiah," I said, glancing into the hallway that was still lit. "We must go."

I had only just said that when a nurse came into the bedroom, where the Soul of Isaiah and I were. She appeared confused when she first saw him, her expression changing as she realized the older man wasn't waking up. All that could be heard was the oxygen machine, but there was no breathing.

The nurse's dark skin got pale, before she inhaled quickly, coming to his bedside, checking the pulse that should've been in his neck. There was nothing. "Oh, Mr. Isaiah," she said quietly. She left the room, going to get the other employees.

I turned toward Isaiah's Soul, who just gulped again.

"Come on," I said. "We have to go."

We both made it into the hallway just as more nurses came into the area, going to examine Isaiah's body. To remove it soon.

My wings came out fully, expanding to their complete span as Isaiah took my extremity.

"It'll be alright," I said as I got a good grip on him. "You'll be okay."

I'd only just gotten to the Heavens with Isaiah when I saw Adiel advancing toward us. He smiled as he met Isaiah's eyes. "Hello," Adiel said. "My name is Adiel. I'm going to watch over you in the Soul Realm. You're safe, I promise," he said, as Isaiah appeared on the verge of tears again.

"Caelum... Caelum... he said that I could see my family," Isaiah rasped. "Is that true?"

Adiel nodded, glancing first at me, and then at Isaiah. "Yes, it is. Us angels, if we lied, we could lose our wings," he said, extending his own black feathered appendages out as he spoke. Isaiah's eyes widened, and then he looked at Adiel, then at me. "Yes, you can see your family. Caelum was telling the truth. You can see your loved ones through the Heavenly River. Since I am going to be your Guardian, just let me know when you would like to use it, and I will grant you permission. Caelum, he can help you use it as well, he uses it himself. He can also help you go to Earth to see your relatives. Again, just let me know when you want to do that. I can recite special words so you can be on Earth." Adiel sighed. "Both of us will be able to help you, if and when you wish."

Isaiah nodded, and then glanced at me. "Can I see them now?" he asked.

"Yes, of course," I told him, gesturing over to the Heavenly River. "Just speak up and say the relative's name that you would like to see."

Isaiah came up to the River nervously, and then peered into the Water, staring at his reflection. He turned and looked at me. I nodded encouragingly, and then he spoke, "Show me Sarah. Show me my daughter."

My eyes met Adiel's as the Water churned, showing the older man that was beside me, Isaiah, his daughter.

Adiel just looked back at me, walking over on the other side of Isaiah. He watched the River, following what the woman was doing.

Sarah was sleeping. That was until her cellphone lit up in the darkness, ringing throughout the silence. She immediately opened her eyes, squinting, before she grasped the phone, putting it to her ear. She cleared her throat, and then spoke. "Hello?"

Instantly, I knew who was calling on the other end. It was the hospice house. They were calling Isaiah's daughter in order to tell her the news.

Sarah automatically sniffled, struggling to breathe. Her eyes glistened, and then she replied to whoever was on the other end of the phone. "Well, thank you for telling me. I'll be there tomorrow morning with my mother. Thank you again," Sarah repeated, her voice breaking as she went to hang up.

The River Water moved around then, the image disappearing.

I peered over at Isaiah, only to see him blink in surprise. His eyes were wet. He took a few deep breaths, and then looked at me. "Thank you, Caelum. Thank you so much."

"You're welcome, Isaiah. I'll be happy to help you in any way I can."

Isaiah nodded, and then peered over at Adiel, who was on the other side of him.

"Are you ready?" Adiel asked Isaiah.

"Yes," Isaiah replied. "Yes, I am."

Adiel smiled, advancing over before walking with him to the Golden Gates. "Come on," Adiel said. "Let's go."

47

"What are you thinking about?"

I brought my attention to Adiel, who had just come back from bringing Isaiah to the Golden Gates. "The mortal that I just brought up to you: Isaiah. I just remembered what he had said, about how he had wished he had never done what he had done when he was younger."

Adiel nodded. "Yes," he said. "Yes, this is true."

I sighed. "I was just thinking about how guilty he seemed to be. He appeared incredibly pained by the decisions he had made previously."

Adiel looked at me, watching my eyes. "Yes, this is true," he repeated. "He did seem quite guilty about his actions, the actions that led to his death. Everything though, happens for a reason. There was a reason the mortal made the decisions he made, which led to him getting emphysema. There was certainly in reason you were summoned to his bedside, to bring him to the Afterlife. Even angels don't always understand it, Caelum. I certainly don't always comprehend it. I do know that you must put your trust in the inevitable."

I squinted, confused, as I peered into Adiel's brown eyes. "The inevitable? Which is?"

"That every mortal, in some point in their life, will meet the end, and they will die. Death is inevitable."

I glanced down at the ground of the Heavens. I should've known Adiel would say that.

"Death is hard to deal with, but it is also an escape from pain. You must look at it differently, Caelum. You can't always be so guarded."

I looked at Adiel. I guess I was usually guarded.

Except now, I was watching over Phoebe and Camilla constantly. My heart was no longer closed off…"Caelum," Adiel said, and I focused on him. "Caelum, I just want you to experience the mortal emotion."

I knew I had to stop being so emotionally distant. It was just that… this duty… this obligation to the mortals; it was easier just to not get attached.

Except with Phoebe and Camilla. The fact that Phoebe was a single mother and her seven-year-old daughter would be left without a parent got me really invested in them. I wanted to check on both constantly, see how they were doing….

"Caelum," Adiel said, and I brought my attention back up at him. "I just want you to understand that there is a reason for everything. Even a reason why you became an angel. That, and that completing this duty with an open heart and mind will help you tremendously. You did a good thing for the Soul of Isaiah, bringing him peace by letting him see into the Heavenly River. That was very kind of you, in helping Isaiah find closure. You just must be careful, Caelum, and be safe, no matter what you do."

I blinked, and then my head tilted slightly. "Adiel?"

He looked into my eyes in response.

"Adiel, why are you constantly saying that? Be careful, and be safe. There must be some sort of reason you are consistently saying it," I said, to which Adiel sighed, and then spoke.

"Caelum, I never told you the story about Lemuel, have I?"

48

I blinked, stunned. "Umm…" I stuttered, and then shook my head. "No. No, you haven't," I said.

Adiel inhaled deeply, before exhaling slowly. "Well, Caelum, Lemuel was a Guardian angel, a Guardian of the mortals. You never met him, I assume?"

I shook my head. I had never heard of an angel named Lemuel.

"Well, he fell in love with a mortal woman, named Chloe. He wanted to give up his immortality and wings permanently to be with her."

I stared, hanging onto every word Adiel said.

"Lemuel Fell but he didn't go into Hell. Instead, he was protected by the words in order to walk among the mortals. He gave up everything so that he could be with Chloe, and afterward, had a normal lifespan of a mortal." Adiel paused, and then continued. "There was one night that Chloe and Lemuel were walking back to where her car was. She got robbed, and almost got shot. Lemuel jumped in front of the gun, taking a bullet for Chloe. Another angel- that I know you know of- named Ezekiel, brought Lemuel's Soul up to Heaven."

I blinked as I thought about Ezekiel. I had met him before- he had the same duty as me, to guide Souls to the Afterlife- but it had been a while since I had seen or heard from him. I focused back on Adiel. "What happened with Chloe? Did Ezekiel have to bring two Souls up?"

Adiel shook his head, and my heart sank at the movement.

Lemuel was separated from the mortal that he loved...

"No. She survived, and now Lemuel is in the Golden Gates, as a Soul, waiting for the day that Chloe will join him." Adiel peered into my eyes as he spoke again. "That is the reason I'm always saying to be careful and be safe. I know now that you love Phoebe with all your heart, and her little Camilla. I just don't want you to become heartbroken, Caelum. I don't want you hurt."

I looking absently at the Golden Gates before turning my attention to the Heavenly River, peering into it and seeing my reflection. I stared at my face, my blue eyes, and then saw Adiel come up to me, glancing at me through the Water.

Adiel... Adiel cared about me. He didn't want me hurt.

I turned toward him, peering into his eyes, before I leaned forward, hugging his body. "Thank you, Adiel," I told him. "I know you're only looking out for me, so thank you," I said.

He just nodded understandingly. "You're welcome, Caelum."

49

"So, where is Phoebe now?" Adiel asked. "What is she doing, now that she is back home, hopefully?"

I blinked. I needed to check on her. "I don't know. I'll check," I said, voicing my thoughts. "I do know that Phoebe needs to see Dr. Isaac again."

I shook my head, trying to clear it.

There was just so much going on with this single mother. The single mother that had grasped my heart....

I watched the Heavenly River, looking at my face. Then I said, "Show me Phoebe Bright."

Phoebe was in her bedroom with her mother. Susanna was helping her daughter pack another bag so they could go back to the neurologist. Phoebe appeared anxious.

Susanna saw this, and paused as her daughter pulled away from the bag that she was packing. Phoebe grasped the bridge of her nose with her fingers, looking like she was in pain.

"Are you alright, honey?" Susanna asked her.

Phoebe just stared at her mother before sniffling.

"Oh, sweetie," Susanna said, pulling her daughter into a hug. "Whatever happens, I'll be with you the entire time, okay?"

"Alright," Phoebe responded, her voice abruptly thick. "Alright," she repeated, and then pulled away from Susanna.

"Mommy? Grandma?"

Camilla's voice floated into the bedroom from the hallway.

Phoebe immediately straightened up. "Yes, Camilla?" Phoebe's voice carried as she spoke to her.

"I'm all packed up," Camilla said.

The little girl poked her head into the doorway hesitantly, before Phoebe smiled at her, glancing at the bag that Camilla had on her shoulder.

"You have your backpack too, right?" Phoebe asked. "Remember, Daddy will be picking you up from school until I get back."

"Yes, Mom. I have my backpack. It's just in my room. It was very heavy."

"I'll help you with that then, Camilla," Susanna said, glancing at Phoebe for a few seconds, and then looked at her granddaughter. "Come on, Camilla. I'll help you," she repeated.

Phoebe smiled at her mother, and then turned toward her bed again. She exhaled in a gust as she stared down at her packed bag. I could tell that she was incredibly uncertain. Uncertain of everything to come.

The River Water trembled as the image disappeared.

I turned my head, glancing at Adiel.

Phoebe was scared.

"Looks like she's going to be back at the neurologist soon," Adiel said, looking back at me. "Seems to me that Camilla is doing alright."

I nodded, twisting my head around, back toward the Heavenly River. I wanted to see the rest of what was going to unfold in the Waters.

Particularly for Camilla. I wanted to watch over her.

"Show me Camilla," I said to the River. "Show me Phoebe Bright's daughter."

Phoebe and Susanna were both relaxing on a couch, talking to each other, with Camilla in the living room as well. She was playing with her plush toys, not really paying attention to what the two adults around her were speaking about. It was only when Phoebe said her name that Camilla moved.

"Camilla," Phoebe said, "Camilla, come here."

Her small daughter walked over to Phoebe, before the mother wrapped her arms around her.

"I'm going to miss you, honey," she said, pulling away from her and then looking Camilla in the eyes. "You're going to be good for Daddy, right?"

Camilla nodded. "Yes, Mom. I will."

"Good," Phoebe said, before Susanna turned toward her grand-daughter.

"Can I get a hug, too?" Susanna asked.

Camilla smiled, before wrapping her arms around her grandparent. "Of course, Grandma. Of course, you can."

The Water rippled as Camilla, Phoebe, and Susanna disappeared, leaving my reflection in the liquid.

My eyes appeared anxious before I glanced up at Adiel, who'd been looking at me through the River.

"I just want to watch over them," I said, knowing that he would understand. "Phoebe especially."

Adiel nodded. "I know, Caelum. That was why I wanted to talk to you."

I watched him, intrigued. "About what?"

"The words which will help you become visible, while also keeping your wings hidden."

My heart seemed to pulse inside my head, and then Adiel continued. "There is also another one so that you can be sensed by the mortals, without being seen. Both I will teach you, but, like always, I want you to promise me that you will be..." He trailed off, and I knew what he was going to say.

"Safe," I finished for him, to which he nodded, smiling.

"Yes, Caelum. Exactly."

My breathing became rapid as I realized what Adiel was going to teach me. I could finally be around Phoebe and be visible to her, or be sensed by her.

This was going to be interesting.

50

O ver the next few days, Adiel began teaching me the words. It took a few tries to get them memorized, but it was easy after that. Once I had mastered both, and I was comfortable enough without Adiel assisting me, he sighed, smiling lightly. "Now, you can go see your Phoebe," he said.

I grinned. "Thank you, Adiel."

I hugged him, breaking away to glance at him. He thumped me on the back.

"You're welcome, Caelum. You're welcome."

Adiel's eyes focused on mine. I knew that he knew that I was going to go over to the Heavenly River.

"Well, Caelum, use the special words wisely," he said.

I nodded. "I will, Adiel. I promise."

"Alright," he said, and then turned around, toward the direction of the Golden Gates. "Let me know if you need anything."

"Okay, I will. I promise, again." I smiled, and that was when I looked over at the Heavenly River. I walked over to it, my heart thudding my ribs. With a clear voice, I said, "Show me Phoebe Bright."

Phoebe stared straight ahead as her mother drove the vehicle. She appeared scared and didn't look like she wanted to talk to Susanna as they entered the parking lot.

"Phoebe," Susanna said, grabbing her daughter's attention. She put a hand on Phoebe's, who was grasping her purse anxiously.

Phoebe just looked at her mother in response.

"Honey, I'll be there, in the room, the entire time. No matter what happens. I'm here for you sweetheart."

Phoebe blinked, before nodding. "Thanks, Mom."

Phoebe sniffled slightly. Susanna gently touched her daughter's hand, and then sighed.

"Alright," she said. "Let's go see the neurologist again."

Susanna peered back over at Phoebe, who nervously unbuckled her seatbelt. Then Phoebe threw her purse over her shoulder, getting out of the car as her mother did the same.

Susanna walked over to Phoebe as soon as they both were outside and grasped her hand. "Alright," Susanna repeated. "Let's go."

Phoebe nodded, and with that, both mother and daughter walked across the lot, going up to the front of the building.

My mouth was dry as I pulled my attention away from the image in the Heavenly River.

Phoebe and Susanna were both going to see Dr. Isaac again. And I would be with them.

51

My wings extended as I landed right behind Susanna and Phoebe. I tucked them into my back as I walked with the mother and daughter. I'd made it just in time so that I could enter the office with the familiar mortals, and I followed Phoebe and Susanna as Phoebe walked up to the front desk. Sweat was beginning to fill my palms.

Phoebe talked a little with the receptionist, getting checked in, before she went to sit down with Susanna. The mother glanced at Phoebe, who breathed deeply, nervously, and Susanna immediately grasped Phoebe's hand. She rubbed her daughter's extremity with her thumb gently.

I just stared at Phoebe, watching her silently.

Phoebe, I thought as I saw her. *Phoebe, you poor thing.*

Phoebe Bright!"

I brought my attention to the brunette woman who was holding the door open. The door that led to the patient rooms.

Susanna and her daughter both got up and went to her.

The woman smiled at them kindly, and then I followed everyone as they walked into the back area. The brunette pointed Susanna and Phoebe in the direction of an empty room, before she spoke. "Dr. Isaac will be with you shortly." She shut the door, leaving Phoebe, Susanna, and I alone.

I stood in the corner of the room while Phoebe was on the patient table; Susanna was in a chair opposite her daughter.

Phoebe, for the most part, appeared incredibly uncomfortable. She kept on fidgeting as Susanna stayed as still as she could, but it was hard for her. Phoebe grasped her necklace nervously, and that was when I realized she was wearing Lola's pawprint. She clutched it for several moments before letting it go.

I swallowed hard against my throat as I understood just how anxious Phoebe was. She was petrified.

Susanna noticed this as well and grabbed her daughter's hand. "Phoebe, I'm right here, honey," she said, in the most comforting manner possible. "I'm here."

I exhaled, watching both Susanna and Phoebe, before Susanna pulled her hands away from her daughter.

"I have to go to the restroom really quick," she said, looking away, toward the closed door. Then she glanced back at Phoebe. "Are you going to be alright until I come back?"

At this, Phoebe smiled slightly. "Yes, Mom. I'll be okay."

Susanna looked at her daughter thoughtfully, and then nodded. "Be right back, honey," she said, getting up from the chair and exiting the patient room. She left Phoebe and I alone, even though I wasn't visible to anyone.

But...I could be sensed by her. I could be sensed by Phoebe. *Phoebe...*

My breathing began to quicken as I saw her gulp, saw her diaphragm spasm as she inhaled.

Phoebe would be able to sense me, with the help of the words. I wanted to touch her...

I blinked before I looked at Phoebe.

I shut my eyes, taking a deep breath before I said one of the words. My heart pounding my chest, I opened them back up to see Phoebe staring at the closed door anxiously. I knew she was waiting for Dr. Isaac to come in. I inhaled deeply, attempting to concentrate, and then walked over to Phoebe, who was still on the examination table. I crossed in front of her.

She suddenly froze, then blinked, glancing from side to side, and I felt my breathing quicken as I noticed her body language.

My heart began to race as I noticed this, and that was when I gazed into her blue eyes. My hand trembling slightly, I reached out and touched her extremity, all while my eyes were glued on hers. My heartrate instantly quickened as I realized that even though I had the touch of death, with the words, my touch didn't hurt Phoebe. I could finally touch her...

She inhaled deeply as she sensed me, startled, looking down at her left hand. The same hand that I was touching.

I watched her as I rubbed my fingers along her flesh gently, seeing her stare at her extremity wonderingly.

I could finally touch Phoebe, and not hurt her.

Before I could stop myself, with no regard as to whether she could hear me or not, I just stared into her crystal blue eyes.

"I'm here," I whispered.

There were sudden footsteps in the hallway, on the other side of the door, and my head snapped up at the noise.

I immediately pulled away from Phoebe, backing into the corner once more. I repeated the words so that she wouldn't sense me again, and that was when Susanna came back. She closed the door behind her, only to see Phoebe squinting, looking confused.

Susanna's eyebrows furrowed as she took in the appearance of her daughter. "What's wrong, Phoebe?"

Phoebe stared right at her mother, shaking her head slightly. "I'm... I'm... not exactly sure," she said.

Susanna looked bewildered. "Are you alright?"

Phoebe blinked. "Yes. Yes, I am." She shook her head, before she spoke. "Nothing. It was nothing."

Her mother watched her for a few seconds, studying Phoebe's body language, and then sighed. She sat down in the chair opposite her daughter.

I gazed at Phoebe's face as both her and her parent waited for the neurologist. My heart was racing.

A knock on the patient room door broke me out of my reverie. Both Susanna and Phoebe's heads snapped up as they heard the sound.

"It's Dr. Isaac," the voice on the other side of the door said. I saw the familiar face of the neurologist from behind the barrier.

I heard Phoebe sigh as she saw him. He went over to Phoebe and Susanna, shaking their hands in a kind manner.

"Hi again, Phoebe, and Susanna," he said, nodding to the mother and daughter, and then sat on a moving chair, glancing at them both. Dr. Isaac then began to speak about how he'd heard about the seizure, the ER visit, as well as the CAT scan. He had a gentle manner, the way he spoke, even though it was horrifying what he was talking about.

Dr. Isaac confirmed that what Phoebe was struggling with was a brain tumor, even though the ER doctors already had. He said that it was good to have multiple opinions on a certain diagnosis, especially such a huge one. "Now," he said. "There are some options in terms of the treatment for the tumor. We can do several things."

The neurologist looked at Susanna, when his attention was diverted.

It was Phoebe, blinking rapidly. She breathed deeply, trying to keep herself together, but then she began crying. Her head fell forward, and she sobbed.

Anxiety filled me at the sight of Phoebe in distress, and I resisted the urge to go up and comfort her.

Her shoulders slumped forward as she appeared defeated. Her blue eyes became red-rimmed, but then she took a breath. "I'm sorry," she said, wiping her face quickly with the back of her hand. "I'm... I'm... just scared," she continued, to which Dr. Isaac just responded. "I understand." He leaned forward, grasping her hands comfortingly. "Whatever happens, we will take care of you the best way we can."

Phoebe stared at the neurologist, clinging to his words, and then nodded understandingly. "Alright," she finally responded. "Okay."

Dr. Isaac watched her for a few moments before he continued with what he was going to say. He was talking about the treatment options, starting over about what could work out the best for Phoebe.

I stayed in the corner of the patient room, taking in as much as I could, all while I was staring at Phoebe, studying her body language and her reactions.

I was waiting for her to cry again, but she was silent. It was as if she'd gone numb.

Phoebe just nodded robotically as the neurologist brought up what could help her: surgery, chemotherapy, or radiation.

He added that whatever Phoebe chose to do, that she would have to get the treatment soon, or the tumor would spread to other parts of her body.

I watched Phoebe wordlessly as she spoke up, glancing at her mother for a split second before talking to the doctor.

She opened her mouth, clearing her throat, and then stated that she wanted to get the surgery. Phoebe said that she just wanted the tumor out of her.

Dr. Isaac nodded understandingly as he heard her words. I sighed, instantly deciding that I was going to be looking over her. Looking over her the entire time.

52

"Alright," Dr. Isaac said, ending the appointment with a handshake for both Susanna and Phoebe. He smiled slightly at Phoebe, who returned the expression. She appeared to be in a daze as the doctor got up from the chair, opening the door, and then twisted around to watch Susanna and her daughter. Phoebe took a deep inhale, and then brought her purse to her shoulder, glancing at her mother. She got up off the examination table, going right to Dr. Isaac as Susanna followed them out of the patient room.

I was the last to exit as I followed Susanna, Phoebe, and Dr. Isaac. He directed Phoebe to the front desk receptionist, and that was when he took her hands a second time. "Remember, I will do my best to help you."

Phoebe sniffled slightly as she watched him. He let her extremities go, and then Phoebe went to the front.

Susanna was right behind her daughter as the woman began saying dates for the next appointment, which would be the meeting with the neurosurgeon. They all agreed on one that was close by. Susanna turned to Phoebe afterward, saying that she would drive her daughter to and from the office, as well as once she got the operation. Phoebe hugged her mother, and I felt relief wash over me at the sight.

Susanna would watch over her daughter the best she could.

"Thank you, Mom," Phoebe said in Susanna's ear. They then walked out of the office together, with me not far behind.

"They worked."

I brought my attention to Adiel as he advanced toward me. I nodded, looking at him when he came to my side.

"The words, they worked," he said, studying my face.

"Yes, they did," I responded.

"You were able to touch Phoebe, and be sensed by her. I saw you go over to her-"

But the rest of Adiel's sentence was cut off.

I'd given him a bear hug. I ignored Adiel's quick, surprised inhale, and said, "Thank you, Adiel. Thank you so much, for everything."

It was a few moments before Adiel replied. "You're welcome, Caelum," he said.

"When will you see Phoebe again?"

"Soon," I responded.

I didn't say how badly I wanted to actually meet Phoebe, and see Camilla. I wanted to be able to be seen by them....

But I didn't say anything.

Anyway, I would wait until Susanna and Phoebe were back home.

The one thing that Phoebe needed right now was comfort. And I was going to be there for her.

53

O ver the next few days, I continued bringing Souls to the Heavens, after Phoebe and Susanna's visit with the neurologist. Not only did I bring the Spirits to Adiel, I also was talking with him after he'd brought them inside the Golden Gates. Talking with him about meeting Phoebe.

Adiel sensed that I was nervous, and gave me a bear hug, holding me close so that he could say in my ear. "Stay safe, Caelum, whatever you do."

I pulled away from Adiel to look at his face, and nodded at his words. "I will, Adiel."

He watched me, as if to take in what I'd just said. Then he thumped me on the back, turning toward the Heavenly River.

I followed where he was looking, and then sighed, walking over to the body of Water.

Adiel advanced, walking behind me, and I brought my attention to it as he came to my side.

I took a deep breath, exhaling slowly, before saying, "Show me Phoebe."

Camilla was excited as she hugged Phoebe.

Phoebe smiled as she put her bag down in the living room before sitting down, exhausted.

"Mom?"

Phoebe turned toward her daughter.

"Are you okay?"

Phoebe grinned at Camilla. "Yes, I'm alright, honey. It was just a long drive, that's all."

Camilla was about to say something else, but then Susanna came into the area, sighing. Susanna sat down on the couch next to her daughter, and then leaned over toward Camilla, tucking a strand of her hair behind her ear. Both Susanna and Phoebe appeared spent.

Camilla picked up on this, looking at both her mother and her grandmother before she walked out of the room.

Phoebe watched her daughter leave, and sighed. Then she turned to Susanna. "How am I going to tell her, Mom?"

Susanna's eyes were glued to her daughter's, before she said, "You're going to just have to be honest." She looked into Phoebe's face; her eyes had gotten watery. Susanna leaned forward, hugging her daughter. "Whatever happens, sweetheart, I'll be here for you. I always will."

The image evaporated, and within a few moments, the Water stopped rippling.

I glanced over at Adiel, who had been by my side the entire time. I inhaled a lungful of air, and then spoke. "I want to go see her," I told him. "I want to go see Phoebe."

Adiel nodded. "Alright, Caelum. Just remember what I told you."

I nodded.

My heart was thudding my ribcage. I was going to finally *meet* Phoebe. Be seen by her…

I inhaled and exhaled slowly, attempting to calm my nerves, and then flew out of the Afterlife. I felt Adiel's eyes on me the entire time.

54

I had just landed in some woods near a trail when I heard children playing in the street.

Looking around quickly as I pulled my wings into my back, I focused on whether there were people around. I couldn't be appearing out of thin air. If someone saw me as I became visible, it could cause problems. There was no one in the area that I was in, though.

I shut my eyes, concentrating on the words which would allow me to become visible to the mortals, as well as keeping my wings hidden. Then I looked around, studying my surroundings before I inhaled, exhaling in a gust.

It's alright, Caelum. Just stay calm…

My heart was pounding in my head as I started to walk out of the woods, going over to the neighborhood where the children were.

It was Phoebe's neighborhood that I was in. I was finally going to meet her…

My arms were shaking as I stepped into the road that led to where the houses were. I swallowed the lump in my throat, focusing on the homes.

I looked at residence after residence… until finally I saw Phoebe's.

My heart was pounding as I saw her come out through the front door, squinting yet again in the bright sun.

I struggled to breathe as I saw her move across the driveway to the car. It took a few seconds to gather myself together, and at that point, I saw Phoebe open the vehicle door. She was getting something out of the backseat. She sucked in a breath in discomfort as a glint of sunlight hit the car window, and that was when I couldn't help it.

I found myself running forward, toward the edge of the driveway. "Are you alright?" I asked her.

It took a few moments for me to even realize what I'd just done.

My heart literally pulverized my chest, hurting my ribs. My feet were unable to move as I stood on the pavement. My eyes were wide.

Caelum. Caelum, what did you just do? I thought as I saw Phoebe pause, and then she turned toward me.

It was once I saw her body twist around that my muscles seemed to unlock, and I took a few cautious steps toward Phoebe in the driveway. She blinked, taken off guard. She sucked in a breath, and her blue eyes hit the sunlight. Crystal blue and gorgeous...

My pulse was in my head as she gathered her composure.

Phoebe inhaled quickly, before she spoke. "Yes. Yes, I'm alright," she said, to which my brain froze up. Phoebe was speaking to me. "Thank you, though. I'm just very sensitive to bright light at the moment," she continued.

I nodded understandingly, pretending that I didn't know what was happening with her, and then turned away from Phoebe.

"Wait."

Just that one word made my insides squirm.

I inhaled deeply, exhaling slowly, and then turned toward her so that I was gazing into her face. I tried to keep my breathing even as she spoke.

"I don't think I've ever met you before," Phoebe said.

I smiled as warmly as I could. "I'm new to this neighborhood," I said, coming up with the lie immediately. "I live quite a while away, through the trail in the woods. I like to go on walks, but I don't know a lot of people up this way. It is my first time being here."

I took a deep breath. I was as careful as possible saying the lie. It wasn't like I could tell Phoebe the *truth*.

"Well, I'm Phoebe," she said. "It's a pleasure to meet you. You'll love it here. It's a really nice neighborhood." She threw her purse over her shoulder, shutting the car door. "What's your name?"

I paused for a split moment before I said, "Caelum."

"Caelum? That's an interesting name."

At that, my heart was now positively bruising my ribs.

"Well, it's nice to meet you, Caelum. I guess I'll see you again sometime."

I smiled at Phoebe, nodding. "Hopefully, I will."

She just grinned back, before she turned around and walked away, toward the front door of her home.

I found myself watching her, before I walked away as well, partly in a daze. I had just spoken to Phoebe.

55

Adiel was in the Afterlife, right beside the Heavenly River, when I made it back. He just stared at me knowingly. I knew that he had seen everything that had happened. Adiel watched me silently, but I still felt like I was in a daze. Everything still felt incredibly surreal.

I just stared back at him, unable to speak.

That was when I saw a slight smile appear on his face, and I blinked. He walked up to me. "You're going to see her again, aren't you?"

I nodded automatically.

"I'm glad that this has given you peace, and made you happy, Caelum."

I grinned back at Adiel. "Thank you. Thank you so much."

Over the next few days, I monitored Phoebe through the Heavenly River. She was mostly sleeping and staying indoors, even though it was sunny most of the time.

One day, Camilla asked Phoebe if she could go out and play.

Phoebe said yes, and then the mother decided to follow her daughter.

I blinked, thinking, and then decided to go see her again.

The last thing I saw in the Heavenly River before I left the Afterlife was Camilla playing in the street, while her mother was by the driveway.

I repeated exactly what I'd done when I'd flown down from the Afterlife a few days previously. I'd landed in the woods, so I quickly said the words, coming out of the area just in time to see Phoebe. I stopped by the edge of her driveway, smiling at her.

As if she could sense that I was looking at her, Phoebe glanced up from what she was doing. She saw me and grinned back.

"Hi," she said.

"Hi," I responded.

It was a few seconds later that I gazed into her face, trying to catch if she was struggling with anything.

Phoebe just stared back, her eyes piercing mine... She finally tilted her head to the side, looking at me quizzically. "What's wrong?" she asked.

"I just wanted to make sure that you weren't in pain. It appeared like you were the last time we talked."

At that, Phoebe blinked, and then regained her composure. "Well, it was just the sun. Today it's not as bright, so I'm okay," she said.

"Good. I'm glad you're feeling better," I told her.

Right as I finished my sentence, I saw Camilla run up to her mother, her breathing rapid. "Mommy, Mommy, who is this?" she asked, glancing at me curiously before she looked back at Phoebe.

I grinned warmly as Phoebe turned to her Camilla, looking into her eyes. "Camilla, this is Caelum," she said, shifting her attention toward me as she spoke.

I smiled, before I crouched down on my knees, getting on Camilla's level. I saw Phoebe stare at me from the corner of my eye, but I just focused on her small daughter, whose blue eyes matched her mother's... "Hi," I said. "How are you, Camilla?"

The child blinked, before staring at me. "Good," she said quietly. "I just have never seen you before. I was wondering who you were."

"Well, I live a while away but I just started coming to this neighborhood. I like walking."

Camilla watched me, nodding, and then I straightened myself up again, bringing my attention back to Phoebe. "I'll get going now," I told her. "I can see that you're probably busy."

She just nodded at my words, and then locked eyes with Camilla, who was looking at her. "Well, it was nice to see you again, Caelum," she said, to which my blood seemed to melt.

"You too," I replied, partly feeling like I could fly as I turned around. Then I walked off, away from them and into the woods.

I paid attention to my surroundings, and then said the words. I turned invisible to the mortals, unveiling my wings before I flew up into the Heavens.

The tight wad of nervousness that had been in my gut dissipated as I made it back to the Afterlife.

I was feeling a lot better now that Phoebe was getting more and more comfortable with me. The fact that she had said that it was nice to see me again was enough to make me fully turn into liquid.

Phoebe...

Just the thought of her looking at me, *seeing me,* made my heart rate spike again. Made my thoughts whirl inside my skull. I could see her now, see her little Camilla.

I shook my head, trying to clear it, when an idea occurred to me. I could go see Lola. It would be nice to go see her again anyway. She was always great company.

I sighed, trying to calm my pounding heart, and then walked off toward the Golden Gates.

56

"Adiel? Adiel, are you there?" I asked. I was standing right in front of the Golden Gates, the magnetic sensation radiating from the barrier. I watched the white fog beyond the enchanted fence for a few seconds before I saw the familiar frame of Adiel walk through the mist, smiling at me.

"Hi, Caelum. How can I help you?" he asked, advancing toward the Gates.

"I...I...I want to see Lola," I said, unsure at first but then becoming confident. "I want to see Lola," I repeated, to which Adiel continued to grin.

"Well, I can certainly help you with that. Back up please, I need to open them," he said. He was referring to the Gates.

I nodded. I retreated several steps before Adiel closed his eyes, reciting the words that would open the barrier.

Adiel beckoned me forward, into the Soul Realm. My heart was pounding my chest the entire time.

"Hi Lola," I said affectionately as she ran up to me, licking my hands immediately. "How are you, sweetie?"

She moaned happily as she pushed her bodyweight into me, almost as if in response, and Adiel laughed.

"Good, huh?" I said, stroking her fur before looking over at Adiel.

He suddenly turned thoughtful. "You want to be reminded of her, don't you?"

I could feel the blood rush into my cheeks, but I just nodded.

"It's not a bad thing, Caelum. You haven't done anything wrong."

I nodded once more before I rubbed the Golden Retriever's ears. She pushed her head into my palm.

"I want to play with Lola," I said. "And I also want to be reminded of them. Phoebe and Camilla. They've both become…"

I trailed off, before Adiel finished for me. "Important," he said.

That was to say the least. I couldn't get either of those two mortals out of my head. I'd been thinking about them so much.

I brought my attention back to Adiel, before I spoke again. "I know I've already said this, but I'll say it again. Thank you so much, Adiel. For everything. Truly, thank you."

He just grinned. "Anything to help a friend," he said, and I felt myself grin back.

Adiel really was special.

57

I made it a habit to check up on Phoebe and Camilla, making sure that nothing else was going on with Phoebe.

Thankfully, she stayed as safe as she could, mostly just staying indoors and sleeping, but it did worry me that she was always in the dark.

Then again, that must've been because of the headaches. It also worried me about Camilla, what would happen with her once her mother had the operation. If she would even understand what Phoebe was going to undergo, since Camilla was so young.

One day, as I was checking on Phoebe through the Heavenly River, that was exactly what she was doing. She was trying to explain what would happen to herself and to Camilla, once Phoebe got the neurosurgery. Phoebe used smaller words that her daughter would understand, and said them slowly and as clear as she could. Camilla focused on her mother, trying her hardest to understand, right when her grandmother walked into the living room. They all sat down on a couch. Phoebe tried to the best of her ability to explain everything, and that was when Susanna joined in, tucking a tendril of hair back behind Camilla's ear.

"Sweetheart, whatever happens, you will always be taken care of," Susanna said, looking into her granddaughter's face. "Camilla, you will probably be staying with Grandpa, or your Daddy, since I will be with Mommy for the surgery, for afterward. She'll need someone to watch over her, so that'll be my job during that time."

Camilla glanced at Phoebe, and then Susanna. "So, this is all for your brain? To make it better?"

"Yes, Camilla," Phoebe said. "There's something in my brain that... that... isn't supposed to be there, so the doctor is going to have to take it out. I'm just going to meet with the surgeon before they perform the operation. The next appointment after that is when they'll have to make... make my brain all better."

Phoebe's breath caught, but then she composed herself. "Hopefully, Camilla, everything will be alright and my brain will fully recover."

The young child looked from her mother, to her grandmother, who nodded along with Phoebe.

"We just wanted to let you know what has been going on, so you know, Camilla," Phoebe said. "You also need to understand that we all love you very much, and everything that regards you is very important."

Phoebe sniffled, and Camilla walked up to her, wrapping her hands around her mother. "Thank you, Mommy," she said. "Thank you for letting me know about your brain. I love you too, Mom."

The Water moved as the image disappeared, with me watching the River afterward, staring at my reflection.

I couldn't help but notice that Phoebe had gotten a hitch to her voice when I'd looked into the Waters. She was going to cry. Again. She'd been breaking down a lot lately, with the pain of her... her brain tumor, and with how uncertain she was. Of her future. Of Camilla's wellbeing. It had all caused Phoebe to cry lately.

The Heavenly River wasn't always good enough, when it came to watching over the mortals. At least not Phoebe and Camilla.

Phoebe was sick, and was always sobbing. I was going to be there for her. It took all of two moments to realize this, that I was going to go and comfort Phoebe.

But I just inhaled deeply before I extended my wings out of my back, flying out of the Afterlife and toward Phoebe's neighborhood.

58

I didn't want to be visible to Phoebe as I landed in the familiar wooded area, surrounded by trees. I wanted to stay invisible. I pulled my wings back before I walked into her neighborhood, my heart racing as I made it to the correct house.

Susanna was still there. She had just exited the front door, leaving it open.

Quickly, I walked across the driveway, making sure I was staying out of Susanna's way before I ducked inside the home. I glanced around, only to see dim lighting from lamps or darkness.

The only other light source was the sun, whose illumination was drifting through the windows.

I sighed.

It all appeared very, very dreary.

Poor Phoebe…

I found myself focusing on a picture of both Phoebe and Camilla smiling, and I gazed into Phoebe's eyes that were in the photo. It was incredible to *really* see her happy.

Most of the time she was the opposite now, always sad…

The sound of a sharp inhale made me shake my head. I turned away from the photo frame by the front door and immediately walked down the hall. Into the guest bedroom, where Phoebe was.

She was hunched over in pain, her eyebrows furrowed and her teeth clenched as she tried not to cry out.

My breathing became rapid as I walked right in front of her, staring at her contorted face.

No. No. No. Phoebe, I thought as I saw her squint, trying to pull through the agony of the headache. *Phoebe, I'm so sorry...*

There was nothing I could do as she groaned, straightening herself back up but still in pain.

"Ugh," she said, pulling her hand away from her skull finally. "Ugh."

It seemed like it had lasted an eternity. It probably lasted about a minute, though. It was just in the nick of time too, because Camilla came into the guest bedroom.

"Mom?" she asked, as her footsteps made the wood underneath the carpet squeak slightly. "Mommy, are you in here?"

The young girl walked right in as Phoebe's head whipped toward the door.

Phoebe instantly attempted to compose herself as Camilla made her way in, but I could see that her eyes were watering.

Phoebe instantly sniffled, blinking rapidly. "Yes, honey. I'm here. I was just making sure that the beds were all made. The rooms looked a little messy."

I knew that Phoebe was just looking for an excuse for Camilla to leave the room.

She didn't want to cry in front of her small daughter. Not again.

I could see the tears building in her eyes though, and the rasp in her voice was audible too.

"Oh," Camilla said, nodding. "Okay."

Like I knew she would do, Camilla exited the room, and the moment she did, Phoebe shut her eyes, inhaling and then exhaling in a gust.

I managed to see tears escaping from her eyes as I gazed into her face, and that was when I couldn't stand it anymore. I wanted to let her know that she wasn't alone…

Closing my eyes, I recited the words that allowed me to be sensed by the mortals, but not seen or heard. I advanced toward Phoebe, standing right in front of her as I stared into her blue eyes…

She couldn't see me as I wiped away the tears that had been falling on her cheeks. I grazed my fingertips along her skin. Phoebe gasped as she felt the sensation, before I whispered, "I'm here."

Phoebe took several steps backward, looking immediately confused. She looked around the room, her eyes darting from side to side, the breath that was going into her lungs frantic and quick. First, she appeared scared, but then she squinted. Her body language changed as she wiped her tears from her cheeks. Phoebe just was staring at her fingertips then, appearing thoughtful.

This was all while I was staring at her, looking into her face…

"Phoebe, where are you?" Susanna's voice caused my head to turn toward the door, where there was the sound of footsteps. "Phoebe?"

I twisted around for a split moment to see Phoebe regain her composure, shaking her head slightly before sighing. She walked over to the door right as her mother came into the area.

"There you are. Are you alright?"

Susanna had caught how Phoebe had started to appear distant.

"Yes," she said, nodding at her mother, who didn't look convinced.

But then Susanna blinked rapidly as I walked behind Phoebe, glancing at Susanna again before advancing toward the bedroom door.

"Do you feel that, Mom?"

Susanna's head went up and down in response.

"What is that?" Susanna asked wonderingly, to which Phoebe's head shook from side to side.

"I don't know," she said.

A grin spread across my face as I realized that both of them could sense my presence.

It didn't matter that they didn't understand what the sensation was. All that mattered was that they had both sensed it. They had both felt the sensation that I was with them.

My breathing was rapid as this came to my attention, my heart pummeling my ribs.

Both Phoebe and Susanna could sense my presence.

59

"They could sense you," Adiel said, looking me in the eyes as I tucked my wings into my back. I nodded.

I'd just gotten back to the Afterlife from Phoebe's house. "I saw everything happen, Caelum."

I gulped, even though I knew that he was telling the truth. Being an angel meant never lying. Plus, the Heavenly River was right by Adiel. It would be easy for him to use the Water to view anything.

I was just a little nervous what he thought. About the way I'd been around Phoebe. Brushing away the tears that had been on her cheeks…

"You're okay, Caelum," Adiel said, yanking me out of my thoughts. "It's alright. I'm just glad that I was able to help you feel better, give you peace of mind."

I grinned at him, automatically feeling as if a gigantic weight had been removed from my chest.

He wasn't judgmental at all. For that, I was grateful.

I peered over at Adiel, away from the Heavenly River.

He just looked at me, before he thumped me on the back, grasping my shoulder. Then he nodded, before he spoke. "Good luck, Caelum. Just be smart, alright?"

I nodded. "Okay."

I focused on Adiel's brown eyes, watching him carefully.

He wanted the best for me. He really, truly did.

Adiel took his hand off my shoulder, and then turned around, but looked back at me once again before he spoke. "Good luck."

He twisted his body after that, walking off to the Golden Gates, leaving me alone. Alone, in the Afterlife.

I sighed, watching my surroundings, before I just flew out of the Heavens. I couldn't be alone here, at least not right now. My mind was racing too much.

I could use some time on a skyscraper or the beach. Either of those places would be perfect to visit right now. I just needed to clear my head.

60

I landed on a skyscraper so far into the atmosphere that I was partly touching the clouds. Pulling my wings into my back, I sighed, closing my eyes. I tried to focus only on the breeze that was blowing all around me. The sunlight that illuminated the sky… I felt the warmth of the light, trying to forget…

"Caelum?"

My eyes flew open as I heard my name. It was as if I'd gotten an electric shock. The sound caused me to freeze. My heart was pounding, and I gulped.

The voice wasn't a familiar one. "Caelum?" it repeated. "Caelum, can I talk to you?"

I took a deep breath, holding it as I twisted my body around, only to release the oxygen from my lungs immediately. My eyes fluttered strangely before I regained my composure. "Ezekiel?" I stammered.

A smile crept up on Ezekiel's lips as he looked at me. "Hi," he said. "Long time."

Long time. That was an understatement. I hadn't seen him in millennia, and only once, for that matter.

"Wha... what?" I struggled to speak as I saw Ezekiel, his chocolate brown skin, his white teeth which were exposed as he grinned. "What…are you doing here?" I asked.

"I just wanted to see you, and talk. I asked Adiel how you were doing. He said that you were here on Earth."

"You found me through the Heavenly River?" I asked.

"Yes," Ezekiel said. "I hadn't seen you in a while, so I figured I'd meet up with you." He sighed. "Like I said before, I also wanted to talk."

I shrugged my shoulders, trying to hide my nervousness.

Please don't be about Phoebe, I thought. *Please don't let this conversation be about her.*

"What about?" I asked, my words completely different from what was going through my head.

"Well, when I looked in the Heavenly River to see where you were, I saw you here, but you looked-look- troubled, Caelum. I've seen that expression before as well. If anything, I just want to make sure that you're alright. I need to catch up with you anyway. Make up for lost time."

Lost time? I'd only seen him once. I didn't voice my thoughts, though. I just shrugged. "Okay. I guess I could use some more angel friends," I said, laughing a little.

Adiel was great to talk to. It was just that it would be nice to speak to more angels.

Ezekiel smiled again as he advanced toward me, although I was sure what this was going to be about.

Phoebe. Phoebe and Camilla.

I knew it, somewhere in my gut. But I grinned back at him, being polite. I had no idea how this was going to go.

"So, how have you been since I've seen you last?" Ezekiel asked. We both walked over to the edge of the skyscraper, to look down at all the cars that resembled ants.

"Good," I said, hoping that Ezekiel wouldn't be able to sense the pounding of my heart. "I've been good. Just doing my duty. It's the same thing all the time, bringing the Souls to Heaven." I shrugged. "Other than that, nothing else has been going on."

I swallowed, before turning and looking at him.

Ezekiel was staring ahead, at another skyscraper in the distance.

"What about you?" I asked.

"Same thing," he said. "Just bringing the Spirits to the Heavens, to Adiel, like always."

I nodded, although what he'd just said made my insides squirm.

Ezekiel was like me, an angel that came to the mortals that would bring Souls to Heaven. He brought the Souls, like he said, to Adiel so that Adiel could bring them to the Golden Gates.

If Ezekiel also saw Adiel, and talked to him, that meant that Adiel must've been talking to Ezekiel about me.

Hopefully not about Phoebe and Camilla.

Adiel promised me that that would stay private.

"So, you spoke with Adiel, then?" I asked Ezekiel, who twisted his body toward me.

"Yes. Like I said, he told me you were here on Earth. I looked in the Heavenly River and saw that you appeared troubled." Ezekiel sighed. "I just wanted to catch up, see how you were."

I looked him in the eyes, trying to catch if there was any judgement that was going to be there, but there was none. "It's just that…" I trailed off for a moment before starting again. "I've fallen for one of the mortals. I don't mean that I've Fallen and am no longer an angel. I mean that I… that I… love her." I stuttered on the last part of the sentence, before I glanced up at Ezekiel. I'd been staring at the ground, avoiding his gaze as I'd talked. I figured I might as well bring up Phoebe and Camilla, since I thought that was where the conversation was going to go. I gulped as I stared at Ezekiel, his brown eyes, and that was when he spoke.

"I thought it was something like that," he said. "I remember Lemuel had a similar expression when he was falling in love. He spoke to me a lot, like the way Adiel speaks to you."

I blinked. I'd almost forgotten about the story that Adiel had told me. About Lemuel and his love…

"Don't worry, Caelum," Ezekiel said, turning his head and looking into my face. "I haven't heard any private conversations between you and Adiel. What you tell Adiel is completely-and only-your business."

I nodded. I was glad about that.

Adiel kept his word, which I knew he had to. There was just a part of me that was a bit unsure.

"I figured that was what was going on," Ezekiel repeated. "That you were in love, I mean. What is going on that is causing you to appear so troubled?"

"She has a brain tumor, and has a child. She's slowly dying, but I'm afraid for her daughter. I don't know what I'll be able to do for her Camilla."

I knew that Adiel had already told me that Derek or Susanna or Mark would be able to help with Camilla, but still… the thought of her without her mother made my hands tremble.

Camilla was only seven years old. She was way too young to understand exactly what her mother was going through. The entire predicament was heartbreaking.

"I just… I think about Phoebe-and her daughter, Camilla-a lot. I even went to visit them," I said, meeting Ezekiel's stare again.

"How did that go?" he asked.

"Great. It was the second time that I'd seen her, but it was the first time I'd met her daughter. Adiel had taught me some words, so I'd decided to use them."

"Are you glad that you did what you did?" Ezekiel asked.

"Yes," I responded automatically. "I want to be in her life, and in Camilla's. I want to be able to watch over them."

I glanced over at Ezekiel, meeting his gaze.

Part of me was waiting for the ridicule, how an angel could fall in love with a mortal woman, but it never came. He just stared at me, watching my face, before he spoke again. "Have you ever met Lemuel?" he asked, still looking at me intently.

I blinked, shaking my head.

All I had heard about him was the story that Adiel had told me. About how Lemuel was a Soul now, waiting for his love to join him…

"No," I said. "No, I haven't."

"I think that it is the perfect time to meet him, then," Ezekiel responded, smiling at me. "I think it is about time you met Lemuel." His wings protruded from his back as he turned away from me slightly. Within seconds, his wings got to their full span. Ezekiel paused, looking behind him. "Come on, Caelum. Follow me."

I tucked my wings into my back as I made it to the Afterlife. Ezekiel turned around. "Come on. Follow me," he said. Then he walked in the direction of the Golden Gates.

I sighed, and followed him, not knowing how this meeting with Lemuel would go.

We both had made it to the Gates when Ezekiel glanced at me, motioning to the barrier, and raising his eyebrows.

Adiel. He wanted me to call out to Adiel.

I smiled, bringing my attention to beyond the Gates. I watched the white fog, felt the magnetic sensation radiating from the massive contraption, and then opened my mouth and spoke. "Adiel? Adiel, are you there?"

There were a few quiet moments as Ezekiel and I were waiting, and then, he was there.

Adiel walked through the mist, a smile on his face as he saw Ezekiel. "Hello, Ezekiel," he said. Then Adiel twisted his head toward me. "Hello, Caelum."

I grinned back at Adiel. "Hi," I responded, looking at him calmly. "Ezekiel, he wants me to meet Lemuel. I told him about… Phoebe." I hesitated slightly, before I continued.

Adiel just watched me as I talked.

"I'd only ever heard the story that you had told me about him. I want to meet Lemuel," I told Adiel, with a half glance at Ezekiel.

Adiel nodded understandingly. "Okay, Caelum. I'll let you both through then. Good luck."

A smile made its way on my face as I looked over at Ezekiel. He glanced over at me before we both backed up, allowing the Golden Gates to open as Adiel said the words. Within moments, the Golden Gates were unlatched, and Adiel was there, looking at me carefully.

Ezekiel walked ahead of me, and I followed behind him, when I felt a hand on my shoulder. I turned my head to see Adiel looking into my eyes. Then he smiled, letting go.

I looked away from Adiel, and saw Ezekiel in the distance, waiting for me. He was patient as I caught up to him, and I was thankful that he didn't talk much as we went through the Soul Realm.

Ezekiel seemed to know exactly where he was going, and after a while, he came up to a Soul of a male with blond hair and blue eyes. The Soul's face seemed to light up when his eyes went from Ezekiel, to me. "Ezekiel, who is this?" he asked curiously.

61

Ezekiel smiled, turning toward me. "Lemuel, this is Caelum. Caelum, this is Lemuel."

I looked at Lemuel, before a warm grin made its way on my face. "It's nice to meet you," I said kindly.

"Nice to meet you as well," Lemuel responded. "I don't think we've ever met."

I shook my head. "No. No, we haven't," I said. "Ezekiel wanted me to meet you."

Lemuel peered over at him, smiling, before Ezekiel spoke. "Caelum here, has a similar situation to what you went through."

Ezekiel stared at Lemuel for a moment.

Lemuel blinked, and then looked back at me.

"It's true," I said, my mouth suddenly feeling dry. "I'm in love with…with…a mortal." I sighed. "I was talking with Ezekiel, and he wanted me to meet you. I've only heard a story about you that was told to me by Adiel. I don't know anything else besides that."

Immediately, Lemuel's face fell. His eyes hit the ground of the Heavens. "My Chloe…" he murmured. "My dear Chloe…" He brought his face back up, so that he was looking at Ezekiel and I, and Lemuel suddenly appeared to be a mortal man who was about a thousand years old. Lemuel's sadness was drowning him as he hunched over in apparent agony, sobs ripping through his body.

I bit my lip as I saw Lemuel, peering over at Ezekiel, who took a half glance at me before bringing his attention back to Lemuel. "I… I'm…. I'm sorry," I stammered as he continued to cry. "I shouldn't have said anything. I'm sorry."

"No," Lemuel said, instantly looking up from the grounds of the Heavens. His face was red and splotchy. "Don't leave. It would be great to have another angel friend. I promise," he said, sniffling. "I'll try not to lose it again. The story, it's just very emotional for me to tell. I love Chloe so much…" Lemuel trailed off, and then glanced at me.

I just looked at him, uncertainty flooding my system.

"Caelum," Lemuel said. "Caelum, did you ever hear the story about how I met Chloe?"

I blinked, before I shook my head.

"No," I said. "No, I've never heard it."

I glanced over at Ezekiel, but his eyes were glued on Lemuel, who took a deep breath.

He spoke. "Caelum, I used to be a Guardian angel. I used to be a Guardian of the Gates specifically, just like Adiel is currently. When I first became a Guardian, I had the choice to be on Earth, protecting the mortals, or to be in the Afterlife, protecting the Souls. I decided to be in the Heavens, bringing the Spirits to the Golden Gates. Ezekiel," Lemuel glanced over at him, and then looked at me. "Ezekiel, he would bring the Souls from Earth to me."

He stopped for a few moments, as if to gather himself together. "One morning, by the mortal's time, I remember, Ezekiel brought the Soul of a young woman up. She had died from cancer. I just remember she was quite young, mid-thirties maybe. Ezekiel and I started to comfort her when she began to cry about her sister. The young woman, who we both found out was named Delilah, was scared about what her family, and her sister, would do now that she was gone." Lemuel paused again, before continuing. "I pointed Delilah in the direction of the Heavenly River and was beside her as she said her sister's name."

He took a deep breath, and I blinked, so engrossed in the story that I was partially startled by the sound.

Lemuel looked me straight in the face and spoke. "Caelum, Delilah was Chloe's sister."

The inhale that went through my lungs as I watched Lemuel was quick. I stared at him for a few moments before I closed my mouth. I'd realized that my jaw had hit the ground of the Heavens.

There were so many questions that I automatically had for Lemuel, but I was just quiet as I waited for him to finish. I watched as he started again, his eyes on Ezekiel.

"Delilah, she'd always been thinking about Chloe, even after she'd seen her in the Heavenly River. "Ezekiel, he would fly down to Earth with Delilah, after I would say the right words to keep her safe. Going to Earth with Delilah's Soul was comforting, to both Delilah and Chloe. In a way, it brought them both peace, I could tell. But I was so drawn to Chloe…"

Lemuel trailed off for a moment, and then shook his head, coming back to the present. "It sounds horrible the way I just said that, so let me explain," he said quickly, watching my eyes. "Delilah was always wondering about Chloe because yes, she was her sister, and yes, they shared a deep bond. But the most important reason Delilah was always thinking about Chloe was because Chloe was- and still is, from what I can see in the Heavenly River-a medium."

Lemuel paused again.

The news was all incredible, what I was hearing.

Lemuel had turned out to fall in love with a mortal. Not just any mortal, though. Chloe could communicate with the Souls of the deceased...

"That was why I was so drawn to her, Caelum. Her knowledge that Delilah was always with her even in death was truly incredible to me. I started to realize that it was something more than just me watching over her and Delilah a few months later. That's just an approximation," Lemuel said, shaking his shoulders and looking at me. "I realized after that," he continued, "that I wanted to become her Guardian angel. A Guardian angel, not a Guardian of the Gates, like I was. I wanted to give up my duty so that I could have another one and be near Chloe. She had continued to understand that her sister wasn't in pain anymore, and was always with her..."

Lemuel glanced at me, before saying, "I wanted... needed to be near her. It felt like almost every second of every day."

I nodded automatically as I heard his words. I understood him completely.

Chloe had engulfed Lemuel's mind. The same way Phoebe had taken over mine...

"I would visit Chloe through the Heavenly River constantly until finally there was one morning when I made the decision that would change my entire existence. I decided that I would join Chloe on Earth, that I would be her Guardian angel."

Lemuel took a breath, and then continued. "It wasn't an easy decision to make, to be switching my duty. But it was the only way to really be near Chloe. I was to be by her side, be her Guardian angel."

"How did you give up being a Guardian of the Gates?" I asked curiously.

"I had to find another angel who would take over for me," he said, and he stared straight into my face.

My breath caught for a moment. "You... Lemuel, you... gave Adiel the ability to be a Guardian of the Gates?"

Lemuel nodded, and I shook my head in astonishment.

I didn't know that. I didn't know that at all.

Adiel never told me any of this.

"I had to learn some of the words in order to hide my wings, as well as just protect me on Earth, since I was used to being in the Afterlife. I had to master several tasks in order to be a Guardian angel, including how to not be so nervous, since being a Guardian meant sometimes being visible to mortals, instead of hiding from them. All these tasks helped me tremendously, and eventually, I was able to meet Chloe... see her for the first time..."

Lemuel trailed off for a moment, and then turned and looked at me. "Everything went well with meeting her, and eventually, after being visible to her and getting to know Chloe for what seemed to be a long time, I made the most important decision that an angel could make: whether to stay an angel or not."

Lemuel peered into my eyes again. His had been on the floor of the Afterlife as he spoke.

He seemed to be getting nervous as he did so.

"I spoke with Ezekiel a lot about what I wanted to do. I wanted to be with Chloe for the rest of her life. I wanted to give up my wings and to become a mortal. I wanted to know what it was like to live like one. To be among the hustle and bustle of their daily lives. Chloe fascinated me with her knowledge of the Afterlife and the Souls. The fact that she knew that her sister was at peace through being a medium fascinated me as well. But the daily life of her was even more intriguing to me. Being an angel for thousands of years by that point had made me more interested in the day-to day lives of the mortals. To me, everything was fascinating about them. The way they slept, the way they ate, even the way they walked. It was interesting to me."

Lemuel's eyes flickered to the ground, and then snapped back up at my face. He turned to Ezekiel for a moment, who was still by my side. "Ezekiel, was a great listener when I brought up the fact that I wanted to give up my wings to be with Chloe. He understood that I…that I…wanted to Fall."

Lemuel brought his eyes back to mine. "How I became a mortal is another half of the story. I wanted to tell you as well, Caelum, since I am telling you everything already."

62

My eyes were glued to Lemuel's. "How did you manage to Fall?" I asked, curiosity and interest flooding my system. His blue eyes focused on me before he spoke. "I flew on top of a gigantic mountain on a massive trail. A high point in the sky so that I could Fall. I had to recite some words to protect me, to guard the essence of who I was to become. If I was a mortal, I would've probably appeared to be someone who… who… would've taken their own life."

Lemuel struggled with the sentence, but I understood what he meant.

He must've appeared to be suicidal, if that was even possible for angels.

I glanced over at Lemuel.

"I recited the words making sure that I was protected, and then I eventually jumped off the mountaintop on which I'd been perched. Anything like that for a mortal would've killed them, the height from the mountain to the water below was so great, but it didn't kill me. Instead, it made me human. Instead, I went into the liquid and swam straight to the surface. I'd been dragged down by the strong current, but I got out of the water safely without drowning."

Lemuel paused, drifting off, and then came back to the present. "I think the reason was because the words, and the other angels in general, were saving me. They didn't want me to die. It wasn't my time. Anyway," Lemuel said, "I made it out of the water before I was found, dripping wet and dirty, by a few hikers in the woods. They called an ambulance for me, and I got a spare set of clothes because of this and was discharged from the hospital a few days later. I thanked them, and then was on my way to see Chloe, who I knew worked close to the park that I'd just gone to."

"How...how...did you keep your cover? I mean, what did you tell the EMTs when they came to you in the woods?" I asked.

"I told them what I told the hikers. That I'd slipped off the rocks above and had fallen from a great height. The first two hikers weren't convinced, I could see it in their faces, but all four of them didn't question me at all. They just went ahead and did what any good mortal would do: they called an ambulance. I used the same excuse on the paramedics, and they seemed to believe me."

Lemuel shifted his shoulders. "It worked. I went to the hospital, and then a few days later I was released." He took a breath. "I had walked over to where Chloe worked one morning. She saw me, and asked if I would want to schedule an appointment with her. I said yes, of course, but I told her I had no money on me, that my wallet had been stolen and that I had nothing to give her. Chloe, at one point, offered the appointment for free. I was impressed. Not only by Chloe's personality but also by how she could help me communicate with the Souls and the angels. She could do it all. I figured out a day I could see Chloe again, and after that meeting, we got to talking. The rest was our romantic relationship that had begun. We-for what the mortals call dating-anyway, we dated for about a year after we met officially."

Lemuel glanced over at Ezekiel.

"Ezekiel said later that for the whole year he was watching over the both of us, Chloe and I, even though that wasn't his duty. You, Ezekiel," he told him. "You are truly a fantastic friend."

I looked over at Ezekiel to see him beaming.

I smiled at the expression. Ezekiel was very flattered.

Lemuel turned back to me, and instantly I saw his face fall. He immediately appeared to be sad, and deep in my gut, I knew what part of the story he was going to talk about next. Lines seemed to appear on his face as he became distraught, and then he spoke. "Caelum, I was going to marry Chloe if I hadn't... hadn't...died and become a Soul."

"You would've married Chloe?" I asked Lemuel, who nodded.

"Yes, Caelum, I would've. I loved her so much. I still love her, but I wanted to spend the rest of my mortal life with Chloe."

He took a deep breath, trying not to cry, but I saw a tear appear in his eye.

Lemuel, I thought. *You poor thing.*

It took a few moments for him to regain his composure, and then, he spoke.

"There was one night that Chloe was working, and, as always when it was late, I came by so that I could walk her to her car. It was parked a long way away from the building where she worked. Maybe it would've been safer if she wasn't parked so far away. Anyway, I came by like any other night, as Chloe was closing, and I was walking her to her car when I heard and saw a gun being positioned. Right at Chloe's head."

Lemuel sniffled before continuing. "Chloe had begun to cry, pleading with whoever had the gun pointed to her head. She even gave him her entire wallet. He pulled the weapon away from her head, and then in a split moment I saw a glint of his eyes in the moonlight. He had a careless look, and in that split moment, I reacted. I jumped right in front of her, catching a bullet straight to the chest. I can still remember the screams that erupted from her…" Lemuel trailed off, and then came back. "The gunshot was deafening. The sound of it going off rang in my ears for a heartbeat before I realized that I wasn't in my body anymore. I was a Soul."

Lemuel peered over at Ezekiel. "Ezekiel, he came right after my Soul had left my body, trying to comfort me as he brought me up to the Afterlife, this time as a Spirit. Now," he said, sighing, glancing back at me. "I am here, in the Spirit Realm, waiting for Chloe to join me in the Heavens. I can still visit her, thanks to Adiel and Ezekiel, but I'll never be able to physically see her, hear her, anything like that, anymore. If anything, I want you to think about your relationship with your mortal, Caelum, and think about this story. Be careful, Caelum, okay?"

I nodded understandingly. I knew what Lemuel was talking about.

He saved Chloe, sacrificing himself for her, but destroyed any future he could've had with her. Now, he had to wait for Chloe to join him as a Spirit, possibly waiting for several seasons.

Lemuel just wanted me to be smart and rational when it came to decide. He knew things from experience, and he didn't want me to repeat his mistakes. Lemuel was, even though I'd just met him, a very thoughtful Soul.

I glanced over at him. His eyes were on the floor of the Heavens, his diaphragm spasming from the sobs that were rattling his body.

"Lemuel?" I asked, getting his attention. "Thank you, for everything. Thank you for telling me the story. It was very interesting. I'm sorry that this happened to you though, that you transitioned into a Soul."

Lemuel was watching me the entire time I spoke, his blue eyes watching my face.

"Just know that Chloe will always think of you for the rest of her life, thinking about how you jumped in front of a gun for her. She'll always have you in her memory, and then when she becomes a Soul, at the end of her days, she'll be reunited with you. Everything will turn out okay, Lemuel," I said, realizing that this would be something that Adiel would say.

Adiel was more of the comforting one, while I was more guarded. But I guessed that that was now changing.

Lemuel stared at my face, absorbing my words, and out of the corner of my eye, I saw Ezekiel doing the same thing.

Both seemed amazed at what I had said. Even I was amazed.

That was when Lemuel ran up to me, engulfing me in a bear hug. I smiled as he pulled away from me.

"Thank you, Caelum," he said, and I could tell that he was being sincere.

"You're welcome, Lemuel. You're welcome."

Lemuel's smile radiated from his face as his blue eyes seemed to become brighter. He looked at me for a few moments, before he finally said, "It was nice to meet you, Caelum. I wish you the best with your mortal love."

I grinned, but inside I felt my insides squirm. I smiled back, trying to hide the way I truly felt.

"Take care of yourself, okay?" Lemuel said again, and I nodded.

"Alright," I told him.

Then he turned to Ezekiel. "It was nice to see you again, Ezekiel. Take care, too," Lemuel told his angel friend, before leaning forward and enveloping him in a hug.

When they both pulled away from each other, Lemuel turned to me. "Feel free to come by anytime you want, Caelum. It would be nice to talk and have more angel friends."

I nodded, understanding immediately what he meant. "I will," I said, truly meaning it.

Ezekiel turned back toward me, before looking at Lemuel.

"Well, we have to go," Ezekiel told him. "Stay safe, Lemuel."

He smiled. "I will. See you both later."

I grinned before I twisted my body around, Ezekiel not far behind me.

63

"I enjoyed meeting Lemuel," I told Ezekiel as we walked through the Spirit Realm, going toward the entrance of the Golden Gates.

"I thought you might like him," he said.

He was now at my side as we walked through the white fog.

"His story was very intense," I said. "But it was also very interesting."

"Everyone-mortal, Soul, or angel-has a story, Caelum. It's just whether or not someone is willing to listen that determines whether or not it is intriguing. But yes, Lemuel's story is interesting. Interesting and one to listen to in order to make sure that mistakes aren't made."

Ezekiel sighed, but then paused, stopping in his tracks as he saw the white mist in front of us move suddenly.

I stopped as well, looking curiously at the fog, before I heard panting along with it.

Ezekiel's eyebrows furrowed in confusion as he glanced at me. But I had a completely different reaction. I grinned as I crouched down on my knees, watching as Lola came bounding out of the substance.

She bolted toward me, licking my hands, and then ran over to Ezekiel, who slowly got on his knees.

He petted her cautiously, and then glanced at me with a questioning look in his dark eyes.

"Lola here, she's Phoebe's dog that passed away. Lola is very well behaved," I told Ezekiel. "Adiel actually was the angel that brought me to the Soul Realm to see her."

The Golden Retriever twisted her head toward me at the mention of Adiel's name. Her tail wagged.

"You know who Adiel is, don't you?" I asked Lola, who licked my hands again.

I focused on her as I spoke to Ezekiel. "Lola though, she helps me."

He looked at me, absorbing my words. "This is great, Caelum," he said. "It's great that you are finding ways to not be stressed, to decompress. It also helps that her dog is so sweet." Ezekiel scratched Lola's ear affectionately. She moaned, and he laughed. "This is good, Caelum. This is very good."

"Thank you," I said. "Lola is great company."

I peered down at the Golden Retriever, who was staring at me. "Would you like to go see Adiel?" I asked her. Her ears automatically perked up, and I laughed.

I glanced over at Ezekiel, who was grinning. "There is no harm in having her as company, it seems," he said, looking over at Lola.

"Then we will bring her with us," I said, smiling at Phoebe's dog's Soul. "Lola is always a joy to be around." I looked down at Lola one more time, before speaking to her again. "Come on, Lola. Let's go see Adiel."

A sigh made its way through my lungs as Ezekiel and I made our way to the entrance of the Golden Gates. Lola was right behind us.

"How was your visit with Lemuel?" Adiel asked, coming out of the white fog, his brown eyes darting from me to Ezekiel.

I just nodded, while Ezekiel said, "Good. It went very well. I think that Caelum made a new angel friend. Lemuel seemed to like him."

Adiel grinned, glancing over at me. "That's fantastic news, Caelum. Very good news."

Ezekiel smiled, looking at my face. "Lemuel certainly did like you," he told me.

He seemed like he was a unique Soul.

Adiel leaned down and petted Lola's ears. She moaned happily, sitting down and wagging her tail before licking his hands. He laughed, and I said, "She decided to say hello, and then came with us through the Soul Realm."

"Lola, you're such a good girl. Good girl," Adiel said, rubbing her ears. He turned his attention to Ezekiel and I afterward.

"You both need to get through the Gates, don't you? Let me do that right now. Stay, Lola," he told the Golden Retriever, who just sat down, waiting patiently. "Okay," Adiel said, walking through the fog into the middle of the Spirit Realm.

Shutting his eyes, he then said the words to open the Gates.

"Thank you, Adiel," Ezekiel said, walking forward once Adiel opened them.

He nodded. "You're welcome, Ezekiel. You're welcome."

I leaned forward, petting Lola's head one last time before I said goodbye to Adiel.

He just nodded, smiling, before I turned and followed Ezekiel out of the Golden Gates and the Spirit Realm. Then we both flew out of the Afterlife.

"It was nice to see you again, Caelum," Ezekiel said, looking into the distance, peering into the clouds. We'd made it back to the skyscraper that I'd been on before.

I nodded, glancing over at him.

Ezekiel looked at me, his brown eyes watching.

"Thank you, Ezekiel. Thank you for coming to see me."

He smiled, the expression taking over his entire face, and then grasped my shoulders affectionately. "I'll see you around, Caelum," Ezekiel said, before walking away, extending his wings, and flying off.

My eyes were glued on the spot where Ezekiel left. My thoughts were both on him, and Lemuel.

I was thinking about how friendly they were toward me. Every angel was. Ezekiel, Lemuel, and Adiel.

I wasn't alone. I never was. I could talk to any of them anytime I wanted to.

I stayed on the top of the skyscraper for hours. By the time I realized that I had to leave, the atmosphere was getting darker, and the sunset was in the distance, above the horizon.

Lemuel's story had taken over my mind though, as well as the fact that Ezekiel had come to me, wanting to know how I was doing.

Phoebe and Camilla had taken over as well. Phoebe, and her brain tumor. Her brain tumor was going to be removed from her skull in a short amount of time. Lemuel. Ezekiel. Phoebe. Camilla. They all were on my mind.

I couldn't get them out of my head.

The sunset in the distance cast the magnificent orange-pink colors in the atmosphere as I stared at it. That was when I finally decided to leave. My wings came out of my back, and I took off, going back into the Afterlife.

64

"A re you okay, Caelum?" Adiel's voice hit my ears as I made it back to the Heavens.

I looked at him to see that he was right beside the River. I nodded as I saw his worried expression. "Yes, Adiel. I'm alright."

"I just thought that there was a lot on your mind. You were on the skyscraper for a while."

So, Adiel had been watching over me.

"Yes. Yes, I was," I said. "I was just thinking about Lemuel, Ezekiel, Phoebe, and Camilla."

"That's a lot to think about, Caelum. A lot of important individuals are in your existence. It'll be alright, though, whatever happens." Adiel sighed, before he spoke again. "Are you feeling better now that you have spoken to more angels and Souls about your Phoebe?"

I knew what he was really asking. He was asking if I was embarrassed or scared about telling Lemuel and Ezekiel.

The truth was that I wasn't really. There was no judgement that seemed to come from telling them. Plus, I got to learn something new. About a Soul that used to be an angel.

"I feel a lot better, yes," I told Adiel, looking into his brown eyes that were focused on me. "I just thought about Phoebe as well. She is supposed to have her brain tumor taken out in a few days. She is supposed to have her surgery. I'm scared for her, Adiel."

Then again, now it seemed like I always was.

He nodded, before I walked over to where he was, beside the Heavenly River.

"I want to check up on her, see how she is doing," I said. I took a deep breath, looking into the Water, and then spoke. "Show me Phoebe Bright."

Phoebe was at a restaurant with her parents. They were waiting for their dinner in the dimly lit, nice establishment.

Mark and Susanna seemed relaxed, but their daughter appeared to be apprehensive, nervous, as her eyes peered around the inside of the area.

Phoebe looked very uncomfortable.

"Honey? Phoebe?" Susanna asked, seeing how her daughter was. "We're just going to get something to eat and then leave, alright? You'll be okay, and so will Camilla."

Susanna reached her hand out, toward her daughter and across the table, grasping Phoebe's extremity.

But that didn't seem to calm her down.

Instead, Susanna touching Phoebe's hand had made Phoebe more anxious.

"Camilla. I need to get to Camilla," she said, her voice on the edge of panic, but both Mark and Susanna appeared calm.

Their daughter, on the other hand, was terrified, almost paranoid.

Mark tried to calm Phoebe, speaking in an even manner. "Phoebe, sweetheart, Camilla is…"

But Phoebe wasn't listening.

Mark trailed off as his daughter quickly got up from the table, instead running toward the bathroom.

Susanna went to follow her, but then she turned around, looking at her mother. "No, Mom. I'm fine. I just need to use the restroom. I'll be right back." And with that, Phoebe twisted back around, going in the direction of the women's bathroom.

She quickly moved the door. She ran into the room, and she was suddenly peering into the huge mirror that was in front of the wall. Phoebe appeared to be shaking as she took in her appearance.

The River Water rippled for several moments before the liquid finally settled down. It went back to normalcy.

I brought my attention to Adiel, who just looked at me with a worried expression on his face.

My eyebrows furrowed, anxiety taking over me as I saw that Adiel was just as scared as I was.

"Caelum, what's…?" he started, but then stopped.

My wings had already erupted from my back. "I'll find out, Adiel," I said, and then flew off, into the direction of where Phoebe was.

My heart was pummeling my ribs as I landed in the deserted road near the restaurant.

Everyone was in the establishment, so I just closed my eyes, reciting the words that would allow me to walk among the mortals.

I had only just opened them back up when I saw Phoebe darting outside of the restaurant, fear soaking her. She immediately shivered in the night but began walking away.

Away, I realized, from her parents. They were still inside. She didn't have a jacket on.

Phoebe, no. Don't... I thought as I saw her walk past the cars that were parked on the side of the road. *No, Phoebe. Please, don't run away...*

She had just gotten to the corner of the street in order to cross it when I ran out in the center of the road. I ran up to Phoebe.

I couldn't just watch her anymore. I had to act.

Something was going on with Phoebe. Something bad.

I hurried over to where she was, crossing right in front of her, right as she was about to walk. Her eyes grew wide, her eyebrows furrowing in bewilderment as she saw me. "What the...?" she started, but then blinked as recognition filled her face. "Caelum?" she asked, and my blood turned to water as she said my name. "Caelum, what are you doing here?"

I stood where I was, blinking for a moment before I came back to myself.

"I was just walking by," I told her. "What's going on? You seem anxious."

At the word *anxious,* Phoebe immediately shook her head, looking from side to side.

It was as if that word was a trigger for a panic attack.

My breathing became rapid as I saw the change in Phoebe. She usually was so relaxed...

"I… I… have to get out of here. Caelum, can you drive me home?" she asked, to which my heart skipped a beat.

Phoebe was comfortable enough to ask me to drive her home. If only I could drive…

"Phoebe," I started, "I don't think that would be appropriate." I sighed at her facial expression. It had automatically seemed to fall. "Are you here alone? Or are you-?"

"Phoebe?"

I was cut off by Mark, who I saw come out of the restaurant. He looked panicked.

His wife came with him, walking out of the entrance. "Phoebe, where are you?" she called.

I looked at Phoebe, who was right in front of me. She shut her eyes as she heard her parents. She almost appeared ashamed.

My heart sank at the sight. What was going on with her?

I peered over at Mark and Susanna, who were both scanning the outside of the restaurant for their daughter, when Phoebe turned around toward them. "I'm here," she said.

She sounded disappointed.

"Phoebe," Susanna cried, running to her daughter. "Phoebe, thank God. We thought that you had disappeared."

Her tone was on the verge of hysteria.

Susanna's eyes flickered from Phoebe to me as her husband caught up with her. "I'm sorry," Phoebe's mother said. "Who are you?" she asked, looking at me cautiously.

I opened my mouth to speak, but instead Phoebe cut me off. "This is Caelum. He's a neighbor of mine. He stopped me from… from…"

But Phoebe trailed off, unable to finish her sentence.

I stared, watching her worriedly, before, to both her parent's and my shock, she began to sob.

Mark looked nervously at me, before his wife and him went on either side of their daughter, comforting her as she cried.

"I'm sorry," I said as they both grasped Phoebe, trying to keep her steady. "Take care," I said, instantly knowing that I was out of my element. I turned to leave, but then Phoebe stopped crying, instead she spoke. "Wait, Caelum." My insides turned to mush as I peered around at her, her red and splotchy face. "I'll see you soon, right?" Phoebe seemed desperate.

Both of her parents glanced at their daughter, before they stared at me.

"Of course, Phoebe," I said, aware of every word that was coming out of my mouth, since her parents were watching me carefully. "Of course." I peered toward Susanna and Mark, nodding. "Take care," I said, before walking off, into the crisp night.

A sigh went through my lungs as I did so, but then I felt my cheeks get cold. I had started to cry.

65

"I don't understand," I said, pulling my wings back as I stood in front of Adiel again.

He looked scared as well.

"Phoebe isn't usually like that. She usually isn't… paranoid…" I trailed off. Adiel stared at me as it seemed to click in my head.

The brain tumor. It was getting worse. It was causing her to become paranoid, maybe even make her hallucinate or have delusions…

Oh, no, I thought as I saw Phoebe's face in my mind.

She was so scared.

It was all because of the tumor that was inside her head. It was growing bigger.

I had been an angel long enough to know Phoebe's behavior when I saw it. She wasn't the only mortal I'd seen that was dealing with a brain tumor.

My face fell as I realized this. Phoebe's brain tumor had gotten bigger.

I watched over Phoebe in the Heavenly River. I saw that the anxiety fits were getting worse, as well as her headaches, which had, over a very short period, gotten debilitating.

Susanna was with Phoebe constantly over the next few days, leading up to the meeting with the surgeon. She had also gotten some over-the-counter medications for her daughter. Phoebe was mostly inside, shrouded in darkness, trying her hardest to stay out of the sun.

Any bright light hurt Phoebe's eyes now. The entire situation was heartbreaking, and I got uneasy seeing her in distress.

I'm sorry, I thought as I saw the images in the Heavenly River. *Phoebe, I'm so sorry.*

"Caelum?"

I looked up to see Adiel watching me carefully. I'd been looking at my reflection in the River.

"Caelum, I know you love Phoebe, but I wanted to tell you something." He sighed, appearing troubled, and then spoke carefully. "Phoebe, she'll only get worse, especially if the brain tumor goes untreated." I opened my mouth to speak, when Adiel spoke. "I know she's going to have surgery to remove it, but until then, she's going to continue to have the symptoms: the paranoia, the strange behavior, the headaches. They will only get worse, as the tumor gets larger."

I bit my lip at what he said.

"I just wanted to let you know. Phoebe isn't the first mortal we've seen that has had a brain ailment."

This was very true.

She was not the first. But the thought of her dealing with a mass in her brain had me worried.

Adiel peered over at me, and my chest buckled as Phoebe's face enveloped my mind.

Phoebe... Phoebe...

Her symptoms would only get worse...

I knew Adiel was right, but it all made me so sad. I bit my lip again, hard, trying to keep myself together, but I failed as my face became damp with tears. I succumbed to the sobs as I thought about Phoebe.

Phoebe, the mortal woman that I'd fallen in love with.

I saw Adiel coming up to me through my tears. He just sighed, and then gave me a hug. "I'm sorry," he said, meaning soaking his words. "I'm so sorry, Caelum."

"Phoebe Bright!"

Phoebe's head snapped up from the floor as her name was called. She gulped, blinking, before her mother grasped her trembling hand.

Phoebe watched Susanna's eyes, before the mother nodded. "Come on, honey. Let's go meet the surgeon."

Phoebe nodded along with her mother, before she steadied herself, walking toward the woman who had called her name.

I stared after both Phoebe and Susanna, and then followed close behind them. I advanced soundlessly into the patient room where they had gone.

66

I was in the patient room, tucked into the corner, invisible to the mortals as Phoebe waited anxiously on the examination table. She waited for the neurosurgeon to come in.

She bit her lip nervously, and my eyes tightened.

Adiel was right.

She was getting worse, as I studied her features.

Her hands clenched, and that was when Susanna spoke. "Honey?"

Phoebe's eyes darted toward her mother.

"It'll be alright. I promise."

Phoebe just looked away, right as I heard footsteps on the other side of the door. The neurosurgeon was here.

I gulped. My heart pounded, the blood seeping into my head as he smiled, looking at Susanna and Phoebe's eyes.

"Hello," he said to them both, introducing himself as he sat down opposite Phoebe. "It's nice to meet you, Phoebe Bright."

The neurosurgeon said that he would try his hardest to help Phoebe. He then went on about the surgery.

Phoebe nodded throughout it all almost robotically. The doctor went on with talking about the kind of operation that was going to happen, given Phoebe's circumstances and symptoms.

He had some MRI scans of Phoebe's brain, which he talked about and explained to the best of his ability.

Phoebe shook her head in a daze before speaking. "So, the operation that is going to happen is a craniotomy, which is where my skull will be partly removed to expose my brain, in order to remove the…the… tumor. It might take about two months to recover, and you saw the MRI results," she said, looking over at the surgeon. "You saw how big the brain…mass… is. I will need to have the surgery the next time I come in."

The neurosurgeon watched Phoebe, before looking over at Susanna.

"Seems like she is listening," he said. "Phoebe," he told her, peering over in her direction, "I will see you in about two weeks, alright?"

Susanna and Phoebe gulped at the same time, but then Susanna shook her head, looking at the doctor as he got up from the chair. He turned toward the door and opened it.

"It was a pleasure to meet you, Ma'am, and Phoebe," he said, glancing in Phoebe's direction as she got off the examination table. He peered first at her, then her mother.

The neurosurgeon twisted around and walked off, heading down the hallway. Phoebe and Susanna went over to the checkout area, to arrange another appointment. An appointment to get the craniotomy to remove the brain tumor.

Phoebe and Susanna walked off into the parking lot.

My wings unfurled from my back as I saw them reach the vehicle, and then I flew to the Afterlife, nervousness soaking my body.

67

"Caelum?" Adiel's voice made me glance at him as I arrived in the Heavens. "How is she? It's different when you actually see the mortals, rather than see them in the River. How is Phoebe, up close?"

I took a deep inhale through my lungs, letting it go slowly. "Phoebe is distracted. She seems incredibly anxious, but was able to retain all the information that the neurosurgeon was saying. She's going to have a craniotomy, which means that the doctor will have to remove her skull partly to get to the brain...the brain...tumor. The neurosurgeon seemed very nice, explaining everything clearly in a way that Phoebe and Susanna could understand. He said his name, but I...I...can't remember what it was..."

I trailed off for a moment, and then brought my attention back to Adiel. "There's just a lot of information when it comes to Phoebe now. I'm nervous for her, Adiel."

He nodded understandingly. "You love her," he stated. "You love her, and that means that she will always be on your mind."

Phoebe would always be on my mind...

"When is the craniotomy?" Adiel asked, taking me out of my reverie.

"Umm...two weeks."

My eyes hit the floor of the Heavens as the thought of Phoebe overcame my mind, when I felt a hand on my shoulder.

I peered over at Adiel, who gave me a relaxed look. "Remember, Caelum, everything will be okay, no matter what happens."

I sniffled a little, before nodding. "I understand, Adiel."

He sighed, staring into my eyes for a few moments, before he squeezed my shoulder affectionately. "You know where I am if you need me, Caelum."

Then he walked off, toward the Golden Gates.

I watched silently as he opened the enchanted barrier before going into the Soul Realm. The Realm that contained Lola, Lemuel, and the other Spirits.

I stared at the Gates that were in the distance, and then finally just went over to them. I wanted to see Lola again, since I was anxious about Phoebe. The Golden Retriever would calm me down.

I went over to the barrier before I called out to Adiel, who instantly grinned at me. "I want to see Lola again, Adiel," I told him, feeling the almost magnetic sensation radiate from the Gates. "I want to see her again."

Anxiety drenched me in the days leading up to the operation.

I was constantly visiting the Soul Realm to see Lola, since she was keeping me as calm as I could be. I was visiting Lola in the Spirit Realm, and was also checking the Heavenly River.

From what I could tell, Phoebe was nervous as well. There were images in the Water of her hugging Camilla and then her mother, which caused me to bite my lip, holding back my emotions as I saw them.

Poor Phoebe, I thought.

She was so anxious.

The night before her operation, she could barely sleep, while I could barely focus on anything else.

Adiel saw how anxious I was. That was when I told him that I was going to be there, in the operating room as Phoebe was getting her craniotomy, her surgery to remove the brain tumor.

I was going to be there, to watch over her like a Guardian angel, even though that wasn't my duty. I would be there for Phoebe.

Adiel nodded as he heard my words. He told me he completely understood. "Good luck, Caelum," he said, before I took off, flying away to see Phoebe.

68

My wings extended out behind me as I landed by the entrance of the surgeon's office, quickly tucking them away afterward. I scanned the parking lot.

Where were Phoebe and Susanna?

My heart pummeled my ribcage, my extremities shaking, before I spotted them advancing through the parking lot. Susanna was holding Phoebe's hand. They both were noticeably nervous.

I sighed as I waited for them, and then they passed me. I entered the waiting room of the office carefully, going into the building with a knot in my stomach.

The appearance of Phoebe's hair in a very low ponytail made me even more anxious for her, since her hairstyle was significant. It was so the surgeon could get to her skull. This would happen after he shaved a portion of her head.

Phoebe... Phoebe.... Phoebe...

I just kept reciting her name in my mind as I watched her.

"Phoebe?"

We both looked up at the sound of the receptionist's voice. She had moved the sliding glass from where the desk was. "Phoebe, I'm going to need you to come here and sign this form really quick, please."

Phoebe glanced at her mother for a moment, before getting up and going to the receptionist, who smiled at her kindly.

"We're just going to need you to sign a consent form for the operation, if you don't mind."

Phoebe just nodded. "No. No, I don't mind. Of course, I'll sign it."

"Okay." The woman passed her a clipboard. "Just sign the line beside the X, and then I'll give the form to the surgeon."

"Alright," Phoebe said, signing it quickly before she gave it back to the receptionist.

"Thank you," she said, before Phoebe just went and sat down next to her mother, who looked apprehensive.

Susanna grasped her daughter's hand again, holding it the entire time.

"Phoebe Bright!"

Phoebe's eyes snapped to the woman holding the door that led to the surgery room.

It was time. It was time. *It was time.*

Phoebe turned to her mother, who just watched her daughter's eyes reassuringly. "I'll be right here when you're done, okay? I'll see you in the recovery room as soon as I'm able."

Susanna smiled, trying to keep Phoebe calm, when her daughter nodded. She went over to the woman.

I followed right behind them, walking into the back operating room, my heart pounding the entire time.

"Hello, Ms. Bright," a man said as he held out his hand to shake Phoebe's. "I'm the anesthesiologist for your surgery. I'm really sorry that this is happening, but I promise we will do our very best for you."

Phoebe nodded silently. I could tell that anxiety had engulfed her, now that she was here, in the OR. Ready to get the brain tumor removed. She shook the anesthesiologist's hand, before he introduced himself calmly.

"One of the other doctors here, Seth, will give you a gown to wear. It's easier for you to wear a gown instead of your clothing for the surgery, since you are having a brain operation. It will be easier to remove."

Phoebe nodded, and I couldn't help but marvel at her behavior. She was doing a great job for having so many things told to her at one time.

A black-haired, thin doctor came up to Phoebe, giving her a blue hospital gown.

"Thank you," Phoebe said, and then looked at him questioningly. "Where are the bathrooms?"

"There is one right here in the hallway," Seth said. "You can change in there."

"Thank you," Phoebe repeated, before disappearing into the bathroom.

It only took a few moments for her to change, and when she came out, the anesthesiologist was there again, watching Phoebe as she walked back into the room. He instructed her to lie down on the laid-back apparatus, where the surgery would take place. Phoebe did so, her hands shaking slightly. I saw the head surgeon, the one that had already met with Susanna and Phoebe, enter the room.

The neurosurgeon looked at her calmly, before the anesthesiologist spoke, grabbing her attention.

"We're just going to insert an IV into your arm in order to get the general anesthesia in your system, okay? We're just going to insert it right now. Are you ready?" he asked, before Phoebe spoke. "Yes."

"Okay," he said, to which he nodded at one of the nurses, who came up to Phoebe and touched her arm carefully. She was inspecting it in order to find a vein.

"Hello, Ms. Bright," she said, a little meek. "My name is Cyndi."

"Hi, Cyndi," Phoebe said.

"That doesn't hurt too bad, does it?" Cyndi asked. She was referring to the needle she was inserting into Phoebe's arm.

Phoebe, to my amazement, didn't even flinch.

"Nope. I didn't feel anything. Thank you," she said to Cyndi, who beamed.

"You're welcome, Ms. Bright."

That was when the anesthesiologist stepped in again, walking up to both Cyndi and Phoebe. "Okay, Phoebe, I want you to count down from ten, can you do that for me?"

Phoebe nodded as the anesthesia started kicking in. Already I could tell that she was getting drowsy.

The specialists watched her patiently as she slowly counted down.

"Ten... nine...eight... seven... six..." Phoebe started, and then trailed off as she became unconscious. Right before she did though, I saw her eyes flicker to mine. She stared at me blankly, before she drifted off into a slumber.

I watched her silently, watched her doze off...

My heart skipped a beat as I came out of my reverie. I looked around at the surgeons and the anesthesiologist as he glanced at the others, nodding once he realized that she was completely sedated.

My breathing hitched slightly.

The operation had begun.

69

I backed away from Phoebe, allowing the surgeon to go over to her. I felt my heart pulverize my rib cage as I saw him move Phoebe's hair with one hand. With the other, he grasped a razor that one of the other doctors had given him.

"Here you go," the other individual said, to which the surgeon nodded.

He glanced at the anesthesiologist, who was looking over Phoebe's vital functions.

I hadn't even noticed that Phoebe had been hooked up to a ventilator, and had a finger monitor on her left hand. I'd just been staring at her sleeping, calm face as the doctors had begun to get her prepared for the surgery. Phoebe was now hooked to a breathing machine, as well as a pulse oximeter and heart rate mechanism. She was about to have the biggest procedure of her life, and I would watch over her, even though it wasn't my obligation.

I heard the head neurosurgeon take a deep breath before beginning to probe around Phoebe's head with his fingertips. He was trying to determine where he should shave it.

He pushed her long hair away from her scalp, and then he slowly and methodically brought the razor up to Phoebe's skull. That was when he carefully began to shave a portion of her head.

My breathing hitched once more. It was becoming more and more real that Phoebe was having the brain mass removed. But I refused to leave the OR.

I was determined to be with Phoebe, determined to be by her side.

Moments passed as Phoebe's head was shaved.

The surgeon had removed a good portion of her hair before he touched it with his gloved hand, feeling it gingerly. Her peach-colored skin was cleaned with a special solution to get rid of any potentially harmful bacteria.

I stared, my heart skipping a beat. I saw the man use a scalpel to cut into the delicate tissue that was Phoebe's head. Her blood was crimson as he carefully made the incision, and another doctor was there to control the bleeding.

First, the neurosurgeon would need to get to her skull, and then they would remove part of it in order to get to the mass that was on her brain.

A wad of nervousness erupted in the pit of my stomach as I watched the operation take place. Sometimes I even walked up close to see what it was the surgeons were doing.

They drilled into her skull using a special instrument, before removing part of it with another one so that they could get to her brain. The sound of the device sent chills up my spine, but I tried to remain as calm as possible as the neurosurgeon continued.

I was biting my lip the entire time.

The whole procedure took around four hours.

I knew this because one of the surgeons told the main one what the time was. He finally got to the mass that had been in Phoebe's brain, and he removed it as carefully as possible, before I swiftly moved out of the way. He placed it away from the apparatus that Phoebe was on, handing it to one of the other specialists.

I gasped as I realized how big it was up close, without the MRI scan.

It was enormous.

After removing the tumor, the neurosurgeon then methodically cleaned up Phoebe's brain, making sure that there were no traces left. He checked her organ before he got a hold of the portion of her skull once more, using a surgical instrument to put the bone back over her brain. He put her skull back together, using numerous objects to make sure that everything in Phoebe's head was as secure as possible. He then sewed her up. I gulped as I saw the sutures being placed over her scalp, as Phoebe was being put back together.

The stitches looked harsh, scary, but it was nothing compared to what I'd just seen. The brain tumor that had been inside her had been even more frightening.

My breathing was rapid, my hands shaking as he finally backed away. He brought his stained, gloved hands up to his chest so that he wouldn't touch anyone else.

I knew what that meant as I saw the other doctors take over, going over to Phoebe as the head neurosurgeon backed away.

It meant the operation was over.

70

Phoebe's crystal blue eyes fluttered as she regained consciousness. The knot in my stomach relaxed as I saw her slowly come around.

I'd waited for three hours for her to wake up, since she had been so heavily sedated. My heart had been in my throat the whole time.

Her appearance was jarring as I looked at her. The bruising from the operation had traveled down to Phoebe's face. She appeared swollen, and black and blue.

I saw her scan her surroundings, and that was when I took in how much equipment that she had hooked to her body. Phoebe had a bandage on her head, as well as an IV drip in her arm that was giving her medication.

I was in the recovery room with her, tucked into a corner, my eyes glued on hers as she groggily moaned.

"Ms. Bright?"

Phoebe looked at Cyndi as she went up to her. Phoebe blinked as she leaned over, touching her hand kindly.

"Ms. Bright, the procedure was successful. You're going to be moved to a recovery ward, but we first want to monitor you here, and then you have some visitors. After that, you will go to the ICU."

Phoebe blinked drowsily, trying to focus on Cyndi's face.

It took a few moments, but Phoebe finally looked around the room, before looking back at Cyndi. Then Phoebe shut her eyes. I could tell that she was trying not to get woozy.

Cyndi seemed to understand this, and that was when she straightened herself back up, taking her hand off Phoebe's. "I'm going to tell your family you're awake, okay? I'll be right back. Just rest for right now. Try to get acclimated."

Phoebe groaned. It took me a few moments to realize that she was agreeing with Cyndi. Phoebe couldn't move because of the bandage, and could barely talk because of the anesthesia, so she just made noises as a way of communicating.

Cyndi blinked before seeming to comprehend what Phoebe was trying to get across. "Okay, Ms. Bright. I will be right back. You rest up, alright?" Cyndi left, leaving Phoebe with one of the other doctors, who was monitoring her.

I copied the doctor, watching Phoebe as she breathed deeply, trying not to get disoriented. I watched her for a while.

I blinked as I heard Cyndi return to the recovery room a few minutes later. Her footsteps echoed down the hallway. She nodded at the other doctor that had been watching over Phoebe, before she said her name softly. "Ms. Bright? Phoebe?" she asked cautiously.

Phoebe opened her eyes, focusing on Cyndi's face.

"Would you like to see what you look like?" Cyndi asked.

Phoebe groaned in response, saying in the smallest whisper, so low that I could barely hear her. "Yes."

Cyndi glanced over at the other doctor, who was still in the room.

He came over to them as Cyndi touched Phoebe's hand gently, reassuring her, when the man gave Cyndi a mirror.

"You still have a lot of healing to do," Cyndi told Phoebe, as she handed her the mirror. Phoebe took it with a trembling hand. "Overall, though, you are doing fantastic. Your head is bandaged to keep from any potential infection, and the stitches underneath will be coming out in about fourteen days."

Phoebe's eyes widened as she looked at her reflection, at the amount of bruising on her face. But Cyndi just smiled reassuringly. "The swelling will go down, I promise," she said.

Phoebe gave the mirror back to Cyndi, and then spoke. "Where's... where's my family?" she asked.

"They are in the waiting room. Adam?" she asked, getting the attention of the doctor that was still in the area. "Will you go tell Ms. Bright's family that she is able to be seen now?"

"Yes, Cyndi," he told her, before walking off.

Phoebe straightened herself up with Cyndi's help, and then gingerly touched her arm that had the IV drip in it.

"It's okay, Ms. Bright," Cyndi said calmly. "You'll be okay."

"She's awake now, but disoriented. She has swelling on her face, but that is normal and will go down within the next few days."

I heard the doctor, Adam, talking before I saw him come back into the room, Susanna and Mark right behind him. I saw Phoebe's parents stop in shock at the sight of their daughter. Susanna blinked rapidly, while Mark breathed quickly. But then they composed themselves as fast as they could, since their daughter was watching them closely.

Cyndi had a kind expression on her face as she saw Phoebe's parents. She took her hand off Phoebe's as they advanced toward both of them. "I'll be right outside. I'll give you all some privacy. If you need something, or if anything happens, let us know."

Susanna and Mark nodded understandingly. Cyndi then got Adam's attention, and they both walked out of the recovery room.

Phoebe's parents sighed, before turning to their daughter, who smiled a tiny smile. "Hi, Mom. Hi, Dad," she said groggily.

Mark grinned back at her, on the verge of tears. Susanna brought her hand up to Phoebe's, gently grasping it. "Hi, honey," she said, in barely a whisper. There was water gathering in her eyes-mimicking her husband- as she took in her daughter, but she immediately sniffled. "The surgeon came to both of us and said that you pulled through amazingly, that the operation was a success," she said, but I could tell that Susanna knew this was something that Phoebe had already known.

"It's nice to see you both," Phoebe said drowsily, watching her mother and father. "How is Camilla doing? Where is she?"

"Good. She's with Derek right now. I called him as soon as the doctors told us you were awake," Susanna said. "I'll let her know that you asked about her. You can see her a bit later. Right now, you need to rest. We just wanted to see you."

"Thank you," Phoebe said to her mother.

"You're welcome, sweetheart. The doctors said that you will be in the ICU for a while to monitor you, so I went ahead and packed a few bags with extra clothes. For you, as well as the both of us," Susanna said, glancing at Mark for a moment. "We'll be here while you're recovering, sweetie."

Phoebe blinked, and then spoke. "Thank you."

She shut her eyes, and that was when Susanna and Mark stood up, taking the cue to let their daughter sleep.

"We love you, Phoebe," Susanna said, before she hugged Mark tightly, walking out of the recovery room. Cyndi and Adam came back in as Phoebe's parents left.

I felt the wad of anxiety in my stomach disappear as I stared at Phoebe. She opened her eyes, taking in both specialists' faces before shutting them again.

That was when I knew it was time to leave. Everything was under control, and it was time to go up to the Heavens.

I sighed, taking one more look at Phoebe before walking out of the recovery room. I advanced outside, exiting the hospital.

My thick black wings appeared from my back, and then I ascended into the atmosphere, relief engulfing me.

71

"A re you alright, Caelum?" Adiel asked. He was beside the Heavenly River, looking cautiously at me.

I could tell from his expression that he had seen everything unfold in the enchanted Water.

Adiel had seen Phoebe getting her operation. He continued to look into my eyes, waiting for an answer. I spoke. "Yes, Adiel, I'm alright. I'm just glad that the surgery is complete. I was getting worried for Phoebe."

Worried was an understatement. I was more terrified for her.

Anything could've happened to Phoebe, but luckily, nothing did. Her operation went smoothly and was successful.

"How long was the procedure?" Adiel asked. "I only saw the beginning and the end of the operation. I couldn't be in front of the Heavenly River for the entire surgery. I had to Guard the Spirits."

I gulped, the memory of Phoebe under anesthesia coming back to me.

"Four hours approximately, and then it was about three hours later when she woke up. She looked very bruised, but she hasn't had any side effects from the operation, at least not yet. Her head was bandaged, and there were stitches in her scalp from the incision. The doctors said the staples, plus the bandage, should come off within the next fourteen days. Phoebe had just met up with her parents again before I left. She's going to be in the ICU for a while so she can improve, and then should be home after that. Phoebe has a long way to go though, in terms of recovery."

Adiel listened carefully as the words that I'd said hit his ears. "She doesn't have anything else going on with her? I mean, in terms of side effects?" he asked.

I shook my head. "Nope. Other than being a little disoriented, she's okay."

Adiel nodded. "That's great, Caelum. Phoebe did have a very intense surgery. It's good that she pulled through. How are you feeling?"

He watched my face, studying it.

"I'm alright," I said, repeating the words that I'd said before.

I looked at Adiel, who nodded. "Okay," he said. "Well, that's good. I'm glad everything is stable."

"It is," I said. "It is."

It took a while for Phoebe to recover, like Cyndi had said, and like I'd thought.

I was there, in the ICU of the hospital, as Phoebe went through days and days of being monitored, guarded by the nurses and doctors to make sure that she was going to be okay. When the fourteenth day finally came, and she was finally ready to get the bandage off and the stitches out, Phoebe seemed relieved.

Cyndi was by her side the whole time as Phoebe got everything removed. Susanna and Mark were there as well, smiling kindly at

Phoebe as their daughter finally gazed into a mirror nearby. She looked at her reflection.

My heart was pounding my chest as I saw Phoebe take in her face, her eyes, and then saw her gasp at her partly shaved head. Her scar was exposed.

Cyndi just smiled at Phoebe through the mirror, seeming to know how scared Phoebe was. "It's alright, Ms. Bright. Your hair will grow back."

Phoebe turned around, glancing at Cyndi again before looking at her parents, who were crying happy tears.

Both had been there the whole fourteen days, coming to visit Phoebe whenever they could. They even brought Camilla in to see Phoebe one day. Camilla was shocked by the way her mother appeared, but then immediately regained her composure, going and sitting by Phoebe's side. Now, days later, Phoebe had finally gotten her stitches out and bandage off.

Within a few more days of monitoring, she was about to go home. Go home and live as much of a normal, mortal life as possible.

I was sure Phoebe was glad about that.

I sighed as I saw the mortal woman grin at her parents, who wiped away their tears.

Phoebe was now, finally, safe.

"Careful. Easy, honey," Susanna said, helping Phoebe out of her car, grasping her hand gently. "Easy, Phoebe."

Phoebe groaned as she shifted her weight to get out of the vehicle, squinting in the sunlight.

"It's alright, I have you," Susanna said as her daughter shuffled along the driveway toward Susanna's home. "I got you," the mother continued as they made it to the front steps. "Careful, now," she said as they both made it up the stairs. "Easy."

Phoebe slowly walked, and that was when Susanna opened the door carefully, with Phoebe walking inside.

They weren't at Phoebe's home yet. Her parents still wanted to watch over her, so Phoebe was at Susannas and Mark's residence.

"Mark!" Susanna called out as she entered the home with her daughter. "Mark, where are you?"

"Right here, Susanna," he responded, walking over to the front door as I quickly went inside with everyone.

Mark shut the door behind his wife and daughter as they went to go sit on the couch.

Phoebe carefully sat down, gingerly making herself comfortable, before Susanna backed away, satisfied that Phoebe was relaxed.

"Thank you, Mom," she said as she sank back into the pillows that were behind her.

"You're welcome, sweetheart. You're welcome."

72

I lost track of how long it took for Phoebe to recover, but it took a while. Days turned into weeks, which then turned into months. All the while, I was still doing my duty, bringing the Souls to the Afterlife. But, like always, I was distracted by the mortal woman who had grasped my heart.

Slowly, little by little, Phoebe was getting her strength back. She was getting better and better the more time passed. Which made me ecstatic.

Phoebe was getting better.

This all meant one thing: I was going to talk to her, for the first time in months.

I caught Phoebe in her driveway right as she was checking her mailbox. Her brown hair had partly grown back, hiding the scar that was over her scalp. The way her hair had grown back looked incredibly unique, an asymmetrical hairstyle. But I could still see the scar.

I didn't care though. The scar meant that she was a survivor, that she had pushed past her ailment....

I felt a smile come across my face as I saw her. "Hi," I said, watching her as she turned around.

Just the sight of Phoebe looking at me made my heart pulverize my ribs.

She smiled back, tucking a strand of her hair back behind her ear. "Hi, Caelum."

"How…how are you?" I asked tentatively. "I haven't seen you in a while."

"Thank you. I've been okay. I've had some health issues and had surgery a few months ago, if you can't tell from the scar. I'm okay now, though. The operation was a success. I have to go back and see if I'm fully in the clear, but I've been alright. Thank you for asking though, Caelum."

I just stared back at her face. "You're welcome, Phoebe."

Right then, I saw Susanna come out of the home, and that was when I took my cue.

"Okay, well, I have to go. It was nice seeing you again, Phoebe."

"You too," she said back, and my breath quickened at her words. "I'll see you again soon, Caelum."

I nodded, grinning, while inside, my intestines were doing backflips. "Okay, Phoebe. Okay."

The Golden Gates towered past my view as I looked up, seeing them disappear. They were gigantic as I brought my eyes back to the front of the barrier. I saw the interior of the Soul Realm.

I looked past the Gates, and then called out to Adiel. "Adiel? Adiel, are you there?"

"I'm here, Caelum. I'm here," he responded as I saw him materialize through the white mist.

Lola showed up behind him, and I smiled.

"I'd like to come into the Spirit Realm again, Adiel. I want to see Lola, as well as speak to Lemuel again."

There were a few questions I wanted to ask him...

Adiel nodded. "Of course, Caelum. I'll let you through. Back up," he said, and I did.

Once he said the words and the monumental Gates opened, I walked through them, petting Lola as she ran up to me. Her tail wagged as she went on her hind legs, licking my cheek, and I grinned.

"Hi, Lola. Hi, sweet girl."

"How is Phoebe?" Adiel asked. I brought my attention back up to his face, nodding.

"Good. She's doing a lot better. She's actually getting better and better the more the days go by. I just talked to her," I said. I felt a blush settle on my cheeks as I looked down at the ground. I brought my eyes back up to Adiel's. "She wants to see me again, Adiel."

His eyes softened as he looked in mine. He smiled. "This is good, Caelum. I'm glad that you are happy, and that Phoebe is alright. I wish you the best."

I grinned at Adiel, before I glanced down at Lola, who was still by my side. I could bring her with me as I walked through the Realm... "Come on, Lola," I told the Golden Retriever, and then I walked off through the fog. "Come on."

"Good luck, Caelum," Adiel said. I turned toward him, smiling.

"Thank you, Adiel," I responded before I twisted my body back around.

And I walked through the mist to find Lemuel, Lola right behind me.

73

I spotted Lemuel after walking through the Realm for a while. His blue eyes lit up as he saw me, and I grinned, stopping right in front of him.

"Caelum," he said. "You came back."

"Yes. Yes, I did," I said. My feet shifted a little as I looked at him, before the words that I wanted to say just spilled out of my mouth. "I wanted to ask you a few questions," I told him.

Lemuel just raised his eyebrows in response.

"Since you became a mortal and Fell, I wanted to ask you about…about the mortal's life. I wanted to know what it was like for you."

Again, I felt my cheeks burn, and I eyed the ground.

"Sure," Lemuel said, and my eyes flashed up to his. "I can help you with that," he stated. "I can certainly help you with that. What would you like to know about the mortals?" Lemuel asked.

My heart pounded against my ribs, but then I just said, "I want to know what they could be like. I want to know how they would act. I wanted to know from the point of view of a former mortal. Lemuel, you were the one I was thinking of when I wanted to talk about this. You've been to Earth, living among the mortals, living among your Chloe. I just… just… wanted to know what it was like."

Lemuel nodded at my words. "Well, it is true that I lived among the mortals. I could certainly tell you about my experience, and about the mortal experience. I could help you." He blinked, and then watched my eyes. "Is this about your love?"

I breathed deeply, responding to him afterward. "Yes. I wanted to see her and be alongside her. I wanted to get to know Phoebe."

Lemuel smiled. "You remind me of myself once I was aware of Chloe being a medium. I just couldn't get her out of my head."

Lemuel glanced into my eyes, and that was when I knew he understood. He was going to help me. "Why are you asking about this?" Lemuel questioned, looking at me curiously.

"I…I… wanted to see Phoebe again, with the words that Adiel taught me. I just wanted to be among the mortals for a little while, be with Phoebe…"

I trailed off, but then glanced back up at Lemuel.

He just watched me carefully.

"Well, I completely understand," he said. "You want to know what everything is like, so you aren't confused by anything, am I right?"

I nodded. "Yes," I said. "Yes, that's right."

"Well," Lemuel said, "I will certainly help you," he repeated. "I will certainly help you with the ways of the mortals."

Lemuel and I talked for a while.

About Phoebe, Camilla, and Chloe. About what the mortals ate, how they slept, how they felt pain in a way that was completely unique to them.

Lemuel explained everything, and I was thankful for him doing so. It all made me seem to understand Phoebe and her family better, as Lemuel explained the ways of the mortals to me. It seemed to be hours later when I smiled at Lemuel, saying goodbye to him.

"Thank you, Lemuel," I said, sincerely meaning it as I looked at him. "Thank you so much for telling me all of this. It really was a huge help."

Lemuel grinned. "Well, you're welcome, Caelum. Come back whenever you need to. I'll be here."

I nodded understandingly. "Alright," I said. "I'll see you around, then. Bye, Lemuel."

"Bye, Caelum. Be safe."

I grinned. "I will."

And with that, I twisted my body around, going toward the Golden Gates entrance and Adiel, the new knowledge of the mortals now in my brain.

74

Heavy panting in the distance made me grin as I walked through the mist.

"Hi, Lola," I said as I saw the Golden Retriever's body materialize. "Hi, sweet girl."

She whined excitedly, running over, before she threw her bodyweight into me.

I laughed, and then straightened myself back up. "Good girl," I said, stroking her ears. "Good girl, Lola."

I looked up to see Adiel in the distance, walking toward me.

He smiled. "Well, someone's very excited to see you," he chuckled. He looked into my face. "Everything okay, Caelum?"

I nodded at him. "Yes. Yes, it is."

Adiel focused on my eyes for a few moments, and then turned away.

I inhaled and exhaled slowly, letting all the breath out of my lungs as I walked behind Adiel. My mind was fixed on Phoebe the whole time.

"Are you going to go see her again?"

I nodded, glancing up at Adiel. "Yes. Yes, I was planning on it."

I looked around the Heavens, watching the Golden Gates that were in the distance.

We'd just walked out of the Soul Realm, and now were over by the Heavenly River. We'd been talking for a short while.

I turned back toward Adiel, who looked into my eyes. "I wish you the best, Caelum," he said, smiling kindly.

I grinned back. "Thank you, Adiel."

And then my wings erupted from my back. I flew out of the Afterlife and to Earth.

My heart was in my throat the entire journey.

Just thinking about it made my insides squirm, but I was determined to get to know Phoebe, to understand her....

I landed on the familiar path partly covered by trees before I shut my eyes, trying to calm my pounding heart. I said the words, opened my eyes back up, and walked on the path toward Phoebe's home. Nervousness was engulfing me the entire time.

I caught sight of Phoebe coming out of her house right as I walked up the street. She smiled at me warmly as she made her way down the steps, and I squinted a little. It was almost as if she'd been waiting for me to go by her residence, stroll by her home.

I grinned back at Phoebe, stopping by her driveway as she walked across it, stopping right in front of me. She had a black baseball cap on, positioned right over her scar, but she appeared ecstatic as her blue eyes locked with mine. It was almost like she was excited to see me.

That made my heart pound my ribs.

The thought that Phoebe was happy to see me...

"Caelum," she said, almost breathlessly, confirming what I was thinking. "Caelum, you're here." Her grin radiated throughout her face, and my heart skipped a beat.

"I just wanted to stop by again, see how you were doing," I said, gulping back my excitement, trying to keep my voice even.

"Well, I'm feeling better every day," Phoebe said. "I'm even able to go outside now, in the sunlight. Before, I couldn't do that. I would get the most severe headaches. I'm better now though. My operation was a success, so that's great."

"Yes, it is," I said, nodding. "I'm glad you are feeling better each day."

Phoebe just smiled. It almost took my breath away, the way she focused on me. Her eyes were so beautiful...

"Would you like me to join you on your walk?" Phoebe suddenly asked, jolting me out of my thoughts. "I need to be out and walking anyway, it'll help with my recovery. I need to be more active, or else my mental state will get bad. Being in the house all the time because of headaches can be kind of sad."

Yes, I thought. *Yes, it can.*

"Sure," I said, blinking at the smile that Phoebe gave me. "I could always walk with someone." I paused, and then looked around her home. "Aren't your parents here though, and Camilla?"

Phoebe blinked, almost astonished that I'd remembered her family, and my breathing hitched.

"Camilla is with her father. She's visiting him for the weekend. My parents are back at their house. I needed some time to readjust, but I can call them if I am having any issues. Camilla needs to see her father, though. I mean, Derek *is* her father."

"I understand," I said, and I completely meant it. "I was just wondering."

"Everything's alright," Phoebe said, gazing at me warmly. "I just wanted to use this time to go out and do something."

That was understandable. She just needed to get out.

I blinked as I looked at Phoebe, before I smiled. "Well, you're welcome to join me. I was just going to walk around the block."

Phoebe nodded, grinning, and then walked to my side. "It will be nice to have someone to talk to," she said, and my intestines squirmed.

I couldn't help but feel flattered. "You're welcome, Phoebe. You're welcome."

The walk around the block turned into a very long stroll around the neighborhood.

I wasn't keeping track of the time as Phoebe and I made our way around the streets, walking on the sidewalk, cutting through the trail that led to the other part of the neighborhood. I was just glad that Phoebe was out of the house and was okay. I was also extremely flattered that she felt as comfortable as she did around me.

Phoebe just needed someone to listen to her. She was very quiet at first, but then she brought up how glad she was. Glad that she was finally able to enjoy the sunshine.

I acted like I didn't know what she was talking about. I couldn't tell her the *truth*.

I could never tell her that.

I asked her about what had happened, and that was when she had stopped beside me.

"I had a brain tumor, Caelum," Phoebe stated, and I saw her eyes begin to water. I held back the urge to hug her as she sniffled. "I... I... had a brain tumor, and because of that I had these horrible headaches." I just stared at her, absorbing her words. "That's actually why I have this on right now," Phoebe continued, referring to the cap on her head. "I had the tumor removed, but I have a massive scar on my scalp because of the operation."

Phoebe moved her hand to the black cap, before bravely taking it off.

I sucked in a breath, stunned, as I saw the scar.

It was massive, taking up almost half of her head, but I could also see that her hair was growing back over it. Growing back to create an interesting, asymmetrical hairstyle.

I brought my eyes back up to Phoebe's.

She looked like she was waiting for judgement or something, to be made fun of, and I squinted.

"You're a fighter," I breathed, partly to myself, before I felt a blush rise in my cheeks. Phoebe just stared at me, astonished.

I blinked. It took several moments for me to come back to myself.

Phoebe had smiled. "Thank you, Caelum," she said, before she began walking again. I followed beside her, amazed that I'd just said that statement out loud.

Phoebe and I walked for a while.

75

"Thank you, Caelum. Thank you for walking with me."
Phoebe smiled.

Her eyes were so blue...

"You're welcome," I replied. It took a few moments to regain my composure.

I stood there, watching her, before I realized that we'd reached Phoebe's home.

Oh, right, I thought as I shook my head, dazed.

"It was nice to talk with you, too, Phoebe," I said.

She grinned. "I'll see you soon, right?" she asked, her voice hopeful.

Always, I thought.

I nodded back at her, smiling warmly. "Of course," I said. "Of course."

Phoebe turned the baseball cap around in her hand, moving the hat anxiously, almost like she was nervous.

I tilted my head to the side, catching her emotion. "Everything alright, Phoebe?"

"I was just... just wondering... if maybe you'd want to go to the park tomorrow? I used to go to one with my dog before she passed. With my dog and Camilla, of course. Now that she's gone, Camilla and I still like to go and have talks about the happy memories of Lola. Since Camilla is with Derek for the weekend, and I need some more fresh air, I was thinking you could come along with me?"

Phoebe again sounded hopeful.

I swallowed, unable to process the fact that she wanted me to be with her more and more. My heart was pounding so hard the blood was in my ears. I blinked as my insides felt like liquid. "Sure," I said automatically. "Sure, I'll come along. What Park?"

Phoebe appeared ecstatic as she answered. Her grin radiated throughout her face. "Spell Park. The name is Spell Park."

I nodded, putting it into my memory. "Is it within walking distance from here?" I asked.

She nodded. "Yes. Yes, it is. I was thinking maybe I could walk with you up to the park. Would that be okay?"

My insides were now almost melted by what she was saying.

Of course, it's okay, Phoebe.

I grinned. "Yes. Of course. I'd love to join you on a walk tomorrow."

Phoebe smiled another smile that took up the entirety of her features. Then she nodded, twisting back around before disappearing into her house.

I watched her leave, my body feeling numb.

Phoebe wanted to spend more time with me.

I took a deep breath as I walked back through the covered area of trees. I said the correct words, and I flew off, feeling as if I was lighter than the air itself.

It took several moments for me to understand what had just happened. Phoebe wanted to see me again.

76

A diel's tanned face was looking right at me as I returned to the Heavens. He was standing right beside the River. Which meant that he had seen everything.

Adiel's eyes locked on mine as a smile crept up on his face, and I couldn't help but smile back.

My wings went into my skin as I walked over to Adiel, feeling slightly dazed.

He was still grinning for several moments before he finally spoke. "Spell Park, huh?"

I nodded.

"Did you know how Spell Park got its name?"

I shook my head, scrunching my eyebrows together.

"A mortal went there for a run and suffered a heart attack. He almost died but was saved by the paramedics. Once he regained consciousness, he said that an angel was watching over him, was his Guardian. Spell Park is said to have supernatural powers, it's said to be protected." Adiel grinned at me. "I think Spell Park is the perfect place for you to meet up with Phoebe again. I think it'll be nice." He walked up to me, before thumping my shoulder affectionately. "I am happy for you, Caelum."

And then he turned around and walked toward the Golden Gates, leaving me alone beside the Heavenly River.

It wasn't long before I flew out of the Afterlife, my mind engulfed with the thought of seeing Phoebe.

A smile crept up on my face as I came out of the wooded area, seeing Phoebe's house in the distance. The sun was bright and shining, so it felt good to be walking in the nice weather.

The grin stayed on my face as I walked toward Phoebe, who had come out of her home and was now looking like she was waiting on me.

She didn't have her cap on this time. She caught sight of me coming closer, and immediately smiled.

I came right up to her. Phoebe was still beaming.

"Hi," she said, in such a way that it made me feel like she truly missed me.

"Hi," I responded in almost a whisper.

I found myself staring at Phoebe for a few moments before I blinked, looking at the ground instead. I cleared my throat, and then Phoebe spoke.

"The Park is right by the neighborhood. There is a shortcut through the trees, there is a path. You don't mind going on it, do you?"

I shook my head. "I don't mind," I said.

"Alright," she told me, taking a step forward.

My heart pounded my ribs, and my breathing hitched.

But Phoebe was just smiling at me as she went to my side. "Alright. Let's go," she said before we both walked away from her residence. "I can show you the Park."

I just nodded at her words. "Okay," I said, partly in a daze as Phoebe began walking with me.

Like before when I saw Phoebe, we walked for a long time, cutting through the trees and the trail. Then we got to the park. After we arrived, we were leisurely strolling through the area, talking the entire way around it.

Phoebe was getting more and more comfortable around me. I could tell because she started to talk about her MRI scan, Camilla, and then her diagnosis that was the brain tumor.

I was just silent, listening without interrupting. My thoughts were racing, though. My mind went back to the moment that she had gotten the MRI, and everything else that had happened after that.

Phoebe talked about Camilla, and even brought up Lola, saying how much she and her daughter missed her. Phoebe began to cry, tears filling her eyes, and that was when I paused, stopping in my tracks. She was looking around at the dogs in the park. Some were off their leash, playing with their owners or other canines, while some of them were walking beside their owners with a leash.

Phoebe just watched everyone, and I could see that expression. That heartbreaking expression that meant that she was thinking back to when she had Lola. Not only that, but Phoebe was also thinking back to when she had taken Lola to the vet to be put down.

My eyes tightened as I looked at Phoebe. She'd turned her head away from me, hiding her face.

Oh, Phoebe, you poor thing, I thought.

"I'm so sorry," I said. "I'm so sorry."

She sniffled, turning her head back around, gazing into my eyes. "I just miss her," Phoebe said. "Camilla does too. Every time we go to the park and see other dogs, Camilla is always talking about Lola. That's why I had a necklace made for the both of us."

Phoebe touched her sternum, and I saw the pawprint necklace resting there. She gripped the jewelry tightly, running her thumb along it. "I... I just.... miss her," Phoebe's voice cracked. "But she's with the angels now. She's safe."

I just tried to keep my face neutral.

I stayed silent, watching Phoebe as she took her hand off the necklace.

"I just miss her," she repeated.

I nodded. "I understand," I responded. "I like that necklace. It is the perfect way to honor Lola."

Phoebe smiled through her tears. "Thank you, Caelum."

"It'll be alright," I said. "Lola is no longer in pain."

Phoebe looked at me, her blue eyes glistening. She nodded, and then we continued walking.

It was a beautiful day. The sun had come out; the light drenching our surroundings.

Phoebe took a deep breath, sucking oxygen into her lungs, before she twisted around, gazing at my face. "I'm glad you are here, Caelum."

I just smiled warmly as she looked in my eyes. "I'm glad to be here too," I said, completely telling the truth.

Phoebe grinned, looking again at the colorful scenery around us. She brought her eyes back to mine. "Do you know why this area is called Spell Park?"

I just stared at her, knowing where the conversation was going. I pretended I didn't know. I shook my head. "No. No, I don't."

Phoebe watched my expression, and then began to talk. She said everything that Adiel had told me when I was up in Heaven.

The story of a man who had a heart attack but was saved by EMTs. The story about an angel watching over him. The story of where the name Spell Park came from.

When Phoebe was finished, she appeared thoughtful, and I knew what she was thinking about. She still was gazing into my eyes, before she sighed. "Maybe there's an angel watching over me," she said.

I stayed silent. I didn't want to slip up on my words. My expression turned calm as she turned away from me, hiding her face. I didn't say a word as she locked eyes with me again. I finally found my voice. "Maybe, Phoebe. Maybe."

We'd just begun to walk around Spell Park again when we both heard a familiar tiny voice.

"Mommy! Mommy, you're here!"

Phoebe turned toward Camilla, and I beamed at how excited the little girl was. Camilla ran over, hugging Phoebe tightly. "Aww, thank you sweetie," Phoebe said, crouching down to her daughter's level. "I missed you too."

I watched Camilla and Phoebe. A slight smile was on my lips, when I saw someone come up to all three of us out of my peripheral vision. I looked up, and that was when I came face-to-face with Derek. I gulped as we watched each other, suddenly incredibly nervous.

We stared at each other, and I hoped Derek couldn't hear the pounding of my heart. Derek nodded slightly.

I looked back down at the ground, watching Phoebe hug Camilla, when the little girl glanced up at me.

"Hello," Camilla said sweetly, slowly taking her hands off her mother.

I smiled. Phoebe got up from her crouch.

"Do you remember Caelum?" Phoebe asked, watching Camilla's face.

"Yes," the little girl said. "I had just forgotten his name," Camilla continued, looking into my eyes.

I crouched down so that I could get to Camilla's level. I was very aware of Derek and Phoebe's eyes on me as I did so.

Camilla looked at me calmly.

"How are you, Camilla?"

Phoebe's daughter nodded her small head. "Good. I was just on a walk with Daddy when I saw you."

I grinned. "Well, I hope you're having a fun time with him," I said.

"I am," Camilla said.

"Good," I replied. "I'm glad."

I straightened myself up, and that was when I saw Derek staring at me. He blinked, clearing his throat before he spoke. "Camilla, come on. We can go find some ice cream."

Camilla took one last look at Phoebe and I, smiling at the both of us, before she went to her father's side.

"I'll see you tomorrow, okay, Camilla?" Phoebe told her daughter.

Camilla nodded understandingly. Derek looked at both Phoebe and I, and then turned around with Camilla beside him.

"Well, that was nice to see Camilla again," Phoebe said, glancing over at me out of my peripheral vision.

I was watching Derek and Camilla walk off, before I looked at Phoebe. "Yes. Yes, that was nice," I told her.

Phoebe looked at me, tilting her head slightly. She could see the look of uneasiness on my face. I was distracted, thinking about Derek's reaction to seeing me.

"What's wrong, Caelum?"

I blinked, before gazing into Phoebe's eyes. "It's Camilla's father. It's Derek," I admitted. "I was nervous meeting him."

Phoebe nodded understandingly, smiling a slight smile. "You have nothing to be afraid of, Caelum," she said. "You have nothing to worry about. Derek is excellent to coparent with, and he's not the jealous type."

I took a deep breath, exhaling slowly as I heard Phoebe's words.

"It's alright," she told me. "It's okay."

"Caelum?"

I looked at Phoebe in response.

"Thank you for walking with me. I needed to get out of the house."

I smiled. "You're welcome," I said.

Phoebe grinned before turning around and going into her home.

I watched her silently as she went up the steps and into her residence. She paused, twisting around when she got up to her front door and smiled. Then she went inside, closing the door behind her.

77

I was partly in a daze as I flew back up to the Afterlife. The Heavenly River was unoccupied, so I went up to it, looking into the Waters. I said, "Show me Phoebe."

Phoebe was staring into a mirror that was in her living room, staring at her reflection. Her eyes were focused on the surgical scar that was on her head. She appeared to be thinking.

Phoebe just sighed. "Thank you, Caelum," she said, running her fingers along the short hair which was growing. "Thank you so much."

The Water rippled before becoming calm, and I peered into it, seeing my own face.

I stared into the Water, my thoughts on Phoebe, and then I turned away, ecstatic.

She liked me, liked my company. She liked being around me.

My heart was pummeling my ribs as I came to this realization. Phoebe liked me.

The next few weeks were a blur.

I brought Souls to the Afterlife and kept an eye on Phoebe.

She was getting stronger and stronger each day that passed. Camilla was also getting the care she needed.

Phoebe wasn't having trouble with hand tremors, or her memory. She was able to take care of her daughter.

It seemed like Phoebe was finally free.

I sighed, letting all the air out of my lungs as I stood on the top of the mountain. I felt the wind blow across my face. I was glad that Phoebe was doing well.

I'd had a wad of nervousness settled in my stomach. Now, though, I felt relaxed.

The sun settled over the horizon as I stood on the rocky terrain. It was gorgeous, the sunset, all the colors that were splattered across the sky. The warmth of the sun and the air made me feel calm. Calm and tranquil.

Phoebe was feeling great over the next few weeks that I checked on her.

She had no symptoms of the brain tumor, and she told Dr. Isaac. I was invisible to Susanna and Phoebe, staying in the corner of the patient room. I was watching.

There was nothing to worry about though, as Phoebe told the doctor how she was feeling.

She didn't have the baseball cap on to cover her head either, so her half-shaved asymmetrical hair style was visible. There were tiny baby hairs growing on her scalp, partly hiding the scar.

Phoebe seemed fine with showing the neurologist the incision, though. She wasn't embarrassed.

That was a good thing. It meant that she was getting more and more confident. Which was great for her health and happiness.

Phoebe was excited.

A bird chirping in the trees made me smile as I walked under them.

I was in Spell Park, visible to the mortals, just walking around and enjoying the sunshine. It felt warm on my face, and a slight breeze went across my skin, making me feel calm. I loved nature, how serene it all was, and I just walked.

I was thinking about Lola when I saw a Golden Retriever running to catch a tennis ball. The dog ran after it happily, and I smiled. The Golden Retriever went back to its owner, and I twisted around, turning my attention to the rest of the park.

It was a large area, but I strolled, partly watching the mortals with their pets, as well as soaking up the sunshine. It helped melt all my anxiety, and I sighed, my body and mind at peace.

"Caelum?"

Adiel's voice floated into my consciousness as he advanced.

I turned, looking. A grin was on my face as I saw him.

Adiel looked at me calmly. "She likes you," he said as he watched me.

I nodded.

"Phoebe likes you," he stated.

My smile took over my entire face and Adiel grinned back. "Caelum, come with me," he abruptly said. "You can go see Lola."

I grinned. "Okay," I said, walking with him as we both went over to the Golden Gates, where I knew Lola was waiting patiently.

"Alright," Adiel said as we got closer. "Time to see the Souls." He opened the barrier, and then we both went inside, walking through the mist and into the Spirit Realm.

78

I followed Adiel as he strolled through the Spirit Realm, looking for Lola.

He was just about to call out to her, when I heard the Golden Retriever panting heavily. Lola ran toward us, appearing through the white mist. "Hi, sweet girl," Adiel said to her as she rubbed her head against his leg. "Good girl, Lola."

I grinned as Lola then came up to me, walking around my legs. She licked my hands happily. "Aww, thank you," I said, peering down at her.

Just watching Lola made me think of the conversation I'd had with Phoebe. About how much Phoebe and Camilla missed Lola.

I glanced over at Adiel, who was right beside me. "I want to bring Lola to Earth again, Adiel," I said. "Phoebe and Camilla, they both miss her terribly. I want to comfort them in a way."

Adiel nodded. "Okay, Caelum," he said, smiling slightly. "I'll allow that for you."

Lola whined as I landed on Phoebe's driveway. The Golden Retriever was excited.

I grinned as I put her down on the ground.

She automatically sat beside me, wagging her tail. She looked at my face expectantly, waiting for me to talk to her.

Aww, I thought. *You really are well behaved.*

I brought my attention to Phoebe's residence that was right in front of me.

Sunlight bounced off the windshield of the vehicle that was parked in the driveway, and the brightness also streamed into the house. The front door was shut as I looked at it, and it also appeared to be locked. That was until I heard Camilla bounding across the inside carpet.

She unlocked the door, skipping down the steps. Camilla passed me as Lola whined again, her tail wagging rapidly as she saw her former owner.

Lola glanced at me, waiting for a command, before I whistled at her. "Come on, Lola. Let's go inside."

And the Golden Retriever went up the front stairs, with me not far behind.

Lola glanced behind her as I advanced up the stairs and into Phoebe's house. Then she just sat down in the front room, her tail wagging across the rug.

I leaned toward her as I went inside, rubbing the Golden Retriever's ears affectionately. "Good girl, Lola. Good girl," I said, petting her as I peered around the front room. But I couldn't find Phoebe anywhere.

Where are you, Phoebe?

But right when I was getting nervous, I heard the wood floor underneath the carpet creak. It was upstairs, where the sound had come from.

I held my breath as I glanced at the steps leading to the bedrooms, only to see Phoebe coming down the staircase. Her long asymmetrical hairstyle was cascading past her shoulders, her body an hourglass shape as she wore a beautiful red dress. Her makeup was stunning, while she wore a cream-colored shawl to go over her shoulders. She also had Lola's pawprint necklace on.

Phoebe slowly made it down the steps as I stared. She was just so stunning...

It took me several moments to compose myself, and when I did, she was already downstairs, oblivious to the fact that I was there. Lola and I were completely invisible.

Phoebe sighed, going into the kitchen to get her purse off the counter. She rummaged through it before she found her cell phone. She quickly dialed a number.

"Hi," Phoebe said, "I'll be ready soon, okay? My daughter is outside playing. I have to get her inside, and then wait for her father to come by and pick her up. I'll let you know when I'm ready to go, I promise."

She hung up, putting her phone back in her purse. I saw her peer into the mirror, looking at her reflection. It seemed like she had no idea how gorgeous she was. Phoebe sighed, and then turned away from the mirror, instead walking over to where I was in the front room. I quickly moved into a corner, Lola following me calmly.

Camilla came back, running up the steps. Phoebe turned around as Camilla opened the door.

"Honey," Phoebe said, "I am going to go out to dinner with a friend of mine tonight. You will be going with Daddy, alright? He'll be watching you."

Camilla looked at her mother, and then spoke. "I'm going to Daddy's for the weekend?"

"Yes, honey," Phoebe said. "Do you have a bag packed?"

"I do," Camilla said, before running off to get it.

"Make sure you have your backpack, too. Get your school stuff in case you need it!" Phoebe called to Camilla.

"Okay, Mom!"

There was a sudden knock on the door, and I looked over to see Phoebe open it up. Derek stood on the other side of it. He cleared his throat as he met Phoebe's eyes.

"Camilla is coming," she said to him. "She just needs to get all of her bags."

Derek silently nodded, but I could see in his eyes he was attracted to the way she looked. Even when Camilla's footsteps resounded in the distance and Phoebe twisted around to see her little girl, I could see Derek staring at Phoebe. His eyes focused on Camilla after a few seconds, shifting away from his former love.

"Daddy!" Camilla yelled excitedly. "Daddy, you're here!"

She was carrying her duffel bag, as well as her backpack.

"Hi, Camilla," Derek said. "Do you have everything with you?"

"Yes, I do," his daughter replied.

"Okay," Derek responded. "Let's get going, then."

Camilla smiled and walked out of the house.

Derek carried Camilla's bags before glancing at Phoebe. "Thank you," he said, and then went down the steps with Camilla.

Phoebe watched the vehicle as Derek started it up, and then he drove off, leaving her driveway.

Phoebe sighed as she shut the front door, going into the kitchen, and getting her purse. She pulled out her phone, ready to call her friend, when it abruptly rang. Phoebe quickly answered it. "Hi," she said. "Yes, I'm ready. My daughter just went out with her father." Phoebe listened to the person on the other line as they spoke to her. "I feel good enough to go out and eat. No, I won't be able to drive," she said. "At least, not yet." Phoebe paused, listening to her friend. "Okay, I'll wait for you then," she said. "Okay, I'll see you in a few minutes."

She pulled the phone away from her ear, putting it into her purse before going into the front area of the house, where Lola and I were silently waiting.

Phoebe went by the front steps leading up to the bedrooms, before sitting down on them. She sat there, waiting patiently, all while Lola and I were in a corner. I gazed into Phoebe's eyes when she unknowingly turned her head toward me.

I felt my heartrate spike.

Lola sighed, the Golden Retriever still by my side as I looked down at her.

I whistled softly, and her ears perked up at the noise. Lola turned and locked eyes with me. "Hi there, sweetheart. Do you want to go see Phoebe?"

Lola continued to peer into my eyes, her tail thumping against the rug. I pointed at Phoebe, who was still on the front steps. Lola whined excitedly. "Go on, Lola," I encouraged. "Go see Phoebe."

Lola wagged her tail as she got up. She ran over to her former owner, her former owner who was oblivious to her presence. That was until Phoebe gasped, looking around as Lola sat right next to her. Phoebe appeared beyond perplexed as she felt her former dog's Soul. Phoebe blinked in confusion, and that was when the Golden Retriever couldn't seem to help herself. She licked Phoebe's hands that were in her lap. Phoebe's eyes darted to her extremity, her eyebrows scrunching up in bewilderment.

Lola whined, excited, while Phoebe just looked incredibly confused.

Phoebe sat on the staircase, bewildered, when there was the sound of a car pulling up into her driveway. She immediately got up, went to the kitchen, grabbed her purse, and went out the door, leaving Lola sitting next to the steps.

The Golden Retriever whined, but then, just as quickly as she'd left, Phoebe came back. She went into the kitchen to grab something that was on the counter. I whistled softly to Lola, and she came right over to me.

We both watched Phoebe for a few moments, before we walked out of the house.

My black wings became visible as I got a good grip on Lola, and I flew off into the Afterlife.

79

I let go of Lola as I entered the Afterlife, going over to the Heavenly River.

She followed me, and that was when I spoke. "Show me Phoebe."

"Thank you for driving me," Phoebe said while in the passenger seat of the vehicle. "I really appreciate it."

"No problem," the man replied, as he drove out of the neighborhood. "I enjoy driving this car. It's an incredibly rare make and model. The horsepower is…" He just trailed off, talking all about his car.

I saw Phoebe glance out of the side passenger window. She stayed silent while he just went on and on.

"…the brakes are awesome too," the man continued.

Phoebe turned to look at him. "Zack, I believe you," she said.

The man, Zack, stopped. "Do you not like my car?"

I do," Phoebe told him. "I'm just not into hearing all about the different features. The vehicle is great, though."

Zack looked away, toward the road. He appeared disappointed. He didn't talk for the rest of the ride. He was quiet even when he got to the restaurant parking lot.

Phoebe sighed as she unbuckled her seatbelt, closing her eyes and then opening them back up.

"What's wrong?" Zack asked.

"Nothing," Phoebe lied. "Nothing. It's nothing," she said, even though I could tell that she was nervous.

"Well, we're here," Zack said.

"Okay."

Zack got out of the driver's side door.

Phoebe waited for a few moments to get out of her seat, gulping as she looked at Zack, who was now heading into the restaurant. It was like he'd completely forgotten about Phoebe.

Phoebe, who looked gorgeous in her red dress, her makeup, and her cream-colored shawl. She gulped, and then eventually got out of Zack's vehicle. She shut the door, joining him. He quickly took his keys out to lock up his car.

It made a sound once it was shut and locked.

Then they both went inside the restaurant. Zack looked oblivious to the way Phoebe appeared, while she was looking uncertain. She didn't say anything though as they both went into the nice establishment, Phoebe following Zack as he headed indoors.

The Water became still as the image disappeared.

Pretty soon, all I was watching was myself: my confused, anxious reflection.

It was obvious that Phoebe was on a date with this man, Zack, that was the reason she was all dressed up, looking stunning.

But this Zack, he wasn't paying attention to her; he was just absorbed in himself.

I peered down at Lola, who was laying patiently beside me. She looked in my eyes.

"Oh, Lola," I said. "What is your former owner doing?" I brought my attention back to the River as it rippled. I stared into the Waters for a few moments before saying again, "Show me Phoebe."

Phoebe and Zack were sitting at a table. She sat at a booth, while he was across from her.

The lighting was dim, the atmosphere calm and relaxing.

Even though the food establishment appeared to be welcoming, Phoebe looked uncomfortable, but was trying to hide the way she felt.

Zack looked at her, his eyes on her scalp. Directly on Phoebe's scar. "That really is huge," Zack commented harshly. "I would be covering that up if I were you."

Phoebe gulped. "I used to, Zack. I didn't want to for tonight, though. I figured it was time to show what I really look like."

"Well, that is hideous," he said, as Phoebe just stared at him. Shock was on her face as she heard the words that he was saying. "I would definitely cover that up," Zack repeated. "How did you get that again?"

"I had brain surgery. I had a tumor growing inside my skull," Phoebe said, taken aback at how rude Zack was being.

"I would stay indoors until I got better, then. I wouldn't want people to see me in public. You look like an experiment gone wrong."

Phoebe just stared at Zack, flabbergasted at how disgustingly rude he was being. He was also very loud.

I saw Zack glance down at one of the menus on the table, and that was when I saw Phoebe peer around uncomfortably. She caught the eyes of one of the waiters, and he quickly walked over to the table. He seemed to understand how unsettled Phoebe was.

"Good evening," he said. "My name is Shaun. I will be your waiter. What can I get you to drink?"

I saw Shaun glance at Phoebe, before looking back at Zack.

She opened her mouth to speak, but Zack cut her off.

"We'll both have water," he said. Phoebe just looked at him, dumbfounded.

Shaun caught this but didn't say a word as he left.

Phoebe stared at Zack, who was still peering over the menu. "I didn't want water, Zack," she said. "Why didn't you let me order?"

"Because," Zack said, not even looking up, "I think that it is the best choice of drink. Just plain water."

"But I didn't want plain water."

"Well, you're on the mend from having major surgery. I need to decide what you can have because you're not well yet. That gigantic scar proves that." Zack peered over at Phoebe finally, glancing up from the menu. "I might as well order the food for you, too, since you're still sick."

Phoebe blinked, taken aback. Right when she was about to open her mouth, though, Shaun returned.

"One water for you, Sir," he said, glancing at Zack. "And one for you, Ma'am."

He put both waters on the table, watching Phoebe's eyes for a moment before walking off. She fidgeted a little in her seat as Zack took a sip of water.

He wasn't even paying attention to her. He was looking everywhere else, but not at Phoebe. She took a sip of her water, but then pushed it away from herself.

"Phoebe, you have to drink that," Zack said, catching what she had just done. "You need your strength back, if not, you won't heal." Phoebe stared at him. "You'll have that ugly scar if you don't follow my advice," Zack continued. "You'll be looking like a monster."

Phoebe's jaw dropped, and tears automatically filled her eyes. Zack didn't catch the reaction. Phoebe blinked away the liquid, before she slid out of the booth. "I need to use the restroom," she said. Zack just nodded.

He wasn't paying attention to her at all as Phoebe walked off, quickly looking for the bathroom that was by the front of the establishment. She opened the restroom door, sniffling as she looked at her reflection, trying to make sure that her makeup wasn't ruined.

Phoebe took a deep breath, looking into the mirror. She bit her lip. She breathed deeply, trying to steady herself, when she bolted out of the restroom. She ran to the front entrance of the restaurant before leaving. Phoebe ran out of the door, going out into the crisp night, leaving Zack behind.

The image disappeared in the Water, leaving me to peer at my reflection, my shocked, angry face.

How could that man be so mean to Phoebe? He was so cruel to her.

My teeth ground against each other as I thought about Zack. He was just so rude…

Phoebe, though, she was walking outside alone, with no one. That thought made me nervous. I had to go see her, make sure that she was okay.

I saw Adiel come from the Golden Gates as I turned around. I sighed.

He could take care of Lola while I went to see Phoebe.

My wings came out automatically then, and I flew out of the Heavens.

I landed near the restaurant, right where Phoebe had been a few moments ago.

No one was in the road, so I quickly said the words to become visible.

I had my eyes closed as I said them, but then opened my eyes back up when I heard sniffling. I saw Phoebe walking alone in the dark, heading away from the restaurant.

My eyebrows went up as I heard her. I had to go see Phoebe, talk to her. I ran over to where she was, walking right behind her before I said her name. "Phoebe?"

Phoebe stopped dead in her tracks as she heard my voice.

"Phoebe?" I asked again.

She slowly twisted her body around when she gasped. "Caelum?" Phoebe said. "Caelum, what are you doing here?"

"I was in the area, what's wrong?"

My eyebrows furrowed as I saw her expression. I walked up to Phoebe, who was sniffling and holding back tears.

"I was supposed to be on a date with someone, but he was so rude. I couldn't stand it. I had to get out of there."

My eyebrows furrowed again. "Who did you go on a date with?" I asked curiously.

"My Dad's boss has a son. His son, Zack, was who I went on the date with," she said. "Both my parents thought that I should see him, but he was being so incredibly rude... He said that my scar was hideous, said that I would look like a monster... I couldn't stand it, so I just left."

I gazed into her face, her beautiful face. "I'm so sorry," I stated. "That's horrible."

"I just had to leave."

Phoebe's face contorted as the pain of the words hit her. I took a few more steps closer to her, when she took me completely by surprise. She stepped forward and hugged me tightly, gasping and crying into my shoulder.

My heartrate quickened as I felt her warmth despite the cold night, and I pulled her close as she wept. I brought one hand up to her hair, touching her scar. She pulled away from me so she could look in my eyes.

Hers were slightly bloodshot as she gazed into my face. Her breath saturated my cheeks as we watched each other. My blood seemed to melt as she leaned forward.... She was inches from me, watching me carefully... My hand was still on her scalp as she pushed herself up on her tiptoes, getting herself to my height...

She gazed first at my eyes, then at my lips, and my heart was racing inside my chest. She kept on doing that, until she backed away, going back to her normal height.

Phoebe looked away from me, and my hand slid down her scalp slowly. I watched her close her eyes as she felt the sensation.

When she opened her eyes back up, she was staring at me. Her crystal blue eyes were watching.

It took a few moments to recover from what had just happened.

Phoebe looked at my face, staring into the essence of me, when she abruptly shivered. "I have to go," she said, taking her hands off my body as I blinked. I came back to the present.

"How are you going to get home?" I asked.

"I was going to call my parents. I have to talk to them anyway."

"Is it alright if I wait with you, Phoebe?"

She smiled. "Of course," she said while she pulled out her phone. "Of course, you can."

Phoebe called her parents while I waited beside her. I was quiet as she spoke into her cell phone.

She hung up, looking at my face. "My parents are on their way," she told me, to which I nodded.

"Okay," I said.

"Thank you waiting with for me, Caelum."

"You're welcome."

We waited a while for Mark and Susanna to get to the restaurant, but when I finally saw the car, I could see them both watching me. They were hesitant as they saw me, but then looked at Phoebe.

It was when I saw Mark and Susanna's stares that I took my cue to leave.

"Alright, Phoebe," I said, feeling anxious. "I'm going to go."

"You'll be back though, right?"

Always, I thought.

"Anytime, Phoebe. Anytime."

I started walking away as Phoebe went to go get in the back seat, when I heard Susanna's voice, and turned around.

"Thank you for waiting with our daughter," she said. I blinked and then smiled warmly.

"You're welcome," I said.

Then I walked off, into the chilled night.

80

I sighed as I watched the Golden Gates in the distance. My heart was pummeling my ribs, my breathing rapid. My thoughts just kept going back to the hug that Phoebe had given me. My blood turned to water as the memory engulfed me, taking over my brain. My insides melted at the mere thought.

Phoebe liked me.

"Adiel?"

"Yes, Caelum?" He emerged from the white mist, Lola beside him.

I grinned as I saw the Golden Retriever behind the Gates. I brought my gaze to Adiel and then backed away so he could open them.

He did so, and Lola ran to me.

Her tail wagged. Her tongue lolled out of her mouth as she walked around my body. She appeared to be smiling and licked my hands.

I smiled as I petted Lola, when Adiel laughed. "She certainly loves you, Caelum," he said. I looked over at him, a grin on my face.

Right as I did so, Lola pushed her bodyweight into my hips. I rubbed her ears as she looked up at me.

"You are just adorable," I told her as I petted the Golden Retriever.

Afterward, I looked up at Adiel. "I just came back from seeing Phoebe," I told him, my heart rate spiking. "I think…. that… that… she's beginning to like me."

Adiel nodded, smiling. "It's great that you're spending time with her," he said. "You're starting to enjoy the mortal experience, their lifespan. That's great, Caelum. That really is. You used to be so cautious when it came to the mortals, and now you're changing. Just remember what I told you before, that you can't show your wings to a healthy mortal. Our existence must be kept secret to them, alright?"

"Yes, I understand."

Lola's tail bumped my hips, and I looked down, immediately relaxing as I petted her.

"It's not just Phoebe that likes you," Adiel said, observing as I petted the Golden Retriever.

I just grinned as I heard his words, my heart pounding my ribs as I looked up at Adiel's brown eyes. "I guess so," I said, the grin still on my face. "I guess so."

A deep breath went through my lungs as I landed on the trail covered with trees. Quickly peering around my surroundings, I checked if anyone was nearby. When I didn't see any people, I said the words.

I walked off the trail, into the neighborhood where Phoebe lived. I headed toward Phoebe's home, just as Camilla opened the front door, bounding down the steps.

I smiled as I saw her. The expression was still on my face when I stopped by Phoebe's mailbox.

Then Camilla caught sight of me. She twisted around completely, instead running up the road in my direction. I smiled at the little girl as she stopped in front of me, looking in my eyes. "Hi," she said in a slightly timid voice. "Hi, Caelum."

I felt a warm grin on my lips. She'd remembered me, remembered my name... I crouched down to her level, the expression still on my face as I spoke to her. "Hi, Camilla," I said. "How are you?"

"Good," she replied. "I'm doing good. Are you here to see Mommy?" she asked.

I nodded at the small child. "Yes. I came to say hello. Is she around?"

Camilla nodded her small head. "Yes, she is. I'm going to go get her," the little girl said, glancing at the house before bolting over to the steps. She opened the front door, going inside before I heard her. "Mommy, Caelum's here!"

My breathing hitched as I focused on the small child, on the front door, and then... Phoebe was visible, looking at me with a happy expression on her face. My insides felt like liquid as we locked eyes, but then Camilla glanced at me, and I looked down at the pavement.

Camilla smiled at me once I was able to meet her eyes, and then she skipped down the steps, with her mother right behind her.

"Caelum," Phoebe breathed, causing my insides to feel like they were melting. "Caelum, you're here." She and Camilla both walked over to me. "How are you?" Phoebe asked.

Right when I was about to answer though, she threw her arms out in front of her, engulfing me in a hug. I hoped that she couldn't feel my heart that was pounding my ribs.

I smiled warmly, and then she backed away from me, gazing into my eyes.

"I'm doing well," I smiled, and then glanced at Camilla, who, despite her only being seven years of age, had a knowing look on her face. My heartrate picked up as I saw Camilla's appearance.

Camilla knew. But she kept quiet as she watched Phoebe and I.

I turned my attention back to Phoebe, who was so excited to see me.

"Would you like to go on a walk again? It is a beautiful day."

It was. The sunshine was illuminating the sky, sending warmth and light to the surroundings around us.

I nodded. "Sure," I said. "I'd be happy to."

"Let me go lock up the house then," Phoebe said, but then looked at her daughter. "Camilla, you're coming with us, since the house will be locked, and I don't want you alone."

Camilla first looked pouty but changed her expression within a few seconds. "Alright," she said, slightly upset. She didn't argue, though.

Instead, she just stood close to me as Phoebe ran to the house, quickly locking it, and then joined Camilla and I.

"I was thinking Spell Park again?" Phoebe looked into my eyes.

I nodded. "Okay," I said, glancing down at Camilla to see a grin on her face.

"Alright," Phoebe said. "Let's go on a walk."

81

Camilla ran ahead of Phoebe and I, skipping on her heels as we all walked along the trail. The trail which led to Spell Park. The little girl bounded along, glancing at her mother and I periodically.

I smiled at Camilla before she turned back around. I caught Phoebe out of the corner of my eye, smiling at her daughter, before I saw her looking at me steadily. Looking at me long enough to cause me to turn and gaze into her eyes.

Phoebe just brought her attention to the ground. A blush had settled on her face when she brought her eyes back to mine.

She opened her mouth to speak, but right when she was about to, Camilla squealed happily.

I looked up to see the trail ending, and Spell Park in the distance.

It was right after that that I saw Camilla holding out her arm. A monarch butterfly was on her extremity, perched on her skin. The colors on the insect were beautiful.

Camilla turned around, her smile radiating through the air, all while the creature stayed on her arm.

"Careful, Camilla," Phoebe said. "Be very careful."

Her little girl nodded, making sure that her arm was as still as possible, all while staring at the winged critter.

I came up to where Camilla was, as slow as I could so I didn't disturb the butterfly. I could hear Phoebe behind me, advancing toward the both of us.

The winged insect was beautiful and multicolored: black and white and orange.

Camilla turned to look at my face, and I saw that the smile had not left her. She was still ecstatic. The child continued to be as still as she could, and that was when the butterfly left her arm, instead flying over to my left shoulder. Camilla giggled as she saw me gaze at it. "Looks like you made a new friend," she said in a sweet, tiny voice.

"It appears that I did," I responded.

Camilla laughed as the butterfly stayed on my shoulder for a few more moments.

It flew off. I turned toward Phoebe, only to see the creature land on her right shoulder.

I squinted, thinking, as Phoebe stood as still as possible, trying not to move. She smiled as I continued to think.

The fact that that butterfly had landed not only on Camilla, but on Phoebe and I as well made me think that this wasn't a coincidence.

This was a sign. A sign that the other angels were watching over all three of us.

The stunning monarch butterfly finally took off. Phoebe turned and looked at me, partly dumbfounded, partly happy. She looked over at her daughter, who was grinning.

"Mommy, the butterfly liked you too," Camilla said, a laugh in her voice.

Phoebe just peered back over at me, appearing mystified. "I've never seen a creature act like that," she said. "To fly on all three of us."

"I haven't either," I replied, remembering exactly what Adiel had told me before.

Don't say anything about the angels, I thought. *Don't say anything.*

I saw Phoebe gazing into my eyes, and that was when I blinked, coming out of my reverie.

"That was interesting," I said, walking over to Phoebe's side. "I wonder what that was all about," I told her, although I was hiding the truth.

I glanced over at Camilla, who was watching Phoebe and I, the knowing look still in her blue eyes. She started giggling again as she twisted her body around. She ran over to where the trail ended, with Phoebe and I right behind her.

The butterfly was still on my mind as we walked. The sun shone brightly in the sky as Phoebe, Camilla, and I walked along Spell Park. Camilla still was skipping in front of us, bounding along.

I heard Phoebe laugh and turned to look at her. We locked eyes, before she spoke. "Camilla is almost always so upbeat. There are very few times that she isn't. She typically has a lot of energy."

I smiled. "Isn't that a good thing?" I asked.

"It is, but she's a handful sometimes," Phoebe stated. "She's a typical seven-year-old."

"She's taken care of though, you are a great parent," I said, to which Phoebe stopped walking, gazing into my eyes with her blue ones.

My heart raced as she stared, but then she blinked, and turned back around. She was looking at Camilla.

Tears were in her eyes as she twisted toward me. She began talking. "I was so scared for her, before. When I had the brain tumor and was in so much agony, I just kept thinking. 'What would happen to Camilla?' I met with my parents and Derek to make sure that they knew what was going on with me."

Phoebe took a breath, before continuing. "Now that the tumor is gone, I feel like a weight is off my chest. I'm so grateful to be alive. Those thoughts that I had when the tumor was in my head, they still come around. 'What will happen with Camilla?' That and the depressing thoughts that I used to have. I just start remembering the thoughts that were circulating in my brain."

Phoebe took a deep breath again, steadying herself as fresh tears stained her cheeks.

Automatically, I took a few steps toward her. "You're still here, Phoebe. You're here. You've recovered, Camilla is safe, and those depressing thoughts are gone. You should just focus on the future. Camilla loves you and you're no longer sick. You're safe," I told her as tears pooled in her blue eyes.

Phoebe blinked, and the tears rolled onto her cheeks.

"You're okay, Phoebe. You're okay," I said.

She sniffled, composing herself before, without even thinking about what I was doing, I brought my hands up to her cheeks. I brushed my fingers along her face, wiping her tears away. I felt Phoebe shudder. She closed her eyes, and then opened them back up, gazing into the essence of me. She did that for a few moments, but then she turned away, nodding.

"You're right, Caelum," she said thickly. "I should just focus on the future. I shouldn't look back."

I glanced at her before my gaze shifted to Camilla, who was still in front of us. She was just sitting on a bench not far from Phoebe and I, waiting patiently.

When her eyes locked with mine though, I could still see that knowing smile. Camilla knew.

The sensation of a warm hand in mine made me look down. Phoebe was grasping my extremity as we all walked around Spell Park.

I gazed at Phoebe, who just smiled in response. It seemed like both Phoebe and Camilla liked me.

That realization made me feel like I was flying, even though my wings were still hidden.

Phoebe and Camilla liked me. They liked *me*.

My heart pounded my chest, threatening to break through my ribcage as Phoebe continued to hold my hand.

She held it until we walked back to the neighborhood, going back to her house.

When we approached her home, she let go, smiling.

"Thank you for coming to the park with Camilla and I. I appreciate it."

"Anytime," was all I could get out. I was pretty sure that my insides were mush as Phoebe looked at me, and then advanced toward the front steps, Camilla right behind her.

Adiel was by the Heavenly River when I made it back up to the Afterlife. My heart was pounding so hard in my excitement that I thought that I was literally going to break my ribcage.

Adiel grinned at me. "I am happy for you, Caelum," he said, seeing how ecstatic I was. "I truly am."

I shook my head, coming back to the present, and then looked at Adiel. "Did you see the butterfly?" I asked. "The monarch butterfly? Or did you send it?"

Adiel smiled. "Caelum," he said, "if you saw a butterfly, that means that you are becoming one with nature. It is beginning to respond to you. Nature, as well as the angels. I didn't send that winged creature to you, or any other supernatural being. It just flew over to you by itself."

I blinked. "I thought you had sent it," I breathed.

"I didn't," Adiel said. "The angels and nature are responding to you now, Caelum. This is a great thing."

I nodded, happier than I'd ever been in my entire existence.

"You're doing great, Caelum," Adiel said to me, coming closer and thumping me on the back affectionately. "You're doing great."

82

T he sunlight warmed my face as I sighed contently.

I was on the top of a mountain, gazing into the gigantic orb of brightness. I watched all the colors dance along the horizon before I shut my eyes, welcoming the warmth as it enveloped me. It all was soothing. It helped me clear my head.

It was clear for a few moments, before Adiel's words came back to my awareness. *'The angels and nature are responding to you, Caelum. This is a great thing.'*

Nature was responding to me. Nature was responding to me. *To me.*

My heart pummeled my ribcage in excitement.

The angels and nature, they were now acknowledging me. That made me incredibly ecstatic.

I twisted around on the hard rock, maneuvering carefully, and then walked down the mountain, going partially on a trail that was nearby.

The sunset on the horizon was stunning as I gazed at it, glancing away for a few moments before I brought my attention back to it.

The sun, the hiking path, the Earth… It was all so beautiful, so hypnotizing, even for an angel. It was all just stunning.

I sighed again as I made my way down the trail, taking one more peek at the sunset before I immediately thought of Lemuel.

Lemuel.

How he Fell and became a mortal. How he fell in love with another mortal. How he turned into a Soul protecting her.

All the thoughts churned around in my head.

But most of all, I was thinking about Phoebe. How she was trusting me now. About how she had started to become comfortable around me. Phoebe. She had begun to trust me.

And that almost made my heart break my ribs.

A gigantic grin took over my face before my wings extended, and I flew off, away from the mountain top and into the atmosphere, the dimming sunlight warming my body as I did so.

Months passed. Months that I spent bringing Souls to the Afterlife. Any other moment was spent with Phoebe and Camilla.

Both were very welcoming as the time progressed. Luckily, the brain tumor which had taken over Phoebe's life wasn't present anymore. After a few months of her being free, she was getting happier and happier. Over the course of the months that went by, I also realized that Camilla was getting more and more comfortable around me.

Phoebe and Camilla, they both trusted me, and that realization was incredible.

Every time I would leave the mother and daughter to go back to Heaven, I would miss them terribly.

Adiel grasped what was happening since I was spending more time with them than ever before. Adiel didn't judge me at all.

He was just excited that I was finally opening up. I was allowing myself to experience the mortal emotion.

I stared at the glistening fluid that was the Heavenly River, staring at my reflection as Adiel came up from behind me. He looked at me through the Water.

"You're going to be checking up on Phoebe and Camilla, aren't you?" he asked.

I nodded. "Yes. Yes, I was going to," I said.

Adiel was beside me as I spoke into the enchanted liquid.

"Show me Phoebe and Camilla," I said.

The Water rippled, waves going across the fluid, and that was when I saw them in the Heavenly River. My heart raced as I saw the image, and Adiel was silent as I focused on what was in front of me.

Phoebe was on a couch, Camilla right beside her as the mother brushed her daughter's long brown hair.

Camilla began to talk as Phoebe went through her thick mane.

Camilla's back was to Phoebe as she spoke to her. "Mom, Mommy, can we go back to the park with the butterflies? That was really fun."

Phoebe smiled at Camilla's words. "Yes, we can, Camilla; we can do that soon."

"Can we go to the park with Caelum?"

Phoebe stopped brushing her daughter's hair as Camilla turned around, looking into Phoebe's eyes.

Phoebe just stared at Camilla.

"Mommy, can we? Can we? He can get all the butterflies."

It took a few moments for Phoebe to regain her composure. She blinked. "Well, honey, I don't know. I haven't seen him for the past few days," she said.

"Well, he needs to come back," Camilla said in a matter-of-fact voice. "He can help me catch butterflies."

Phoebe was still partly in shock as she looked at her daughter. "Maybe, Camilla. Maybe he'll come back."

"For my birthday, can he come visit?" the little girl asked.

"I'll ask Caelum once I see him again, okay?" Phoebe responded, smiling slightly at Camilla. "I'll ask him, sweetheart. I'll ask him."

Phoebe's smiling face faded as the Water churned, turning smooth.

My breathing was rapid, my heart pounding as I glanced over at Adiel. He was grinning.

The expression took over his entire face, and I just stared at him, feeling like my insides were doing somersaults.

Camilla. Camilla not only trusted me now. She wanted me around her, too.

She really liked me. She was excited to see me.

Adiel's smile caused me to feel like I was airborne. He then brought his hand up, walking over to me and thumping my shoulder affectionately. "Good luck, Caelum," he said encouragingly. "Good luck."

83

"Caelum?"

I glanced over at Phoebe, who was right beside me. We'd gone on another walk to Spell Park and then come back to Phoebe's house. She had just wanted someone to talk to, she'd said, someone to talk to besides her family. We were in the kitchen. I was sipping a glass of water as Phoebe spoke.

I answered her as I pulled the glass away from my lips. "Yes?" I responded.

"Would you be able to come to Camilla's birthday party? Her big day is coming up soon, and I wanted to make it special. She loves you, and I wanted to know if you would be able to be there. She'll be turning eight."

Phoebe gazed into my eyes, while my insides turned to mush.

I would never get used to this. Camilla asking about me when I looked in the Heavenly River, and then Phoebe saying, when I was beside her and visible, that Camilla loved me. Phoebe said that Camilla loved me.

I looked at Phoebe, focusing on her for a few moments before I cleared my throat to keep it from tremoring. "I'd love to come," I said as my heart pulverized my chest. "I'd love to come to Camilla's birthday party."

Phoebe grinned. It was a wide smile, one that I didn't even know existed. I'd never seen such happiness from her before.

"Thank you, Caelum. I can't wait to tell Camilla. She's going to be so excited!" Phoebe laughed, and instantly took me by surprise by giving me a bear hug. When she pulled away from me, she kissed my cheek, causing it to immediately get warm. "Thank you, Caelum! Thank you, thank you, thank you! This is going to make Camilla so happy!"

I smiled at Phoebe. "Anything for the both of you." Phoebe grinned. Anything for Phoebe and Camilla. Anything for the mother and daughter.

"Camilla, she really, really, likes you. She talks a lot about you, too."

I blinked, taken aback. "What does she talk about? What does she bring up about me?"

Phoebe looked me straight in the face. "Well, ever since she saw the monarch butterfly perch on your shoulder, she is determined to say that that was a sign. A sign that an angel was watching over us at Spell Park. Camilla is convinced that you're…. that you're… an angel."

I tried to not react to that one. My heart was pounding though, and I struggled to keep my breathing even. I tried not to show any expression at what Phoebe had just said.

"That's very sweet of Camilla to think that. She's a sweetheart." I smiled. "Both you and your daughter are very sweet."

I said it without thinking.

Phoebe just stared at me. Her face was frozen in a smile. I watched her expression for a moment before speaking.

"Both you and your daughter have been so kind to me over the past few months," I said to which Phoebe responded. "Camilla hasn't stopped talking about you since the last time she saw you,

Caelum. It's great that you will be at her birthday party. It'll be a delightful surprise for her."

"Where is she right now?" I asked, curious.

"Camilla is spending time with her father, and her grandparents. She hasn't seen Derek's parents in a long time, so I told Derek that he could spend the weekend with Camilla. She was excited to see him. They'll be back on Sunday," Phoebe said. "It'll be nice that you'll come for her birthday party though, Caelum."

"Well, tell her that I said hello," I said, grinning.

Phoebe just smiled back at me. "I will, Caelum," she said. "I will."

84

"Adiel?" I asked, pulling my wings into my back. I'd just come to the Afterlife, and Adiel was watching me carefully.

"Am I doing the right thing, being with Phoebe and Camilla, going over and seeing them? I know that you've already said that I am finally experiencing the mortal emotion, and that you are happy with me. I just... I'm just...not exactly sure what...what I'm doing."

I took a deep breath through my lungs, exhaling slowly as I brought my eyes back up to Adiel. They had been on the ground of the Heavens.

He just stared at me knowingly. "It's alright, Caelum," he said. "You're going to be okay. Every angel, and mortal, for that matter, has to start somewhere. I think it's amazing that you are finally not only letting the mortals in, you are also being so kind to them that they like you back. As for everything else, I think you are overthinking and being too hard on yourself. You are going to be just fine, Caelum. I now know how much you care for Phoebe, and her small child. Let the nervousness go, and just be yourself," Adiel said. "Just be yourself, Caelum. Be the best angel that *you* can be."

I sighed, taking in Adiel's words.

He looked at me steadily, trying to see if anything that he said had soaked into my consciousness.

I nodded, to which Adiel spoke. "Caelum, you'll be alright, I promise."

My black wings flew out in front of me, going to the left and right of my body as I landed in the woods near Phoebe's house. I closed my eyes, taking a deep breath before saying the words to make me visible. It was after that that I went along the path to the familiar neighborhood. I found it quickly.

I was surprised at how many cars were in the driveway, and I grinned instantly. A lot of mortals came for Camilla's birthday party.

A grin was on my face as I advanced toward the house, walking past the parked vehicles and up the steps.

I rang the doorbell, my heart in my throat, before I heard someone walk over to answer the door. Within moments, it opened, revealing Phoebe. "Caelum," she breathed. She sounded surprised and excited. "Caelum, you came."

I smiled once more at Phoebe, before I heard a squeal from inside the residence. Footsteps followed, and a few moments later I saw Camilla come into view. Phoebe laughed. Camilla was just so excited. She saw me, and that was when she ran outside, instantly hugging me around my middle.

I heard Phoebe gasp, and I looked up at her, my smile taking over my entire face. Phoebe's jaw was open in surprise as she saw her daughter hug my abdomen.

I glanced down at the little girl, before saying her name, getting her attention. "Camilla?" I asked. She looked up at me. "Camilla, how old are you today?"

The child's blue eyes locked on mine. "I'm eight today. Today is my birthday, and I'm eight years old, Caelum. Caelum, I missed you," she stated.

At that, I thought my heart was going to explode.

"Aww, thank you, Camilla. I missed you too, sweetheart."

I rubbed her back affectionately.

Camilla's hands fell to her sides, away from my abdomen. I crouched down on my knees, looking the little girl straight in the eyes. "How's your big day going so far? How's your birthday?"

"Good," Camilla said. "My mom and dad are here, and Grandma and Grandpa are coming too."

"That's really nice, Camilla," I said, peering into her face.

She had the facial structure of her mother, as well as her blue eyes. It was like looking at a mini-Phoebe.

My heart was pounding as I glanced at Phoebe, who was just smiling at the whole interaction between her daughter and I.

"Don't forget, Camilla, that your dad's parents are coming as well," Phoebe told her child.

Camilla's entire face lit up as she twisted around, looking at her mother. She then glanced over at me. "Yes, Grandma and Grandpa are coming, as well as my Daddy's mom and dad!"

The little girl squealed, excitement soaking her.

Oh, you cute little one, I thought as I watched Camilla.

Phoebe was grinning from ear-to-ear as she spoke. "Come on, Camilla. We all need to go inside."

The small child brought her attention to her mother, glanced over at me, and then ran back into the house. Phoebe glanced at her daughter before she looked back at me, grinning some more.

I straightened myself up from my crouch, and then walked up to Phoebe, walking past her and into the house. I stood at the entrance to the door, and then she motioned toward the inside of the home.

She followed close behind me, shutting the door and coming to my side as I began to walk into the living room, where Camilla's family members all were.

I gulped, glancing over at Phoebe for a split moment.

She just had a relaxed expression on her face.

I saw a small nod from her, and that was when I realized that she was letting me know that everything would be okay. Everything was going to be alright, meeting Phoebe and Camilla's family and friends.

The tight knot in my stomach dissipated as I continued to walk into the interior of the home. Phoebe was right beside me as I did so.

"Happy birthday, Camilla," I said as the small child blew out all the candles that were on her cake.

All eight of them.

Camilla looked up and smiled at me. "Thank you, Caelum," she said. Her grin was so wide that I could see two missing teeth.

"Aww," I said. "Did the Tooth Fairy visit you?".

I'd been an angel long enough to know that the small mortals believed in the Tooth Fairy, Santa Claus, even monsters under their bed.

"Yes, she did," Camilla responded. "She gave me five dollars!"

Out of the corner of my eye, I saw Phoebe laughing. She was right beside me, but I didn't want to glance at her, giving Camilla the clue that meant that her mother had given her the cash.

I just continued to focus on Camilla, her bright blue eyes, her excited energy. The little girl was just so precious.

Aww, Camilla, you are too cute. She kept her focus on me.

She held my attention for several moments, before turning toward everyone else who had come to the party. It was a good turnout. Phoebe, and her parents were there, as well as Derek and his parents.

There were even some children that were there that lived down the street. I recognized them but didn't know their names. The children were with their parents. Altogether, there were about eight to ten mortals who were present at Camilla's birthday party.

It was a great turnout for the little girl.

I brought my attention back to Camilla, and then glanced at Phoebe.

"I think it's time to cut the cake!" the mother said excitedly, looking at Camilla. The small child had a headband on that said, '*Birthday Girl.*'

Camilla beamed as Phoebe came to her side, grabbing the cake, holding it steady with one hand, while she cut it into pieces.

Phoebe sliced through the dessert, giving one to Camilla first, before glancing at everyone around the table.

"There's plenty of the cake for everyone," Phoebe stated. "If anyone wants some, it's here."

I saw the mortals that were around the table nod, and then smiled at Camilla as she ate the dessert.

I was smiling as Phoebe walked into the kitchen, getting some napkins for everyone. She then came back to my side.

I took a half glance at her, grinning, before I suddenly felt eyes on me. I looked around and saw that all the mortals were watching me.

Everyone, including Camilla.

I gulped nervously, and then found Derek, whose eyes were glued to mine. We looked at each other for what felt like an eternity, before breaking eye contact.

His gaze then went to Camilla, who was happily eating her dessert. He glanced at her, and then glanced at me.

I caught him raising his eyebrows a little, as he looked at Camilla, and then back at me. I knew what he was silently asking.

Are you taking care of Camilla? Are you taking care of my little girl?

My head moved slightly as I looked at Derek.

I gave him a nod, and then he blinked, bringing his attention back to his daughter.

The happy expression on Camilla's face gave me the strength to watch the mortals, smiling at all of them, including Phoebe. They all just grinned back, before turning their attention to the small child, who still had the *'Birthday Girl'* headband on.

I glanced at her, before turning to Phoebe, who gave me a relaxed expression. An expression that meant that I was okay, that I was welcome at the party.

I sighed before I followed Phoebe, who had walked over at the table where her daughter was.

Phoebe grabbed a paper plate that was nearby, cutting a slice of the birthday cake. She then handed the piece to me. I took it tentatively as Phoebe cut another portion. As she did so, she came to sit down at the table, next to where Camilla was.

I sat next to Phoebe, who just smiled at me.

That was when I realized that everything was going to be alright, that they all accepted me.

I was going to be okay.

85

"So, how was little Camilla's birthday party?" Adiel asked as I pulled my wings into my back.

I'd just arrived at the Afterlife. A grin appeared on my lips as I answered him. "It was great. Camilla gave me a hug, and then everyone, including me, ate some of the birthday cake. Everyone, including Derek, seemed to be welcoming."

"Who else was there?" Adiel asked.

"It was Phoebe, Camilla, Phoebe's parents, Derek, and Derek's mother and father. Camilla's friends were there too." I looked at Adiel. "There was a decent number of mortals there, all there for Camilla. So, it was fun."

Adiel had a soft expression on his face. "Well, it seems like you had a fun experience with the mortals. I'm excited for you. Caelum, you've opened yourself up so much since meeting Phoebe."

I smiled at him. I never thought, in all the millennia that I was doing my obligation to the mortals, that I'd ever become close friends with one. With a mortal. A mortal and her daughter.

I never thought that I would become so drawn to their lives. The single mother and her little girl. The two mortals that had my heart.

I exhaled slowly as I peered into the Heavenly River, studying my reflection. I glanced over at Adiel, who was watching me.

He just looked, a knowing expression on his face. Adiel knew that I was going to check on Phoebe and her eight-year-old daughter. He knew by now that I was now completely in their lives.

I glanced over at him for a split moment, and then spoke to the liquid. "Show me Phoebe and Camilla." The River Water rippled, before it became smooth, revealing the image in the fluid.

"Camilla! Come here, sweetie! Grandma and Grandpa are here!" Phoebe called out to her daughter, who was in her bedroom.

The mother was in the living room. The doorbell had just rung, so Phoebe went to open the door. Susanna and Mark were both on the opposite side of the threshold. They smiled at Phoebe, who just said, "Thank you for doing this. I think Camilla will love it."

At that moment, Camilla bounded into the room, happiness soaking her. "Grandma! Grandpa!" she yelled excitedly. She then ran toward Susanna and Mark, hugging them both, before turning around and looking at Phoebe. "Mommy, Mom, what's going on?" Camilla asked curiously.

It was Susanna who answered. "Camilla, honey, Grandpa and I have a surprise for you. Do you have a bag packed?"

Camilla nodded, and then her eyebrows creased together as she tried to think about where she was going, what the surprise was. The little girl glanced at her mother, who just smiled.

"Camilla, go get your bag, honey," Phoebe said. Camilla bounded away, going into her bedroom.

Mark, Susanna, and Phoebe waited patiently. Phoebe's parents had stepped inside the house.

Camilla ran back and looked at her mother, her Grandma, and Grandpa. Her bag was on her shoulder. "What's going on?" Camilla asked, curiosity drenching her.

Phoebe grinned, before she asked a question. "Camilla, did you pack for a week? For all seven days?"

The child blinked and then looked into her mother's face. She nodded.

"Yes. Yes, I did, Mommy," Camilla said, still curious. "What's going on?"

She brought her attention to her mother, and then her grandparents. They were all smiling at her.

Phoebe looked over at her parents, raising her eyebrows questioningly.

Her parents nodded, before Phoebe turned to her daughter. "Camilla, honey, Grandma and Grandpa have a surprise for you. For your big day, even though it has passed, Grandma and Grandpa still want to take you somewhere."

Phoebe grinned, glancing at her parents for a split moment.

Camilla immediately perked up. The little girl watched all three of the mortals that were around her.

"Camilla," Susanna said, "we're going to go to your favorite amusement park, as well as the aquarium. They are all out-of-town, so that's why you had to pack for seven days. We're going to go to a lot of places this week, in celebration of your birthday."

Camilla's eyes widened as her Grandma spoke, and then froze as the words soaked in. She ran over to Susanna, hugging her around her middle. "Thank you, Grandma and Grandpa! Thank you, thank you, thank you!"

"You're welcome, sweetie," Susanna said as she put her hand on Camilla's back affectionately. "You're welcome, Camilla. You're welcome."

The little girl was beaming as she looked at Susanna and Mark. She looked at them, a smile radiating throughout her face.

But then Camilla paused, the grin frozen on her lips. She turned her head to the side and brought her attention to her mother. "Mom, Mommy, are you coming too?"

Phoebe crouched onto her knees to get to her daughter's level. She spoke. "Camilla, honey, I won't be going with you. This trip is only for you, Grandma, and Grandpa. You behave for them, alright? I expect you to be good, okay?"

Phoebe raised her eyebrows slightly as she spoke to Camilla.

"But what are you going to do?" her daughter questioned.

At that, Susanna, Mark, and Camilla all stared at Phoebe. She shrugged.

"I don't know," Phoebe said. "You're in good hands though, Camilla. Grandma and Grandpa will take care of you. I might just clean the house when you are gone. I might do all the boring stuff."

Camilla blinked. "Oh, okay, Mommy."

Phoebe glanced at her mother and father, before looking at her daughter. "You're going to have to tell me all about your trip when you come back, okay, sweetie?"

Camilla nodded.

"Alright, honey," Phoebe said. She hugged her child, and then looked at her parents once more. She nodded at them silently, and then smiled. "Have a great trip, Camilla," she told her little one before her parents turned away with their granddaughter. They went down the steps and into their vehicle.

Phoebe just watched them leave. "Bye, Camilla," she said softly. "Be safe."

The River moved as the image disappeared.

Within moments, I was just looking at my own reflection. My blue eyes and short brown hair.

Adiel was staring at me through the Water. I brought my attention to him, taking a deep breath, and then exhaling. He just looked at me.

I looked at him for a few moments before I spoke.

I had just remembered what Phoebe had told me. It was the day that she'd asked me if I could come to Camilla's birthday party.

"Adiel," I said, the conversation springing into my mind. "Phoebe told me once that Camilla thought that I was an angel."

Adiel blinked, and then stared at me. "When did little Camilla start thinking that?" he asked.

"Phoebe told me after all three of us went to Spell Park. She said that her daughter thought that because of the way the butterfly was acting that day. She thought that I was an angel because of the creature landing on all three of us when we were at the park."

Adiel looked at me, watching me closely. "How did you respond, Caelum?"

"I tried to keep my face neutral when Phoebe said that."

Adiel nodded. "That's good, Caelum. Just remember, if you want to still see Phoebe and Camilla, you *must* keep your wings invisible."

"I'll remember," I told him.

"That's interesting though, that Camilla had that thought," he said.

Interesting and true, but I couldn't tell her that she was right. I would never be able to tell the little girl or her mother. I couldn't tell either of them that the child was right.

I wouldn't be able to tell the little one the *truth*.

I would have to hide it. Hide it every time I saw Phoebe and Camilla.

Every time I interacted with them.

86

A diel looked me in the eyes, holding them with his. "Caelum, I want you to be careful, but I also want you to be happy. I know I constantly tell you this, but just… stay safe, alright? Promise me. Promise me, Caelum."

Adiel's brown eyes stayed on my blue ones.

I nodded. "I promise," I told him. "I promise to be careful and safe."

Adiel looked at me for several moments before nodding and turning around, walking off in the direction of the Golden Gates. He left me alone. I was just standing right in front of the Heavenly River, taking in my reflection before the wings came out of my back. I flew off.

I kept a close eye on Phoebe throughout the week, when she was alone. I knew that she was going to be alright, but I still worried. I still worried about Phoebe. The mortal that I was in love with.

"Hi, Lola," I said happily, stroking the Golden Retriever's head.

I'd just come back to the Afterlife. I'd brought a Soul to Heaven, a Soul of a woman who had a heart attack because of diabetes. She'd passed away after not following her diet.

Adiel had taken the Soul, walking with her to the Golden Gates, but I had followed them.

I'd told Adiel that I wanted to see Lola, and now was just playing with Phoebe's former pet. She was still incredibly sweet, running around in circles, her tail wagging rapidly.

"Aww, sweetie," I said, rubbing her ears, which caused her to moan. "You're a good dog. Good girl, Lola. Good girl."

It was when the Golden Retriever stopped and looked into the white mist that I turned around, bringing my attention to Adiel. He'd materialized out of it. He grinned as he saw Lola, and then looked over at me.

"Still attached to Lola, I see," he said, his expression taking over it entirely.

I grinned back at him, nodding wordlessly.

"Phoebe is always on your mind," he said.

That was a statement. A true statement.

I sighed before I spoke. "I want to go to the Heavenly River again. I want to see her again."

I was constantly worried about her. She was always on my mind.

Adiel knew that already. He knew how much I cared for Phoebe. He looked at me before he nodded. "Okay, Caelum," he said. "Let's go."

Lola's ears perked up as Adiel said that, and she whined, her tail wagging.

She ran up to Adiel, licking his hands. He just smiled. "Hi, honey. You can come too, Lola," he said, the expression still on his face. "You can come too."

Adiel glanced up at me. I still had a grin on my lips as he turned, going toward the Golden Gates.

I was right behind him, Lola beside me as we walked away from the Soul Realm.

My heart was pounding in my chest as I gazed down at the Heavenly River. Adiel was beside me as I did so.

I took a glance at him quickly, our eyes meeting for a split moment before I looked back into the Water. I inhaled slowly, exhaling as I tried to steady myself.

It took a few seconds. I closed my eyes before opening them back up. It was after that that I spoke, with as much confidence that I could have. "Show me Phoebe Bright."

The house was dimly lit as Phoebe walked around inside, pacing a few times before she just sank into a nearby couch.

She ran her fingers through her hair, moving it quickly. Phoebe blinked several times, throwing half of her hair to the other side of her head. Then she gazed down at the carpet, sighing. She looked straight at a lamp, a lamp that was illuminating the surroundings, causing a soft sunset color to be in the home.

Phoebe was lost in thought, putting her hands in her lap, lacing them together in order to stay still.

She just sat on the couch, thinking.

Phoebe sat like that for a while.

The Heavenly River rippled as the image evaporated. I squinted in confusion, my eyebrows furrowing as I looked at Adiel, who watched my face.

He blinked, appearing a little confused as well. A moment later though, it seemed like realization slammed into him. His breath caught, and he stared at me.

My facial expression was confusion again as I watched Adiel.

"What, Adiel?" I asked him, my bewilderment visible through my body language.

But Adiel just stared, blinking every few seconds. He continued to stare at me until he finally sighed.

Wordlessly, he walked up to me, grasping my shoulder. I looked in his eyes.

I felt Lola's fur brush against my hand. I blinked before I glanced down at the Golden Retriever. I'd completely forgotten that she was there.

When I looked back at Adiel, he was still holding my shoulder, a look in his eyes that I'd never seen before.

It was a mixture of calm and anxiety, if that could ever happen to an angel. It was also an expression of hesitation.

Adiel continued to look at me before he released my shoulder, glancing down at Phoebe's former pet. "Come on, Lola. Let's go, girl," he said, and the Golden Retriever bounded after him as he walked off toward the Soul Realm, leaving me near the Heavenly River.

Only once did Adiel twist his body around, looking at me before he reached the Golden Gates.

"Stay safe, Caelum," he told me as I focused on him. "Stay safe."

87

I stood next to the Heavenly River, lost in thought as I peered into the Water, looking at my reflection.

I stared at my face, my confused expression. Adiel's reaction to Phoebe in the enchanted liquid puzzled me. He'd never acted like that before.

Blinking for a few moments before my wings came out of my back, I flew off. I headed in the direction of Phoebe's house.

It didn't take long for me to get to her residence.

The sky was ink-black as I landed in the street. There were very few lights on inside the homes in the neighborhood.

Which was a good thing. I could easily say the words that would make me visible.

Quickly, I did so, but when I opened my eyes, I saw that the lights were still on inside Phoebe's home.

I blinked several times, trying to understand, but then just walked over to the driveway before advancing toward the front door.

I knocked a few times and then waited patiently for a response.

Within seconds, I heard footsteps, and then… the door opened, revealing Phoebe.

She blinked several times in surprise, and then finally spoke. "Caelum?"

"Caelum?" Phoebe repeated, opening the door farther when she saw me. She shifted her feet a little as she looked at my face.

"Hi, Phoebe. Are you alright?" I asked.

She blinked several times again. It took her a moment to respond. "Yes. Yes, I'm okay." She sighed for a moment, glancing into her home before she spoke. "Come on in, Caelum. I don't want you to freeze outside. The temperature is supposed to drop."

I smiled at Phoebe as she opened the door wide, allowing me to enter.

"Come on in, Caelum," she said, backing up as I walked in, before shutting the door.

The warm light was still flooding the area, and I gazed around the inside of the home, a little confused. Usually, mortals were asleep currently, during this phase of night.

I guessed that Phoebe couldn't sleep. Something had kept her up late. I scrunched my eyebrows together at that thought.

But then, suddenly, I was wondering why I'd come here, to Phoebe's residence at this time of night, for the mortals.

That was all that was going through my head before Phoebe spoke, bringing me back to the present.

I turned to look at her.

"What are you doing out so late?" she asked curiously, gazing into my face.

I blinked. "I... I... forgot what time it was when I left. I got caught in the dark on the way back to my place, and just saw that the lights were still on at your home." I took a deep breath, my heart pounding as I told the lie.

The truth was that I really didn't know why I'd come to Phoebe's home, this late at night...

"I just wanted to check up on you," I continued as she turned her head a little, squinting at what I was telling her.

"I guess Camilla was right then," Phoebe said softly, so gently that I could barely hear her.

I blinked a few times before I spoke. I was suddenly clueless. "Camilla was right about what?"

"About you," she said. "About you being a Guardian angel. You've come here to watch over me."

My heartrate sped up as my breathing became rapid, and I felt my muscles become rigid. I tried breathing through my nose, trying to calm my pummeling organ inside my ribcage.

She just looked at me as I stared at her. It took me several moments to talk again. "I... I was just making sure you were safe, Phoebe," I said, stuttering a little when I began the sentence.

"Well, I am," she said. "Thank you."

Why are you in Phoebe's house, Caelum? I asked myself this question in my head, quickly knowing I was out of my element. *Why are you here? Why are you here? Why are you here?*

I swallowed the lump that had risen in my throat, before I just looked at Phoebe, completely feeling out of place. "I... I'm... I'm sorry," I stammered. "I'm glad you're alright, but I have to go," I said, quickly glancing down at the carpet.

I looked at Phoebe's face, turning around afterward. I guessed that my cheeks were beet red as I began to walk across the soft ground toward the door. "I'm just going to… Leave now," I told her as I walked away. I didn't look around at her for fear of her seeing my burning cheeks. "I'm going to… go," I continued.

My heart was pounding so hard my pulse was in my skull. I'd only just touched the door handle when I heard Phoebe's voice.

"Wait, Caelum." Her soft tone soaked my arteries, and I automatically shut my eyes as I heard her. "Caelum," she said again, and I heard the floor slightly creak as she walked closer.

I twisted around, my insides liquid. I saw her advance toward me, but I felt like my entire body had just locked up.

All I could do was just look at her. Her blue eyes, her beautiful complexion…

My muscles were completely locked into place. I couldn't move as she walked toward me; my heart was racing inside my ribcage as my eyes locked with Phoebe's. She just gazed at me intently, studying my reaction as she moved.

"Caelum," she repeated. My blood turned to water.

I inhaled deeply, exhaling as Phoebe peered into my face. My pulse was now in my head, my insides feeling like liquid as she watched me.

Phoebe walked even closer, and I felt my breathing become hitched. I couldn't take in air, couldn't think, as I began to feel her exhale on my skin. She got within touching distance, but I couldn't register what was happening.

I was frozen. I was frozen as Phoebe put her hands on my chest, settling them on my pounding heart, and I closed my eyes automatically. The feeling drenched my arteries. Phoebe's hands were so warm…

Her breath went into my skin, soaking into my pores, and it was a split second later that I registered the feeling of Phoebe's lips on my cheek.

It sent a shockwave through my body as she continued to trail her kisses down my face, but I stayed still as her mouth met mine. The sensation was so soft, so tender, it felt like butterfly wings against my lips. It caused my heart to flutter inside my chest, before I felt Phoebe pull away.

A few moments passed as the feeling soaked into my being, and then I opened my eyes, opened them to see her staring.

Our oxygen was entangled at this point, she was so close to me, but she had backed away. It was as if she was checking to make sure if she had done anything wrong.

Phoebe just continued to peer into my eyes.

The gaze she was giving, the way we were so close together with our breathing intertwined, the butterfly-soft kiss that she had just given me...

Phoebe hadn't done anything wrong.

Her exhale soaked my face as I leaned toward her, bringing my right hand up to her left cheek as I kissed her back. I stroked her warm skin gently, and I felt a shudder ripple through her.

Phoebe inhaled quickly as she reacted to me immediately, and suddenly I felt like a starving being, hungry for her kisses. I felt her mouth against mine, and it was like lightning through my arteries. I was quickly drowning in the need for her, the need to be close to her.

I loved Phoebe. I loved her. I kissed her and the sensation caused my insides to become liquid.

Our panted breaths soaked our skin as we broke away from each other. Phoebe's hands abruptly went down my chest, and I felt the warm feeling trail after it. Then her hands were on my hips, moving up my bare skin underneath my clothing.

My breathing stopped as I realized what she was doing, what she wanted.

She paused, her hands on my bare chest under the fabric, on my pummeling heart. But then I just pulled her close, tasting her oxygen...

Phoebe's mouth was on mine again, and by that point, my mind had completely caught on fire. I agreed with her. She broke away for a moment, the air from her lungs saturating my skin. Phoebe breathed into my lips, but then I abruptly had to ask her.

I had to. I *needed* to.

"May I?"

My hands were on the corners of her ribcage, but I wouldn't move them. Not until I watched her nod. She gazed into my eyes. "Yes," she murmured, and her lips were on mine once more.

My fingertips grazed along the fabric of her shirt before moving downward, along the skin of her hips.

She broke away, only to drench my pores with the air she exhaled. Her hands roamed once more down my chest, and I could feel my entire body blazing. All I wanted was Phoebe.

She brought my sweat-soaked shirt up and exposed my flesh, and I helped her as she took the piece of clothing off my body. She threw it on the carpet before kissing me.

Phoebe, I thought as she sent lightning through my veins. *Phoebe...*

But I couldn't continue my brainwave as a groan shook through my throat.

Phoebe had begun to run her hands over my abdominal muscles, and then my chest, trailing her palms up to my neck. My body was burning as I continued to feel Phoebe's midriff. I swiftly picked her up, causing her to inhale.

Her breath drenched my face as I lifted her off the carpet, carrying her across it, all while her lips were on mine… I brought us both to the bedroom nearby, all while we were enamored with each other…

Vaguely, I was aware of all our garments ending up on the floor, and Phoebe kissing my cheek. Heat continued to rage through me, taking every thought in my brain with it.

I kissed Phoebe as my flesh glistened, and a moan escaped her windpipe as my lips met her jaw gently, trailing down her throat to her sternum… I tasted the perspiration on her skin, and could feel her heart pulse under my touch…

Her breath drenched my skin, her voice causing my heartrate to quicken. "Caelum," she sighed softly. "Caelum."

Phoebe pulled me close as my mouth met hers.

All I wanted was Phoebe. All I wanted was her as my body burned, raging with all the flames that consumed me.

The inferno blazed for a while.

88

I shut my eyes, inhaling deeply before exhaling slowly. My thoughts were running wild inside my head. My heart was pummeling my ribs, while the same brainwaves were rapidly circulating inside my mind.

Caelum…Caelum, what have you done? What have you done? What have you done? I opened my eyes back up, staring at the bedroom ceiling. *What am I doing?*

My mind was racing, but it had been doing that throughout the night, since I couldn't sleep. Angels were unable to get any shut-eye, since our obligation required us to be alert always. So, I had been awake throughout the darkness, trying to get a grip on what had happened earlier.

Just thinking about it made heat rush through my cheeks. It made my entire body feel like an electrical wire.

My heart was racing as I tried to keep my breathing even, but then I heard a moan beside me, and realized that Phoebe was awake. I heard her sigh as she turned around in the bed, smiling at me as she rested her head on my chest. I just gazed into her blue eyes, and was so taken aback by her beauty that I couldn't speak for several seconds.

Phoebe rested her head on my left shoulder, just looking at me and smiling, before she spoke. "Good morning, Caelum."

She put her hand on my bare chest, over my pounding heart, and I found myself staring at her, transfixed by how gorgeous she was.

My eyes were on her before she leaned forward, moving her hand to my neck, and kissed me.

The sensation jolted through my bones, but then I quickly felt the warmth of sunlight streaming through the window, soaking my skin. I brought my hand to Phoebe's cheek, stroking it gently as my lips brushed against hers. I pulled away when I felt the illumination hit my face. I sighed, the sound echoing through the room. I grinned at Phoebe before I spoke. "Hi," I said, looking at her, her crystal blue eyes.

Her expression was happy as she leaned in toward me, speaking softly into my lips. It sent tingles down my spine.

"Hi, Caelum," she breathed, kissing me. "Good morning," she repeated.

My body turned into mush as our oxygen became intertwined. It was a few moments later that she backed away.

Phoebe looked at me steadily, and I realized that I had forgotten to breathe.

I inhaled, and that was when the sunlight had begun to shine right into my eyes. It was as if the angels were telling me that it was the right moment to get up.

I squinted slightly at the bright illumination, and that was when I finally got out of the bed, putting my clothing on. I could see Phoebe watching me from my peripheral vision.

She propped up on one elbow, pulling the bedsheets to cover herself. "Do you need to go somewhere?" she asked.

I turned around to look at Phoebe, gazing into her face. "Yes," I said, watching her. "Yes, I do. I will be back though, I promise."

Phoebe and I watched each other, before I walked over, taking her head in my hands, and kissed her.

"I'll be back, I promise," I breathed into her lips after I broke away.

I felt her nod. "Okay," she said softly. "Alright."

"Adiel? Adiel, are you there?" I stood in front of the Golden Gates, staring through the gargantuan fence, waiting for him to walk through the mist.

I needed to talk to him. I just needed to talk to him.

Moments passed as I just stood on the other side of the barrier, the memories from the night before swirling around in my head. Just like the white fog that surrounded the Soul Realm.

Adiel? Adiel, where are you?

I sucked in a lungful of oxygen as he appeared through the substance, his facial expression unreadable as his eyes connected with mine.

It seemed like he wasn't showing a lot of emotion, but he was also very cautious about what he was going to say.

I breathed deeply, trying to keep my emotions in check, as well as my heartrate. I exhaled in a gust.

I opened my mouth to speak. Nothing could come out as I struggled for the words though. I tried once more, but then I just stopped.

Adiel made his way toward me, nodding slightly. I backed away from the Golden Gates, allowing him to say the words so they would open. He did so, and then walked over. His expression was still unreadable. He still appeared incredibly stoic.

I blinked several times, trying hard to keep calm, before I started to speak. "I... I..." I began, but then paused. "I... Am I... Am I going to lose my wings, Adiel?" I asked, stuttering a little as I spoke. "Am I going to get my wings taken away from me?" My heart was pounding so hard I could feel it in my head. "Adiel. Adiel, I..." But then I trailed off, unable to speak because I was so nervous.

Adiel's brown eyes locked on mine then, and I paused.

He stared for several seconds. Afterward, he spoke. "Caelum," he said. "Caelum, was what happened... was it done with consent? Consent from both of you?"

I blinked, the memories of the night before taking over my brain.

My heart pummeling my ribcage as I sighed Phoebe's name... My lips meeting her neck, kissing her flesh, tracing down to her collarbone...

Heat flooded through my face at the thought, but then another one made its way through my mind.

Phoebe's hair cascaded down her shoulders when she ran her palms over my bare chest... My eyes had closed as warmth crept up my body, and the movement of her hands caused my skin to immediately prickle. Her long hair tickled my cheeks as she brought her mouth to mine...

I shook my head, coming back to the present again, and I saw Adiel staring at me, waiting for an answer. An answer to a question that I'd forgotten immediately.

"Caelum?" Adiel asked. "Caelum, was everything that happened, did it happen with consent? With both of yours?" He repeated the question, raising his eyebrows, wanting to know the response.

The memories from the night before were so strong…

It took a moment to think though about what Adiel was asking. But then I nodded. Everything had happened with both of us agreeing, so yes, the answer was yes. "Yes," I said, my voice slightly scratchy. "Yes, it did," I told Adiel.

Our eyes met as he watched me. Adiel inhaled, exhaling deeply, before he spoke. "Caelum, if everything that was done, if both of you agreed to it, you will not lose them. If you were violent toward her, then you would immediately lose your wings. Since that will never happen, you are safe."

Me? Hurt Phoebe? Never in millennia would I ever hurt Phoebe.

But if everything was done with us agreeing, there was nothing to worry about. So, I was basically nervous about nothing.

"Caelum," Adiel said, causing me to blink and then look at him. "Caelum, you are going to be alright. You won't lose your wings."

I instantly felt like a huge rock had gotten lifted off my chest. My breathing became even again, and I nodded.

"Okay, Adiel," I said. "Alright."

89

My heartbeat was in my skull as I brought my attention to the Heavenly River, watching the clear Water for a few moments before I said, "Show me Phoebe."

Phoebe was sitting on a couch in the living room, her gaze on nothing as she sighed. It was a loud exhale, but I could also hear a noise come from her. It was almost like a groan, mixed with a sob.

"Oh, Phoebe," she said out loud to herself. "Oh, Phoebe, what have you done?"

She crossed her legs on the couch she was on, and then she put her head in her hands, running her fingers through her hair quickly once more.

"What did you do? What did you do that for? Now you scared him off…"

Her voice hitched at that last statement, and immediately tears started coming from her eyes. Her crystal blue eyes turned raw, and she gasped for air.

No, no, no, I thought as I saw the River ripple, going back to its normal state. *No, Phoebe, don't cry...* I looked up from the Water, only to see Adiel looking back at me.

I hadn't seen or heard him come up to the enchanted liquid at all.

My mind was racing as I saw him, and then I felt my black wings come out, and I flew out of the Afterlife.

My feet hit the pavement before my wings flew in front of me, stopping my body from falling forward. My thoughts were whirling around inside my head, but all I could really focus on was the way Phoebe was beating herself up.

Thinking that I had run off after what had happened... Thinking that I had left her for good after what we did...

My eyes were on Phoebe's residence for a few moments before I looked around at the surroundings.

There was no one outside, but I still walked under the shade of the large tree in the front yard. It was dark enough that nobody would be able to see me.

I shut my eyes, said the words, and then sighed, making my way over to the front door of Phoebe's house.

I knocked twice, my breathing rapid, before the door opened, and Phoebe was there.

Her blue eyes were still slightly raw. She spoke with an uneven tone, like her voice was broken. "Caelum?" she said.

I just stood there, looking at her before she backed up, allowing me to come inside. I did so, turning around and staring into her face. Her facial expression still looked slightly contorted in guilt, sadness, and anger. Anger, it seemed, at herself.

Why would she be angry at herself?

"Caelum," Phoebe started, but I cut her off, instead taking her chin in my palms and kissing her. It was several moments until I broke away. Even then, my lips went on Phoebe's again.

I heard a moan build in the back of her throat, and pulled away from her, my fingertips grazing across Phoebe's cheeks. Her eyes were closed, and I felt her tilt her head into my right hand, leaning into it.

She brought her hand up to mine, grasping my arm gently. Phoebe brought my hand to her lips, kissing the center of my palm, sending tingles down my spine. Then she watched me, piercing my whole being with her gorgeous look.

"Phoebe," I said, but then it was her turn to cut me off.

Her mouth was on mine before I could finish what I was going to say. She was suddenly kissing me in a way that was taking over the entire essence of my being. Phoebe engulfed my mind for a while.

I felt it when Phoebe began to back away.

The sensation of her kiss lingered though, burning its way into my brain so that it wouldn't leave for the rest of my existence.

The feeling made my heart flutter, and I felt Phoebe's oxygen brush against my face, causing me to shiver. Her lips pressed against my cheek, but then she pulled away, her voice soft as she spoke.

"Caelum," she whispered into my ear, causing me to shudder. "Caelum, I love you."

90

P hoebe pulled away. Her breath hitting my skin was enough to make my eyelids flutter and close.

I just gazed at her, unable to say anything because my voice had been stolen from me. Stolen by her beauty.

I couldn't speak as she watched me steadily. I instead leaned forward, bringing my mouth to hers. It was only afterward that my voice returned.

I pulled away slightly, her breath tickling my cheeks as I did so.

"I love you too, Phoebe," I said softly, before backing away a little to kiss her cheek. Her skin felt so warm…

It was a few seconds later when I backed away once more, looking into her blue eyes.

The sunlight streamed through the window nearby, and under the illumination, Phoebe's eyes made her look like a supernatural being, like myself.

She was just so stunning…

A young child's squeal made me blink, instantly alert. It pulled me back to reality.

I turned my head toward the window, automatically thinking of Camilla, before I just relaxed. It was just a child playing outside.

But then my mind was on Camilla. Camilla. *Camilla…*

I brought my attention back to Phoebe, and I could tell from the look on her face that her thoughts were on her daughter.

"Camilla," she said, blinking. "Camilla," she repeated, trailing off before looking at me nervously. She hesitated, and then opened her mouth to speak. "Caelum. Caelum, I'm sorry, but you have to leave." Phoebe suddenly appeared extremely anxious. "My parents, they'll…" she trailed off, but I knew what she was going to say.

Even though I knew Susanna and Mark personally, through Camilla's birthday party, I wasn't sure if they would approve of me.

Meeting me in this manner, where I had spent the night with Phoebe. Both of us-Phoebe and I-were unsure on that one.

Phoebe breathed deeply, running past me as she quickly straightened up her home.

I squinted, following behind her slowly, before I finally brushed her arm. She turned around, pausing. She gazed at me. That was when I spoke.

"Whatever happens, you are loved, Phoebe."

I moved in close, kissing her softly. I pulled away, looking into her eyes.

Phoebe nodded understandingly, before I walked over to the front door and left her residence.

91

The guttural, bone-crunching, almost instantaneous crack rang in my ears as I stood on the sidelines of the football game. High school football.

The victim had fallen to the ground after the tackle, but, like I knew would happen, he didn't get up. Even though he had just gotten pushed to the ground, given the equipment that he had on, I didn't know what the bone-crunching crack was.

I knew though, that the young man had broken something. Something important.

I found out, moments later, that it was the guy's back.

He had recently had surgery, and, as soon as he had been cleared to play again, he had. Only this time, tragedy struck. He had a spine injury.

I found out all this information as people who were on the sidelines ran to the field. This was after the referee stopped the game. They were talking to each other as they ran past me, totally oblivious to my presence.

I glanced up at the stands as the coach ran up to the high schooler on the grass. He came up with the other players. But the victim just laid there, unresponsive.

I looked up at the stands as the doctor on the field came up, beginning CPR. There was a petrified look from an older, tan-skinned gentleman in the seats. I knew by the expression on the man's face that he was the young guy's father. He quickly darted past the onlookers. The onlookers had tears in their eyes as they watched the school doctor perform chest compressions, but to no avail.

"Let me through! Let me through!" he screamed, to which people dispersed instantly.

The father clambered down from the bleachers. The color on his face turned completely gray as he saw his son on the football field, unresponsive to the care that was being given to him.

The fellow players ran to the father, putting their hands on his shoulder as the dad crumpled to his knees. Agony and sadness drenched him. His cries made me clench my teeth, holding back a sob, and I overheard the paramedics talk to the doctor. This was before I saw one of the EMTs come up with a gurney.

They gingerly put the young highschooler in a neck brace, and then on the apparatus. They then went to take him to the ambulance. I watched the commotion silently, watched the medics race to the emergency vehicle, and that was when I heard a voice.

"Hello?"

I twisted my body around, only to see a brown-haired, brown eyed, and tanned skin Soul looking at me.

He appeared taken aback. He looked like a miniature of his father. They were related. His Soul made him also look like he had just barely reached seventeen years of age.

My eyes met his as he began to panic, and I automatically felt my black wings come out. "You're alright," I said to calm him. "You're going to be okay."

The young boy watched my face, tears in his eyes. "My…my…father…" he said. He glanced over at the older man, who was now hugging his son's coach, holding him in a vice-like grip.

The young boy's father continued to sob. "Samuel," he choked. "Samuel."

I saw the son clench his teeth, trying to keep it together, before he was betrayed by a single trail of water coming out of his eye.

"Oh, no. Dad…" Samuel's Soul said, right as the ambulance holding the boy's body took off. "Dad…"

Samuel's Soul's face became stricken. He looked at his father, who was now appearing inconsolable. He looked to rip out his own hair.

Samuel then turned his attention back to me. "Can I… Can I…?" he began to ask, and I knew automatically what he wanted to know.

"Yes. Yes, you can say goodbye," I said, glancing first over at Samuel's Soul, then at his father, who had been drenched in agony.

Samuel looked at me for about two seconds before he ran up to his dad, gripping him tightly as the father got up from his knees. "Dad," I heard the young man say. "Dad, I love you."

He let go of his father, coming back up to me afterward. Samuel watched my face, and then I asked him a question. A question that, as soon as I thought of it, made my mind partly drift to Phoebe.

"Samuel?" I asked the Soul next to me, who was now watching the sky.

The sunset was painting the atmosphere with pink, yellow, and orange. I glanced over at Samuel, who looked at me as I watched him.

"Did you believe in angels when you were alive?"

He seemed to have a sparkle in his brown eyes immediately. He reminded me of Adiel in that sense.

"Yes. I believed that there were always Guardian angels watching over me. I had a rough start in life… multiple, complicated doctor's appointments and very invasive surgeries. So yes, I believed. And now, seeing an angel in front of me confirms everything. Now, I know." Samuel began staring again at the illumination from the setting orb of light. "I always knew that at one point a supernatural being would take me to Heaven," he said, while his eyes were glued to the brightness.

I blinked. I wasn't expecting him to be so optimistic. It almost reminded me of the way Phoebe might act.

I thought about that for a few more moments before I blinked once more, coming out of my reverie.

The sunlight in my face made me realize that the angels, yet again, were watching over me. Over me, and Samuel.

I felt my wings come out as I looked over at the Soul beside me. "Okay, Samuel," I said, grabbing his attention. "Time to go."

92

I stood beside the Heavenly River, patiently waiting for Adiel to come back from the Golden Gates, from the Spirit Realm. I just wanted to speak with him.

About Samuel, Phoebe, and Camilla. About how all of them believed in angels.

Especially little Camilla. The small child had already told her mother what she thought I was.

But it wasn't like I could tell her the *truth*. I had to keep that part a secret.

"Do you have something you wish to tell me about?"

I turned to see Adiel walking over toward me, looking at me curiously. "Well…. well…yes," I said, stammering a bit on my words. Ever since the conversation that I'd had with him about Phoebe, I'd been having a hard time getting my words out. "I wanted to talk about… the mortals. Some of them seem to be so accepting of the angels, and then there are some that are absolutely petrified of death. It's just… the mortals… they can be so different from one another," I admitted, looking at Adiel's brown eyes.

He watched me as he listened to my words. "Well, that's the mortals for you," he said. "Everyone is different, no one is the same, even when it comes to the angels. Everyone is unique, unique in their own eclectic way."

Adiel watched my expression as he continued to speak. "Death is also something that every mortal must go through, but mortals all have different ways of thinking when it comes to how it'll happen, or when it'll be. Some mortals, especially the religious ones, are anxious about what will happen with their Soul. Others, not so much. The one thing though, that you must understand Caelum, is that not every mortal will believe. And that's okay. You must be understanding and comprehend that not everybody believes in us. And again, that is alright."

I nodded, looking at Adiel.

"Be openminded, Caelum, and everything will be okay," he said.

I opened my mouth to speak once more. "Why would mortals be so terrified of death, though?" I asked, trying to wrap my head around it.

I truly didn't know exactly why they would.

Even though I was an angel, sometimes the mortal emotion and thought process didn't make sense. Make sense to me, at least.

"Caelum, some mortals are petrified because it, death, isn't always easy on them. Some mortals cross over and die quickly, or within a few minutes or hours, by the mortal's time. Death can happen quickly, or death can happen slowly, where it can take months, or maybe years to slowly deteriorate. The process of crossing over is different for different mortals, which is why it is so scary for some."

I blinked for several moments, attempting to keep tears from building in my eyes, but I sniffled, the water cutting trails into my cheeks instead.

Phoebe, I thought as Adiel's words soaked into my brain. *Phoebe. Poor Phoebe.*

I saw Adiel come over to me through my tears. He put his hand on my shoulder, looking in my eyes, before just giving me a bear hug. "Caelum," he told me as I gripped him hard, sobbing into his clothing. "Caelum, it's better to have a relationship with a mortal and experience their emotions then not to experience anything at all."

Adiel backed away from me to look at my face. My tear-stained, raw face.

I nodded, before my mind instantly drifted to the night I had spent with Phoebe.

"Caelum," Adiel said, grasping my eyes with his. "You're going to be okay."

Over the course of the next few days, I watched over Phoebe and Camilla, and, at one point, decided to go over to visit.

Once I got there, Phoebe opened the door. Camilla was ecstatic that I'd come.

She'd automatically begun to ask me a bunch of questions. Questions all regarding one subject.

That I was an angel.

Phoebe, I could see, was watching me out of my peripheral vision the entire time I talked with her small daughter. So, I was very careful about what I told Camilla.

"Camilla, sweetie, if you'd like me to be a Guardian angel, then I'll be one."

The little girl beamed, hugging me tightly. I glanced up at Phoebe, who was grinning at me.

Thank you, she mouthed, continuing to smile.

I nodded, my own happy expression taking over my face as I felt Camilla's hug.

Now, I had trust from both mortals. The two mortals that I loved.

93

The young, red-haired woman had choked on her own saliva as she had been convulsing. It only took a few moments for her to cross over, but the gagging noises were unnerving to listen to as she lay there in bed. She was on her back, asphyxiating.

I couldn't help her, though. All I could do was watch or touch her and speed up the process of her becoming a Soul. I walked up to the side of the young woman's bed in the darkness, ready to end her suffering, when I heard it. The noise meant that she had passed away.

All the air went out of her lungs, and she went still. The redhaired woman was no longer among the mortals.

I bit my lip, staring at her now unmoving body, looking at the drool and blood that was all over her chin. I squinted, wondering where the blood had come from, and then realized that she had bitten her tongue.

Bit her tongue and her lip.

A gasp resounded behind me. I instantly let my wings out from behind my body. Now it had just become a habit, in order to calm the Souls.

"Wh…what…?" she started, and I looked at her as she struggled to speak. "Am I… am I…?" she began once more, but then stopped as she looked at her body that was in her bed.

She looked back at me, her blue eyes hitting the moonlight that cut through the room. She began to tear up and sniffle, but I just watched her, trying to help.

"My name is Caelum," I said. "I'm here to bring you to Heaven."

The redhaired woman glanced at me, breathing in deeply.

"What's your name?" I asked her calmly.

She sighed, her breathing hitching slightly as she responded.

"Beth...Bethany. My name is Bethany."

"It's nice to meet you, Bethany," I told her, sincerely meaning it.

I saw her sigh, gulping in more oxygen, before she said, "I always had it. I always had the epilepsy. The seizures were awful. My parents were trying to figure out a way so that I wouldn't have the tremors anymore, but apparently, I succumbed to one before they could successfully find a cure. I used to bite my tongue so much that there would be gashes all over it..."

Bethany trailed off, staring at her body in her bed. It looked horrific. Saliva and blood covered her, making a jarring look.

I instantly, through listening to Bethany's story, was brought back to when Phoebe had her seizure. About how she almost lost her life that day...

"Are you okay?" Bethany asked, taking me out of my thoughts.

It was only then that I realized that my breathing was rapid, my pulse in my head.

I looked at Bethany. "Yes," I said, nodding. "I just... I've never really gotten over seeing seizures, even after all the millennia."

That part was true. That part I could say.

Bethany nodded understandingly. "I know. They can... well... could... be terrifying to experience as well. I was knocked unconscious most of the time, but occasionally, I would be awake during the seizure. That was absolutely horrifying."

I tried to keep my expression neutral as she said that last sentence.

Having a seizure while still conscious just sounded petrifying. Having the ability to experience it all though…

I shivered, suddenly feeling cold as I saw Bethany nod once more at my reaction.

"Yeah, I know," she said. "They were horrific to go through."

Luckily now, she wouldn't be dealing with the seizures, with the fits, anymore. Bethany was now at peace.

"Oh, no," she said, instantly grabbing my attention, to which she nudged me.

Her alarm clock on her dresser near her bed, it said six-thirty.

"My parents are going to come in right around now," Bethany said. A few moments later, there was a series of creaks across the carpet outside.

I turned to Bethany's Soul, who looked panicked, even in the moonlight. "We must leave as soon as they turn on the light. You must trust me, alright?" I told her.

She looked at me, before nodding.

"Okay," I said.

Sure enough, the bedroom lights turned on as the door opened, followed by a horrified gasp.

It was her mother.

"Paul! Paul! Wake up, it's Bethany!"

She instantly leaned over her daughter, trying desperately to prop her up. She was trying to clear Bethany's throat, even though her daughter was gone.

I nudged the Soul of the young woman as she began to sob. "Say goodbye, Bethany. But do it quickly, because we must leave." She blinked, looking at me with a confused expression. "You can go hug your mother," I said, to which Bethany gasped, wiping the tears away from her cheeks.

She ran to her mom, holding her close as she sobbed. The mother inhaled sharply as Bethany grasped her parent. "Bye, Mom. I'll miss you," the young woman said as she let go of her mother, looking right at me as her father darted into the room.

"What...? Anna...?"

But then I saw his stricken look as agony engulfed his face, as he looked at his daughter's bloodied and vacant body. I saw Bethany's Soul turn around, looking at her father, before she spoke. "Bye, Dad. I'll miss you, too."

She walked up to me afterward. She was ready to leave.

"I'm going to bring you to the Afterlife," I said.

I encouraged her toward me, and she wrapped her hands around my body.

"Alright," I said to her. "Hold on, Bethany."

And we took off into the night, the similarities between Phoebe and Bethany's seizures in my brain as we did so.

94

Lola's panting filled my ears as I played with the Golden Retriever. I was in the Afterlife, but outside the Golden Gates, near the River.

I'd been on my knees, playing with Phoebe's dog's Soul, before I got to my feet, petting Lola's head. "Come on, girl. Let's go see Phoebe," I said, to which the dog's ears immediately perked up.

I chuckled, walking over to the Water, commanding it. It rippled, but that was when my heart seemed to drop to my stomach. Phoebe was wincing, and stumbling slightly as she walked throughout the house. She winced again, and that was when I knew that her foot had fallen asleep once more.

Oh, no, I thought, before I glanced up to see Adiel coming out of the Gates toward me.

"Adiel, can you take care of Lola for me? I have to go check on Phoebe."

"Go on, Caelum. I'll watch her."

My wings burst out of my back, and I instantly flew off, heading in the direction of Phoebe's house.

95

I flew into the trees beside Phoebe's neighborhood, deciding to just say the words there, since it was the middle of the day. The sun was out, bright and shining.

I ran into the road, bounding up the steps to Phoebe's house. I knocked on her door, my heart partly in my throat. I waited anxiously for Phoebe to answer… but then was surprised by little Camilla opening the front door.

A smile radiated throughout her entire face. "Caelum!" she yelled excitedly, running up and wrapping her arms around my abdomen.

A grin automatically made its way on my lips as she hugged me. *Oh, sweetie,* I thought. *Camilla, you are too cute.*

Camilla looked up at my face after a few moments, her voice affectionate as she spoke. "Caelum, are you here to see Mommy?"

I nodded, but right at that moment, I heard a sigh that instantly made my organs turn into mush.

Camilla immediately let go of my body before I walked up to Phoebe. Camilla shut the door as I crouched down on one knee by her mother, who was sitting on the couch.

Phoebe suddenly stared quizzically, after she got over the shock of seeing me. I saw her wince slightly, but then she just continued to watch my eyes. "Caelum," she breathed. I could tell that she was surprised. "Caelum, did you know?"

I felt her hand in mine, causing my heartrate to spike.

I looked up at her, before saying, "I...I...I had a bad feeling that something was wrong," I said, glancing over at Camilla for a moment. She came up to both Phoebe and me.

"You're Mommy's Guardian angel," the tiny daughter said, to which I instantly stared at the carpet. I could see that Phoebe was watching me the entire time the little girl was speaking. Finally, I just looked at the mother, rubbing my thumb along her hand that was still in mine.

"I'll be whatever you want me to be," I said, watching Phoebe's gaze.

She blinked.

The grin that was on Camilla's face made me turn toward her, since I could see the child out of my peripheral vision.

I just smiled at Camilla, before hugging her.

"You're an amazing little girl, Camilla," I told her, to which she gripped me tight in a hug. I looked at Phoebe, who was smiling so widely the expression engulfed her entire face. "You really are," I finished, grinning at Camilla when she looked at me.

I checked up on Phoebe ever since that day. It was either by looking through the Heavenly River, or by physically going by her house and seeing her and her daughter.

Unfortunately, though, Phoebe's symptoms got worse, and, over time, she began to decline. Over the course of the next few months, the mortal that I was in love with started to have rapid, frequent mood swings, as well as pounding headaches. She was also sleeping constantly and becoming forgetful.

All of which was extremely out of character.

Adiel was always there to vent to, or to be a shoulder to cry on whenever I broke down. Which was a lot, now that Phoebe was deteriorating.

I also sought comfort with Lola. I now believed in the animals, their unconditional love and caring nature. The Golden Retriever helped me.

I broke down a lot over the course of the next few months, but Adiel kept on telling me that what I was doing was a good thing. Caring for Phoebe and Camilla was a good thing.

96

There was one day that I checked on Phoebe through the Heavenly River. I knew this time though, deep in my gut, that the brain tumor was back, and that the mass would cause Phoebe to cross over. I instantly flew over to her side, invisible, as she and her mother were at Dr. Isaac's again, at the neurologist's office.

I went there, only to hear what I was dreading but expecting... that the cancer was back, and that it was terminal.

I was broken.

Phoebe's health was failing.

I knew that it was going to be hard for me to deal with, but this... this was agony.

Adiel told me once when I was talking with him that anguish could be extremely difficult. That some mortals blame themselves for a loved one's death, or that they get upset over the fact that they weren't there in the mortal's final moments.

For an angel, me being one, it was different. Since I'd never really felt this way about anyone.

Mortal or angel.

Adiel was there for me though, through it all. He stuck by my side. He stuck by my side for a long span of time.

Phoebe's health was absolutely disintegrating before my eyes, both as I checked on her in the Heavenly River, and when I was there with her physically. And if I wasn't there with her physically, then I was by her side, invisible, watching over her. Poor Camilla though, she only understood that her mother's brain was sick.

That was the only way she could comprehend what was going on with Phoebe.

As Phoebe started to become sicker and sicker, Camilla became more and more sad, anxious, and fearful.

Camilla was crying more and more, but it didn't help that Susanna, Derek, and Mark were all feeling the same way.

They were all horrified by the idea of losing Phoebe and knew that she wasn't doing any of her strange behavior on purpose.

It was the cancer, the mass on her brain which was causing it. It was the tumor.

97

I followed Phoebe as she came back into her home.
She had just walked, and I'd been with her.
I'd been invisible, though.

Ever since she'd gotten worse and worse, I wasn't able to be with her physically anymore, where she could see me.

Not in life, anyway.

Phoebe stumbled partly as I stood next to her, invisible, and I turned my head to the side in confusion once I saw how she was acting. But then again, at this point, nothing made sense.

Phoebe shut her eyes tight, and suddenly I could sense that she was in throbbing agony from the headache that had engulfed her. She winced, grumbling slightly before she gasped for air. She'd begun to cry, her face contorted in agony. She opened her eyes, tears cutting trails into her cheeks, but then abruptly bolted upstairs.

I paused, alarmed and confused as I followed her.

What are you doing, Phoebe? What are you doing?

She grabbed a disposable razor off the bathroom counter with one hand, while with the other she began filling the bathtub nearby with water. With fumbling fingers, she took the protective covering off of the blade. Phoebe eventually got the sharp edge of the razor in her fingers. She successfully broke apart the device, so there were just sharp razor blades in her hands.

There were just sharp razor blades in her hands. There were just.... sharp... razor blades...

I blinked as I saw Phoebe put them on the tub, while with the other hand she shut off the water...

Right as she was about to slide into the liquid with all her clothing on, I said the words so that I would be able to be sensed. Which was good, because now, I was sobbing uncontrollably. I was gasping as I finished the words, right as Phoebe pulled up her shirt sleeves... *"NO!"* I screamed, throwing myself forward, grasping her wrists with my hands. I pressed my fingertips into her wrists, gently but firmly, effectively stopping her.

Phoebe gasped, watching her hands that were now enveloped in mine, even though she couldn't see them.

Phoebe, I thought, staring into her eyes, trying to see the crystal blue, but even that had seemed to disappear.

It was clear that she was unwell. She appeared delirious.

She blinked though, at the change in the energy around her. Phoebe could sense me, I knew that.

I continued to just stare into her eyes, holding my thumbs to her wrists.

And that was when.... Phoebe began to sob.

Her head fell forward, her chin partially splashing both of us with water, and she just cried. An anguished yell escaped her, and that was when I couldn't help it anymore as I cried along with her.

I leaned forward, kissing her cheek.

I tasted the tears that were streaming down her face as my lips touched her skin. They made mine prickle.

Even after all the months I'd spent with Phoebe, I loved her, and I was so sorry that the cancer had come back, that her life had drastically changed. I was so sorry...

"I'm sorry," was all I could say as I pressed my fingertips into her wrists, even though she wouldn't be able to see or hear me. "I'm so sorry."

"Phoebe?"

My eyes darted toward the bathroom door, and I heard Susanna shut the front one from downstairs.

She had just come inside the home.

"Phoebe? Where are you?"

I just looked back at Phoebe, watching her as tears flooded her cheeks. She gasped in a lungful of air, and then another anguished scream escaped her.

Footsteps instantly were on the stairs as I heard Susanna run, and that was when I turned to see her anxious face near the bathroom door.

"Phoebe?" she asked, her voice almost in hysterics. I saw her take in the scene for two seconds before she rushed to her daughter's side.

Susanna began to sob along with Phoebe, and she ran toward her, right behind me. That was when I took my cue.

I'm so sorry, I thought as I watched Susanna and Phoebe hugging. My eyes began to water. *I'm so sorry.*

That night I was interested in how Camilla was.

Camilla wasn't home at the time, she was at Derek's residence, which was a relief. If I hadn't been there at the right moment, that situation could've ended a lot differently...

Camilla was with Derek, and had just been told a simpler version of what had happened to Phoebe. She was just told that her mother had almost gotten hurt, and Camilla had run upstairs to her bedroom. That was where I was, invisible, as I had overheard the conversation between Derek and his tiny daughter.

Camilla just shut the door to her bedroom tightly, climbing into her bed instantly, before curling up in a ball and crying.

Oh, Camilla. You poor sweet thing.

I bit my lip as she sobbed, but then she started talking softly, since her bedroom window was open.

My heart skipped a beat as I realized that she'd begun to speak. Speak to me.

"Caelum," she said in her little voice. "Caelum, please be a Guardian angel, and... and... watch over Mommy, please. Especially when she passes away."

She immediately curled into another ball. I rushed to her bedside then, a lump automatically in my throat.

"Please... please..."

She sobbed, and I couldn't help it then.

"Aww, sweetie,'" I said, even though she wouldn't be able to hear me.

I quickly said the words so that she could sense me. "Mommy will be taken care of," I said out loud, stroking the little girl's cheeks gently. "I promise, sweetheart."

Camilla gasped, and I smiled. The words, the words that I had spoken, they had worked.

I tasted tears, and that was when I realized that I'd started crying.

"Mommy will be alright," I told Camilla, before I gave her a hug, tucking a strand of hair behind her ear afterward..

Sighing deeply as I let her go, I felt the liquid cut trails into my skin.

"I'm sorry," I found myself telling the small child. I was saying the same thing I'd told her mother. "I'm so sorry."

98

The day came when I knew it was time for Phoebe to cross over.

The magnetic, almost electric sensation had been getting stronger and stronger, but this time around, the feeling was palpable.

I knew that by the end of that day, that she was going to pass away. I knew, but her family didn't.

They thought that they still had some more time left to spend with Phoebe. Susanna, Derek, Mark, and Camilla didn't realize it would be so soon.

The day that Phoebe had crossed over was also the day that she had been admitted to the hospital with pneumonia because of a bacterial infection. She had a lower immune system because the cancer had spread throughout her body, and Phoebe, the poor mortal, was in agony.

Her head, joints, and chest all hurt, while all the color had drained from her face, and her eyes were no longer crystal blue. She was so ill. Phoebe was also hallucinating, since the brain tumor had disintegrated her organ.

I said the special words so that I could only be seen by mortals who were dying, but Phoebe was so sick she was saying that I was the Devil reincarnated. She pointed to me while she'd begun speaking with one of the nurses, who had immediately put her on medication.

"Can you see him?" Phoebe had asked in her disorganized way of thinking. "Can you see the scary Devil in the corner?"

My feelings shattered into a million pieces. Phoebe thought I was the Devil…

But that was when I truly knew that she was dying, and that Adiel was right. Sometimes, it wasn't always easy for the mortals to pass away.

It was later in the evening, by the tail end of the visitor's hours, that Camilla was there to say goodbye to her mother. She tried to keep a brave face on as her frail mom hugged her. Hugged her for the final time.

Susanna and Mark were there as well, holding their daughter before leaving the room.

I stayed in the corner of the area, visible only to Phoebe as she woke up several hours later, since she'd been taking multiple moments of shut-eye. I stared at Phoebe as she opened her eyes, disoriented and confused.

"Phoebe," I said, walking slowly, feeling the almost tangible sensation that emanated off her. "Phoebe, it's time to go," I said as calmly as I could, although I could feel that I'd begun to cry. "Phoebe," I said, my voice thick.

She blinked rapidly, pushing herself up, attempting to scramble away from me, and I stopped, looking straight at her eyes.

"You're going to be alright, Phoebe. I'll take care of you," I said.

She paused, her mouth was open as if she was about to scream, but then she asked a question, tears in her eyes. "How do you know? How do you know I'll be okay?"

I took a step closer as she watched me warily. She didn't flinch, though.

"I'm an angel," I told her. "I'm an angel, Phoebe, and I'll take care of you."

Phoebe blinked again, her face in disbelief. "What's your name?" she asked me.

Inside, my heart dropped, but I knew in my gut that it wasn't her fault. It was the brain cancer.

I answered her. "Caelum. My name is Caelum," I said, as gently as I could. I went over to her bedside, leaning over her, and thankfully she wasn't scared. "Everything's going to be alright, Phoebe," I breathed, moving in close. My lips touched her cheek. "It'll be okay, I promise," I whispered before I kissed her.

Automatically, I heard the heart monitor that she was hooked to beep loudly, flatlining.

Phoebe was gone.

I pulled away from the mortal that I'd fallen in love with. I just stepped away. But then I heard a familiar voice behind me, a voice that was breathless and in disbelief.

"Caelum?"

99

My heartrate spiked, and I twisted around slowly, only to see Phoebe's Soul blinking, unable to take everything in. "Caelum?" she repeated, to which I let my wings out of my back.

Phoebe smiled, the expression taking over her whole face. The color was back in her skin, as the healthy look took control inside her Soul. She was stunning. "Camilla was right," she said. "She was right. You *are* an angel."

I nodded, unknowingly taking a step toward her.

Phoebe inhaled sharply, looking at the ground, and then back up at me. "You're an angel."

The loud noises of the personnel entering the room caught both of us by surprise. I quickly ran over to Phoebe's Soul. I paused, glancing at her as she looked at me. "Do you trust me, Phoebe?" I asked as I gazed at her, her stunningly blue eyes.

She looked at me for about two moments before nodding.

I then held her close to my body. I unfurled my wings and took off into the Heavens.

100

A diel was the one to greet us as we made it to the Afterlife. Phoebe's hand was on my pounding heart as I looked at Adiel, who was also playing with Lola.

I let go of Phoebe's Soul just as the dog saw her former owner. The Golden Retriever came bounding over to Phoebe, who was ecstatic and shocked at the same time.

"Lola?" she asked, surprised, to which Lola wagged her tail, whining happily at the sound of Phoebe's voice.

Lola then jumped up on her hind legs, licking Phoebe's cheek. Tears began to pool in Phoebe's eyes.

"Lola. Oh, Lola," she said, petting her dog, before gripping me in a tight hug. She was crying into my clothing. I held her close. "Thank you. Thank you so much."

It was several moments before she let me go.

I could feel it when she loosened her grip. I pulled away, noticing Adiel.

Phoebe blinked, her mouth was open in surprise as he smiled at her, his wings came out of his back as he did so.

I could tell instantly that Phoebe knew that Adiel knew about her, knew who she was. There was recognition in his face, understanding in his eyes. "Hello, Phoebe," Adiel told her. I watched him as he spoke as well. "My name is Adiel. I'll be protecting you inside the Golden Gates." He turned to show her the towering barrier, to which her eyes widened. "I'll be in the Golden Gates, which is inside the Soul Realm. You may see your family whenever you like. Caelum, he can take you whenever you want. You are safe, Phoebe Bright."

Phoebe just blinked, in complete and utter shock. She looked over at me, and then at Adiel, who was smiling.

But I just found myself staring at Phoebe. The Soul that was once a mortal. A mortal that I loved.

I realized quickly that I'd taken another step toward her again, and then paused.

Phoebe turned toward Adiel, who just moved his head a little, encouragingly.

She inhaled, looking at me again, but I was just frozen, unable to move. Phoebe took me by surprise. She ran to me, leaping into my arms.

My muscles unlocked, and I lifted her off the ground as she wrapped her arms around my neck. Her mouth met mine. She kissed me, and immediately, I kissed her back.

I loved her so much. And I would love her for the rest of my existence.

For the rest of my supernatural lifespan.

Glossary

Caelum- (Ki-lum)

Adiel- (Add-de-el)

Lemuel- (Lem-you-l)

Ezekiel- (E-z-ke-l)

Phoebe- (Fee-be)

About the Author

Elizabeth Wittekind has always been creative. Constantly thinking of unique plotlines for different stories and having an imagination, she loves the fantasy genre in books and movies. She published her debut novel *Ethereal Imprints* in 2022 and soon after came up with the idea for a second story. *Arcadian Divinity* was the result. Elizabeth has several additional works in progress.

Also by: Elizabeth Wittekind

The Ethereal Chronicles

Ethereal Imprints: Book 1